ALSO BY GREG EGAN FROM GOLLANCZ

DISTRESS
GREG EGAN

The right of Greg Egan to be identified as the author
of this work has been asserted by him in accordance with
the Copyright, Designs and Patents Act 1988.

First published in Great Britain in 1995 by Millennium

This edition published in Great Britain in 2008 by Gollancz
an imprint of the Orion Publishing Group
Orion House, 5 Upper St Martin's Lane, London WC2H 9EA
An Hachette Livre UK Company

10 9 8 7 6 5 4 3 2 1

A CIP catalogue record for this book is
available from the British Library

ISBN 978 0 57508 1 734

Typeset at The Spartan Press Ltd,
Lymington, Hants

Printed and bound at Mackays of Chatham plc,
Chatham, Kent

The Orion Publishing Group's policy is to use papers that
are natural, renewable and recyclable products and made
from wood grown in sustainable forests. The logging and
manufacturing processes are expected to conform to the
environmental regulations of the country of origin.

www.orionbooks.co.uk

It is not true that the map of freedom will be complete
    with the erasure of the last invidious border
when it remains for us to chart the attractors of thunder
    and delineate the arrhythmias of drought
to reveal the molecular dialects of forest and savanna
    as rich as a thousand human tongues
and to comprehend the deepest history of our passions
    ancient beyond mythology's reach

So I declare that no corporation holds a monopoly on
    numbers
no patent can encompass zero and one
no nation has sovereignty over adenine and guanine
no empire rules the quantum waves

And there must be room for all at the celebration of
    understanding
for there is a truth which cannot be bought or sold
imposed by force, resisted
or escaped.

– From *Technolibération* by Muteba Kazadi, 2019

PART ONE

1

'All right. He's dead. Go ahead and talk to him.'

The bioethicist was a laconic young asex with blond dreadlocks and a T-shirt which flashed up the slogan SAY NO TO TOE! in between the paid advertising. Ve countersigned the permission form on the forensic pathologist's notepad, then withdrew to a corner of the room. The trauma specialist and the paramedic wheeled their resuscitation equipment out of the way, and the forensic pathologist hurried forward, hypodermic syringe in hand, to administer the first dose of neuropreservative. Useless prior to legal death – massively toxic to several organs, on a time scale of hours – the cocktail of glutamate antagonists, calcium channel blockers, and antioxidants would halt the most damaging biochemical changes in the victim's brain, almost immediately.

The pathologist's assistant followed close behind her, with a trolley bearing all the paraphernalia of post-mortem revival: a tray of disposable surgical instruments; several racks of electronic equipment; an arterial pump fed from three glass tanks the size of water-coolers; and something resembling a hairnet made out of grey superconducting wire.

Lukowski, the homicide detective, was standing beside me. He mused, 'If everyone was fitted out like you, Worth, we'd never have to do this. We could just replay the crime from start to finish. Like reading an aircraft's black box.'

I replied without looking away from the operating table; I could edit out our voices easily enough, but I wanted a continuous take of the pathologist connecting up the surrogate

3

blood supply. 'If everyone had optic nerve taps, don't you think murderers would start hacking the memory chips out of their victims' bodies?'

'Sometimes. But no one hung around to mess up this guy's brain, did they?'

'Wait until they've seen the documentary.'

The pathologist's assistant sprayed a depilatory enzyme on to the victim's skull, and then wiped all the close-cropped black hair away with a couple of sweeps of his gloved hand. As he dropped the mess into a plastic sample bag, I realised why it was holding together instead of dispersing like barber's shop waste; several layers of skin had come with it. The assistant glued the 'hairnet' – a skein of electrodes and SQID detectors – to the bare pink scalp. The pathologist finished checking the blood supply, then made an incision in the trachea and inserted a tube, hooked up to a small pump to take the place of the collapsed lungs. Nothing to do with respiration; purely as an aid to speech. It was possible to monitor the nerve impulses to the larynx, and synthesise the intended sounds by wholly electronic means, but apparently the voice was always less garbled if the victim could experience something like the normal tactile and auditory feedback produced by a vibrating column of air. The assistant fitted a padded bandage over the victim's eyes; in rare cases, feeling could return sporadically to the skin of the face, and since retinal cells were deliberately not revived, some kind of temporary ocular injury was the easiest lie to explain away the pragmatic blindness.

I thought again about possible narration. *In 1888, police surgeons photographed the retinas of one victim of Jack the Ripper, in the vain hope that they might discover the face of the killer embalmed in the light-sensitive pigments of the human eye . . .*

No. Too predictable. And too misleading; revival was not a process of extracting information from a passive corpse. But

4

what were the alternative references? Orpheus? Lazarus? 'The Monkey's Paw'? 'The Tell-Tale Heart'? *Reanimator*? Nothing in myth or fiction had really prefigured the truth. Better to make no glib comparisons. Let the corpse speak for itself.

A spasm passed through the victim's body. A temporary pacemaker was forcing his damaged heart to beat – operating at power levels which would poison every cardiac muscle fibre with electro-chemical by-products, in fifteen or twenty minutes at the most. Pre-oxygenated ersatz blood was being fed into his heart's left atrium, in lieu of a supply from the lungs, pumped through the body once only, then removed via the pulmonary arteries and discarded. An open system was less trouble than recirculation, in the short term. The half-repaired knife wounds in his abdomen and torso made a mess, leaking thin scarlet fluid into the drainage channels of the operating table, but they posed no real threat; a hundred times as much blood was being extracted every second, deliberately. No one had bothered to remove the surgical larvae, though, so they kept on working as if nothing had changed: stitching and chemically cauterising the smaller blood vessels with their jaws, cleaning and disinfecting the wounds, sniffing about blindly for necrotic tissue and clots to consume.

Maintaining the flow of oxygen and nutrients to the brain was essential but it wouldn't reverse the deterioration which had already taken place. The true catalysts of revival were the billions of liposomes – microscopic drug capsules made from lipid membranes – being infused along with the ersatz blood. One key protein embedded in the membrane unlocked the blood-brain barrier, enabling the liposomes to burrow out of the cerebral capillaries into the interneural space. Other proteins caused the membrane itself to fuse with the cell wall of the first suitable neuron it encountered, disgorging an elaborate package of biochemical machinery to re-energise the cell, mop up some of the molecular detritus of ischaemic damage, and protect against the shock of re-oxygenation.

Other liposomes were tailored for other cell types: muscle fibres in the vocal fold, the jaw, the lips, the tongue; receptors in the inner ear. They all contained drugs and enzymes with similar effects: hijacking the dying cell and forcing it, briefly, to marshal its resources for one final – unsustainable – burst of activity.

Revival was not resuscitation pushed to heroic extremes. Revival was permitted only when the long-term survival of the patient was no longer a consideration, because every method which might have achieved that outcome had already failed.

The pathologist glanced at a display screen on the equipment trolley. I followed her gaze; there were wave traces showing erratic brain rhythms, and fluctuating bar graphs measuring toxins and breakdown products being flushed out of the body. Lukowski stepped forward expectantly. I followed him.

The assistant hit a button on a keypad. The victim twitched and coughed blood – some of it still his own, dark and clotted. The wave traces spiked, then became smoother, more periodic.

Lukowski took the victim's hand and squeezed it – a gesture which struck me as cynical, although for all I knew it might have reflected a genuine compassionate impulse. I glanced at the bioethicist. Vis T-shirt now read CREDIBILITY IS A COMMODITY. I couldn't decide if that was a sponsored message or a personal opinion.

Lukowski said, 'Daniel? Danny? Can you hear me?' There was no obvious physical response, but the brain waves danced. Daniel Cavolini was a music student, nineteen years old. He'd been found around eleven, bleeding and unconscious, in a corner of the Town Hall railway station – with watch, notepad, and shoes still on him, unlikely in a random mugging gone wrong. I'd been hanging out with the homicide squad for a fortnight, waiting for something like this. Warrants for revival were issued only if the evidence favoured the victim's being able to name the assailant; there was little prospect of obtaining a useable verbal description of a stranger, let alone an identikit of the killer's face. Lukowski had woken a magistrate just after midnight, the minute the prognosis was clear.

Cavolini's skin was turning a strange shade of crimson, as more and more revived cells began taking up oxygen. The alien-hued transporter molecule in the ersatz blood was more efficient than haemoglobin – but like all the other revival drugs, it was ultimately toxic.

The pathologist's assistant hit some more keys. Cavolini twitched and coughed again. It was a delicate balancing act; small shocks to the brain were necessary to restore the major coherent rhythms, but too much external interference could wipe out the remnants of short-term memory. Even after legal death, neurons could remain active deep in the brain, keeping the symbolic firing-pattern representations of recent memories circulating for several minutes. Revival could temporarily restore the neural infrastructure needed to extract those traces, but if they'd already died away completely – or been swamped by the efforts to recover them – interrogation was pointless.

Lukowski said soothingly, 'You're okay now, Danny. You're in hospital. You're safe. But you have to tell me who did this to you. Tell me who had the knife.'

A hoarse whisper emerged from Cavolini's mouth: one faint, aspirated syllable, then silence. My skin crawled with predictable monkey's paw horror – but I felt an idiotic surge of exultation, too, as if part of me simply refused to accept that this sign of life *could not be* a sign of hope.

Cavolini tried again, and the second attempt was more sustained. His artificial exhalation, detached from voluntary control, made it sound like he was gasping for breath; the effect was pitiful – but he wasn't actually short of oxygen at all. His speech was so broken and tortuous that I couldn't make out a single word, but an array of piezoelectric sensors

7

was glued to his throat, and wired to a computer. I turned to the display panel.

Why can't I see?

Lukowski said, 'Your eyes are bandaged. There were a couple of broken blood vessels, but they've been repaired; there'll be no permanent damage, I promise. So just . . . lie still, and relax. And tell me what happened.'

What time is it? Please. I better call home. I better tell them—

'We've spoken to your parents. They're on their way, they'll be here as soon as possible.'

That much was true – but even if they showed up in the next ninety seconds, they would not be allowed into the room.

'You were waiting for the train home, weren't you? Platform four. Remember? Waiting for the ten-thirty to Strathfield. But you didn't get on. What happened?' I saw Lukowski's gaze shift to a graph below the transcript window, where half a dozen rising curves recording improved vital signs were extended by dashed computer projections. All of the projected curves hit their peaks a minute or so in the future, then swiftly declined.

He had a knife. Cavolini's right arm began to twitch, and his slack facial muscles came to life for the first time, taking on a grimace of pain. **It still hurts. Please help me.** The bioethicist glanced calmly at some figures on the display screen, but declined to intervene. Any effective anaesthetic would damp down neural activity too much to allow the interrogation to continue; it was all or nothing, abort or proceed.

Lukowski said gently. 'The nurse is getting some painkillers. Hang in there, man, it won't be long. But tell me: *who had the knife?*' The faces of both of them were glistening with sweat now; Lukowski's arm was scarlet up to the elbow. I thought: If you found someone dying on the pavement in a pool of blood, you'd ask the same questions, wouldn't you? And tell the same reassuring lies?

'Who was it, Danny?'

My brother.

'Your brother had the knife?'

No, he didn't. I can't remember what happened. Ask me later. My head's too fuzzy now.

'Why did you say it was your brother? Was it him, or wasn't it?'

Of course it wasn't him. Don't tell anyone I said that. I'll be all right if you stop confusing me. Can I have the painkillers now? Please?

His face flowed and froze, flowed and froze, like a sequence of masks, making his suffering seem stylised, abstract. He began to move his head back and forth; weakly at first, then with manic speed and energy. I assumed he was having some kind of seizure: the revival drugs were overstimulating some damaged neural pathway.

Then he reached up with his right hand and tore away the blindfold.

His head stopped jerking immediately; maybe his skin had grown hypersensitive, and the blindfold had become an unbearable irritation. He blinked a few times, then squinted up at the room's bright lights. I could see his pupils contract, his eyes moving purposefully. He raised his head slightly and examined Lukowski, then looked down at his own body and its strange adornments: the pacemaker's brightly coloured ribbon cable; the heavy plastic blood-supply tubes; the knife wounds full of glistening white maggots. Nobody moved, nobody spoke, while he inspected the needles and electrodes buried in his chest, the strange pink tide washing out of him, his ruined lungs, his artificial airway. The display screen was behind him, but everything else was there to be taken in at a glance. In a matter of seconds, *he knew*; I could see the weight of understanding descend on him.

He opened his mouth, then closed it again. His expression shifted rapidly; through the pain there was a sudden flash of pure astonishment, and then an almost amused comprehension of the full strangeness – and maybe even the perverse virtuosity – of the feat to which he'd been subjected. For an instant, he really did look like someone admiring a brilliant, vicious, bloody practical joke at his own expense.

Then he said clearly, between enforced robotic gasps: 'I . . . don't . . . think . . . this . . . is . . . a . . . good . . . id . . . dea. I . . . don't . . . want . . . to . . . talk . . . any . . . more.'

He closed his eyes and sank back on to the table. His vital signs were descending rapidly.

Lukowski turned to the pathologist. He was ashen, but he still gripped the boy's hand. 'How could the retinas function? What did you do? You *stupid*—' He raised his free hand as if to strike her, but he didn't follow through. The bioethicist's T-shirt read: ETERNAL LOVE IS A LOVEPET. MADE FROM YOUR LOVED ONE'S OWN DNA. The pathologist, standing her ground, screamed back at Lukowski, 'You had to push him, didn't you? You had to keep *on and on* about the brother, while his stress hormone index climbed straight into the red!' I wondered who'd decided what a normal level of adrenaline was, for the state of being dead from knife wounds but otherwise relaxed. Someone behind me emitted a long string of incoherent obscenities. I turned to see the paramedic, who would have been with Cavolini since the ambulance; I hadn't even realised that he was still in the room. He was staring at the floor, his fists clenched tight, shaking with anger.

Lukowski grabbed my elbow, staining me with synthetic blood. He spoke in a stage whisper, as if hoping to keep his words off the soundtrack. 'You can film the next one, okay? This has *never* happened before – *never* – and if you show people a one-in-a-million glitch as if it was—'

The bioethicist ventured mildly, 'I think the guidelines from the Taylor Committee on optional restraints make it clear—'

The pathologist's assistant turned on ver, outraged. 'Who

asked you for an opinion? Procedure is none of your business, you pathetic—'

An ear-splitting alarm went off, somewhere deep in the electronic guts of the revival apparatus. The pathologist's assistant bent over the equipment and bashed on the keypad like a frustrated child attacking a broken toy until the noise went away.

In the silence that followed, I almost closed my eyes, invoked **Witness**, stopped recording. I'd seen enough.

Then Daniel Cavolini regained consciousness, and began to scream.

I watched as they pumped him full of morphine, and waited for the revival drugs to finish him off.

2

It was just after five as I walked down the hill from Eastwood railway station. The sky was pale and colourless, Venus was fading slowly in the east – but the street itself already looked exactly as it did by daylight. Just inexplicably deserted. My carriage on the train had been empty, too. Last-human-on-Earth time.

Birds were calling – loudly – in the lush bushland which lined the railway corridor, and in the labyrinth of wooded parks woven into the surrounding suburb. Many of the parks resembled pristine forest – but every tree, every shrub, was engineered: at the very least drought and fire resistant, shedding no messy, flammable twigs, bark or leaves. Dead plant tissue was resorbed, cannibalised; I'd seen it portrayed in time-lapse (one kind of photography I never carried out myself): an entire brown and wilting branch shrinking back into the living trunk. Most of the trees generated a modest amount of electricity – ultimately from sunlight, although the chemistry was elaborate, and the release of stored energy continued twenty-four hours a day. Specialised roots sought out the underground superconductors snaking through the parks, and fed in their contributions. Two and a quarter volts was about as intrinsically safe as electric power could be – but it required zero resistance for efficient transmission.

Some of the fauna had been modified, too; the magpies were docile even in spring, the mosquitoes shunned mammalian blood, and the most venomous snakes were incapable of harming a human child. Small advantages over their wild cousins, tied to the biochemistry of the engineered vegetation, guaranteed the altered species dominance in this microecology – and small handicaps kept them from flourishing if they ever escaped to one of the truly wild reserves, distant from human habitation.

I was renting a small detached unit in a cluster of four, set in a zero-maintenance garden which merged seamlessly with the tendril of parkland at the end of a cul-de-sac. I'd been there for eight years, ever since my first commission from SeeNet, but I still felt like a trespasser. Eastwood was just eighteen kilometres from the centre of Sydney, which – although ever fewer people had reason to travel there – still seemed to hold an inexplicable sway over real-estate prices; I couldn't have bought the unit myself in a hundred years. The (barely) affordable rent was just a felicitous by-product of the owner's elaborate tax evasion schemes – and it was probably only a matter of time before some quiver of butterfly wings in world financial markets rendered the networks slightly less generous, or my landowner slightly less in need of a write-off, and I'd be picked up and flung fifty kilometres west, back to the outer sprawl where I belonged.

I approached warily. Home should have felt like a sanctuary after the night's events, but I hesitated outside the front door, key in hand, for something like a minute.

Gina was up, dressed, and in the middle of breakfast. I hadn't seen her since the same time the day before; it was as if I'd never left.

She said, 'How was filming?' I'd sent her a message from the hospital, explaining that we'd finally *got lucky*.

'I don't want to talk about it.' I retreated into the living room and sank into a chair. The action of sitting seemed to replay itself in my inner ears; I kept descending, again and again. I fixed my gaze on the pattern in the carpet; the illusion slowly faded.

'Andrew? What happened?' She followed me into the room. 'Did something go wrong? Will you have to reshoot?'

'I said I don't want to—' I caught myself. I looked up at her, and forced myself to concentrate. She was puzzled, but not yet angry. *Rule number three: tell her everything, however unpleasant, at the first opportunity. Whether you feel like it or not. Anything less will be treated as deliberate exclusion and taken as a personal affront.*

I said, 'I won't have to reshoot. It's over.' I recounted what had happened.

Gina looked ill. 'And was anything he said worth . . . *extracting*? Did mentioning his brother make the slightest sense – or was he just brain-damaged and ranting?'

'That's still not clear. Evidently the brother does have a history of violence; he was on probation for assaulting his mother. They've taken him in for questioning . . . but it could all come to nothing. If the victim's short-term memories were lost, he could have pieced together a false reconstruction of the stabbing, using the first person who came to mind as being capable of the act. And when he changed his story he might not have been covering up at all; he might simply have realised that he was amnesic.'

Gina said, 'And even if the brother *did* kill him . . . no jury is going to accept a couple of words, instantly retracted, as any kind of proof. If there's a conviction, it will have nothing to do with the revival.'

It was difficult to argue the point; I had to struggle to regain some perspective.

'Not in this case, no. But there have been times when it's made all the difference. The victim's word alone might never stand up in court – but there've been people tried for murder who would never have been suspected otherwise. Cases when the evidence which actually convicted them was only pieced together because the revival testimony put the investigation on the right track.'

Gina was dismissive. 'That may have happened once or twice – but it's still not worth it. They should ban the whole procedure, it's obscene.' She hesitated. 'But you're not going to use that footage, are you?'

'Of course I'm going to use it.'

'You're going to show a man dying in agony on an operating table – captured in the act of realising that everything which brought him back to life is guaranteed to kill him?' She spoke calmly; she sounded more incredulous than outraged.

I said, 'What do you want me to use instead? A dramatisation, where everything goes according to plan?'

'No. But why not a dramatisation where everything goes wrong, in exactly the way it did last night?'

'*Why?* It's already happened, and I've already filmed it. Who benefits from a reconstruction?'

'The victim's family. For a start.'

I thought: *Possibly*. But would a reconstruction really spare their feelings? And no one was going to force them to watch the documentary, in either case.

I said, 'Be reasonable. This is powerful stuff; I can't just throw it away. And I have every right to use it. I had permission to be there – from the cops, from the hospital. And I'll get the family's clearance—'

'You mean the network's lawyers will brow-beat them into signing some kind of waiver "in the public interest".'

I had no answer to that; it was exactly what would happen. I said, 'You're the one who just declared that revival is obscene. You want to see it banned? This can only help your cause. It's as good a dose of frankenscience as any dumb luddite could ask for.'

Gina looked stung; I couldn't tell if she was faking. She said, 'I have a doctorate in materials science, you peasant, so don't call *me*—'

'I didn't. You know what I meant.'

'If anyone's a luddite, you are. This entire project is

beginning to sound like Edenite propaganda. "*Junk DNA!*" What's the subtitle? "The biotechnology nightmare?" '

'Close.'

'What I don't understand is why you couldn't include a single positive story—'

I said wearily, 'We've been over this before. It's not up to me. The networks won't buy anything unless there's an angle. In this case, the downside of biotech. That's the choice of subject, that's what it's about. It isn't meant to be "balanced". Balance confuses the marketing people; you can't hype something which contains two contradictory messages. But at least it might counteract all the hymns of praise to genetic engineering everyone's been gagging on lately. And – taken along with everything else – it *does* show the whole picture. By adding what they've all left out.'

Gina was unmoved. 'That's disingenuous. "Our sensationalism balances their sensationalism." It doesn't. It just polarises opinion. What's wrong with a calm, reasoned presentation of the facts – which might help to get revival and a few other blatant atrocities outlawed – without playing up all the old transgressions-against-nature bullshit? Showing the excesses, but putting them in context? You should be helping people make informed decisions about what they demand from the regulatory authorities. *Junk DNA* sounds more likely to inspire them to go out and bomb the nearest biotech lab.'

I curled into the armchair and rested my head on my knees. 'All right, I give up. Everything you say is true. I'm a manipulative, rabble-rousing, anti-science hack.'

She frowned. 'Anti-science? I wouldn't go that far. You're venal, lazy, and irresponsible – but you're not quite Ignorance Cult material yet.'

'Your faith is touching.'

She prodded me with a cushion, affectionately I think, then

went back to the kitchen. I covered my face with my hands, and the room started tipping.

I should have been jubilant. *It was over.* The revival was the very last piece of filming for *Junk DNA*. No more paranoid billionaires mutating into self-contained walking ecologies. No more insurance firms designing personal actuarial implants to monitor diet, exercise, and exposure to pollutants – for the sake of endlessly recomputing the wearer's most probable date and cause of death. No more Voluntary Autists lobbying for the right to have their brains surgically mutilated so they could finally attain the condition nature hadn't quite granted them . . .

I went into my workroom and unreeled the fibre-optic umbilical from the side of the editing console. I lifted my shirt and cleared some unnameable debris from my navel, then extracted the skin-coloured plug with my fingernails, exposing a short stainless-steel tube ending in an opalescent laser port.

Gina called out from the kitchen, 'Are you performing unnatural acts with that machine again?'

I was too tired to think of an intelligent retort. I snapped the connectors together, and the console lit up.

The screen showed everything as it came through. Eight hours' worth in sixty seconds – most of it an incomprehensible blur, but I averted my gaze anyway. I didn't much feel like reliving any of the night's events, however briefly.

Gina wandered in with a plate of toast; I hit a button to conceal the image. She said, 'I still want to know how you can have four thousand terabytes of RAM in your peritoneal cavity, and no visible scars.'

I glanced down at the connector socket. 'What do you call that? Invisible?'

'Too small. Eight-hundred-terabyte chips are thirty millimetres wide. I looked up the manufacturer's catalogue.'

'Sherlock strikes again. Or should I say Shylock? Scars can be erased, can't they?'

17

'Yes. But . . . would you have obliterated the marks of your most important rite of passage?'

'Spare me the anthropological babble.'

'I do have an alternative theory.'

'I'm not confirming or denying anything.'

She let her gaze slide over the blank console screen, up to the *Repo Man* poster on the wall behind it: a motorcycle cop standing behind a dilapidated car. She caught my eye, then gestured at the caption: DON'T LOOK IN THE TRUNK!

'Why not? *What's in the trunk?*'

I laughed. 'You can't bear it anymore, can you? You're just going to have to watch the movie.'

'Yeah, yeah.'

The console beeped. I unhooked. Gina looked at me curiously; the expression on my face must have betrayed something. 'So is it like sex – or more like defecation?'

'It's more like Confession.'

'You've never been to Confession in your life.'

'No, but I've seen it in the movies. I was joking, though. It's not like anything at all.'

She glanced at her watch, then kissed me on the cheek, leaving toast crumbs. 'I have to run. Get some sleep, you idiot. You look terrible.'

I sat and listened to her bustling around. She had a ninety-minute train journey every morning to the CSIRO's wind turbine research station, west of the Blue Mountains. I usually got up at the same time myself, though. It was better than waking alone.

I thought: *I do love her. And if I concentrate, if I follow the rules, there's no reason why it can't last.* My eighteen-month record was looming – but that was nothing to fear. We'd smash it, easily.

She reappeared in the doorway. 'So, how long do you have to edit this one?'

'Ah. Three weeks exactly. Counting today.' I hadn't really wanted to be reminded.

'Today doesn't count. Get some sleep.'

We kissed. She left. I swung my chair around to face the blank console.

Nothing was over. I was going to have to watch Daniel Cavolini die a hundred more times, before I could finally disown him.

I limped into the bedroom and undressed. I hung my clothes on the cleaning rack, and switched on the power. The polymers in the various fabrics expelled all their moisture in a faint humid exhalation, then packed the remaining dirt and dried sweat into a fine, loose dust, and discarded it electro-statically. I watched it drift down into the receptacle; it was always the same disconcerting blue – something to do with the particle size. I had a quick shower, then climbed into bed.

I set the alarm clock for two in the afternoon. The pharm unit beside the clock said, 'Shall I prepare a melatonin course to get you back in synch by tomorrow evening?'

'Yeah, okay.' I stuck my thumb in the sampling tube; there was a barely perceptible sting as blood was taken. Non-invasive NMR models had been in the shops for a couple of years, but they were still too expensive.

'Do you want something to help you sleep now?'

'Yes.'

The pharm began to hum softly, creating a sedative tailored to my current biochemical state, in a dose in accordance with my intended sleeping time. The synthesiser inside used an array of programmable catalysts, ten billion electronically reconfigurable enzymes bound to a semiconductor chip. Im-mersed in a small tank of precursor molecules, the chip could assemble a few milligrams of any one of ten thousand drugs. Or at least, any of the ones for which I had software, for as long as I kept paying the licence fees.

The machine disgorged a small tablet, still slightly warm.

I bit into it. 'Orange-flavoured after a hard night! You remembered!'

I lay back and waited for the drug to take effect.

I'd watched the expression on his face – but those muscles were palsied, uncontrollable. I'd heard his voice – but the breath he spoke with was not his own. I had no real way of knowing what he'd experienced.

Not 'The Monkey's Paw' or 'The Tell-Tale Heart'.

More like 'The Premature Burial'.

But I had no right to mourn Daniel Cavolini. I was going to sell his death to the world.

And I had no right even to empathise, to imagine myself in his place.

As Lukowski had pointed out, it could never have happened to me.

3

I'd seen a 1950s Moviola once, in a glass case in a museum. Thirty-five-millimetre celluloid travelled a tortuous path through the guts of the machine, moving back and forth between two belt-driven spools held up on vertical arms behind the tiny viewing screen. The whine of the motor, the grinding of the gears, the helicopter whir of the shutter blades – sounds coming from an AV of the machine in action, showing on a panel below the display case – had made it seem more like a shredding device than any kind of editing tool.

An appealing notion. *I'm very sorry . . . but that scene has been lost forever. The Moviola ate it.* Standard practice, of course, had been to work only with a copy of the camera original (usually an unviewable negative, anyway) – but the idea of one slip of a cog transforming metres of precious celluloid into confetti had stuck in my head ever since, a glorious, illicit fantasy.

My three-year-old 2052 Affine Graphics editing console was incapable of destroying anything. Every shot I downloaded was burnt into two independent write-once memory chips – and also encrypted and sent automatically to archives in Mandela, Stockholm and Toronto. Every editing decision that followed was just a rearrangement of references to the untouchable original. I could quote from the raw footage (and *footage* it was – only dilettantes used pretentious neologisms like 'byteage') as selectively as I wished. I could paraphrase, substitute, and improvise. But not one frame of the original could ever be damaged or misplaced, beyond repair, beyond recovery.

I didn't really envy my analogue-era counterparts, though; the painstaking mechanics of their craft would have driven me mad. The slowest step in digital editing was human decision-making, and I'd learnt to get most judgements right by the tenth or twelfth attempt. Software could tweak the rhythms of a scene, fine-tune every cut, finesse the sound, remove unwanted passersby; even shift whole buildings, if necessary. The mechanics was all taken care of; there was nothing to distract from the content.

So all I had to do with *Junk DNA* was transform one hundred and eighty hours of real-time into fifty minutes of sense.

I'd filmed four stories, and I already knew how I'd order them: a gradual progression from grey to black. Ned Landers the walking biosphere. The HealthGuard actuarial implant. The Voluntary Autists lobby group. And Daniel Cavolini's revival. SeeNet had asked for excess, for transgressions, for frankenscience. I'd have no trouble giving them exactly what they wanted.

Landers had made his money in dry computers, not bio-tech, but he'd gone on to buy several R&D-intensive molecular genetics corporations to help him achieve his personal transformation. He'd begged me to film him in a sealed geodesic dome full of sulphur dioxide, nitrogen oxides, and benzyl compounds – me in a pressure suit, himself in swimming trunks. We'd tried it, but my face plate kept fogging up on the outside with oily carcinogenic residues, so we'd had to meet again in downtown Portland. Promising as the noxious dome had seemed, the immaculate blue skies of the state which was racing California to zero-emission laws for every known pollutant had turned out to be a more surreal back-drop by far.

'I don't need to breathe at all if I don't want to,' Landers had confided, surrounded by a visible abundance of clean, fresh air. This time, I'd persuaded him to do the interview in a small, grassy park opposite the NL Group's modest headquarters. (There were children playing soccer in the background – but the console would keep track of any continuity problems, and offer solutions to most of them with a single keystroke.) Landers was in his late-forties, but he could have passed for twenty-five. With a robust build, golden hair, blue eyes, and glowing pink skin, he looked more like a Hollywood version of a Kansas farm worker (in good times) than a rich eccentric whose body was swarming with engineered algae and alien genes. I watched him on the console's flatscreen, and listened through simple stereo speakers. I could have fed the playback straight into my optic and auditory nerves, but most viewers would be using a screen or a headset – and I needed to be sure that the software really *had* constructed a steady, plausible, rectilinear grid of pixels out of my own retinas' highly compressed visual shorthand.

'The symbionts living in my bloodstream can turn carbon dioxide back into oxygen indefinitely. They get some energy through my skin, from sunlight, and they release any glucose they can spare – but that's not nearly enough for me to live on, and they need an alternative energy source when they're in darkness. That's where the symbionts in my stomach and intestines come in; I have thirty-seven different types, and between them, they can handle anything. I can eat grass. I can eat paper. I could live off old tyres, if I had a way of cutting them into pieces small enough to swallow. If all plant and animal life vanished from the face of the Earth tomorrow, I could survive off tyres for a thousand years. I have a map showing all the tyre dumps in the continental USA. The majority are scheduled for biological remediation, but I have court actions in progress to see that a number of them survive. Apart from my own personal reasons, I think they're a part of our heritage which we owe to future generations to leave untouched.'

I went back and intercut some microscope footage of the tailored algae and bacteria inhabiting his blood and digestive tract, then a shot of the tyre dump map, which he'd displayed for me on his notepad. I played with an animation I'd been preparing, a schematic of his personal carbon, oxygen, and energy cycles, but I wasn't yet sure where it belonged.

I'd prompted him: 'So you're immune to famine and mass extinctions – but what about viruses? What about biological warfare, or some accidental plague?' I cut my words out; they were redundant, and I preferred to intrude as little as possible. The change of topic was a bit of a *non sequitur* as things stood, though, so I synthesised a shot of Landers saying, 'As well as using symbionts,' computed to merge seamlessly with his actual words, 'I'm gradually replacing those cell lines in my body which have the greatest potential for viral infection. Viruses are made of DNA or RNA; they share the same basic chemistry as every other organism on the planet. That's why they can hijack human cells in order to reproduce. But DNA and RNA can be manufactured with totally novel chemistry – with non-standard base pairs to take the place of the normal ones. A new alphabet for the genetic code: instead of guanine with cytosine, adenine with thymine – instead of G with C, A with T – you can have X with Y, W with Z.'

I changed his words after 'thymine' to: '—you can use four alternative molecules which don't occur in nature at all.' The sense was the same, and it made the point more clearly. But when I replayed the scene, it didn't ring true, so I reverted to the original.

Every journalist paraphrased vis subjects; if I'd flatly refused to employ the technique, I wouldn't be working. The trick was to do it honestly – which was about as difficult as imposing the same criterion on the editing process as a whole.

I cut in some stock molecular graphics of ordinary DNA,

showing every atom in the paired bases which bridged the strands of the helix, and I colour-coded and labelled one example of each base. Landers had refused to specify exactly which non-standard bases he was using, but I'd found plenty of possibilities in the literature. I had the graphics software substitute four plausible new bases for the old ones in the helix, and repeated the slow zoom-in and rotation of the first shot with this hypothetical stretch of Landers-DNA. Then I cut back to his talking head.

'A simple base-for-base substitution in the DNA isn't enough, of course. Cells need some brand new enzymes to synthesise the new bases – and most of the proteins which interact with DNA and RNA need to be adapted to the change, so the genes for those proteins need to be *translated*, not just rewritten in the new alphabet.' I improvised some graphics illustrating the point, stealing an example of a certain nuclear binding protein from one of the journal articles I'd read but redrawing the molecules in a different style, to avoid copyright violation. 'We haven't yet been able to deal with every single human gene which needs translation, but we've made some specific cell lines which work fine with mini-chromosomes containing only the genes they need.

'Sixty per cent of the stem cells in my bone marrow and thymus have been replaced with versions using neo-DNA. Stem cells give rise to blood cells, including the cells of the immune system. I had to switch my immune system back into an immature state, temporarily, to make the transition work smoothly – I had to go through some of the childhood clonal deletion phases all over again, to weed out anything which might have caused an autoimmune response – but basically, I'm now able to shoot up pure HIV, and laugh about it.'

'But there's a perfectly good vaccine—'

'Of course.' I cut my own words out, and made Landers say: 'Of course, there's a vaccine for that.' Then: 'And I have symbionts providing a second, independent immune sytem anyway. But who knows what's coming along next? I'll be prepared, whatever it is. Not by anticipating the specifics – which no one could ever do – but by making sure that no vulnerable cell in my body still speaks the same biochemical language as any virus on Earth.'

'And in the long term? It's taken a lot of expensive infrastructure to provide you with all of these safeguards. What if that technology doesn't survive long enough for your children and grandchildren?' This was all redundant, so I ditched it.

'In the long term, of course, I'm aiming to modify the stem cells which produce my sperm. My wife Carol has already begun a program of ova collection. And once we've translated the entire human genome, and replaced all twenty-three chromosomes in sperm and ova . . . everything we've done will be heritable. Any child of ours will use pure neo-DNA – and all the symbionts will pass from mother to child in the womb.

'We'll translate the genomes of the symbionts as well – into a third genetic alphabet – to protect them from viruses, and to eliminate any risk of accidental gene exchange. They'll be our crops and our herds, our birthright, our inalienable dominion, living in our blood forever.

'And our children will be a new species of life. More than a new species – a whole new kingdom.'

The soccer players in the park cheered; someone had scored a goal. I left it in.

Landers beamed suddenly, radiantly, as if he was contemplating this strange arcadia for the very first time.

'That's what I'm creating. *A new kingdom.*'

I sat at the console eighteen hours a day, and forced myself to live as if the world had shrunk, not to the workroom itself, but to the times and places captured in the footage. Gina left me to it; she'd survived the editing of *Gender Scrutiny Overload*, so she already knew exactly what to expect.

She said blithely, 'I'll just pretend that you're out of town. And that the lump in the bed is a large hot water bottle.'

My pharm programmed a small skin patch on my shoulder to release carefully timed and calibrated doses of melatonin, or a melatonin blocker – adding to, or subtracting from, the usual biochemical signal produced by my pineal gland, re-shaping the normal sine wave of alertness into a plateau followed by a deep, deep trough. I woke every morning from five hours of enriched REM sleep, as wide-eyed and energetic as a hyperactive child, my head spinning with a thousand disintegrating dreams (most of them elaborate remixes of the previous day's editing). I wouldn't so much as yawn until eleven forty-five – but fifteen minutes later, I'd go out like a light. Melatonin was a natural circadian hormone, far safer and more precise in its effects than crude stimulants like caffeine or amphetamines. (I'd tried caffeine a few times; it made me believe I was focused and energetic, but it turned my judgement to shit. Widespread use of caffeine explained a lot about the twentieth century.) I knew that when I went off the melatonin, I'd suffer a short period of insomnia and daytime drowsiness – an overshoot of the brain's attempts to count-eract the imposed rhythm. But the side-effects of the alter-natives were worse.

Carol Landers had declined to be interviewed, which was a shame – it would have been quite a coup to have chatted with the next Mitochondrial Eve. Landers had refused to comment on whether or not she was currently using the symbionts; perhaps she was waiting to see if he'd continue to flourish, or whether he'd suffer a population explosion of some mutant bacterial strain, and go into toxic shock.

I'd been permitted to speak to a few of Landers' senior employees – including the two geneticists who were doing most of the R&D. They were coy when it came to discussing anything beyond the technicalities, but their general attitude seemed to be that any freely chosen treatment which helped safeguard an individual's health – and which posed no threat to the public at large – was ethically unimpeachable. They had a point, at least from the biohazard angle; working with neo-DNA meant there was no risk of accidental recombination. Even if they'd flushed all their failed experiments straight into the nearest river, no natural bacterium could have taken up the genes and made use of them.

Implementing Landers' vision of the perfect survivalist family was going to take more than R&D, though. Making heritable changes in any human gene was currently illegal in the US (and most other places) – apart from a list of a few dozen 'authorised repairs' for eliminating diseases like muscular dystrophy and cystic fibrosis. Legislation could always be revoked, of course – although Landers' own top biotech attorney insisted that changing *the base pairs* – and even translating a few genes to accommodate that change – wouldn't actually violate the anti-eugenics spirit of the existing law. It wouldn't alter the external characteristics of the children (height, build, pigmentation). It wouldn't influence their IQ, or personality. When I'd raised the question of their presumed sterility (barring incest), he'd taken the interesting position that it would hardly be Ned Landers' fault if *other people's children* were sterile with respect to his own. There were no infertile people, after all – only infertile couples.

An expert in the field at Columbia University said all of this was bullshit: substituting whole chromosomes, whatever the phenotypic effects, would simply be illegal. Another expert, at the University of Washington, was less certain. If I'd had the time, I could probably have collected a hundred sound-bites of eminent jurists expressing every conceivable shade of opinion on the subject.

I'd spoken to a number of Landers' critics, including Jane Summers, a freelance biotech consultant based in San

Fransisco, and a prominent member of Molecular Biologists for Social Responsibility. Six months earlier (writing in the semi-public MBSR netzine, which my knowledge miner always scrutinised diligently), she'd claimed to have evidence that several thousand wealthy people, in the US and elsewhere, were having their DNA translated, cell type by cell type. Landers, she'd said, was merely the only one to have gone public – to act as a kind of decoy: a lone eccentric, defusing the issue, making it seem like one man's ridiculous (yet almost Quixotic) fantasy. If the research had been exposed in the media with no specific person associated with it, paranoia would have reigned: there would have been no limit to the possible membership of the nameless elite who planned to divorce themselves from the biosphere. But since it was all out in the open, and all down to harmless Ned Landers, there was really nothing to fear.

The theory made a certain amount of sense – but Summers' evidence hadn't been forthcoming. She'd reluctantly put me in touch with an 'industry source' who'd supposedly been involved in gene translation work for an entirely different employer – but the 'source' had denied everything. Pressed for other leads, Summers had become evasive. Either she'd never had anything substantial or she'd made a deal with another journalist to keep the competition away. It was frustrating, but in the end I hadn't had the time or resources to pursue the story independently. If there really was a cabal of genetic separatists, I'd just have to read the exclusive in the *Washington Post* like everyone else.

I closed with a medley of other commentators – bioethicists, geneticists, sociologists – mostly dismissing the whole affair. 'Mr Landers has the right to live his own life, and raise his own children any way he sees fit. We don't persecute the Amish for their inbreeding, their strange technology, their desire for independence. Why persecute him, for essentially the same "crimes"?'

29

The final cut of the story was eighteen minutes long. In the broadcast version, there'd only be room for twelve. I pared away mercilessly, summarising and simplifying – taking care to do a professional job, but not too worried by the loss of detail. Most real-time broadcasts on SeeNet served no purpose but to focus publicity, and to guarantee reviews in some of the more conservative media. *Junk DNA* was scheduled for 11 p.m. on a Wednesday; the vast majority of the audience would log on to the full, interactive version at their convenience. As well as a slightly longer linear backbone, the interactive would be peppered with optional detours to other sources: all the technical journal articles I'd read for my own research (and all the articles they in turn cited); other media coverage of Landers (and of Jane Summers' conspiracy theory); the relevant US and international statutes – and even trails leading into the quagmire of potentially relevant case law.

On the evening of the fifth day of editing – right on schedule, reason enough for minor jubilation – I tidied up all the loose ends, and ran through the segment one last time. I tried to clear away all my memories of filming, and all my preconceptions, and watch the story like a SeeNet viewer who'd seen nothing at all on the subject before (save a few misleading promotions for the documentary itself).

Landers came across surprisingly sympathetically. I'd thought I'd been harsher. I'd thought I'd at least given him every opportunity to damn himself with his earnest account of his surreal ambitions. Instead, he seemed far more good-humoured than po-faced; he almost appeared to be sharing all the jokes. *Living off tyre dumps? Shooting up HIV?* I watched, amazed. I couldn't decide if there really was a faint undercurrent of deliberate irony, a hint of self-deprecation in his manner which I'd somehow missed before – or whether the subject matter simply made it impossible for a sane viewer to interpret his words any other way.

What if Summers was right? What if Landers was a decoy,

a distraction, a consummate performing clown? What if thousands of the planet's wealthiest people really were planning to grant themselves, and their offspring, perfect genetic isolation, and absolute viral immunity?

Would it matter? The rich had always cut themselves off from the rabble, one way or another. Pollution levels would continue to decline, whether or not algal symbionts rendered fresh air obsolete. And anyone who chose to follow in Landers' footsteps was no great loss to the human gene pool.

There was only one small question which remained unanswered, and I tried not to give it too much thought.

Absolute viral immunity . . . against what?

4

Delphic Biosystems had been too generous by far. Not only had they arranged for me to interview ten times as many of their Public Relations staff as I could ever have made time for, they'd showered me with ROMs packed with seductive micrographs and dazzling animation. Software flow-charts for the HealthGuard implant were rendered as airbrushed fantasies of impossible chromed machines, jet-black conveyor belts moving incandescent silver nuggets of 'data' from subprocess to subprocess. Molecular schematics of interacting proteins were shrouded with delicately beautiful – and utterly gratuitous – electron-density maps, veils of pink and blue aurorae melting and merging, transforming the humblest chemical wedding into a microcosmic fantasia. I could have set it all to Wagner – or Blake – and flogged it to members of Mystical Renaissance, to play on a loop whenever they wanted to go slack-jawed with numinous incomprehension.

I slogged my way through the whole morass, though – and it finally paid off. Buried amongst all the technoporn and science-as-psychedelia were a few shots worth salvaging.

The HealthGuard implant employed the latest programmable assay chip: an array of elaborate proteins bound to silicon, in many respects like a pharm's synthesiser, but designed to count molecules, not make them. The previous generation of chips had used a multitude of highly specific antibodies, Y-shaped proteins planted in the semiconductor in a chequerboard pattern, like adjoining fields of a hundred different crops. When a molecule of cholesterol, or insulin, or whatever, happened to strike exactly the right field and collide with a matching antibody, it bound to it long enough for the tiny change in capacitance to be detected, and logged in a microprocessor. Over time, this record of serendipitous collisions yielded the amount of each substance in the blood.

The new sensors used a protein which was more like a Venus flytrap with brains than an antibody's passive, single-purpose template. 'Assayin' in its receptive state was a long, bell-shaped molecule, a tube opening out into a broad funnel. This conformation was metastable; the charge distribution on the molecule rendered it exquisitely sensitive, spring-loaded. Anything large enough colliding with the inner surface of the funnel caused a lightning-fast wave of deformation, engulfing and shrink-wrapping the intruder. The micro-processor, noting the sprung trap, could then probe the captive molecule by searching for a shape of the assayin which imprisoned it even more snugly. There were no more wasted, mismatched collisions – no more insulin molecules striking cholesterol antibodies, yielding no information at all. Assayin always knew what had hit it.

It was a technical advance worth communicating, worth explaining, worth *demystifying*. Whatever the social implications of the HealthGuard implant, they could no more be presented in a vacuum, divorced from the technology which made the device possible, than *vice versa*. Once people ceased to understand how the machines around them actually functioned, the world they inhabited began to dissolve into an incomprehensible dreamscape. Technology moved beyond control, beyond discussion, evoking only worship or loathing, dependence or alienation. Arthur C. Clarke had suggested that any sufficiently advanced technology would be indistinguishable from magic – referring to a possible encounter with an alien civilisation – but if a science journalist had one responsiblity above all else, it was to keep Clarke's Law from applying to human technology in human eyes.

(Lofty sentiments . . . and here I was peddling franken-science, because that was the niche that had needed filling. I salved my conscience – or numbed it for a while – with platitudes about Trojan horses, and changing the system from within.)

I took the Delphic Biosystems graphics of assayin in action, and had the console strip away the excessive decoration so it was possible to see clearly what was going on. I threw out the gushing commentary and wrote my own. The console deliv-ered it in the diction profile I'd chosen for all of *Junk DNA*'s narration, cloned from samples of an English actor named Juliet Stevenson. The long-vanished 'Standard English' pro-nunciation – unlike any contemporary UK accent – remained easily comprehensible across the vast Anglophone world. Any viewer who wished to hear a different voice could cross-translate at will, though; I often listened to programs re-dubbed into the regional accents I had most trouble following – US south-east, northern Irish, and east-central African – hoping to sharpen my ear for them.

Hermes – my communications software – was programmed to bounce almost everyone on Earth, while I was editing. Lydia Higuchi, SeeNet's West Pacific Commissioning Execu-tive Producer, was one of the few exceptions. It was my notepad that rang, but I switched the call through to the console itself; the screen was larger and clearer – and the camera stamped its signal with the words AFFINE GRAPHICS EDITOR MODEL 2052-KL, and a time code. Not very subtle, but it wasn't meant to be.

Lydia got straight to the point. She said, 'I saw the final cut of the Landers stuff. It's good. But I want to talk about what comes next.'

'The HealthGuard implant? Is there some problem?' I didn't hide my irritation. She'd seen selections of the raw footage, she'd seen all my post-production notes. If she wanted anything significant changed, she'd left it too damned late.

She laughed. 'Andrew, take one step back. Not the next story in *Junk DNA*. Your next project.'

I eyed her as if she'd casually raised the prospect of imminent travel to another planet. I said, 'Don't do this to me, Lydia. Please. You know I can't think rationally about anything else right now.'

She nodded sympathetically but said, 'I take it you've been monitoring this new disease? It's not anecdotal static anymore; there are official reports coming out of Geneva, Atlanta, Nairobi.'

My stomach tightened. 'You mean Acute Clinical Anxiety Syndrome?'

'A.k.a. *Distress*.' She seemed to savour the word, as if she'd already adopted it into her vocabulary of deeply telegenic subjects. My spirits sank even further.

I said, 'My knowledge miner's been logging everything on it, but I haven't had time to stay up to date.' *And frankly, right now . . .*

'There are over four hundred diagnosed cases, Andrew. That's a thirty per cent rise in the last six months.'

'How can anyone *diagnose* something when they don't have a clue what it is?'

'Process of elimination.'

'Yeah, I think it's bullshit, too.'

She mimed brief sarcastic amusement. 'Get serious. This is a brand new mental illness. Possibly communicable. Possibly caused by an escaped military pathogen—'

'Possibly fallen from a comet. Possibly a punishment from God. Amazing how many things are possible, isn't it?'

She shrugged. 'Whatever the cause, it's spreading. There are cases everywhere now but Antarctica. This is headline news – and more. The board decided last night: we're going to commission a thirty-minute special on Distress. High profile, blitz promotion, culminating in synchronous primetime broadcasts, worldwide.'

Synchonous didn't mean what it should have, in netspeak; it meant the same calendar date and local time for all viewers. 'Worldwide? You mean Anglophone world?'

'I mean world world. We're tying up arrangements to on-sell to other-language networks.'

'Well . . . good.'

Lydia smiled, a tight-lipped impatient smile. 'Are you being coy, Andrew? Do I have to spell it out? We want you to make it. You're our biotech specialist, you're the logical choice. And you'll do a great job. So . . . ?'

I put a hand to my forehead, and tried to work out why I felt so claustrophobic. I said, 'How long do I have, to decide?'

She smiled even more widely, which meant she was puzzled, annoyed, or both. 'We're broadcasting on 24 May – that's ten weeks from Monday. You'll need to start pre-production the minute *Junk DNA* is finished. So we need your answer as soon as possible.'

Rule number four: Discuss everything with Gina first. Whether or not she'd ever admit to being offended if you didn't.

I said, 'Tomorrow morning.'

Lydia wasn't happy, but she said, 'That's fine.'

I steeled myself. 'If I say no, is there anything else going?'

Lydia looked openly astonished now. 'What's wrong with you? Primetime world broadcast! You'll make five times as much on this as on *Gender*.'

'I realise that. And I'm grateful for the chance, believe me. I just want to know if there's . . . any other choice.'

'You could always go and hunt for coins on the beach with a metal detector.' She saw my face, and softened. Slightly. 'There's another project about to go into pre-production. Although I've very nearly promised it to Sarah Knight.'

'Tell me.'

'Ever heard of Violet Mosala?'

'Of course. She's a . . . physicist? A South African physicist?'

'Two out of two, very impressive. Sarah's a huge fan, she chewed my ear off about her for an hour.'

'So what's the project?'

'A profile of Mosala . . . who's twenty-seven, and won the Nobel Prize two years ago – but you knew that all along, didn't you? Interviews, biography, appraisals by colleagues, blah blah blah. Her work's purely theoretical, so there's nothing much to show of it except computer simulations – and she's offered us her own graphics. But the heart of the program will be the Einstein Centenary conference—'

'Wasn't that back in the 1970s?' Lydia gave me a withering look. I said, 'Ah. Centenary of his death. Charming.'

'Mosala is attending the conference. On the last day of which, three of the world's top theoretical physicists are scheduled to present rival versions of the Theory of Everything. And you don't get three guesses as to who's the alpha favourite.'

I gritted my teeth and suppressed the urge to say: *It's not a horse race, Lydia. It might be another fifty years before anyone knows whose TOE was right.*

'So when's the conference?'

'The fifth to the eighteenth of April.'

I blanched. 'Three weeks from Monday.'

Lydia looked thoughtful for a moment, then pleased. 'You don't really have time, do you? Sarah's been prepared for this for months—'

I said irritably, 'Five seconds ago you were talking about me starting pre-production on *Distress* in less than three weeks.'

'You could walk straight into *that*. How much modern physics do you know?'

I feigned indignation. '*Enough!* And I'm not stupid. I can catch up.'

'When?'

'I'll make time. I'll work faster; I'll finish *Junk DNA* ahead of schedule. When's the Mosala program going to be broadcast?'

'Early next year.'

Which meant eight whole months of relative sanity – once the conference was over.

Lydia glanced at her watch, redundantly. 'I don't understand you. A high-profile special on Distress would be the logical endpoint of everything you've been doing for the last five years. After that, you could think about switching away from biotech. And who am I going to use instead of you?'

'Sarah Knight?'

'Don't be sarcastic.'

'I'll tell her you said that.'

'Be my guest. I don't care what she's done in politics, she's only made one science program – and that was on fringe cosmology. It was good – but not good enough to ramp her straight into something like this. She's earned a fortnight with Violet Mosala, but not a primetime broadcast on the world's alphamost virus.'

Nobody had *found* a virus associated with Distress; I hadn't seen a news bulletin for a week, but my knowledge miner would have told me if there'd been a breakthrough of that magnitude. I was beginning to get the queasy feeling that if I didn't make the program myself, it would be subtitled: *How an escaped military pathogen became the twenty-first-century AIDS of the mind.*

Pure vanity. What did I think, that I was the only person on the planet capable of deflating the rumours and hysteria surrounding Distress?

I said, 'I haven't made any decision yet. I need to talk it over with Gina.'

Lydia was sceptical. 'Okay, fine. "Talk it over with Gina", and call me in the morning.' She glanced at her watch again. 'Look, I really have to go. Some of us actually have *work* to do.' I opened my mouth to protest, outraged; she smiled sweetly and aimed two fingers at me. 'Gotcha. No sense of irony, you *auteurs*. 'Bye.'

I turned away from the console and sat staring down at my clenched fists, trying to untangle what I was feeling – if only enough to enable me to put it all aside and get back to *Junk DNA*.

I'd seen a brief news shot of someone with Distress, a few months before. I'd been in a hotel room in Manchester, flicking channels between appointments. A young woman – looking healthy, but dishevelled – was lying on her back in a corridor in an apartment building in Miami. She was waving her arms wildly, kicking in all directions, tossing her head and twisting her whole body back and forth. It hadn't looked like the product of any kind of crude neurological dysfunction, though: it had seemed too coordinated, too purposeful.

And before the police and paramedics could hold her still – or still enough to get a needle in – and pump her full of some high-powered court-order paralytic like Straitjacket or Medusa – they'd tried the sprays, and they hadn't worked – she'd thrashed and screamed like an animal in mortal agony, like a child in a solipsistic rage, like an adult in the grip of the blackest despair.

I'd watched and listened in disbelief – and when, mercifully, she'd been rendered comatose and dragged away, I'd struggled to convince myelf that it had been nothing out of the ordinary: some kind of epileptic fit, some kind of psychotic tantrum, at worst some kind of unbearable physical pain, the cause of which would be swiftly identified and dealt with.

None of which was true. Victims of Distress rarely had a history of neurological or mental illness, and bore no signs of injury or disease. And no one had the slightest idea how to *deal with* the cause of their suffering; the only current 'treatment' consisted of sustained heavy sedation.

I picked up my notepad and touched the icon for **Sisyphus**, my knowledge miner.

I said, 'Assemble a briefing on Violet Mosala, the Einstein Centenary conference, and the last ten years' advances in Unified Field Theories. I'll need to digest it all in about . . . a hundred and twenty hours. Is that feasible?'

There was pause while **Sisyphus** downloaded the relevant sources and scrutinised them. Then it asked, 'Do you know what an ATM is?'

'An Automatic Teller Machine?'

'No. In this context, an ATM is an All-Topologies Model.'

The phrase sounded vaguely familiar; I'd probably skimmed through a brief article on the topic, five years before.

There was another pause, while more elementary background material was downloaded and assessed. Then: 'A hundred and twenty hours would be good enough for listening and nodding. Not for asking intelligent questions.'

I groaned. 'How long for . . . ?'

'A hundred and fifty.'

'Do it.'

I hit the icon for the pharm unit, and said, 'Recompute my melatonin doses. Give me two more hours of peak alertness a day, starting immediately.'

'Until when?'

The conference began on 5 April; if I wasn't an expert on Violet Mosala by then, it would be too late. But I couldn't risk cutting loose from the forced rhythms of the melatonin – and rebounding into erratic sleep patterns – in the middle of filming.

'April the eighteenth.'

The pharm said, 'You'll be sorry.'

That was no generic warning – it was a prediction based on five years' worth of intimate biochemical knowledge. But I had no real choice – and if I spent the week after the conference suffering from acute circadian arrhythmia, it would be unpleasant, but it wouldn't kill me.

I did some calculations in my head. Somehow, I'd just conjured up five or six hours of free time out of thin air.

It was a Friday. I phoned Gina at work. *Rule number six: Be unpredictable. But not too often.*

I said, 'Screw *Junk DNA*. Want to go dancing?'

5

It was Gina's idea to go deep into the city. The Ruins held no attraction for me – and there was far better nightlife closer to home – but (rule number seven) it wasn't worth an argument. When the train pulled into Town Hall station, and we took the escalators up past the platform where Daniel Cavolini had been stabbed to death, I blanked my mind and smiled.

Gina linked arms with me and said, 'There's something here I don't feel anywhere else. An energy, a buzz. Can't you feel it?'

I looked around at the station's black-and-white tiled walls, graffiti-proof and literally antiseptic.

'No more than in Pompei.'

The demographic centre of greater Sydney had been west of Parramatta for at least half a century – and had probably reached Blacktown, by now – but the demise of the historical urban core had begun in earnest only in the 30s, when office space, cinemas, theatres, physical galleries and public museums had all become obsolete at more or less the same time. Broadband optical fibres had been connected to most residential buildings since the teens but it had taken another two decades for the networks to mature. The tottering edifice of incompatible standards, inefficient hardware, and archaic operating systems thrown together by the fin-de-siècle dinosaurs of computing and communications had been razed to the ground in the 20s, and only then – after years of premature hype and well-earned backlashes of cynicism and ridicule –

could the use of the networks for entertainment and tele-commuting be transmuted from a form of psychological torture into a natural and convenient alternative to ninety per cent of physical travel.

We stepped out on to George Street. It was far from deserted, but I'd seen footage from days when the country's population was half as much, and it shamed these meagre crowds. Gina looked up, and her eyes caught the lights; many of the old office towers still dazzled, their windows decorated for the tourists with cheap sunlight-storing luminescent coatings. 'The Ruins' was a joke, of course – vandalism, let alone time, had scarcely made a mark – but we *were* all tourists here, come to gawk at the monuments left behind, not by our ancestors, but by our older siblings.

Few buildings had been converted for residential use; the architecture and economics had never added up – and some urban preservationists actively campaigned against it. There were squatters, of course – probably a couple of thousand, spread throughout what was still referred to as the Central Business District – but they only added to the post-apocalyptic mood. Live theatre and music survived, out in the suburbs – with small plays in small venues, or crowd-pulling colosseum bands in sports stadia – but mainstream theatre was per-formed in real-time VR over the networks. (The Opera House, foundations rotting, was currently predicted to slide into Sydney Harbour in 2065 – a delightful prospect, though I suspected that some group of saccharine-blooded killjoys would raise the money to rescue the useless icon at the last moment.) Walk-in retailing, such as it was, had long ago moved entirely to regional centres. There were a few hotels still open on the fringes of the city, but restaurants and nightclubs were all that remained in the dead heart, spread out between the empty towers like souvenir stalls scattered amongst the pyramids in the Valley of the Kings.

We headed south into what had once been Chinatown; the

43

crumbling decorative façades of deserted emporia still attested to that, even if the cuisine didn't.

Gina nudged me gently and directed my attention to a group of people strolling north, on the opposite side of the street. When they'd passed, she said, 'Were they . . . ?'

'What? Asex? I think so.'

'I'm never sure. There are naturals who look no different.'

'But that's the whole point. You can never be sure – but why did we ever think we could discover anything that mattered about a stranger, at a glance?'

Asex was really nothing but an umbrella term for a broad group of philosophies, styles of dress, cosmetic-surgical changes, and deep-biological alterations. The only thing that one asex person necessarily had in common with another was the view that vis gender parameters (neural, endocrine, chromosomal and genital) were the business of no one but verself, usually (but not always) vis lovers, probably vis doctor, and sometimes a few close friends. What a person actually did in response to that attitude could range from as little as ticking the 'A' box on census forms, to choosing an asex name, to breast or body-hair reduction, voice timbre adjustment, facial resculpting, empouchment (surgery to render the male genitals retractable), all the way to full physical and/or neural asexuality, hermaphroditism, or exoticism.

I said, 'Why bother staring at people and guessing? En-male, en-fem, asex . . . who cares?'

Gina scowled. 'Don't make me out to be some kind of bigot. I'm just curious.'

I squeezed her hand. 'I'm sorry. That's not what I meant.'

She pulled free. '*You* got to spend a year thinking about nothing else – being as voyeuristic and intrusive as you liked. And getting paid for it. I only saw the finished documentary. I don't see why I should be expected to have reached some final position on gender migration just because *you've* rolled credits on the subject.'

I bent over and kissed her on the forehead.

'What was that for?'

'For being the ideal viewer, above and beyond all your many other virtues.'

'I think I'm going to throw up.'

We turned east, towards Surry Hills, into an even quieter street. A grim young man strode by alone, heavily muscled and probably facially sculpted . . . but again, there was no way to be sure. Gina glanced at me, still angry, but unable to resist. '*That* – assuming he was umale – I understand even less. If someone wants a build like that . . . fine. But why the face, as well? It's not as if anyone would be likely to mistake him for anything but an en-male, without it.'

'No – but being mistaken for an en-male would be an insult, because he's migrated out of that gender as surely as any asex. The whole point of being umale is to distance yourself from the perceived weaknesses of contemporary natural males. To declare that their "consensual identity" – stop laughing – is so much less masculine than your own that you effectively belong to another sex entirely. To say: no mere en-male can speak on my behalf, any more than a woman can.'

Gina mimed tearing out hair. 'No *woman* can speak on behalf of all *women*, as far as I'm concerned. But I don't feel obliged to have myself sculpted ufem or ifem to make that point!'

'Well . . . exactly. I feel the same way. Whenever some Iron John cretin writes a manifesto "in the name of" all men, I'd much rather tell him to his face that he's full of shit than desert the en-male gender and leave him thinking that he speaks for all those who remain. But . . . that *is* the commonest reason people cite for gender migration: they're sick of self-appointed gender-political figureheads and pretentious Mystical Renaissance gurus claiming to represent them. And sick of being libelled for real and imagined gender crimes. If all men are violent, selfish, dominating, hierarchical . . . what can you do except slit your wrists, or migrate from male to imale, or asex? If all women are weak, passive, irrational victims—'

Gina thumped me on the arm admonishingly. 'Now you're caricaturing the caricaturists. I don't believe anyone talks like that.'

'Only because you move in the wrong circles. Or should I say the right ones? But I thought you watched the program. There were people I interviewed who made exactly those assertions, word for word.'

'Then it's the fault of the media for giving them publicity.'

We'd arrived at the restaurant, but we lingered outside. I said, 'That's partly true. I don't know what the solution is, though. When will someone who stands up and proclaims, "I speak for no one but myself" get as much coverage as someone who claims to speak for half the population?'

'When people like you give it to them.'

'You know it's not that simple. And . . . imagine what would have happened with feminism – or the civil rights movements, for that matter – if no one could ever be permitted to speak "on behalf of" any group, without their certified, unanimous consent? Just because some of the current lunatics are like parodies of the old leaders, it doesn't mean we'd be better off now if TV producers had said: "Sorry, Dr King, sorry, Ms Greer, sorry, Mr Perkins, but if you can't avoid these sweeping generalisations and confine your statements to your personal circumstances, we'll have to take you off the air." '

Gina eyed me sceptically. 'That's ancient history. And you're only arguing that position to try to squirm out of your own responsibilities.'

'Of course. But the point is . . . gender migration is ninety per cent *politics*. Some coverage still treats it as a kind of decadent, gratuitous, fashionable mimicry of gender reassignment for transsexuals – but most gender migrants go no further than superficial asex. They don't cross right over;

they have no reason to. It's a protest action, like resigning from a political party, or renouncing your citizenship . . . or deserting a battlefield . . . but whether it will stabilise at some low level, and shake up attitudes enough to remove the whole reason for migration, or whether the population will end up evenly divided between all seven genders in a couple of generations, I have no idea.'

Gina grimaced. 'Seven genders – and all of them perceived as monolithic. Everyone stereotyped at a glance. Seven pigeon-holes instead of two isn't progress.'

'No. But maybe in the long run there'll only be asex, umale and ufem. Those who want to be pigeon-holed will be – and those who don't will remain mysterious.'

'No, no – in the long run we'll have nothing but VR bodies, and we'll all be mysterious or revelatory in turns, as the mood takes us.'

'I can't wait.'

We went inside. Unnatural Tastes was a converted department store, cavernous but brightly lit, opened up by the simple expedient of cutting a large elliptical hole in the middle of every floor. I waved my notepad at the entry turnstile; a voice confirmed our reservation, adding, 'Table 519. Fifth floor.'

Gina smiled wickedly. 'Fifth floor: stuffed toys and lingerie.'

I glanced up at our fellow diners – mostly umale and ufem couples. I said, 'You behave yourself, redneck, or next time we're eating in Epping.'

The place was three-quarters full, at least, but the seating capacity was less than it seemed; most of the volume of the building was taken up by the central well. In what was left of each floor, human waiters in tuxedos weaved their way between the chromed tables; it all looked archaic and stylised, almost Marx Brothers, to me. I wasn't a big fan of Experimental Cuisine; essentially, we'd be guinea pigs, trying out medically safe but otherwise untested bioengineered produce.

Gina had pointed out that at least the meal would be sub-sidised by the manufacturers. I wasn't so sure; Experimental Cuisine had become so fashionable lately that it could prob-ably attract a statistically significant sample of diners for each novelty, even at full price.

The tabletop flashed up menus as we took our seats – and the figures seemed to confirm my doubts about a subsidy. I groaned. ' "Crimson bean salad"? I don't care what colour they are, I want to know what they *taste like*. The last thing I ate here that looked like a kidney bean tasted exactly like boiled cabbage.'

Gina took her time, prodding the names of half a dozen dishes to view the finished products, and screens of data on the design of the ingredients. She said, 'You can work it all out, if you pay attention. If you know what genes they moved from where, and why, you can make a fair stab at predicting the taste and texture.'

'Go ahead, dazzle me with science.'

She hit the CONFIRM ORDER button. 'The green leafy stuff will taste like spinach-flavoured pasta – but the iron in it will be absorbed by your body as easily as the haem iron in animal flesh, leaving spinach for dead. The yellow things which look like corn will taste like a cross between tomato and green cap-sicum spiced with oregano – but nutrients and flavour will be less sensitive to poor storage conditions and over-cooking. And the blue puree will taste almost like parmesan cheese.'

'Why blue?'

'There's a blue pigment, a photoactivated enzyme, in the new self-fermenting lactoberries. They could remove it during processing, but it turns out we metabolise it directly into vitamin D – which is safer than making it the usual way, with UV on the skin.'

'Food for people who never see the sun. How can I resist?' I ordered the same.

The service was swift – and Gina's predictions were more

or less correct. The whole combination was actually quite pleasant.

I said, 'You're wasted on wind turbines. You could be designing the spring collection for United Agronomics.'

'Gee, thanks. But I already get all the intellectual stimulation I can handle.'

'How is Big Harold coming along, anyway?'

'Still very much Little Harold, and likely to stay that way for a while.' Little Harold was the one-thousandth-scale prototype of a projected two-hundred-megawatt turbine. 'There are chaotic resonance modes turning up which we missed in the simulations. It's starting to look like we're going to have to re-evaluate half the assumptions of the software model.'

'I can never quite understand that. You know all the basic physics, the basic equations of air-flow dynamics, you have access to endless supercomputer time . . .'

'So how can we possibly screw up? Because we can't compute the behaviour of thousands of tonnes of air moving through a complex structure on a molecule-by-molecule basis. *All* the bulk flow equations are approximations, and we're deliberately operating in a region where the best-understood approximations break down. There's no magical new physics coming into play – but we're in a grey zone between one set of convenient simplifying assumptions and another. And so far, the best new set of compromise assumptions are neither convenient nor simple. And they're not even correct, as it turns out.'

'I'm sorry.'

She shrugged. 'It's frustrating – but enough of it's frustrating in an interesting way to keep me from going insane.'

I felt a stab of longing; I understood so little about this part of her life. She'd explained as much as I could follow, but I still had no real idea of what spun through her head when she was sitting at her work station juggling airflow simulations, or clambering around the wind tunnel making adjustments to Little Harold.

I said, 'I wish you'd let me film some of this.'

Gina regarded me balefully. 'Not a chance, Mr Franken-science. Not until you can tell me categorically whether wind turbines are Good or Evil.'

I cringed. 'You know that's not up to me. And it changes every year. New studies are published, the alternatives come in and out of favour—'

She cut me off bitterly. '*Alternatives?* Planting *photovoltaic engineered forests* on ten thousand times as much land per megawatt sounds like environmental vandalism to me.'

'I'm not arguing. I could always make a Good Turbine documentary . . . and if I can't sell it straight away, just wait for the tide to turn again.'

'You can't afford to make anything on spec.'

'True. I'd have to fit it in between other shooting.'

Gina laughed. 'I wouldn't try it. You can't even manage—'

'What?'

'Nothing. Forget it.' She waved a hand, retracting the comment. I could have pressed her, but I would have been wasting my time.

I said, 'Speaking of filming . . .' I described the two projects Lydia had offered me. Gina listened patiently, but when I asked for her opinion, she seemed baffled.

'If you don't want to make *Distress* . . . then don't. It's really none of my business.'

That stung. I said, 'It affects you, too. It would be a lot more money.' Gina looked affronted. 'All I mean is, we could afford to take a holiday or something. We could go overseas next time you have leave. If that's what you wanted.'

She said stiffly, 'I'm not taking leave for another eighteen months. And I can pay for my own holidays.'

'All right. Forget it.' I reached over to take her hand; she pulled away, irritated.

We ate in silence. I stared down at my plate, running through the rules, trying to decide where I'd gone wrong. Had I broken some taboo about money? We kept separate accounts, sharing the rent fifty-fifty – but we'd both helped each other out, many times, and given each other small luxuries. What should I have done? Gone ahead and made *Distress* – purely for the money – and only then asked if there was anything we could spend it on together that would make it worthwhile?

Maybe I'd made it sound as if I thought she expected to dictate the projects I chose – offending her by seeming to have failed to appreciate the independence she allowed me. My head spun. The truth was, I had no idea what she was thinking. *It was all too hard, too slippery.* And I couldn't imagine what I could say that might begin to put it right, without the risk of making everything far worse.

After a while, Gina said, 'So where's the big conference being held?'

I opened my mouth, then realised I didn't have a clue. I picked up my notepad and quickly checked the briefing Sisyphus had prepared.

'Ah. On Stateless.'

'*Stateless?*' She laughed. 'You're a burnt-out case on biotech . . . so they're sending you to the world's largest engineered-coral island?'

'I'm only fleeing Evil biotech. Stateless is Good.'

'Oh, really? Tell that to the governments who keep it embargoed. Are you sure you won't get thrown in prison when you come home?'

'I'm not going to trade with the wicked anarchists. I'm not even going to film them.'

'Anarcho-syndicalists, get it right. Though they don't even call themselves that, do they?'

I said, 'Who's "they"? It depends who you ask.'

'You should have had a segment on Stateless in *Junk*

DNA. Embargoed or not, they're prospering – and all thanks to biotechnology. That would have balanced the talking corpse.'

'But then I couldn't have called it *Junk DNA*, could I?'

'Exactly.' She smiled. Whatever I'd done, I'd been forgiven. I felt my heart pounding, as if I'd been dragged back at the last moment from the edge of an abyss.

The dessert we chose tasted like cardboard and snow, but we obligingly filled out the tabletop questionnaires before leaving.

We headed north up George Street to Martin Place. There was a nightclub called The Sorting Room in the old Post Office building. They played Zimbabwean *njari* music, multi-layered, hypnotic, pounding but never metronomic, leaving splinters of rhythm in the brain like the marks of fingernails raked over flesh. Gina danced ecstatically, and the music was so loud that speech was, mercifully, almost impossible. In this wordless place I could do no wrong.

We left just after one. On the train back to Eastwood, we sat in a corner of the carriage, kissing like teenagers. I wondered how my parents' generation had ever driven their precious cars in such a state. (Badly, no doubt.) The trip home was ten minutes – almost too short. I wanted everything to unfold as slowly as possible. I wanted it to last for hours.

We stopped a dozen times, walking down from the station. We stood outside the front door for so long that the security system asked us if we'd lost our keys.

When we undressed and fell on to the bed together, and my vision lurched, I thought it was just a side-effect of passion. When my arms went numb, though, I realised what was happening.

I'd pushed myself too far with the melatonin blockers, depleting neurotransmitter reserves in the region of the hypo-thalamus where alertness was controlled. I'd borrowed too much time, and the plateau was crumbling.

Stricken, I said, 'I don't believe this. I'm sorry.'

'About what?' I still had an erection.

I forced myself to concentrate; I reached over and hit a button on the pharm. 'Give me half an hour.'

'No. Safety limits—'

'Fifteen minutes,' I pleaded. 'This is an emergency.'

The pharm hesitated, consulting the security system. 'There is no emergency. You're safe in bed, and the house is under no threat.'

'You're gone. You're recycled.'

Gina seemed more amused than disappointed. 'See what happens when you transgress natural limits? I hope you're recording this for *Junk DNA*.' Mockery only made her a thousand times more desirable – but I was already lapsing into microsleeps. I said dolefully, 'Forgive me? Maybe . . . tomorrow, we could—'

'I don't think so. Tomorrow you'll be working till 1 a.m. And I'm not waiting up.' She took me by the shoulders and rolled me on to my back, then knelt astride my stomach.

I made sounds of protest. She bent over and kissed me on the mouth, tenderly. 'Come on. You don't really want to waste this rare opportunity, do you?' She reached down and stroked my cock; I could feel it respond to her touch, but it barely seemed to be a part of me anymore.

I murmured, 'Ravisher. Necrophiliac.' I wanted to make a long earnest speech about sex and communication, but Gina seemed intent on disproving my whole thesis before I could even begin. 'Talk about *Bad Timing*.'

She said, 'Is that a yes or a no?'

I gave up trying to open my eyes. 'Go ahead.'

Something vaguely pleasant began to happen, but my senses were retreating, my body was spinning off into the void.

I heard a voice, light-years away, whisper something about 'sweet dreams'.

But I plunged into blackness, feeling nothing. And I dreamt of silent oceanic depths.

Of falling through dark water. Alone.

6

I'd heard that London had suffered badly from the coming of the networks, but was less of a ghost town than Sydney. The Ruins were more extensive, but they were being exploited far more diligently; even the last glass-and-aluminium towers built for bankers and stockbrokers at the turn of the millennium, and the last of the 'high tech' printing presses which had 'revolutionised' newspaper publishing (before becoming completely obsolete), had been labelled 'historic' and taken under the wing of the tourism industry.

I hadn't had time, though, to visit the hushed tombs of Bishopsgate or Wapping. I'd flown straight to Manchester – which appeared to be thriving. According to **Sisyphus**'s potted history, the balance between real-estate prices and infrastructure costs had favoured the city in the 20s, and thousands of information-based companies – with a largely telecommuting workforce, but the need for a small central office as well – had moved there from the south. This industrial revival had also shored up the academic sector, and Manchester University was widely acknowledged to be leading the world in at least a dozen fields, including neurolinguistics, neo-protein chemistry, and advanced medical imaging.

I replayed the footage I'd taken of the city centre – swarming with pedestrians, bicycles and quadcycles – and picked out a few brief establishing shots. I'd hired a bicycle, myself, from one of the automated depots outside Victoria Station; ten ecus and it was mine for the day. It was a recent model Whirlwind, a beautiful machine: light, elegant, and nearly indestructible –

made in nearby Sheffield. It could simulate a pushbike if required (a trivial option to include, and it kept the masochistic purists happy), but there was no mechanical connection between pedals and wheels; essentially, it was a human-powered electric motorbike. Superconducting current loops buried in the chassis acted as a short-term energy store, smoothing out demands on the rider, and taking full advantage of the energy-reclaiming brakes. Forty k.p.h. took no more effort than a brisk walk, and hills were almost irrelevant, ascent and descent nearly cancelling each other out in energy lost and gained. It must have been worth about two thousand ecus – but the navigation system, the beacons and locks, were so close to tamper-proof that I would have needed a small factory, and a PhD in cryptology, to steal it.

The city's trams went almost everywhere, but so did the covered cycleways, so I'd ridden the Whirlwind to my afternoon appointment.

James Rourke was Media Liaison Officer for the Voluntary Autists Association. A thin, angular man in his early-thirties, in the flesh he'd struck me as painfully awkward, with poor eye contact and muted body language. Verbally articulate, but far from telegenic.

Watching him on the console screen, though, I realised how wrong I'd been. Ned Landers had put on a dazzling performance, so slick and seamless that it left no room for any question of what was going on beneath. Rourke put on no performance at all – and the effect was both riveting and deeply unsettling. Coming straight after Delphic Biosytems' elegant, assured spokespeople (teeth and skin by Masarini of Florence, sincerity by Operant Conditioning plc), it would be like being jolted out of a daydream by a kick in the head.

I'd have to tone him down, somehow.

I had a fully autistic cousin myself – Nathan. I'd met him only once, when we were both children. He was one of the lucky few who'd suffered no other congenital brain damage, and at the time he was still living with his parents in Adelaide. He'd shown me his computer, cataloguing its features exhaustively, sounding scarcely different from any other enthusiastic thirteen-year-old technophile with a new toy. But when he'd started demonstrating his favourite programs – stultifying solo card games, and bizarre memory quizzes and geometric puzzles that had looked more like arduous intelligence tests than anything I could think of as recreation – my sarcastic comments had gone right over his head. I'd stood there insulting him, ever more viciously, and he'd just gazed at the screen, and smiled. Not tolerant. Oblivious.

I'd spent three hours interviewing Rourke in his small flat; VA had no 'central office', in Manchester or anywhere else. There were members in forty-seven countries – almost a thousand people, worldwide – but only Rourke had been willing to speak to me, and only because it was his job.

He was not fully autistic, of course. But he'd shown me his brain scans.

I replayed the raw footage.

'Do you see this small lesion in the left frontal lobe?' There was a tiny dark space, a minuscule gap in the grey matter, above the pointer's arrow. 'Now compare it with the same region in a twenty-nine-year-old fully autistic male.' Another dark space, three or four times larger. 'And here's a non-autistic subject of the same age and sex.' No lesion at all. 'The pathology isn't always so obvious – the structure can be malformed, rather than visibly absent – but these examples made it clear that there's a precise physical basis to our claims.'

The view tilted up from the notepad to his face. **Witness** manufactured a smooth transition from one rock-steady 'camera angle' to another – just as it smoothed away saccades: the rapid darting movements of the eyeballs, restlessly scanning and re-scanning the scene even when the gaze was subjectively fixed.

57

I said, 'No one would deny that you've suffered damage in the same part of the brain. But why not be thankful that it's minor damage, and leave it at that? Why not count yourself lucky that you can still function in society, and get on with your life?'

'That's a complicated question. For a start, it depends what you mean by "function".'

'You can live outside of institutions. You can hold down skilled jobs.' Rourke's main occupation was research assistant to an academic linguist – not exactly sheltered employment.

He said, 'Of course. If we couldn't, we'd be classified as fully autistic. That's the criterion which defines "partial autism": we can survive in ordinary society. Our deficiencies aren't overwhelming – and we can usually fake a lot of what's missing. Sometimes we can even convince ourselves that nothing's wrong. For a while.'

'For a while? You have jobs, money, independence. What else does it take to *function*?'

'Interpersonal relationships.'

'You mean sexual relationships?'

'Not necessarily. But they are the most difficult. And the most . . . illuminating.'

He touched a key on his notepad; a complex neural map appeared. 'Everyone – or almost everyone – instinctively attempts to understand other human beings. To guess what they're thinking. To anticipate their actions. To . . . "know them". People build symbolic models of other people in their brains, both to act as coherent representations, tying together all the information which can actually be observed – speech, gestures, past actions – and to help make informed guesses about the aspects which can't be known directly – motives, intentions, emotions.' As he spoke, the neural map dissolved, and re-formed as a functional diagram of a 'third person' model: an elaborate network of blocks labelled with objective and subjective traits.

'In most people, all of this happens with little or no conscious effort: there's an *innate ability* to model other people. It's refined by use in childhood – and total isolation would cripple its development . . . in the same way as total darkness would cripple the visual centres. Short of that kind of extreme abuse, though, upbringing isn't a factor. Autism can only be caused by congenital brain damage, or later physical injuries to the brain. There are genetic risk factors which involve susceptibility to viral infections *in utero* – but autism itself is not a simple hereditary disease.'

I'd already filmed a white-coated expert saying much the same things, but VA members' detailed knowledge of their own condition was a crucial part of the story . . . and Rourke's explanation was clearer than the neurologist's.

'The brain structure involved occupies a small region in the left frontal lobe. The specific details describing individual people are scattered throughout the brain – like all memories – but this structure is *the one place* where those details are automatically integrated and interpreted. If it's damaged, other people's actions can still be perceived and remembered – but they lose their special significance. They don't generate the same kind of "obvious" implications; they don't make the same kind of immediate sense.' The neural map reappeared – this time with a lesion. Again, it was transformed into a functional diagram – now visibly disrupted, overlaid with dozens of dashed red lines to illustrate lost connections.

Rourke continued, 'The structure in question probably began to evolve towards its modern human form in the primates, though it had precursors in earlier mammals. It was first identified and studied – in chimpanzees – by a neuroscientist called Lamont, in 2014. The corresponding human version was mapped a few years later.

'Maybe the first crucial role for Lamont's area was to help make deception possible – to learn how to hide your own true motives, by understanding how others perceive you. If you know how to *appear* to be servile or cooperative – whatever's really on your mind – you have a better chance of stealing food, or a quick fuck with someone else's partner. But then . . . natural selection would have upped the ante, and favoured those who could see through the ruse. Once lying had been invented, there was no turning back. Development would have snowballed.'

I said, 'So the fully autistic can't lie – or judge someone else to be lying. But the partially autistic . . . ?'

'Some can, some can't. It depends on the specific damage. We're not all identical.'

'Okay. But what about relationships?'

Rourke averted his gaze, as if the subject was unbearably painful – but he continued without hesitation, sounding like a fluent public speaker delivering a familiar lecture. 'Modelling other people successfully can aid cooperation, as well as deception. *Empathy* can act to improve social cohesion at every level. But as early humans evolved a greater degree of monogamy – at least, compared to their immediate ancestors – the whole cluster of mental processes involved in *pair-bonding* would have become entangled. Empathy for our breeding partner attained a special status: their life could be, in some circumstances, as crucial to the passing on of your genes as your own.

'Of course, most animals will instinctively protect their young, or their mates, at a cost to themselves; altruism is an ancient behavioural strategy. But how could *instinctive altruism* be made compatible with human self-awareness? Once there was a burgeoning ego, a growing sense of self in the foreground of every action, how was it prevented from over-shadowing everything else?

'The answer is, evolution invented *intimacy*. Intimacy makes it possible to attach some, or all, of the compelling qualities associated with the ego – the model of the self – to models of other people. And not just possible – pleasurable. A pleasure reinforced by sex, but not restricted to the act, like orgasm. And not even restricted to sexual partners, in humans. Intimacy is just the belief – rewarded by the brain – that you *know* the people you love in almost the same fashion as you know yourself.'

The word 'love' had come as a shock, in the middle of all that sociobiology. But he'd used it without a hint of irony or self-consciousness – as if he'd seamlessly merged the vocabularies of emotion and evolution into a single language.

I said, 'And even partial autism makes that impossible? Because you can't model anyone well enough to really *know them* at all?'

Rourke didn't believe in yes-or-no answers. 'Again, we're not all identical. Sometimes the modelling is accurate enough – as accurate as anyone's – but it's not rewarded: the parts of Lamont's area which make most people feel good about intimacy, and actively seek it out, are missing. Those people are considered to be "cold", "aloof". And sometimes the reverse is true: people are driven to seek intimacy, but their modelling is so poor that they can never hope to find it. They might lack the social skills to form lasting sexual relationships – or even if they're intelligent and resourceful enough to circumvent the social problems, *the brain itself* might judge the model to be faulty, and refuse to reward it. So the drive is never satisfied – because it's physically impossible for it to be satisfied.'

I said, 'Sexual relationships are difficult for everyone. It has been suggested that you've merely invented a neurological syndrome which allows you to abdicate responsibility for problems which everyone faces, as a matter of course.'

Rourke stared down at the floor and smiled indulgently. 'And we should just pull ourselves together, and try harder?'

'Either that, or have autografts to correct the damage.' A small number of neurons and glial cells could be removed from the brain without harm, regressed to an embryonic state, multiplied in tissue culture, then reinjected into the damaged region. Artificially maintained gradients of embryonic marker hormones could fool the cells into thinking that they were back in the developing brain, and guide them through a fresh attempt to build the necessary synaptic connections. The success rate was unimpressive for the fully autistic – but for people with relatively small lesions, it was close to forty per cent.

'The Voluntary Autists don't oppose that option. All we're campaigning for is the legalisation of the alternative.'

'Enlargement of the lesion?'

'Yes. Up to and including the complete excision of Lamont's area.'

'*Why?*'

'Again, that's a complicated question. Everyone has a different reason. For a start, I'd say that as a matter of principle, we should have the widest possible range of choices. Like transsexuals.'

That was a reference to another kind of brain surgery which had once been highly controversial: NGR. Neural gender reassignment. People born with a mismatch between neural and physical gender had been able to have their bodies resculpted – with increasing precision – for almost a century. In the 20s, though, another option had become feasible: changing the gender of the brain; altering the hardwired neural map of the body image to bring it into line with the existing flesh and blood. Many people – including many transsexuals – had campaigned passionately against legalising NGR, fearing coercion, or surgery carried out on infants. By the 40s, though, it had become generally accepted as a legitimate option, freely chosen by about twenty per cent of transsexuals.

I'd interviewed people undergoing every kind of reassignment operation, for *Gender Scrutiny Overload*. One neural man born with a female body had proclaimed ecstatically –

after being resculpted en-male – 'This is it! I'm free, I'm home!' And another – who'd opted for NGR – had gazed into a mirror at her unchanged face and said, 'It's like I've broken out of some kind of dream, some kind of hallucination, and I can finally see myself as I really am.' Judging from audience feedback to *Gender*, the analogy would attract enormous sympathy – if it was allowed to stand.

I said, 'The endpoint of either operation on transsexuals is a *healthy* man or woman. That's hardly the same as becoming autistic.'

Rourke countered, 'But we do suffer a mismatch, just like transsexuals. Not between body and brain, but between the drive for intimacy and the inability to attain it. No one – save a few religious fundamentalists – would be cruel enough to tell a *transsexual* that they'll just have to learn to live with what they are, and that medical intervention would be a wicked self-indulgence.'

'But no one's stopping you from choosing medical intervention. The graft is legal. And success rates are sure to improve.'

'And as I've said, VA don't oppose that. For some people, it's the right choice.'

'But how can it ever be *the wrong choice*?'

Rourke hesitated. No doubt he'd scripted and rehearsed everything he'd wanted to say – but this was the heart of it. To have any hope of winning support for his cause, he was going to have to make the audience understand why he did *not* want to be cured.

He said carefully, 'Many fully autistic people suffer additional brain damage, and various kinds of mental retardation. In general, we don't. Whatever damage we've suffered to Lamont's area, most of us are intelligent enough to understand our own condition. We *know* that non-autistic people are capable of believing that they've achieved intimacy. But in VA, we've decided we'd be better off without that talent.'

63

'Why better off?'

'Because it's a talent for self-deception.'

I said, 'If autism is a lack of understanding of others . . . and healing the lesion would grant you that lost under-standing—'

Rourke broke in, 'But how much *is* understanding – and how much is a *delusion of understanding*? Is intimacy a form of knowledge – or is it just a comforting false belief? Evolution isn't interested in whether or not we grasp the truth, except in the most pragmatic sense. And there can be equally pragmatic falsehoods. If the brain needs to grant us an exaggerated sense of our capacity for knowing each other – to make pair-bonding compatible with self-awareness – it will lie, shame-lessly, as much as it has to, in order to make the strategy succeed.'

I'd fallen silent, not knowing how to respond. Now I watched Rourke waiting for me to continue. Though he appeared as awkward and shy as ever, there was something in his expression which chilled me. He honestly believed that his condition had granted him an insight no ordinary person could share – and if he didn't exactly *pity us* our hardwired capacity for blissful self-deception, he couldn't help but perceive himself as having the broader, clearer view.

I said haltingly, 'Autism is a . . . tragic, disabling disease. How can you . . . *romanticise it* into nothing more than some kind of . . . viable alternative lifestyle?'

Rourke was polite, but dismissive. 'I'm not doing any such thing. I've met over a hundred fully autistic people, and their families. I *know* how much pain is involved. If I could banish the condition tomorrow, I'd do it.

'But we have our own histories, our own problems, our own aspirations. We're *not* fully autistic – and excision of Lamont's area, in adulthood, won't render us the same as someone who was born that way. Most of us have learnt to compensate by modelling people consciously, explicitly – it takes far more effort than the innate skill, but when we lose what little we have of that, we won't be left helpless. Or "selfish", or "merciless", or "incapable of compassion" – or any of the other things the murdochs like to claim. And being granted the surgery we've asked for won't mean loss of employment, let alone the need for institutional care. So there'll be no cost to the community—'

I said angrily, 'Cost is the least of the issues. You're talking about deliberately – surgically – ridding yourself of something . . . *fundamental to humanity*.'

Rourke looked up from the floor and nodded calmly, as if I'd finally made a point on which we were in complete agreement.

He said, 'Exactly. And we've lived for decades with a *fundamental* truth about human relationships – which we choose not to surrender to the comforting effects of a brain graft. All we want to do now is make that choice complete. To stop being punished for our refusal to be deceived.'

Somehow, I whipped the interview into shape. I was terrified of paraphrasing James Rourke; with most people, it was easy enough to judge what was fair and what wasn't, but here I was on treacherous ground. I wasn't even sure that the console could convincingly mimic him – when I tried it, the body language looked utterly wrong, as if the software's default assumptions (normally used to flesh out an almost-complete gestural profile gleaned from the subject) were being pumped out in their entirety to fill the vacuum. I ended up altering nothing – merely extracting the best lines, and setting them up with other material – and resorting to narration, when there was no other way.

I had the console show me a diagram of the segments I'd used in the edited version, slivers scattered throughout the long linear sequence of the raw footage. Each take – each unbroken sequence of filming – was clearly 'slated': labelled

65

with time and place, and a sample frame at the start and end. There were a few takes from which I'd extracted nothing at all; I played them through one last time, to be sure I hadn't left out anything important.

There was some footage where Rourke was showing me into his 'office' – a corner of the two-room flat. I'd noticed a photograph of him – probably in his early-twenties – with a woman about the same age.

I asked who she was.

'My ex-wife.'

The couple stood on a crowded beach, somewhere Mediterranean-looking. They were holding hands and trying to face the camera – but they'd been caught out, unable to resist exchanging conspiratorial sideways glances. Sexually charged, but . . . *knowing*, too. If this wasn't a portrait of intimacy, it was a very good imitation.

Sometimes we can even convince ourselves that nothing's wrong. For a while.

'How long were you married?'

'Almost a year.'

I'd been curious, of course, but I hadn't pressed him for details. *Junk DNA* was a science documentary, not some sleazy exposé; his private life was none of my business.

There was also an informal conversation I'd had with Rourke, the day after the interview. We'd been walking through the grounds of the university, just after I'd taken a few minutes' footage of him at work – helping a computer scour the world's Hindi-speaking networks in search of vowel shifts (which he usually did from home, but I'd been desperate for a change of backdrop, even if it meant distorting reality). The University of Manchester had eight separate campuses scattered throughout the city; we were in the newest, where the landscape architects had gone wild with engineered vegetation. Even the grass was impossibly lush and verdant; for the first few seconds, even to me, the shot looked like a badly forged composite: sky filmed in England, ground filmed in Brunei.

Rourke said, 'You know, I envy you your job. With VA, I'm forced to concentrate on a narrow area of change. But you'll have a bird's eye view of everything.'

'Of what? You mean advances in biotechnology?'

'Biotech, imaging, AI . . . the lot. The whole battle for the H-words.'

'The H-words?'

He smiled cryptically. 'The little one and the big one. That's what this century is going to be remembered for. A battle for two words. Two definitions.'

'I don't have the slightest idea what you're talking about.' We were passing through a miniature forest in the middle of the quadrangle; dense and exotic, as wayward and brooding as any surrealist's painted jungle.

Rourke turned to me. 'What's the most patronising thing you can offer to do for people you disagree with, or don't understand?'

'I don't know. What?'

'Heal them. That's the first H-word. *Health*.'

'Ah.'

'Medical technology is about to go supernova. In case you hadn't noticed. So what's all that power going to be used for? The maintenance – or creation – of "health". But what's "health"? Forget the obvious shit that everyone agrees on. Once every last virus and parasite and oncogene has been blasted out of existence, what's the ultimate goal of "healing"? All of us playing our preordained parts in some Edenite "natural order"' – he stopped to gesture ironically at the orchids and lilies blossoming around us – 'and being restored to the one condition our biology is optimised for: hunting and gathering, and dying at thirty or forty? Is that it? Or . . . opening up every technically possible mode of existence?

Whoever claims the authority to define the boundary between *health* and *disease* claims . . . everything.'

I said, 'You're right: the word's insidious, the meaning's open-ended – and it will probably always be contentious.' I couldn't argue with *patronising*, either; Mystical Renaissance were forever offering to 'heal' the world's people of their 'psychic numbing', and transform us all into 'perfectly balanced' human beings. In other words: perfect copies of themselves, with all the same beliefs, all the same priorities, and all the same neuroses and superstitions.

'So what's the other H-word? The big one?'

He tipped his head and looked at me slyly. 'You really can't guess? Here's a clue, then. What's the most intellectually lazy way you can think of, to try to win an argument?'

'You're going to have to spell it out for me. I'm no good at riddles.'

'You say that your opponent lacks *humanity*.'

I'd fallen silent, suddenly ashamed – or at least embarrassed – wondering just how deeply I'd offended him with some of the things I'd said the day before. The trouble with meeting people again after interviewing them was that they often spent the intervening time thinking through the whole conversation, in minute detail – and concluding that they'd come out badly.

Rourke said, 'It's the oldest semantic weapon there is. Think of all the categories or people who've been classified as *non-human*, in various cultures, at various times. People from other tribes. People with other skin colours. Slaves. Women. The mentally ill. The deaf. Homosexuals. Jews. Bosnians, Croats, Serbs, Armenians, Kurds—'

I said defensively, 'Don't you think there's a slight difference between putting someone in a gas chamber, and using the phrase rhetorically?'

'Of course. But suppose you accuse me of "lacking humanity". What does that actually mean? What am I likely to have done? Murdered someone in cold blood? Drowned a puppy?

Eaten meat? Failed to be moved by Beethoven's Fifth? Or just failed to have – or to seek – an emotional life identical to your own in every respect? Failed to share all your values and aspirations?'

I hadn't replied. Cyclists whirred by in the dark jungle behind me; it had begun to rain, but the canopy protected us.

Rourke continued cheerfully. 'The answer is: "any one of the above". Which is why it's so fucking lazy. Questioning someone's "humanity" puts them in the company of serial killers – which saves you the trouble of having to say anything intelligent about their views. And it lays claim to some vast imaginary consensus, an outraged majority standing behind you, backing you up all the way. When you claim that Voluntary Autists are trying to rid themselves of their *humanity*, you're not only defining the word as if you had some divine right to do that . . . you're implying that everyone else on the planet – short of the reincarnations of Adolf Hitler and Pol Pot – agrees with you in every detail.' He spread his arms and declaimed to the trees, *'Put down that scalpel, I beseech you . . . in the name of all humanity!'*

I said lamely, 'Okay. Maybe I should have phrased some things differently, yesterday. I didn't set out to insult you.'

Rourke shook his head, amused. 'No offence taken. It's a battle, after all – I can hardly expect instant surrender. You're loyal to a narrow definition of Big H – and maybe you even honestly believe that everyone else shares it. I support a broader definition. We'll agree to disagree. And I'll see you in the trenches.'

Narrow? I'd opened my mouth to deny the accusation, but then I hadn't known how to defend myself. What could I have said? That I'd once made a sympathetic documentary about gender migrants? (How magnanimous.) And now I had to balance that with a frankenscience story on Voluntary Autists?

So he'd had the last word (if only in real-time). He'd shaken my hand, and we'd parted.

I played the whole thing through, one more time. Rourke was remarkably eloquent – and almost charismatic, in his own strange way – and everything he'd said was relevant. But the private terminology, the manic outbursts . . . it was all too weird, too messy and confrontational.

I left the take unused, unquoted.

I'd gone on to another appointment at the university: an afternoon with the famous Manchester MIRG – Medical Imaging Research Group. It had seemed like too good a chance to miss – and imaging, after all, lay behind the definitive identification of partial autism.

I skimmed through the footage. A lot of it was good – and it would probably make a worthwhile five-minute story of its own, for one of SeeNet's magazine programs – but it was clear now that Rourke's own concise notepad demonstration had supplied all the brain scans *Junk DNA* really needed.

The main experiment I'd filmed involved a student volunteer reading poetry in silence, while the scanner subtitled the image of her brain with each line as it was read. There were three independently computed subtitles, based on primary visual data, recognised word-shapes, and the brain's final semantic representations . . . the last sometimes only briefly matching the others, before the words' precise meanings diffused out into a cloud of associations. However eerily compelling this was, though, it had nothing to do with Lamont's area.

Towards the end of the day, one of the researchers – Margaret Williams, head of the software development team – had suggested that I climb into the womb of the scanner, myself. Maybe they wanted to turn the tables on me – to scrutinise and record me with their machinery, just as I'd been doing to them for the past four hours. Williams had certainly been as insistent as if she'd believed it was a matter of justice.

She said, 'You could record the subject's-eye view. And we could get a look at all your hidden extras.'

I'd declined. 'I don't know what the magnetic fields would do to the hardware.'

'Nothing, I promise. Most of it must be optical – and everything else will be shielded. You get on and off planes all the time, don't you? You walk through the normal security gates?'

'Yes, but—'

'Our fields are no stronger. We could even try reading your optic nerve activity, via the scanner – and then comparing the data with your own direct record.'

'I don't have the download module with me. It's back at the hotel.'

She pursed her lips, frustrated – obviously dying to tell me to shut up, do as I was told, and get inside the scanner. 'That's a pity. And I suppose you'd have problems with the warranty if we improvised something – our own cable and interface?'

'I'm afraid so. The software would log the use of non-standard equipment, and then I'd be in deep trouble at the next annual service.'

But she still wasn't ready to give up. 'You were talking about the Voluntary Autists, before. If you wanted something spectacular to illustrate *that* . . . we could image your own Lamont's area – while you brought to mind a sequence of different people. We could record it all, and play it back for you. Then you could show your viewers a real-time working copy of the thing itself. Not some glossy animation: Flesh and blood, caught in the act. Neurons pumping calcium ions, synapses firing. We could even transform the neural architecture into a functional diagram, calibrate it, identify trait symbols. We have all the software—'

I said, 'It's very kind of you to offer. But . . . what kind of tenth-rate journalist would I be, if I started resorting to using myself as the subject of my own stories?'

7

Two weeks before the Einstein Centenary conference was due to begin, I signed a contract with SeeNet for *Violet Mosala: Symmetry's Champion*. As I scrawled my name on the electronic document with my notepad's stylus, I tried to convince myself that I'd been given the job because I'd do it well – not merely because I'd pulled rank and begged for a favour. There was no doubt that Sarah Knight was inexperienced – she was five years younger than me, and she'd spent most of her career in political journalism. Being a self-confessed 'fan' of Mosala might even have worked against her; no one at SeeNet would have wanted a gushing hagiography. But for all my alleged professionalism, I'd still only glanced at **Sisyphus**'s briefing, I still had no real idea what I was taking on.

The truth was, I didn't care about the details; all that mattered was putting *Junk DNA* behind me, and running as far away from *Distress* as I could. After twelve months drowning in the worst excesses of biotechnology, the pristine world of theoretical physics shone in my mind's eye like some anaesthetised mathematical heaven, where everything was cool and abstract and gloriously inconsequential . . . an image which merged seamlessly with the white coral snow-flake of Stateless itself, growing out into the blue Pacific like a perfect fractal star. Part of me understood full well that if I took these beautiful mirages to heart, I was certain to be disappointed – and I even struggled to imagine the most unpleasant ways in which I might be brought back down to

Earth. *I could suffer an attack of multiple-drug-resistant pneumonia or malaria, a strain to which the locals were immune. High-level pharms which could analyse the pathogenic organisms and design a cure on the spot would be unavailable, thanks to the boycott, and I'd be too weak for the flight back to civilisation* . . . It wasn't an impossible scenario; the boycott had killed hundreds of people over the years.

Still, anything had to be better than coming face-to-face with a victim of Distress.

I left a message for Violet Mosala. I assumed she was still at her home in Cape Town, though the software which answered her number was giving nothing away. I introduced myself, thanked her for generously agreeing to give her time to the project, and generally spouted polite clichés. I said nothing to encourage her to call me back; I knew it wouldn't take much real-time conversation to reveal my total ignorance of her life and work. *Pneumonia, malaria* . . . *making a complete fool of myself.* I didn't care. All I could think of was escape.

I'd psyched myself up to be 'forced to relive' Daniel Cavolini's revival – but I should have known all along how absurd that was. Editing never re-created the past; it was more like performing an autopsy on it. I worked on the sequence dispassionately – and every hour I spent reshaping it made the job of imagining the responses of a viewer, seeing it all for the first time, more and more a matter of calculation and instinct – and less and less connected to anything I felt about the events myself. Even the final cut, superficially fluid and immediate, was for me a kind of post-mortem revival of a post-mortem revival. It had happened, it was over; whatever brief illusion of life the technology managed to create, it was no more capable of climbing out of the screen and walking down the street than any other twitching corpse.

Daniel's brother, Luke, had been charged with the murder

– and had already pleaded guilty. I logged on to the court records system and skimmed through footage of the three hearings which had taken place so far. The magistrate had ordered a psychiatric report, which had concluded that Luke Cavolini suffered from occasional bouts of 'inappropriate anger' which had never quite put him far enough out of touch with reality to have him classified as mentally ill and treated against his will. He was competent, and culpable, and understood precisely what he'd done – and he'd even had a 'motive': an argument the night before, about a jacket of Daniel's which he'd borrowed. He'd end up in an ordinary prison, for at least fifteen years.

The court footage was public domain, but there was no time to use any of it in the broadcast version. So I wrote a brief postscript to the revival story, stating the bare facts: the charges laid, the guilty plea. I didn't mention the psychiatric report; I didn't want to muddy the waters. The console read the words over a freeze-frame of Daniel Cavolini screaming.

I said, 'Fade-out. Roll credits.'

It was Tuesday, 23 March, 4:07 p.m.

Junk DNA was over.

I left a note in the hall for Gina and walked up to Epping to get myself inoculated for the journey ahead. Scientists on Stateless broadcast local 'weather reports' – both meteorological and epidemiological – into the net, and despite all the other bizarre acts of political ostracism, the relevant UN bodies treated this data just as if it had emerged from a sanctified member state. As it turned out, neither pneumonia nor malaria shots were indicated – but there'd been recent outbreaks of several new strains of adenovirus, none of them life-threatening but all of them potentially debilitating enough to ruin my stay. Alice Tomasz, my GP, downloaded sequences for some small peptides which mimicked appropriate viral surface proteins, synthesised their RNA, and then spliced the fragments into a tailored – harmless – adenovirus. The whole process took about ten minutes.

As I inhaled the live vaccine, Alice said, 'I liked *Gender Scrutiny Overload.*'

'Thank you.'

'That part at the end, though . . . Elaine Ho on gender and evolution. Did you honestly believe that?'

Ho had pointed out that humans had spent the last few million years reversing the ancient mammalian extremes of gender dimorphism and behavioural differences. We'd gradually evolved biochemical quirks which actively *interfered with* ancient genetic programs for gender-specific neural pathways; the separate blueprints were still inherited, but hormonal effects in the womb kept them from being fully enacted – essentially 'masculinising' the brain of every female embryo, and 'feminising' the brain of every male. (Homosexuality resulted when the process went – very slightly – further than normal.) In the long term – even if we took an Edenite stand and refused all genetic engineering – the sexes were already converging. Whether or not we tampered with nature, nature was tampering with itself.

'It seemed like a good way to end the program. And everything she said was true, wasn't it?'

Alice was noncommittal. 'So what are you working on these days?'

I couldn't bring myself to own up to *Junk DNA* . . . but I was just as afraid to mention Violet Mosala, in case my own doctor turned out to know more about Mosala's TOE-in-progress than I did. It wasn't an idle fear; Alice was obscenely well read on everything.

I said, 'Nothing, really. I'm on holiday.'

She glanced again at my notes on her desk screen – which would have included data from my pharm. 'Good for you. Just don't relax too hard.'

I felt like an idiot, caught out in an obvious lie – but as I walked out of the surgery, it ceased to matter. The street was dappled with leaf-shadows, the breeze from the south was soft and cool. *Junk DNA* was over, and I felt as unburdened as if I'd just been granted a reprieve from a fatal disease. Epping was a quiet suburban centre: a doctor, a dentist, a small supermarket, a florist, a hairdresser, and a couple of (non-experimental) restaurants. No Ruins; the commercial sector had been bulldozed fifteen years before and given over to engineered forest. No billboards (though advertising T-shirts almost made up for the loss). On rare Sunday afternoons when nothing else claimed our time, Gina and I walked up here for no reason at all, and sat beside the fountain. And when I came back from Stateless – with eight whole months to edit *Violet Mosala* into shape – there'd be more of those days than there'd been for a long while.

When I opened the front door, Gina was standing in the hall, as if she'd been waiting for me to return. She seemed agitated. Distraught. I moved towards her, asking, 'What's wrong?' She backed away, raising her arms, almost as if she was fending off an attacker.

She said, 'Andrew, I know there's no good time. But I waited—'

At the end of the hall were three suitcases.

The world drew itself away from me. Everything around me took one step back.

I said, 'What's going on?'

'Don't get angry.'

'I'm not angry.' That was the truth. 'I just don't understand.'

Gina said, 'I gave you every chance to fix things. And you just kept right on, as if nothing had changed.'

Something odd was happening to my sense of balance; I felt as if I was swaying wildly, though I knew I was perfectly still. Gina looked miserable. I held out my arms to her – as if I could comfort her.

I said, 'Couldn't you tell me something was wrong?'

'Did I need to? Are you blind?'

'Maybe I am.'

'You're not a child, are you? You're not stupid.'

'I honestly don't know what I'm supposed to have done.'

She laughed bitterly. 'No, of course you don't. You just started treating me like some kind of . . . arduous obligation. Why should you think there was anything wrong with that?'

I said, 'Started treating you . . . when? You mean the last three weeks? You always knew about editing. I thought—'

Gina screamed, 'I'm not talking about your fucking *job*!'

I wanted to sit down on the floor – to steady myself, to regain my bearings – but I was afraid the action might be misinterpreted.

She said coldly, 'Please don't stand there blocking the way. You're making me nervous.'

'What do you think I'm going to do? Take you prisoner?' She didn't reply. I squeezed past her into the kitchen. She turned and stood in the doorway, facing me. I had no idea what to say to her. I had no idea where to begin.

'I love you.'

'I'm warning you, don't start.'

'If I've screwed up, just give me a chance to put things right. I'll try harder—'

'There's nothing worse than when you *try harder*. The strain is so fucking obvious.'

'I always thought I'd—' I met her eyes: dark, expressive, impossibly beautiful. Even now, the sight of them cut through everything else I was thinking and feeling, and transformed part of me into a helpless, infatuated child. But I'd still, always, concentrated, I'd always paid attention. *How had it come to this?* What signs could I have missed . . . when, how? I wanted to demand dates and times and places.

Gina looked away and said, 'It's too late to change any-thing. I've found someone else. I've been seeing someone else for the last three months. If you really didn't know that . . . what kind of message did you need? Did I have to bring him home and screw him in front of you?'

I closed my eyes. I didn't want to hear this; it was just noise that made everything more complicated. I said slowly, 'I don't care what you've done. We can still—'

She took a step towards me and shouted, '*I care!* You selfish moron! *I care!*' Tears were streaming down her face. Beneath everything I was struggling to understand, I just ached to hold her; I still couldn't believe I was the reason for all her pain.

She said contemptuously, 'Look at you! I'm the one who's just told you I've been screwing someone else behind your back! I'm the one who's walking out! And it still hurts me a thousand times more than anything will ever hurt you—'

I must have thought about what I did next, I must have planned it, but I don't remember turning to the sink and hunting for a knife, I don't remember opening my shirt. But I found myself standing by the kitchen doorway, carving lines back and forth across my stomach with the point of the blade, saying calmly, 'You always wanted scars. Here are some scars.'

Gina threw herself at me, knocking me off my feet. I pushed the knife away, under the table. Before I could get up, she sat on my chest, and started slapping and punching me. She screamed, 'You think that *hurts*? You think that's the same? You don't even know the difference, do you? *Do you?*'

I lay on the floor and looked away from her, while she pummelled my face and shoulders. I felt nothing at all, I was just waiting for it to be over – but when she stood up and started to leave, making snivelling noises as she staggered around the kitchen, I suddenly wanted to hurt her, badly.

I said evenly, 'What did you expect? I can't cry on cue like you do. My prolactin level's not up to it.'

I heard her dragging the suitcases along the hall. I had a vision of following her out the door, offering to carry something, making a scene. But my desire for revenge had already faded. I loved her, I wanted her back . . . and everything I could imagine doing to try to prove that seemed guaranteed to hurt her, guaranteed to make everything worse.

The front door slammed shut.

I curled up on the floor. I was bleeding messily – and gritting my teeth as much against the metallic stench, and a sense of helpless incontinence, as against the pain – but I knew I wasn't cut deeply. I hadn't gone insane with jealousy and rage and severed an artery; I'd always known exactly what I was doing.

Was I meant to feel ashamed of that? Ashamed that I hadn't broken the furniture, disembowelled myself – or tried to kill her? I could still feel the sting of Gina's contempt – and if I'd never really known her thoughts before, I'd understood one thing as she knocked me to the floor: because I hadn't been overwhelmed by emotion, because I hadn't lost control . . . in her eyes, I was somehow less than human.

I wrapped a towel around my superficial wounds, then told the pharm what had happened. It buzzed for several minutes, then exuded a paste of antibiotics, coagulants, and a collagen-like adhesive. It dried on my skin like a tight-fitting bandage.

The pharm had no eye of its own, but I stood by the phone and showed it our handiwork.

It said, 'Avoid strenuous bowel movements. And try not to laugh too hard.'

8

Angelo said glumly, 'I've been sent.'

'Then you'd better come in.'

He followed me down the hall into the living room. I asked, 'How are the girls?'

'Good. Exhausting.'

Maria was three, Louise was two. Angelo and Lisa both worked from home – in soundproof offices – taking the childcare in shifts. Angelo was a mathematician with a net-based, nominally Canadian university; Lisa was a polymer chemist with a company which manufactured in the Netherlands.

We'd been friends since university, but I hadn't met his sister until Louise was born. Gina had been visiting mother and daughter in hospital; I'd fallen for her in the elevator, before I had any idea who she was.

Seated, Angelo said cautiously, 'I think she just wants to know how you are.'

'I sent her ten messages in ten days. She knows exactly how I am.'

'She said you stopped suddenly.'

'*Suddenly?* Ten acts of ritual humiliation is all she gets, without a reply.' I hadn't meant to sound bitter, but Angelo was already beginning to look like a peace envoy stranded on a battlefield. I laughed. 'Tell her whatever she wants to hear. Tell her I'm devastated . . . but recovering rapidly. I don't want her to feel insulted . . . but I don't want her to feel guilty, either.'

He smiled uncertainly, as if I'd made a tasteless joke. 'She's taking it badly.'

I clenched my fists and said slowly, 'I know that, and so am I, but don't you think she'd feel better if you told her . . .' I stopped. 'What did she say you should tell me if I asked if there was any chance of her coming back?'

'She said to say no.'

'Of course. But . . . did she mean it? What did she tell you to say if I asked if she meant it?'

'Andrew—'

'Forget it.'

A long, awkward silence descended. I considered asking where she was, who she was with, but I knew he wouldn't tell me. And I didn't really want to know.

I said, 'I'm meant to be flying out to Stateless tomorrow.'

'Yeah, I heard. Good luck.'

'There is another journalist who'd be willing to take over the project. I'd only have to make one call—'

He shook his head. 'There's no reason to do that. It wouldn't change anything.'

The silence returned. After a while, Angelo reached into a jacket pocket and pulled out a small plastic vial of tablets. He said, 'I've got some Ds.'

I groaned. 'You never used to take that shit.'

He glanced up at me, wounded. 'They're harmless. I like to switch off sometimes. What's wrong with that?'

'Nothing.'

Disinhibitors were non-toxic and non-addictive. They created a mild sensation of well-being, and increased the effort required for considered thought – rather like a moderate dose of alcohol or cannabis, with few of the side effects. Their concentration in the bloodstream was self-limiting – above a certain level, the molecule catalysed its own destruction – so taking a whole bottle was exactly the same as swallowing a single D.

Angelo offered me the vial. I took out a tablet reluctantly, and held it in my palm.

Alcohol had almost vanished from polite society by the time I was ten years old, but its use as a 'social lubricant' always seemed to be lauded in retrospect as unequivocally beneficial, and only the violence and organic damage it induced were viewed as pathological. To me, though, the magic bullet which had taken its place seemed like a distillation of the real problem. Cirrhosis, brain damage, assorted cancers, and the worst traffic accidents and crimes of stupefaction had been mercifully banished . . . but I still wasn't prepared to concede that human beings were physically incapable of communicating or relaxing without the aid of psychoactive drugs.

Angelo swallowed a tablet and said admonishingly, 'Come on, it's not going to kill you. Every known human culture has used some kind of—'

I mimed putting the thing in my mouth, but palmed it. *Screw every known human culture.* I felt a momentary pang of guilt at the deception, but I didn't have the energy for an argument. Besides, my dishonesty was well intentioned. I could imagine more or less what Gina had told her brother: *Get him D'd, it's the only way he'll start talking.* She'd sent Angelo here in the hope that I'd unburden myself, spill my guts, and be *healed*. It was a touching gesture – on the part of both of them – and the least I could do in return was reduce the number of lies he'd have to tell her to make her believe she'd done some good.

Angelo's eyes glazed over slightly, as the chemical shut down various pathways in his brain. It occurred to me that James Rourke should have added a third disputed H-word to his list: honesty. Freud had saddled Western culture with the bizarre notion that the least considered utterances were always, magically, the truest – that reflection added nothing, and the ego merely censored or lied. It was an idea born more of convenience than anything else: he'd identified the part of the mind easiest to circumvent – with tricks like free association – and then declared the product of all that remained to be 'honest'.

But now that my words were chemically sanctified, and would at last be taken seriously, I got straight to the point. 'Look: tell Gina I'm going to be okay. I'm sorry I hurt her. I know I was selfish. I'm going to try to change. I still care about her . . . but I know it's over.' I hunted for more, but there really was nothing else she needed to know.

Angelo nodded significantly, as if I'd said something new and profound. 'I could never understand why you were always breaking up with women. I thought you were just unlucky. But you're right: you're a selfish bastard. All you really care about is your work.'

'That's right.'

'So what are you going to do about it? Find a new career?'

'No. Live alone.'

He grimaced. 'But that's worse. That makes you twice as selfish.'

I laughed. 'Really? Do you want to explain why?'

'Because then you're not even trying!'

'What if *trying* is at other people's expense? What if I'm tired of hurting people, and I choose not to do that anymore?'

This simple idea seemed to confound him. He'd taken up Ds late in life; maybe they addled his brain more than they did for someone who'd developed a tolerance for the drug in adolescence.

I said, 'I honestly used to think I could make someone happy. And myself. But after six attempts, I think I've proved that I can't. So I'm taking the Hippocratic oath: Do no harm. What's wrong with that?'

Angelo gave me a dubious look. 'I can't exactly picture you living like a monk.'

'Make up your mind: First I'm being selfish, then I'm being

83

pious. And I hope you're not impugning my masturbatory skills.'

'No, but there's one small problem with sexual fantasies: they make you want the real thing even more.'

I shrugged. 'I could always go neural asex.'

'Very funny.'

'Well, it's always there as a last resort.' I was already growing sick of the whole stupid ritual, but if I threw him out too soon there was the risk that he'd give Gina a less-than-satisfactory catharsis report. The details didn't matter, he'd be allowed to keep them to himself – but he had to be able to say with a straight face that we'd kept on baring our souls right into the small hours.

I said, 'You always claimed that you'd never get married. Monogamy was for the weak. Casual sex was more honest, and better for all concerned—'

Angelo laughed, but gritted his teeth. 'I was *nineteen* when I said that. How'd you like it if I dug up a few of your wonderful films from the same era?'

'If you've got copies . . . name your price.' It seemed inconceivable, but I'd spent four years of my life – and thousands of dollars from assorted part-time jobs – making half a dozen terminally pretentious experimental dramas. My underwater *butoh* version of *Waiting for Godot* was perhaps the single worst creation of the digital video era.

Angelo stared at the carpet, suddenly pensive. 'I meant it, though. At the time. The whole idea of a family—' He shuddered. 'It sounded like being buried alive. I couldn't imagine anything worse.'

'So you grew up. Congratulations.'

He glared at me angrily. 'Don't be so fucking glib.'

'I'm sorry.' He didn't seem to be joking; I'd struck a nerve.

He said, 'No one *grows up*. That's one of the sickest lies they ever tell you. People change. People compromise. People get stranded in situations they don't want to be in . . . and they make the best of it. But don't try to tell me it's some kind of . . . glorious preordained ascent into *emotional maturity*. It's not.'

I said uneasily, 'Has something happened? Between you and Lisa?'

He shook his head apologetically. 'No. Everything's fine. Life is wonderful. I love them all. But . . .' He looked away, his whole body visibly tensing. 'Only because I'd go insane if I didn't. Only because *I have to make it work*.'

'But you do. Make it work.'

'Yes!' He scowled, frustrated that I was missing the point. 'And it's not even that hard, anymore. It's pure habit. But . . . I used to think there'd be more. I used to think that if you changed from . . . valuing one thing to valuing another, it was because you'd learnt something new, understood something better. *And it's not like that at all*. I just value what I'm stuck with. That's it, that's the whole story. People make a virtue out of necessity. They sanctify what they can't escape.

'I *do* love Lisa, and I *do* love the girls . . . but there's no deeper reason than the fact that that's the best I can make of my life, now. I can't argue with a single thing I said when I was nineteen years old – because I don't *know better* now. I'm not *wiser*. That's what I resent: all the fucking pretentious lies we were fed about *growth* and *maturity*. No one ever came clean and admitted that "love" and "sacrifice" were just what you did to stay sane when you found yourself backed into a different kind of corner.'

I said, 'You really are full of shit. I hope you don't take Ds at parties.'

He looked stung for a moment, then he understood: I was promising to keep my mouth shut. I wasn't going to throw a word of this back at him when he was sober.

I walked him to the station just before midnight. There was a warm breeze blowing, and ten thousand stars.

'Good luck with Stateless.'

'Good luck with your debriefing.'

'Ah. I'll tell Gina . . .' He trailed off, frowning like an aphasic.

'You'll think of something.'

'Yeah.'

I watched the train until it disappeared, thinking: She did help me, after all. I actually forgot about both of us, for a while. And she'll survive. And I'll survive. And tomorrow, I'll be on a South Pacific island . . . trying to bluff my way through two weeks with Violet Mosala.

Backed into a different kind of corner.

What more could I have asked for?

PART TWO

9

The living, artificial island of Stateless was anchored to an unnamed guyot – a submerged, flat-topped, extinct volcano – in the middle of the South Pacific. At thirty-two degrees latitude, it lay outside the ocean resource zones of the Polynesian nations to the north, in uncontested international waters. (Laughable ambit claims by Antarctic squatters aside.) It sounded remote – but it was only four thousand kilometres from Sydney; a direct flight would have taken less than two hours.

I sat in the transit lounge in Phnom Penh, trying to unknot the muscles in the back of my neck. The airconditioning was icy, but the humidity seemed to penetrate the building unchecked. I thought about wandering out into the city – which I'd never seen firsthand – but I only had forty minutes between flights, and it would probably have taken half that time to obtain the necessary visa.

I'd never understood why the Australian government was such a vehement supporter of the boycott against Stateless. For twenty-three years, successive Ministers of Foreign Affairs had ranted about its 'destabilising influence on the region' – but in fact it had acted to relieve tensions considerably, by accepting more Greenhouse refugees than any nation on the planet. And it was true that the creators of Stateless had broken countless international laws, and used thousands of patented DNA sequences without permission . . . but a nation founded by invasion and mass-murder (acts demurely regretted in a treaty signed two hundred and fifty years later) could hardly claim to be on higher moral ground.

It was clear that Stateless was being ostracised for purely political reasons. But no one in power seemed to feel obliged to make those reasons explicit.

So I sat in the transit lounge, stiff from a four-hour flight in the wrong direction, and tried to read the sections of **Sisyphus**'s physics lesson which I'd skimmed over the first time. They were highlighted in accusing blue, eyeball-track analysis gallingly right on every count.

> *At least two conflicting generalised measures can be applied to* T, *the space of all topological spaces with countable basis. Perrini's measure [Perrini, 2012] and Saupe's measure [Saupe, 2017] are both defined for all bounded subsets of* T, *and are equivalent when restricted to* M – *the space of n-dimensional paracompact Hausdorff manifolds* – *but they yield contradictory results for sets of more exotic spaces. However, the physical significance (if any) of this discrepancy remains obscure—*

I couldn't concentrate. I gave up, closed my eyes and attempted to doze off – but a siesta appeared to be biochemically impossible. I blanked my mind and tried to relax. Eventually, my notepad chimed and announced my connection to Dili – picking up the news from the room's IR broadcast a few seconds before the multilingual audio began. I headed for the security gate – and, stepping through, recalled the scanner in Manchester, extracting poetry from a student's brain. No doubt in twenty years' time, weaponless hijackers would have their intentions exposed as easily as any explosive or knife. My passport file carried details of my suspicious internal anomalies, to reassure nervous security officials that I wasn't wired to explode . . . and maybe people who were plagued by unwanted dreams of running amok at twenty thousand metres would need analogous certificates of innocuousness in future.

There were no flights to Stateless from Cambodia. China, Japan and Korea were all pro-boycott, so Cambodia fell into line with its major trading partners to avoid causing offence. As did Australia – but its enthusiastic punishment of the 'anarchists' went above and beyond the call of *realpolitik*. There were flights from Phnom Penh to Dili, though, and from there I could finally reach my destination.

It was no mystery why Sydney-to-Dili was out of the question. After Indonesia annexed East Timor in 1976, they'd split the profits – the Timor Gap oilfields – with their silent partner, Australia. In 2036, with half a million East Timorese dead, and the oil wells irrelevant – *hydrocarbons* being molecules which engineered algae made from sunlight, in any shape and size, for a tenth of the cost of milk – the Indonesian government, under pressure more from its own citizens than from any of its allies, had finally, reluctantly, acceded to demands for autonomy for the province of Timor Timur. Formal independence had followed in 2040. But fifteen years later, the lawsuits against the oil thieves still hadn't been settled.

I boarded through the umbilical, and took my seat. A few minutes later, a woman in a bright red sarong and white blouse sat down beside me. We exchanged nods and smiles.

She said, 'You wouldn't believe the rigmarole I'm going through. Once in a blue moon my people hold a conference off the nets – and they had to choose the most difficult place in the world to reach.'

'You mean Stateless?'

She regarded me sympathetically. 'You too?'

I nodded.

'You poor man. Where have you come from?'

'Sydney.'

Her accent was almost certainly Bombay but she said, 'I'm from Kuala Lumpur. So you've had it worse. I'm Indrani Lee.'

'Andrew Worth.'

We shook hands. She said, 'Of course, I'm not giving a paper myself. And the proceedings will be on-line the day after the conference finishes. But . . . if you don't turn up, you miss all the gossip, don't you?' She smiled conspiratorially. 'People grow so desperate to talk off the nets – knowing there'll be no record, no audit trail. By the time each face-to-face meeting comes around, they're ready to tell you all their secrets in five minutes. Don't you find?'

'I hope so. I'm a journalist – I'm covering the conference for SeeNet.' A risky confession, but I wasn't about to try imitating a TOE specialist.

Lee showed no obvious signs of disdain. The plane began its almost vertical ascent. I was in the cheap centre aisle, but my screen showed Phnom Penh as it receded beneath us – an astonishing jumble of styles, from vine-covered stone temples (real and *faux*) to faded French colonial (ditto), to gleaming black ceramic. Lee's screen began to display an emergency procedures audiovisual; my recent-enough spate of flights on identical planes qualified me for an exemption.

When the AV was over, I said, 'Do you mind if I ask what your field is? I mean, TOEs, obviously, but which approach—?'

'I'm not a physicist. What I do is much closer to your own line of work.'

'You're a journalist?'

'I'm a sociologist. Or if you want my full job description: I study the Dynamics of Contemporary Ideas. So . . . if physics is about to come to an end, I thought I'd better be on hand to witness the event.'

'You want to be there to remind the scientists that they're "really just priests and story-tellers"?' I'd meant that as a joke – her own comment had been tongue-in-cheek, and I'd tried to match her tone – but my words came out sounding like an accusation.

She gave me a reproving glare. 'I'm not a member of any Ignorance Cult. And I'm afraid you're twenty years out of date if you think sociology is some kind of hotbed for Humble Science! or Mystical Renaissance. In academia, they're all in the History Departments now.' Her expression softened to a kind of weary resignation. 'We still get all the flak, though. It's unbelievable: a couple of badly framed studies from the 1980s still get thrown in my face by medical researchers, as if I was personally responsible.'

I apologised; she waved the offence away. A robot trolley offered us food and drink; I declined. It was absurd, but the first leg of my zig-zag path to Stateless had left me feeling worse than any non-stop flight across the entire Pacific.

As lush Vietnamese jungle gave way to choppy grey water, we exchanged a few pleasantries about the view – and further commiserations about the ordeal of reaching the conference. Despite my gaffe, I was intrigued by Lee's profession, and I finally worked up the courage to raise the subject again. 'What's the attraction for you, in devoting your time to studying physicists? I mean . . . if it was the science itself, you'd *be* a physicist. You wouldn't be standing back and watching them.'

She shook her head in disbelief. 'Isn't that exactly what you plan to do, yourself, for the next fortnight?'

'Yes – but my job's very different from yours. Ultimately, I'm just a communications technician.'

She gave me a look which seemed to say: *I'll deal with that one later*. 'The physicists at this conference will be there to make progress on TOEs, right? To trash the bad ones and refine the good ones. They're only interested in the end product: a theory that works, that fits the known data. That's their job, their vocation. Agreed?'

'More or less.'

'Of course, they're *aware* of all the processes they use to do this, beyond the actual mathematics: the communication of ideas, the withholding of ideas; acts of cooperation, acts of rivalry. They could hardly fail to know all about the politics, the cliques, the alliances.' She smiled, a proclamation of innocence. 'I'm not using any of those words pejoratively. Physics is not *debunked* – as groups like Culture First continue to insist – just because some perfectly ordinary things like nepotism, jealousy, and occasional acts of extreme violence play a part in its history. But you can hardly expect *the physicists themselves* to waste their time writing it all down for posterity. They want to purify and polish their little nuggets of theory, and then tell brief, elegant lies about how they found them. Who wouldn't? And it makes no difference, on one level: most science can be assessed without knowing anything about its detailed human origins.

'But *my* job is to get my hands on as much of the real history as possible. Not for the sake of "dethroning" physics. For its own sake, as a separate discipline. A separate branch of science.' She added, in mock reproof, 'And believe me, we *don't* suffer from equation envy anymore. We're due to out-strip them any day now. The physicists keep merging theirs, or thowing them out. We just keep inventing new ones.'

I said, 'But how would you feel if there were meta-sociologists looking over your shoulder, recording all your messy day-to-day compromises? Keeping you from getting away with your own elegant lies?'

Lee confessed without hesitation: 'I'd hate it, of course. And I'd try to conceal everything. But that's what the game's all about, isn't it?

'The physicists have it easy – with their subject, if not with me. The universe can't hide anything: forget all that anthro-pomorphic Victorian nonsense about "prising out nature's secrets". The universe can't lie; it just does what it does, and there's nothing else to it.

'People are the very opposite. There's nothing to which we'll devote more time, and energy, and cunning, than burying the truth.'

East Timor from the air was a dense patchwork of fields along the coast, and what looked like native jungle and savanna in the highlands. A dozen tiny fires dotted the mountains, but the blackened pinpricks beneath the smoke trails were dwarfed by the scars of old open-cut mines. We spiralled down over the island in a helical U-turn, hundreds of small villages coming into sight and then slipping away.

The fields displayed no trademark pigments (let alone the logos of fourth-generation biotech); visibly, at least, the farmers were refusing the temptation to go renegade, and were using only old, out-of-patent crops. Agriculture for export was almost dead; even hyper-urbanised Japan could feed its own population. Only the poorest countries, unable to afford the licence fees for state-of-the-art produce, struggled for self-sufficiency. East Timor imported food from Indonesia.

It was just after midday as we touched down in the tiny capital. There was no umbilical; we walked across the sweltering tarmac. The melatonin patch on my shoulder, pre-programmed by my pharm, was nudging me relentlessly towards Stateless time, two hours later than Sydney's – but Dili was two hours in the other direction. I felt jet-lagged for the first time in my life, physically affronted by the sight of the blazing midday sun – and it struck me just how eerily effective the patch ordinarily was, when I could alight in Frankfurt or Los Angeles without the slightest sense of violated expectations. I wondered how I would have felt if I'd had my hypothalamic clock slavishly synched to the local time zones, all the way along the absurd loop of my flight path. Better, worse . . . or just disturbingly normal, one part of my perception of time laid bare as the simplest of biochemical phenomena?

The single-storey airport building was crowded – with

more people seeing off, or greeting, travellers than I'd ever witnessed in Bombay, Shanghai, or Mexico City, and more uniformed staff that I'd seen in any other airport on the planet. I stood in line behind Indrani Lee to pay the two-hundred-dollar transit tax on the near-monopoly route to Stateless. It was pure extortion . . . but it was hard to begrudge the opportunism. How else was a country this size supposed to raise the foreign exchange it needed in order to buy food? I hit a few keys on my notepad, and **Sisyphus** replied: with great difficulty.

East Timor had none of the few exotic minerals which still needed to be mined to meet net global demand after recycling, and it had been stripped long ago of anything which might have been useful to local industry. Trade in native sandalwood was forbidden by international law, and in any case engineered plantation species produced a better, cheaper product. A couple of electronics multinationals had built appliance-assembly factories in Dili, during a brief period when the independence movement appeared to have been crushed, but they'd all closed in the 20s, when automation became cheaper than the cheapest sweated labour. That left tourism and culture. But how many hotels could be filled, here? (Two small ones; a total of three hundred beds.) And how many people could make their living on the world nets as writers, musicians, or artists? (Four hundred and seven.)

In theory, Stateless faced all the same basic problems, and more. But Stateless had been renegade from the start – its very land built with unlicensed biotech. And no one went hungry there.

It must have been the jet-lag, but it only dawned on me slowly that most of the people in the airport weren't there to greet friends, after all. What I'd mistaken for luggage and gifts was merchandise; these people were traders and their customers: tourists, travellers, and locals. There were a couple of stuffy-looking official airport shops in one corner . . . but the whole building seemed to double as a marketplace.

Still in the queue, I closed my eyes and invoked **Witness**; a sequence of eyeball movements woke the software in my gut, which generated the image of a control panel and fed it down my optic nerve. I stared at the LOCATION slot on the panel, which still read SYDNEY; it obligingly blanked. I mimed vertical one-handed typing, and entered DILI. Then I looked squarely at BEGIN RECORDING, highlighting the words, and opened my eyes.

Witness confirmed: 'Dili, Sunday, 4 April, 2055. 4:34:17 GMT.' *Beep*.

The Customs Department collected the transit tax – and apparently their hardware was down. Instead of our notepads dealing with everything via a brief exchange of IR, we had to sign papers, show our physical ID cards, and receive a cardboard boarding pass with an official rubber stamp. I'd been half expecting some petty harassment if the opportunity arose, but the Customs officer, a softly spoken woman with a dense Papuan frizz beneath her cap, gave me the same patient smile as she'd given everyone else, and processed my paperwork just as swiftly.

I wandered through the airport, not really looking to buy anything, just filming the scene for my scrapbook. People were shouting and haggling in Portuguese, Bahasa and English – and, according to **Sisyphus**, Tetum and Vaiqueno, local languages undergoing a slow resurrection. The airconditioning was probably working, but the body heat of the crowd must have almost balanced its effect; after five minutes, I was dripping with sweat.

Traders were selling rugs, T-shirts, pineapples, oil paintings, statues of saints. I passed by a stall of dried fish, and had to concentrate to keep my stomach from heaving; the smell was no problem, but however many times I confronted it, the sight of dead animals offered for human consumption still left

97

me reeling, more than a human corpse ever did. Engineered crops could match or exceed all the nutritional benefits of meat; a small flesh trade still existed in Australia, but it was discreet and heavily cosmeticised.

I saw a rack of what looked like Masarini jackets, on sale for a tenth of the price they would have fetched in New York or Sydney. I waved my notepad at them; it found one in my size, interrogated the tag in the collar, and chimed approval – but I had my doubts. I asked the thin teenage boy who was standing by the rack. 'Are these *real* authentication chips or . . . ?' He smiled innocently and said nothing. I bought the jacket, then ripped out the tag and handed the chip back to him. 'You might as well get some more use out of it.'

I ran into Indrani Lee beside a software stall. She said, 'I think I've spotted someone else who's headed for the conference.'

'Where?' I felt a mixture of excitement and panic; if it was Violet Mosala herself, I was still unprepared to face her.

I followed Lee's gaze to an elderly Caucasian woman, who was arguing heatedly with a trader selling scarves. Her face was vaguely familiar, but in profile I couldn't put a name to it.

'Who is that?'

'Janet Walsh.'

'No. You're joking.'

But it was her.

Janet Walsh was an award-winning English novelist – and one of the world's most prominent members of Humble Science! She'd first come to fame in the 20s with *Wings of Desire* ('a delicious, mischievous, incisive fable' – *The Sunday Times*), a story set among an 'alien race', who happened to look exactly like humans . . . except that their males were born with large butterfly wings growing out of their penises, which were necessarily and bloodily severed when they lost their virginity. The alien females (who lacked hymens), were all callous and brutal. After being raped and abused by everyone in sight for most of the novel, the hero discovers a magical technique for making his lost wings grow back – on his shoulders – and flies off into the sunset. ('Gleefully subverts all gender stereotypes' – *Playboy*.)

Since then, Walsh had specialised in morality tales concerning the evils of 'male science' (sic), an ill-defined but invariably calamitous activity – which even women could perform if they were led sufficiently astray, although apparently that was no excuse to change the label. I'd quoted her pithiest comment on the subject in *Gender Scrutiny Overload*: 'If it's arrogant, hubristic, dominating, reductionist, exploitative, spiritually impoverished, and dehumanising – what else should we call it but *male*?'

I said, '*Why*? Why is she here?'

'Hadn't you heard? But you were probably travelling; I saw it on the net just before I left. One of the murdochs hired her as a special correspondent to cover the Einstein Conference. Planet News, I think.'

'*Janet Walsh* is going to report on progress in Theories of Everything?' Even for Planet Noise, that was surreal. Sending members of the British royal family to cover famines, and soap opera stars to cover summit meetings, didn't come close.

Lee said drily, ' "Report" may not be quite the word for it.'

I hesitated. 'Can I ask you something? I . . . never really had a chance before I left to look into the cults' response to the conference.' **Sisyphus** would have picked up any relevant stories – but I'd requested a briefing pared down to the essentials. 'I don't suppose you've heard whether or not they're . . . taking much interest?'

Lee regarded me with amazement. 'They've been chartering direct flights from all over the planet for the past week. If Walsh is coming the long way, at the last minute, it's only to keep up appearances for her employer's sake – to maintain a veneer of non-partisanship. Stateless will be swarming with her supporters.' She added gleefully, '*Janet Walsh!* Now that makes the trip worthwhile!'

I felt a stab of betrayal. 'You said you weren't—'

She scowled. 'Not because I'm a follower! Janet Walsh is a hobby of mine. By day I study the rationalists. By night I study their opposites.'

'How very . . . Manichean.' Walsh bought the scarf and started walking away from the stall, not quite towards us. I turned so my face was hidden from her. We'd met once, at a bioethics conference in Zambia; it hadn't been pleasant. I laughed numbly. 'So this is going to be your ideal working holiday?'

Lee was puzzled. 'And yours, too, surely? You must have been hoping desperately for something more than a few sleepy seminars to film. Now you'll have Violet Mosala versus Janet Walsh. Physics versus the Ignorance Cults. Maye even riots in the streets: anarchy comes to Stateless at last. What more could you possibly ask for?'

Denied access to Australian, Indonesian and Papua-New-Guinean airspace, the Portuguese-registered plane headed south-west across the Indian Ocean. The waters looked wind-swept, grey-blue and threatening, though the sky above was clear. We'd curve right round the continent of Australia, and we wouldn't sight land again until we arrived.

I was seated beside two middle-aged Polynesian men in business suits, who conversed loudly and incessantly in French. Mercifully, their dialect was so unfamiliar to me that I could almost tune them out; there was nothing on the plane's headset worth listening to, and without a signal the device made a poor substitute for earplugs.

Sisyphus could reach the net via IR and the plane's satellite link, and I considered downloading the reports I'd missed about the cult presence on Stateless – but I'd be there soon enough; anticipation seemed masochistic. I forced my attention back to the subject of All-Topology Models.

The concept of ATMs was simple enough to state: the universe was considered to possess, at the deepest level, a mixture of every single mathematically possible topology.

Even in the oldest quantum theories of gravity, the 'vacuum' of empty space-time had been viewed as a seething mass of virtual wormholes, and other more exotic topological distortions, popping in and out of existence. The smooth appearance at macroscopic lengths and human timescales was just the visible average of a hidden riot of complexity. In a way, it was like ordinary matter: a sheet of flexible plastic betrayed nothing to the naked eye of its microstructure − molecules, atoms, electrons, and quarks − but knowledge of those constituents allowed the bulk substance's physical properties to be computed: its modulus of elasticity, for example. Space-time wasn't made of atoms, but its properties could be understood by viewing it as being 'built' from a hierarchy of ever more convoluted deviations from its apparent state of continuity and mild curvature. Quantum gravity had explained why observable space-time, underpinned by an infinite number of invisible knots and detours, behaved as it did in the presence of mass (or energy): curving in exactly the fashion required to produce the gravitational force.

ATM theorists were striving to generalise this result: to explain the (relatively) smooth ten-dimensional 'total space' of the Standard Unified Field Theory − whose properties accounted for *all four forces*: strong, weak, gravitational, and electromagnetic − as the net result of an infinite number of elaborate geometrical structures.

Nine spatial dimensions (six rolled up tight), and one time, was only what total space appeared to be if it wasn't examined too closely. Whenever two subatomic particles interacted, there was always a chance that the total space they occupied would behave, instead, like part of a twelve-dimensional hypersphere, or a thirteen-dimensional doughnut, or a fourteen-dimensional figure eight, or just about anything else. In fact – just as a single photon could travel along two different paths at once – any number of these possibilities could take effect simultaneously, and 'interfere with each other' to produce the final outcome. Nine space, one time, was nothing but an average.

There were two main questions still in dispute among ATM theorists.

What, exactly, was meant by 'all' topologies? Just how bizarre could the possibilities contributing to the average total space become? Did they have to be, merely, those which could be formed with a twisted, knotted sheet of higher-dimensional plastic – or could they include states more like a (possibly infinite) handful of scattered grains of sand – where notions like 'number of dimensions' and 'space-time curvature' ceased to exist altogether?

And how, exactly, should the average effect of all these different structures be computed? How should the sum over the infinite number of possibilities be *written down and added up* when the time came to test the theory: to make a prediction, and calculate some tangible, physical quantity which an experiment could actually measure?

On one level, the obvious response to both questions was: 'Use whatever gives the right answers' – but choices which did that were hard to find . . . and some of them smacked of contrivance. Infinite sums were notorious for being either intractable, or too pliable by far. I jotted down an example – remote from the actual tensor equations of ATMs, but good enough to illustrate the point:

$$\text{Let } S = 1 - 1 + 1 - 1 + 1 - 1 + 1 - \ldots$$
$$\text{Then } S = (1-1) + (1-1) + (1-1) + \ldots$$
$$= 0 + 0 + 0 \ldots$$
$$= 0$$

$$\text{But S} = 1 + (-1+1) + (-1+1) + (-1+1) \ldots$$
$$= 1 + 0 + 0 + 0 \ldots$$
$$= 1$$

It was a mathematically naive 'paradox'; the correct answer was, simply, that this particular infinite sequence didn't add up to any definite sum at all. Mathematicians would always be perfectly happy with such a verdict, and would know all the rules for avoiding the pitfalls – and software could assess even the most difficult cases. When a physicists's hard-won theory started generating similarly ambiguous equations, though, and the choice came down to strict mathematical rigour and a theory with no predictive power at all . . . or, a bit of pragmatic side-stepping of the rules, and a theory which churned out beautiful results in perfect agreement with every experiment . . . it was no surprise that people were tempted. After all, most of what Newton had done to calculate planetary orbits had left contemporary mathematicians apoplectic with rage.

Violet Mosala's approach was controversial for a very different reason. She'd been awarded the Nobel prize for rigorously proving a dozen key theorems in general topology – theorems which had rapidly come to comprise a standard mathematical toolbox for ATM physicists, obliterating stumbling blocks and resolving ambiguities. She'd done more than anyone else to provide the field with solid foundations, and the means of making careful, measured progress. Even her fiercest critics agreed that her *mathematics* was meticulous, beyond reproach.

The trouble was, she told her equations too much about the world.

The ultimate test of a TOE was to answer questions like: 'What is the probability of a ten-gigaelectronvolt neutrino fired at a stationary proton scattering off a down quark and emerging at a certain angle?' . . . or even just: 'What is the mass of an electron?' Essentially, Mosala prefixed all such questions with the condition: 'Given that *we know* that space-time is roughly four-dimensional, and total space is roughly ten-dimensional, and the apparatus used to perform the experiment consists, approximately, of the following . . .'

Her supporters said she was merely setting everything in context. No experiment happened in isolation; quantum mechanics had been hammering that point home for the last hundred and twenty years. Asking a Theory of Everything to predict the chance of observing some microscopic event – without adding the proviso that 'there is a universe, and it contains, among other things, equipment for detecting the event in question' – would be as nonsensical as asking: 'If you pick a marble out of a bag, what are the odds that it will be green?'

Her critics said she used circular reasoning, assuming from the very beginning all the results she was trying to prove. The details she fed into her computations included *so much* about the known physics of the experimental apparatus that – indirectly, but inevitably – they gave the whole game away.

I was hardly qualified to come down on either side, but it seemed to me that Mosala's opponents were being hypocrit-ical, because they were pulling the same trick under a different guise: the alternatives *they* offered all invoked a cosmological fix. They declared that 'before' the Big Bang and the creation of time (or 'adjoining' the event, to avoid the oxymoron), there had been nothing but a perfectly symmetrical 'pre-space', in which all topologies carried equal weight . . . and the 'average result' of most familiar physical quantities would have been infinite. Pre-space was sometimes called 'infinitely hot'; it could be thought of as the kind of perfectly balanced chaos which space-time would become if so much energy was poured into it that literally everything became equally pos-sible. Everything and its opposite; the net result was that nothing happened at all.

But some local fluctuation had disturbed the balance in such a way as to give rise to the Big Bang. From that tiny accident, our universe had burst into existence. Once that had happened, the original 'infinitely hot', infinitely even-handed mixture of topologies had been forced to become ever more biased, because 'temperature' and 'energy' now had meaning – and in an expanding, cooling universe, most of the 'hot' old symmetries would have been as unstable as molten metal thrown into a lake. And when they'd cooled, the shapes into which they'd frozen had just happened to favour topologies close to a certain ten-dimensional total space – one which gave rise to particles like quarks and electrons, and forces like gravity and electromagnetism.

By this logic, the only correct way to sum over all the topologies was to incorporate the fact that our universe had – by chance – emerged from pre-space in a certain way. Details of the broken symmetry had to be fed into the equations 'by hand' – because there was no reason why they couldn't have been utterly different. And if the physics resulting from this accident seemed improbably conducive to the formation of stars, planets, and life . . . then this universe was just one of a vast number which had frozen out of pre-space, each with a different set of particles and forces. If every possible set had been tried, it was hardly surprising that at least one of them had turned out to be favourable to life.

It was the old anthropic principle, the fudge which had saved a thousand cosmologies. And I had no real argument with it – even if all the other universes were destined to be forever hypothetical.

But Violet Mosala's methods seemed neither more nor less circular. Her opponents had to 'fine tune' a few parameters in their equations, to take account of the particular universe 'our' Big Bang had created. Mosala and her supporters merely described real experiments in the real world so thoroughly that they 'showed the equations' the very same thing.

It seemed to me that both groups of physicists were confessing, however reluctantly, that they couldn't quite explain how the universe was built . . . without mentioning the fact that they were there inside it, looking for the explanation.

Silence filled the cabin as we flew into darkness. Display screens blinked out, one by one, as passengers dozed off; everyone had had a long journey, wherever they'd started from. I watched the cloud banks behind us darken – a swift, violent sunset, metallic and bruised – then I switched to a route map as we headed north-east, just beyond sight of New Zealand. I thought of space probes on slingshot orbits to Venus via Jupiter. It was as if we'd had to take the long way round to build up enough velocity – as if Stateless was moving too fast to be approached any other way.

An hour later, the island finally appeared ahead of us, like a pale stranded starfish. Six arms sloped gently down from a central plateau; along their sides, grey rock gave way to banks of coral, which thinned from a mass of solid outcrops to a lacelike presence barely breaking the surface of the water. A faint blue bioluminescent glow outlined the convoluted borders of the reefs, enclosed by a succession of other hues – the colour-coded depth lines of a living navigation chart. A small cloud of flashing orange fireflies was clustered in the nearest of the starfish's armpits; whether they were boats anchored in the harbour, or something more exotic, I couldn't tell.

Inland, a sprinkling of lights hinted at a city's orderly grid. I felt a sudden rush of unease. Stateless was as beautiful as any atoll, as spectacular as any ocean liner . . . with none of the reassuring qualities of either. *How could I trust this bizarre artifact not to crumble into the sea?* I was accustomed to standing on solid rock a billion years old, or riding machines of a suitably modest human scale. In my own lifetime, this whole island had been nothing but a cloud of minerals adrift over half the Pacific – and from this vantage, it didn't seem beyond belief that the ocean might surge in through a thousand invisible pores and channels to dissolve it all, reclaim it all, at any moment.

As we descended, though, the land spread out around us, streets and buildings came into view, and my insecurity faded. One million people had made this their home, staking their lives on its solidity. If it was humanly possible to keep this mirage afloat, then I had nothing to fear.

10

The plane emptied slowly. Passengers pressed forward, sleepy and irritable; many were clutching cushions and small blankets, looking like children up past their bedtime. It was only about nine p.m. here – and most people's body clocks would have agreed – but we were all still dazed and cramped and weary. I looked around for Indrani Lee, but I couldn't spot her in the crowd.

There was a security gate at the end of the umbilical, but no airport staff in sight, and no obvious device for interrogating my passport. Stateless placed no restrictions on immigration, let alone the entry of temporary visitors – but they did prohibit certain imports. Beside the gate was a multilingual sign which read:

> *Feel free to try to bring through weapons.*
> *We'll feel free to try to destroy them.*
> STATELESS AIRPORT SYNDICATE

I hesitated. If my passport wasn't read, and the seal of approval for my implants taken into account . . . what would this machine do to me? Incinerate a hundred thousand dollars worth of hardware – and fry a large part of my digestive tract in the process?

I knew that was paranoid: I could hardly have been the first journalist to set foot on the island. And the message was probably aimed at visitors from certain privately owned South American islands – 'libertarian havens' established by self-styled 'political refugees' from the US gun law reforms of the 20s – some of whom had tried to bring Stateless around to their special way of thinking on a number of occasions.

Nevertheless, I stood back for several minutes, hoping that someone in uniform would appear to put my mind at ease. My insurance company had declined to offer me any kind of cover once I was on Stateless, and when my bank found out I'd been here, they wouldn't be pleased; they still owned most of the chips in my gut. Legally, the risk wasn't mine to take.

No one turned up. I walked through. The frame of the scanner was loose, and it shuddered slightly – my body pinning a tiny portion of the magnetic flux, dragging it forward, then releasing it to rebound like elastic – but no microwave pulses seared my abdomen, and no alarms went off.

The gate led into a modern airport, not much different from many I'd seen in small European cities, with clean-lined architecture and moveable seating which groups of people had arranged in inward-facing rings. There were only three airline counters and they all displayed much smaller versions of their logos than usual, as if not wishing to attract too much attention. Booking passage here, I'd found no flights advertised openly on the net; I'd had to post a specific query in order to obtain any information. The European Federation, India, and several African and Latin American countries only enforced the minimal boycott of selected high technology which the UN demanded; these airlines were operating entirely within the laws of their home nations. Still, irritating the Japanese, Korean, Chinese and US governments – not to mention the biotech multinationals – would always carry a risk. Committing the offence discreetly wouldn't conceal anything, but no doubt it acted as a gesture of obeisance, and lessened the perceived need for examples to be made of the collaborators.

I collected my suitcase and stood by the baggage roundabout, trying to get my bearings. I watched my fellow passengers drift away, some greeted by friends, some going on alone. Most spoke in English or French; there was no official language here, but almost two-thirds of the population had migrated from other Pacific islands. Choosing to live on Stateless might always be a political decision in the end – and some Greenhouse refugees apparently preferred to spend years in Chinese detention camps instead, in the hope of eventually being accepted into that entrepreneurial dreamland – but after seeing your home washed into the ocean, I could imagine that a self-repairing (and currently increasing) landmass might hold a special attraction. Stateless represented a reversal of fortune: sunlight and biotechnology playing the whole disaster movie backwards. Better than raging at the storm. Fiji and Samoa were finally growing new islands of their own, but they weren't yet habitable – and both governments were paying several billion dollars for the privilege, in licence fees and consultants' charges. They'd carry the debt into the twenty-second century.

In theory, a patent lasted only seventeen years – but biotec companies had perfected the strategy of reapplying for the same coverage from a different angle when the expiration date loomed: First for the DNA sequence of a gene, and all its applications . . . then for the corresponding amino acid sequence . . . then for the *shape* and *functionality* (irrespective of precise chemical makeup) of the fully assembled protein. I couldn't bring myself simply to shrug off the theft of knowledge as a victimless crime – I'd always been swayed by the argument that no one would waste money on R&D if engineered lifeforms couldn't be patented – but there was something insane about the fact that the most powerful tools against famine, the most powerful tools against environmental damage, the most powerful tools against *poverty* . . . were all priced beyond the reach of everyone who needed them the most.

As I began to cross towards the exit, I saw Janet Walsh heading in the same direction, and I hung back. She was walking with a group of half a dozen men and women – but one man walked a few metres outside the entourage, with a practised smooth gait and a steady gaze directed straight at Walsh. I recognised the technique at once, and the practitioner a moment later: David Connolly, a photographer with Planet Noise. Walsh needed a second pair of eyes, of course – she would hardly have let them put all that nasty dehumanising technology inside her own body . . . and, worse, her own POV would have left her out of every shot. Not much point employing a celebrity journalist if she wasn't on-screen.

I followed at a discreet distance. A group of forty or fifty supporters were standing outside in the warm night air, holding up luminescent banners – more telegenic in the relative darkness than they would have been inside – which switched in synch between HUMBLE SCIENCE!, WELCOME JANET! and SAY NO TO TOE! They cheered in unison as Walsh came through the doors. She broke away from her halo of companions to shake hands and receive kisses; Connolly stood back to capture it all.

Walsh made a short speech, wisps of grey hair blowing in the breeze. I couldn't fault her skills with camera or crowd: she had the knack of appearing dignified and authoritative, without seeming stern or aloof. And I had to admire her stamina: she displayed more energy after the long flight than I could have summoned if my life had been in danger.

'I want to thank all of you for coming here to greet me; I really am touched by your generosity. And I want to thank you for undertaking the long, arduous journey to this island, to lend your voices to our small song of protest against the forces of scientific arrogance. There are people gathering here who believe they can crush every last source of human dignity, every last wellspring of spiritual nourishment, every last precious, sustaining mystery, under the weight of their "intellectual progress" – grind us all down into one equation, and write it on a T-shirt like a cheap slogan. People who believe they can take all the wonders of nature and the secrets of the heart and say: "This is it. This is all there is." Well, we're here to tell them—'

The small crowd roared, 'NO!'

Beside me, someone laughed quietly. 'But if they *can't* take away your precious dignity, Janet, why make such a fuss?'

I turned. The speaker was a . . . twentyish? asex? Ve tipped vis head and smiled, teeth flashing white against deep black skin, eyes as dark as Gina's, high cheekbones which had to be a woman's – except, of course, they didn't. Ve was dressed in black jeans and a loose black T-shirt; points of light appeared on the fabric sparsely, at random, as if it was meant to be displaying some kind of image, but the data feed had been cut.

Ve said, 'What a windbag. You know she used to work for D-R-D? You'd think she'd have snappier rhetoric, with credentials like that.' *Cre-den-tials* was pronounced with an ironic (Jamaican?) drawl; D-R-D was Dayton-Rice-Daley, the Anglophone world's largest advertising firm. 'You're Andrew Worth.'

'Yes. How—?'

'Come to film Violet Mosala.'

'That's right. Do you . . . work with her?' Ve looked almost too young even to be a doctoral student – but then, Mosala had completed her own PhD at twenty.

Ve shook vis head. 'I've never met her.'

I still couldn't pin down vis accent, unless the word I was looking for was mid-Atlantic: halfway between Kingston and Luanda. I put down my suitcase and held out a hand. Ve shook it firmly. 'I'm Akili Kuwale.'

'Here for the Einstein Conference?'

'Why else?'

I shrugged. 'There must be other things happening on Stateless.' Ve didn't reply.

Walsh had moved on, and her cheer squad were dispersing. I glanced down at my notepad and said, 'Transport map.'

Kuwale said, 'The hotel's only two kilometres away. Unless

that suitcase is heavier than it looks . . . it would be just as easy to walk, wouldn't it?'

Ve had no luggage, no backpack, nothing; ve must have arrived earlier, and returned to the airport . . . to meet me? I had a serious need to be horizontal, and I couldn't imagine what ve wanted to tell me that couldn't wait until morning – and couldn't be said on a tram – but that was probably all the more reason to hear it.

I said, 'Good idea. I could use some fresh air.'

Kuwale seemed to know where ve was going, so I put my notepad away and followed along. It was a warm, humid night, but there was a steady breeze which took the edge off the oppressiveness. Stateless was no closer to the tropics than Sydney; overall, it was probably cooler.

The layout of the centre of the island reminded me of Sturt, an inland South Australian neopolis built at about the time Stateless was seeded. There were broad, paved streets and low buildings, most of them small blocks of apartments above shopfronts, six storeys high at the most. Everything in sight was made from reef-rock: a form of limestone, strengthened and sealed by organic polymers, which was 'farmed' from the self-replenishing quarries of the inner reefs. None of the buildings was bleached-coral white, though; trace minerals produced all the colours of marble: rich greys, greens and browns, and more rarely dark crimson, shading to black.

The people around us seemed relaxed and unhurried, as if they were all out for leisurely strolls with no particular destination in mind. I saw no cycles at all, but there'd have to be a few on the island; tram lines stretched less than half-way to the points of the star, fifty kilometres from the centre.

Kuwale said, 'Sarah Knight was a great admirer of Violet Mosala. I think she would have done a good job. Careful. Thorough.'

That threw me. 'You know Sarah?'

'We've been in touch.'

I laughed wearily. 'What is this? Sarah Knight is a big fan of Mosala . . . and I'm not. *So what?* I'm not some Ignorance Cult member here to do a hatchet job; I'll still treat her fairly.'

'That's not the issue.'

'It's the only issue I'm willing to discuss with you. Why do you imagine it's any of your business how this documentary's made?'

Kuwale said calmly, 'I don't. The documentary's not important.'

'Right. Thanks.'

'No offence. But it's not what I'm talking about.'

We walked on a few metres, in silence. I waited to see if keeping my mouth shut and feigning indifference would prompt a sudden revelatory outburst. It didn't.

I said, 'So . . . what exactly are you doing here? Are you a journalist, a physicist . . . or what? A sociologist?' I'd almost said: *A cultist* – but even a member of a rival group like Mystical Renaissance or Culture First would never have mocked the deep wisdom of Janet Walsh.

'I'm an interested observer.'

'Yeah? That explains everything.'

Ve grinned appreciatively, as if I'd made a joke. I could see the curved façade of the hotel in the distance, straight ahead now; I recognised it from the conference organisers' AV.

Kuwale became serious. 'You'll be with Violet Mosala a lot, over the next two weeks. Maybe more than any other person. We've tried to get messages through to her, but you know she doesn't take us seriously. So . . . would you at least be willing to keep your eyes open?'

'For what?'

Ve frowned, then looked around nervously. 'Do I have to spell it out? I'm AC. *Mainstream* AC. We don't want to see her hurt. And I don't know how sympathetic you are, or how far you're prepared to go to help us, but all you'd have to do is—'

114

I held up a hand to stop ver. 'What are you talking about? *You don't want to see her hurt?*'

Kuwale looked dismayed, then sudddenly wary. I said, ' "Mainstream AC"? Is that supposed to mean something to me?' Ve didn't reply. 'And if Violet Mosala doesn't take you seriously, why should anyone else?'

Kuwale was clearly having grave second thoughts about me. I still wanted to know what the first ones had been. Ve said derisively, 'Sarah Knight never agreed to anything – not in so many words – but at least she understood what was going on. What kind of journalist are you? Do you ever go looking for information? Or do you just grab an electronic teat and see what comes out when you *suck?* '

Ve broke away, and headed down a side street. I called out, 'I'm not a mind-reader! Why don't you *tell me* what's going on?'

I stood and watched ver disappear into the crowd. I could have followed, demanding answers, but I was already beginning to suspect that I could guess the truth. Kuwale was a fan of Mosala's, affronted by the planeloads of cultists who'd come to mock ver idol. And though it wasn't, literally, impossible that an even more disturbed member of Humble Science! or Mystical Renaissance meant Violet Mosala harm . . . most likely it was all just Kuwale's elaborate fantasy.

I'd call Sarah Knight in the morning; she'd probably had a dozen weird mesages from Kuwale, and finally fobbed ver off by replying: *It's not even my job anymore. Go pick on the arsehole who stole it from me, Andrew Worth. Here's a recent picture.* I could hardly blame her; it was a small enough act of revenge.

I continued on towards the hotel. I was dead on my feet, sleepwalking.

I asked **Sisyphus**, 'So what does AC stand for?'

'In what context?'

'Any context. Besides *alternating current*.'

There was a long pause. I glanced up at the sky, and spotted the faint row of evenly spaced dots, drifting slowly eastward against the stars, which still bound me to the world I knew.

'There are five thousand and seventeen other meanings, including specialist jargon, subcultural slang, and registered businesses, charities, and political organisations.'

'Then . . . anything which might fit the way it was used by Akili Kuwale a few minutes ago.' My notepad kept twenty-four hours of audio in memory. I added, 'Kuwale is probably asex.'

Sisyphus digested the conversation, rescanned its list, and said, 'The thirty most plausible meanings are: Absolute Control, a Fijian security consultancy who work throughout the South Pacific; Asex Catholique, a Paris-based group which advocates reform of the policies of the Roman Catholic Church towards asex gender migrants; Advanced Cartography, a South African satellite data reduction firm . . .' I listened to all thirty, then thirty more, but the connections were all so ludicrous as to amount to nothing but noise.

'So what's the meaning which makes perfect sense – but isn't listed in any respectable database? What's the one answer I can't get out of my favourite electronic teat?'

Sisyphus didn't dignify that with a reply.

I nearly apologised, but I caught myself in time.

11

I woke at six-thirty, a few seconds before my alarm sounded. I caught fragments of a retreating dream: images of waves crashing against disintegrating coral and limestone – but if the mood had been threatening, it was rapidly dispelled. Sunlight filled the room, shining off the smooth silver-grey walls of polished reef-rock. There were people talking on the street below; I couldn't make out any words, but the tone sounded relaxed, amiable, civilised. If this was anarchy, it beat waking up to police sirens in Shanghai or New York. I felt more refreshed and optimistic than I had for a very long time.

And I was finally going to meet my subject.

I'd received a message the night before, from Mosala's assistant, Karin De Groot. Mosala was giving a media conference at eight; after that, she'd be busy for most of the day – starting at nine, when Henry Buzzo from Caltech was delivering a paper which he claimed would cast doubt on a whole class of ATMs. Between the media conference and Buzzo's paper, though, I'd have a chance to discuss the documentary with her, at last. Although nothing had to be concluded on Stateless – I'd be able to interview her at length back in Cape Town, if necessary – I'd been beginning to wonder if I'd be forced to cover her time here as just another journalist in the pack.

I thought about breakfast, but after forcing myself to eat on the flight from Dili, my appetite still hadn't returned. So I lay on the bed, reading through Mosala's biographical notes one more time, and rechecking my tentative shooting schedule for the fortnight ahead. The room was functional, almost ascetic compared to most hotels . . . but it was clean, modern, bright, and inexpensive. I'd slept in less comfortable beds, in rooms with plusher but gloomier decor, at twice the cost.

It was all too good, by far. Peaceful surroundings and an untraumatic subject – what had I done to deserve this? I'd never even found out who Lydia had sent into the breach to make *Distress*. Who'd be spending the day in a psychiatric hospital in Miami or Berne, while tranquillisers were withdrawn from one strait-jacketed victim after another, to test the effects of some non-sedative drug on the syndrome, or to obtain scans of the neuropathology unsullied by pharmacological effects?

I brushed the image away, angrily. Distress wasn't my responsibility; I hadn't created the disease. And I hadn't forced anyone to take my place.

Before leaving for the media conference, I reluctantly called Sarah Knight. My curiosity about Kuwale had all but faded – it was sure to be a sad story, with no surprises – and the prospect of facing Sarah for the first time since I'd robbed her of *Violet Mosala* wasn't appealing.

I didn't have to. It was only ten to six in Sydney, and a generic answering sytem took my call. Relieved, I left a brief message, then headed downstairs.

The main auditorium was packed, buzzing with expectant chatter. I'd had visions of hundreds of protesters from Humble Science! picketing the hotel entrance, or brawling with security guards and physicists in the corridors, but there wasn't a demonstrator in sight. Standing in the entrance, it took me a while to pick out Janet Walsh in the audience, but once I'd spotted her it was easy to triangulate to Connolly in a forward row – perfectly placed to turn from Walsh to Mosala with a minimum of neck strain.

I took a seat near the back of the room, and invoked **Witness**. Electronic cameras on the stage would capture the

118

audience, and I could buy the footage from the conference organisers if there was anything worth using.

Marian Fox, President of the International Union of Theoretical Physicists, took the stage and introduced Mosala. She uttered all the words of praise that anyone would have used in her place: *respected, inspirational, dedicated, exceptional.* I had no doubt that she was perfectly sincere . . . but the language of achievement always seemed to me to crumble into self-parody. How many people on the planet could be *exceptional*? How many could be *unique*? I had no wish to see Violet Mosala portrayed as no different from the most mediocre of her colleagues, but all the laudatory clichés conveyed nothing. They just rendered themselves meaningless.

Mosala walked to the podium, trying to look graceful under hyperbole; a section of the audience applauded wildly, and several people rose to their feet. I made a mental note to ask Indrani Lee for her thoughts as to when and why these strange adulatory rituals – observed almost universally with actors and musicians – had begun to be followed for a handful of celebrity scientists. I suspected it was all down to the Ignorance Cults; they'd struggled so hard to raise popular interest in their cause that it would have been surprising if they hadn't ended up generating some equally vehement opposing passions. And there were plenty of social strata where the cults were pure establishment, and there could be no greater act of rebellion than idolising a physicist.

Mosala waited for the noise to die down. 'Thank you, Marian. And thank you all for attending this session. I should just briefly explain what I'm doing here. I'll be on a number of panels taking questions on technical matters, throughout the conference. And, of course, I'll be happy to discuss the issues raised by the paper I'm giving on the eighteenth, after I've presented it. But time is always short on those occasions, and we like to keep the questions tightly focused – which, I know,

119

often frustrates journalists who'd like to cover a broader range of topics.

'So, the organising committee has persuaded a number of speakers to hold media sessions where those restrictions won't apply. This morning it's my turn. So if you have anything you'd like to ask me which you're afraid might be ruled out as irrelevant at later sessions . . . this is your chance.'

Mosala came across as relaxed and unassuming; she'd been visibly nervous in the footage I'd seen of earlier appearances – the Nobel ceremony, especially – but if she wasn't yet a seasoned veteran, she was definitely more at ease. She had a deep, vibrant voice – which might have been electrifying if she ever took to making speeches – but her tone was conversational, not oratorial. All of which boded well for *Violet Mosala*. The awkward truth was, some people just didn't belong on a living-room screen for most of fifty minutes. They didn't *fit* – and they emerged distorted, like a sound too loud or too soft to record. Mosala, I was sure now, would survive the limitations of the medium. So long as I didn't screw up completely, myself.

The first few questions came from the science correspondents of the non-specialist news services . . . who diligently resurrected all the old non sequiturs: *Will a Theory of Everything mean an end to science? Will a TOE render the future totally predictable? Will a TOE unlock all the unsolved problems of physics and chemistry, biology and medicine . . . ethics and religion?*

Mosala dealt with all of this patiently and concisely. 'A Theory of Everything is just the simplest mathematical formulation we can find which encapsulates all the underlying order in the universe. Over time, if a candidate TOE survives sustained theoretical scrutiny and experimental testing, we should gradually become confident that it represents a kind of *kernel of understanding* . . . from which – in principle, in

120

the most idealised sense – everything around us could be explained.

'But that won't make anything "totally predictable". The universe is full of systems which we understand completely – systems as simple as two planets orbiting a star – where the mathematics is chaotic, or intractable, and long-term predictions will always be impossible to compute.

'And it doesn't mean "an end to science". Science is much more than the search for a TOE; it's the elucidation of the relationships between order in the universe at every level. Reaching the foundations doesn't mean hitting the ceiling. There are dozens of problems in fluid dynamics – let alone neurobiology – which need new approaches, or better approximations, not the ultimate, precise description of matter on a subatomic scale.'

I pictured Gina at her workstation. And I pictured her in her new home, recounting all her problems and small triumphs to her new lover. I felt unsteady for a moment, but it passed.

'Lowell Parker, Atlantica. Professor Mosala, you say a TOE is the "simplest mathematical formulation of the underlying order in the universe". But aren't all these concepts culturally determined? "Simplicity"? "Order"? Even the range of formulations available to contemporary mathematics?' Parker was an earnest young man with a Boston accent; Atlantica was a highculture netzine, produced mainly by part-time academics from east coast universities.

Mosala replied, 'Certainly. And the equations we choose to call a TOE won't be unique. They'll be like . . . say, Maxwell's Equations for electromagnetism. There are half a dozen equally valid ways Maxwell's Equations can be written – constants can be shuffled around, different variables used . . . they can even be expressed in either three or four dimensions. Physicists and engineers still can't agree as to which formulation is the simplest – because that really depends on what you

121

want to use them for: designing a radar antenna, calculating the behaviour of the solar wind, or describing the history of the unification of electrostatics and magnetism. But they all give identical results in any particular calculation – because they all describe the same thing: electromagnetism itself.'

Parker said, 'That's often been said about the world's religions, hasn't it? They all express the same basic, universal truths – merely in a different manner, to suit different times and places. Would you concede that what you're doing is essentially just a part of the same tradition?'

'No. I don't believe that's true.'

'But you've admitted that cultural factors will determine the TOE we accept. So how can you claim that what you're doing is any more "objective" than religion?'

Mosala hesitated, then said carefully, 'Suppose every human being was wiped off the face of the planet tomorrow, and we waited a few million years for the next species with a set of religious and scientific cultures to arise. What do you think the new religions would have in common with the old ones – the ones from our time? I suspect the only common ground would be certain ethical principles which could be traced to shared biological influences: sexual reproduction, child rearing, the advantages of altruism, the awareness of death. And if the biology was very different, there might be no overlap at all.

'But if we waited for the new scientific culture to come up with their idea of a TOE, then I believe that – however different it looked "on paper" – it would be something which either culture would be able to show was mathematically equivalent in every respect to our TOE . . . just as any physics undergraduate can prove that all the forms of Maxwell's Equations describe exactly the same thing.

'That's the difference. Scientists may start off disagreeing wildly – but they converge on a consensus, regardless of their culture. There are physicists at this conference from over a hundred different countries. Their ancestors three thousand years ago might have had twenty or thirty mutually contradictory explanations between them for any phenomenon you care to think of in the natural world. And yet there are only *three* conflicting candidate TOEs being presented here. And in twenty years' time, if not sooner, I'd bet there'll only be one.'

Parker appeared dissatisfied with this reply, but he took his seat.

'Lisbeth Weller, GrünWeisheit. It seems to me that your whole approach to these issues reflects a male, Western, reductionist, left-brained mode of thought.' Weller was a tall, sober-looking woman, who sounded genuinely saddened and perplexed. 'How can you possibly reconcile this with your struggle as an African woman against cultural imperialism?'

Mosala said evenly, 'I have no interest in surrendering the most powerful intellectual tools I possess, because of some quaint misconception that they're the property of any particular group of people: male, Western, or otherwise. As I said, the history of science is one of convergence towards a shared understanding of the universe – and I'm not willing to be excluded from that convergence for any reason. And as for "left-brained modes of thought", I'm afraid that's a rather dated – and reductionist – concept. Personally, I use the whole organ.'

There was loud applause from the fans, but it sounded plaintive as it died out. The atmosphere in the room was changing: becoming strained, polarised. Weller, I knew, was a proud member of Mystical Renaissance – and although most journalists here would have no cult affiliation, the minority with strong anti-science sentiments could still make their presence felt.

'William Savimbi, Proteus Information. You speak approvingly of a convergence of ideas which has no respect for ancestral cultures – as if your own heritage were of no importance to you at all. Is it true that you received death threats from the Pan-African Cultural Defence Front, after you publicly stated that you didn't consider yourself to *be* an African woman?' Proteus was the South African branch of a large Canadian family company; Savimbi was a solid, grey-haired man, who spoke with casual familiarity, as if he'd been covering Mosala for some time.

Mosala struggled visibly to contain her anger. She reached into a pocket and took out her notepad, and began typing on the keyboard.

Without pausing, she said, 'Mr Savimbi, if you find the technology of your profession too daunting, perhaps you should look for something less challenging. *This* is the quote, from the original Reuters story, filed in Stockholm on 10 December, 2053. And it's only taken me fifteen seconds to find it.'

She held up the notepad, and her recorded voice said: 'I don't wake up every morning and say to myself: "I'm an African woman, how should this be reflected in my work?" I don't think that way at all. I wonder if anyone asked Dr Wozniak how being European influenced his approach to polymer synthesis.'

There was more applause – from more of the audience, this time – but I sensed a growing predatory undercurrent. Mosala was becoming visibly agitated, and however sympathetic the pack were – in principle – I had no doubt that they'd be overjoyed if she was provoked into losing control.

'Janet Walsh, Planet News. Ms Mosala, perhaps you could clarify something for me. This Theory of Everything you keep talking about, which is going to sum up the final truth about the universe . . . it sounds absolutely wonderful to me, but I would like to hear exactly what it's based on.'

Mosala must have known who Walsh was, but she be-trayed no sign of hostility. She said, 'Every TOE is an attempt to find a deeper explanation for what's called the Standard

Unified Field Theory. That was completed in the late-20s – and it's survived all experimental tests, so far. Strictly speaking, the SUFT is already a "Theory of Everything": it does give a unified account of all the forces of nature. But it's a very messy, arbitrary theory – based on a ten-dimensional universe with a lot of strange quirks which are difficult to take at face value. Most of us believe that there's a simpler explanation underlying it, just waiting to be found.'

Walsh said, 'But this SUFT you're trying to supplant – what was *that* based on?'

'A number of earlier theories which each, separately, accounted for one or two of the four basic forces. But if you want to know where those earlier theories came from, I'd have to recount five thousand years of scientific history. The short answer is, ultimately, a TOE will be based on observations of every aspect of the world, and the search for patterns in those observations.'

'*That's it?*' Walsh mimed happy disbelief. 'Then we're all scientists, aren't we? We all use our senses, we all make observations. And we all see patterns. I see patterns in the clouds above my home, every time I walk out into the garden.' She smiled a modest, self-deprecating smile.

Mosala said, 'That's a start. But there are two powerful steps beyond that kind of observation, which have made all the difference. Carrying out deliberate, controlled experiments, instead of only watching nature as it unfolds. And carrying out quantitative observations: making measurements, and trying to find patterns in the numbers.'

'Like numerology?'

Mosala shook her head, and said patiently. 'Not any pattern, for the sake of it. You have to have a clear hypothesis to start with, and you have to know how to test it.'

'You mean . . . use all the right statistical methods, and so on?'

'Exactly.'

125

'But *given* the right statistical methods . . . you think the whole truth about the universe is spelt out in the patterns you can find by peering at a endless list of numbers?'

Mosala hesitated, probably wondering if the tortuous process of explaining anything more subtle would be worse than accepting that characterisation of her life's work.

'More or less.'

'Everything's in the numbers? The numbers never lie?'

Mosala lost all patience. 'No, they don't.'

Walsh said, 'That's very interesting. Because a few months ago, I came across a preposterous – very offensive! – idea that was being spread on some of the far-right-wing European networks. I thought it deserved to be properly – scientifically! – refuted. So I bought a little statistical package, and I asked it to test the hypothesis that a certain portion – a certain *quota* – of the Nobel Prizes since the year 2010 have been explicitly reserved on political grounds for the citizens of African nations.' There was a moment of stunned silence, then a wave of outraged exclamations spread across the room. Walsh held up her notepad and continued, raising her voice over the outcry, 'And the answer was, there was a ninety-five per cent chance—' Half a dozen people in the fan club rows sprang to their feet and started shouting at her; the two men on either side of me began hissing. Walsh pressed on, with an expression of bemusement, as if she couldn't understand what all the fuss was about. 'The answer was, there was a *ninety-five percent chance that it was true*.'

A dozen more people stood up to abuse her. Four journalists stormed out of the auditorium. Walsh remained on her feet, waiting for a response, smiling innocently. I saw Marian Fox move tentatively towards the podium; Mosala gestured to her to stay back.

Mosala began typing on her notepad. The shouting and hissing gradually subsided, and then everyone but Walsh took their seats again.

The silence can't have lasted more than ten seconds, but it was long enough for me to realise that my heart was pounding. I wanted to punch someone. Walsh was no racist, but she was an expert manipulator. She'd slipped a barb under everyone's skin; if she'd had two hundred screaming, placard-waving followers at the back of the auditorium, she couldn't have raised stronger passions.

Mosala looked up and smiled sweetly.

She said, 'The African scientific renaissance has been examined in detail, in over thirty papers in the last ten years. I'd be happy to give you the references, if you can't track them down yourself. You'll find there are several more sophisticated hypotheses for explaining the sharp rise in the number of articles by African scientists published in peer-reviewed scientific journals, the rates of citation of those articles, the number of patents awarded – and the number of Nobel Prizes for physics and chemistry.

'When it comes to your own field, though, I'm afraid you're on your own. I can't find a single study which offers any alternative explanation to the *ninety-nine percent likelihood* that since its inception, a quota of Booker Prizes has been set aside for a clearly delineated, intellectually challenged minority: hacks who should have stayed in advertising.'

The auditorium exploded with laughter. Walsh remained standing for a few seconds, then took her seat with remarkable dignity: unrepentant, unashamed, unfazed. I wondered if all she'd wanted was for Mosala to hit back on the same level. There was no question that Planet Noise would find a way to twist the exchange into a victory for Walsh: SCIENCE PRODIGY, CONFRONTED WITH THE FACTS, INSULTS RESPECTED AUTHOR. But most of the media would report that Mosala had responded with great restraint to deliberate provocation.

There were a few more questions – all of them innocuous and mildly technical – then the session was declared at an end.

I walked around to the back of the stage where Karin De Groot was waiting for me.

De Groot was unmistakably ifem – a look which was not at all 'halfway towards' androgynous; it was far more distinctive than that. While ufems and umales exaggerated well-established facial gender cues, and asexes eliminated them, the first ifems and imales had modelled the human visual system and found completely new clusters of parameters which would set them apart at a glance – without rendering them all homogeneous.

She shook my hand then led me towards one of the hotel's small meeting rooms. She said quietly, 'Go easy on her, will you? That wasn't pleasant back there.'

'I can't imagine anyone handling it better.'

'Violet's not someone I'd want as an enemy; she never hits back without thinking it through. But that doesn't mean she's made of stone.'

The room had a table and seating for twelve, but only Mosala was waiting there. I'd been half expecting a private security guard – but then, the fan club notwithstanding, she wasn't quite in the rock star league. And Kuwale's dire intimations notwithstanding, there was probably no need.

Mosala greeted me warmly. 'I'm sorry we couldn't do this earlier, but I'm afraid I hadn't set aside any time for it. After all those meetings with Sarah Knight, I'd assumed the whole planning stage was over.'

All those meetings with Sarah Knight? Pre-production should never have gone that far without SeeNet's approval.

I said, 'I'm sorry to put you through it again. There's always some unavoidable duplication when a new director takes over a project.'

Mosala nodded, distracted. We sat and went through the whole conference timetable together, comparing notes. Mosala asked not to be filmed at more than fifty per cent of the sessions she attended. 'I'd go mad if you were watching me all the time, catching me out whenever I pulled a face at something I disagreed with.' I agreed, but then we haggled over the particular fifty per cent – I definitely wanted reaction shots for all the talks where her work would be explicitly discussed.

We decided on three interview sessions, two hours each, the first on Wednesday afternoon.

Mosala said, 'I still have some trouble understanding what your aim is with this program. If the subject is TOEs, why not just cover the whole conference instead of putting the spotlight on me?'

'Audiences find the theories more accessible if they come packaged as something which a particular person has done.' I shrugged. 'Or so the network executives have convinced themselves – and probably convinced the audiences as well, by now.' SeeNet stood for Science, Education and Entertainment Network, but the S-word was often treated as a source of embarrassment incapable of being intrinsically interesting, and requiring the maximum possible sugar-coating. 'With a profile we can touch on some broader issues, though, in terms of the way they affect your day-to-day life. The Ignorance Cults, for example.'

Mosala said drily, 'You don't think they get enough publicity already?'

'Yes – but most of it's on their own terms. The profile could be a chance for people to see them through your eyes.'

She laughed. 'You want me to tell your audience what I think of the cults? You won't have time for anything else, if I get started.'

'You could stick to the big three.'

Mosala hesitated. De Groot flashed me a warning look, but I ignored it. I said, 'Culture First?'

'Culture First is the most pathetic. It's the last refuge for people desperate to think of themselves as "intellectuals" – while remaining complete scientific illiterates. Most of them are just nostalgic for the era when a third of the planet was controlled by people whose definition of a *civilised* education was Latin, European military history, and the selected doggerel of a few overgrown British schoolboys.'

I grinned. 'Mystical Renaissance?'

Mosala smiled ironically. 'They start from such good intentions, don't they? They say most people are blind to the world around them: sleepwalkers in a zombie's routine of mundane work and mind-numbing entertainment. I couldn't agree more. They say they want everyone on the planet to become "attuned" to the universe we're living in, and to share the awe they feel when they confront the deep strangeness of it all: the dizzying length and time scales of cosmology, the endlessly rich complexities of the biosphere, the bizarre paradoxes of quantum mechanics.

'Well . . . all of those things inspire awe in me, too – some of the time – but Mystical Renaissance treats that response as *an end in itself*. And they want science to pull back from investigating anything which gives them a high in its pristine, unexplained state – in case they don't get the same rush from it, once it's better understood. Ultimately, they're not interested in the universe at all, any more than people who romanticise the life of animals into a cartoon world where no blood is spilt . . . or people who deny the existence of ecological damage, because they don't want to change the way they live. Followers of Mystical Renaissance only want the truth if it suits them, if it *induces the right emotions*. If they were honest, they'd just stick a hot wire in their brain at whatever location made them believe they were undergoing a constant mystical epiphany – because in the end, that's all they're after.'

This was priceless; no one of Mosala's stature had ever really let fly against the cults like this. Not on the public record.

'Humble Science!?'

Mosala's eyes flashed with anger. 'They're the worst, by far. The most patronising, the most cynical. Janet Walsh is just a tactician and a figurehead; most of the real leaders are far better educated. And in their collective wisdom, they've decided that the fragile blossom of human culture just can't survive any more revelations about what *human beings* really are, or how the universe actually functions.

'If they spoke out against the abuse of biotechnology, I'd back them all the way. If they spoke out against weapons research, I'd do the same. If they stood for some coherent system of values which made the most pitiless scientific truths less alienating to ordinary people . . . without denying those truths . . . I'd have no quarrel with them at all.

'But when they decide that *all knowledge* – beyond a border which is theirs to define – is anathema to civilisation and sanity, and that it's up to some self-appointed cultural elite to generate a set of hand-made "life-affirming" myths *to take its place* . . . to imbue human existence with some suitably uplifting – and politically expedient – meaning . . . they become nothing but the worst kind of censors and social engineers.'

I suddenly noticed that Mosala's slender arms, spread out on the table in front of her, were trembling; she was far angrier than I'd realised. I said, 'It's almost nine, but we could take this up again after Buzzo's lecture, if you have time?'

DeGroot touched her elbow. They leant towards each other, and conversed *sotto voce*, at length.

Mosala said, 'We have an interview scheduled for Wednesday, don't we? I'm sorry, but I can't spare any time before then.'

'Of course, that's fine.'

'And those comments I just made are all off the record. They're not to be used.'

My heart sank. 'Are you serious?'

'This was supposed to be a meeting to discuss our filming schedule. Nothing I said here was intended to be made public.'

I pleaded, 'I'll put it all in context: Janet Walsh went out of her way to insult you – and at the media conference you kept your cool, you were restrained – but afterwards, you expressed your opinions in detail. What's wrong with that? Or do you want Humble Science! to start censoring *you*?'

Mosala closed her eyes for a moment then said carefully, 'Those are my opinions, yes, and I'm entitled to them. I'm also entitled to decide who hears them and who doesn't. I don't want to inflame this whole ugly mess any further. So would you please respect my wishes and tell me that you won't use any of it?'

'We don't have to sort this out immediately. I can send you a rough cut—'

Mosala gestured dismissively. 'I signed an agreement with Sarah Knight, saying I could veto anything, on the spot, with no questions asked.'

'If you did, that was with her, personally, not with SeeNet. All SeeNet have from you is a standard clearance.'

Mosala did not look happy. 'You know what I've been meaning to ask you? Sarah said you'd explain why you had to take over the project at such short notice. After all the work she put into it, all she left was a ten-second message saying: I'm off the profile, Andrew Worth is the new director, he'll tell you the reason why.'

I said carefully, 'Sarah may have given you the wrong impression. SeeNet had never officially chosen her to make the documentary. And it was SeeNet who approached you and set things up initially – not Sarah. It was never a freelance project she was developing independently, to offer to them. It was a SeeNet project which she *wanted* to direct, so she sank a lot of her own time into trying to make that happen.'

De Groot said, 'But why *didn't it* happen? All that research, all that preparation, all that enthusiasm . . . why didn't it pay off?'

What could I say? That I'd stolen the project from the one

132

person who truly deserved it . . . so I could have a fully paid South Pacific holiday, away from the stresses of serious frankenscience?

I said, 'Network executives are in a world of their own. If I could understand how they made their decisions, I'd probably be up there with them myself.'

De Groot and Mosala regarded me with silent disbelief.

12

TechnoLalia, SeeNet's major rival, insisted on labelling Henry Buzzo 'the revered guru of trans-millennial physics' – and frequently implied that he should retire as soon as possible, leaving the field open to younger colleagues who rated more dynamic clichés: *wunderkinder und enfants terrible* 'surfing pre-space's infinite-dimensional *nouvelle vague*'. (Lydia dismissed TL as a guccione, 'all hip and no brain'. I couldn't argue with that, but I often feared that SeeNet was heading for a similar fate.) Buzzo had shared the Nobel back in 2036, with the seven other architects of the Standard Unified Field Theory – but he, too, was now trying to demolish, or at least supersede, it. I was reminded of two early-twentieth-century physicists: J. J. Thomson, who'd established the existence of electrons as distinct particles, and George Thomson, his son, who'd shown that they could also behave like waves. It was an enlargement of vision, not a contradiction – and no doubt Buzzo was hoping to perform a similar feat in a single generation.

Buzzo was a tall, bald, heavily wrinkled man, eighty-three years old but showing no signs of frailty. He was a lively speaker, and seemed to strike sparks off the audience of ATM specialists . . . but even his arcane jokes, which left them in stitches, went over my head. His introduction contained plenty of familiar phrases, and plenty of equations which I'd seen before – but once he started *doing things* with those equations, I was completely out of my depth. Every now and then he'd display graphics: knotted grey-white tubes, with green-gridded surfaces and bright red geodesic lines snaking across them. Triplets of mutually perpendicular arrowed vectors would blossom from a point, then move around a loop or a knot, tipping and twisting along the way. No sooner would I start to feel that I was making sense of these diagrams, though, than Buzzo would wave a hand at the screen dismissively and say something like: 'I can't show you the most crucial aspect – what's happening in the bundle of linear frames – but I'm sure you can all picture it: just imagine embedding this surface in twelve dimensions . . .'

I sat two (empty) seats to the left of Mosala, but I hardly dared glance her way. When I did, she kept her eyes on Buzzo, but her expression became stony. I couldn't imagine what means she suspected I'd employed to win the contract for the documentary. (Bribery? Extortion? *Sex?* If only SeeNet could have been so divertingly Byzantine.) It didn't really matter how I'd done it, though; the injustice of the end result was self-evident, regardless.

'So this path integral,' said Buzzo, 'gives us an invariant!' His latest crisp diagram of knotted tubes suddenly blurred into an amorphous grey-green haze – symbolising the shift from a particular space-time to its generalisation in pre-space – but the three vectors he'd sent to circumnavigate the simulated universe remained fixed. 'Invariants' in an All-Topologies Model were physical quantities which could be shown to be independent of such things as the curvature of space-time in the region of interest, and even how many dimensions it possessed; finding invariants was the only way to make any kind of coherent physics emerge from the daunting indeterminacy of pre-space. I fixed my gaze on Buzzo's steady vectors; I wasn't entirely lost yet, after all.

'But that's obvious. Now comes the tricky part: imagine extending the same operator to spaces where the Ricci curvature is *nowhere-defined*—'

Now I was lost.

I gave serious thought to calling Sarah again, and asking if she'd be willing to take back *Violet Mosala*. I could have handed her the footage I'd shot so far, smoothed out the administrative glitches with Lydia, and then crawled away somewhere to recover – from Gina's departure, from *Junk DNA* – without having to pretend that I was doing anything but convalescing. I'd told myself that I couldn't afford to stop working, even for a month . . . but that was a question of what I was used to, not a question of starvation – and without someone to share the rent, I was going to have to move house anyway. *Distress* would have kept me in leafy, tranquil East-wood for a year or more – but whatever I did now, I was headed back to the outer sprawl.

I don't know what stopped me from walking out of that incomprehensible lecture and away from Mosala's justified distaste. Pride? Stubbornness? Inertia? Maybe it came down to the presence of the cults. Walsh's tactics could only become uglier – but that only made it seem more of a betrayal to abandon the project. I'd given in to SeeNet's demands for frankenscience in *Junk DNA*; this was a chance to atone, by showing the world someone who was standing up against the cults. And it wasn't as if the rhetoric was about to give way to violence, Kuwale notwithstanding. This was arcane physics, not biotechnology, and even at the Zambian bioethics confer-ence, where I'd last seen Walsh, it was God's Image as usual – not Humble Science! – who'd pelted speakers with monkey embryos and doused unsympathetic journalists in human blood. No religious fundamentalists had bothered with the Einstein Centenary Conference; TOEs were either beyond their comprehension, or beneath their contempt.

Mosala said softly, 'That's nonsense.'

I glanced at her warily. She was smiling. She turned to me, all hostilities momentarily forgotten, and whispered, 'He's wrong! He thinks he's found a way to discard the isolated-point topologies; he's cooked up an isomorphism which maps them all into a set of measure zero. But he's using *the wrong measure*. In this context, he has to use Perrini's, not Saupe's! How could he have missed that?'

I had only the vaguest idea of what she was talking about. Isolated-point topologies were 'spaces' where nothing actually touched anything else. A 'measure' was a kind of generalisation of length, like a higher-dimensional area or volume – only they included *much* wilder abstractions than that. When you summed something over all the topologies, you multiplied each contribution to the infinite sum by a 'measure' of 'how big' the topology was . . . a bit like weighting the worldwide average of some statistic according to the population of each country, or according to its land area, or its Gross Domestic Product, or some other measure of its relative significance.

Buzzo believed he'd found a way of tackling the calculation of any real physical quantity which made the effective contribution of all the universes of isolated points equal to zero.

Mosala believed he was mistaken.

I said, 'So, you'll confront him when he's finished?'

She turned back to the proceedings, smiling to herself. 'Let's wait and see. I don't want to embarrass him. And someone else is sure to spot the error.'

Question time arrived. I strained my limited grasp of the subject, trying to decide if any of the issues raised were Mosala's in disguise – but I thought not. When the session ended and she still hadn't spoken, I asked point blank: 'Why didn't you tell him?'

She became irritated. '*I* could be mistaken. I'll have to give it more thought. It's not a trivial question; he may have had a good reason for the choice he made.'

I said, 'This was a prelude to his paper on Sunday week, wasn't it? Clearing the ground for his masterpiece?' Buzzo, Mosala and Yasuko Nishide were scheduled to present their rival TOEs – in strict alphabetical order – on the last day of the conference.

'That's right.'

'So . . . if he's wrong about the choice of measure, he could end up falling flat on his face?'

Mosala gave me a long, hard look. I wondered if I'd finally managed to push the decision out of my hands: if she'd withdraw her cooperation entirely, leaving me with no subject to film, no reason to remain.

She said coldly, 'I have enough trouble deciding when my own techniques are valid; I don't have time to be an expert on everyone else's work as well.' She glanced at her notepad. 'I believe that's all the filming we agreed on for today. So if you'll excuse me, I'm meeting someone for lunch.'

I saw Mosala heading for one of the hotel restaurants, so I turned the other way and walked out of the building. The midday sky was dazzling; in the shadows of awnings the buildings retained their subtle hues, but in the glare of full sunlight they took on an appearance reminiscent of the oldest quarters of some North African cities, all white stone against blue sky. There was an ocean-scented breeze from the east, warm but not unpleasant.

I walked down side streets at random, until I came to an open square. In the middle there was a small circular park, some twenty metres wide, covered with luxuriant grass – wild and unmown – and dotted with small palms. It was the first vegetation I'd seen on Stateless, except for potted plants in the hotel. Soil was a luxury here; all the necessary minerals could be found in the ocean, in trace amounts, but trying to provide the island with enough topsoil for agriculture would have meant trawling several thousand times the area of water required for the algae-and-plankton-based food chain which met all the same needs.

I gazed at this modest patch of greenery – and the longer I stared, the more the sight of it unnerved me. It took me a while longer to understand why.

The whole island was *an artifact*, as much as any building of metal and glass. It was maintained by engineered lifeforms – but their wild ancestors were as remote to them as ancient buried ore bodies were to gleaming titanium alloy. This tiny park, which was really just an overgrown potted plant, should have driven that home mercilessly, puncturing the illusion that I was standing on anything but the deck of a vast machine.

It didn't.

I'd seen Stateless from the air, spreading its tendrils out into the Pacific, as organically beautiful as any living creature on the planet. I knew that every brick and tile in this city had been grown from the sea, not fired in any kiln. The whole island appeared so 'natural', on its own terms, that it was *the grass and the trees* which looked artificial. This patch of wild – 'authentic' – nature seemed alien and contrived.

I sat on a bench – reef-rock, but softer than the paving beneath it; more polymer, less mineral? – half shaded by one of the (ironic?) palm-tree-shaped sculptures which ringed the edge of the square. None of the locals were walking on the grass, so I stayed back. I hadn't regained my appetite, so I just sat and let the warm air and the sight of the people wash over me.

Unwillingly, I recalled my ludicrous fantasy of endless carefree Sunday afternoons with Gina. Why had I ever imagined that she'd want to sit by a fountain in Epping with me, for the rest of her life? How could I have believed, for so long, that she was happy . . . when all I'd made her feel, in the end, was ignored and invisible, suffocated and trapped?

My notepad beeped. I slid it from my pocket and **Sisyphus** announced, 'WHO epidemiology statistics for March have just been released. Notified cases of Distress now number five hundred and twenty-three. That's a thirty per cent increase in a month.' A graph appeared on the screen. 'There have been more new cases reported in March than in the previous six months combined.'

I said numbly, 'I don't remember asking to be told this.'

'August the seventh last year. 9:43 p.m.' The hotel room in Manchester. 'You said, "Let me know if the numbers ever really take off."'

'Okay. Go on.'

'There have also been twenty-seven new journal articles published on the topic since you last enquired.' A list of titles appeared. 'Do you want to hear their abstracts?'

'Not really.'

I glanced up from the screen, and noticed a man working at an easel on the far side of the square. He was a stocky Caucasian, probably in his fifties, with a tanned, lined face. Since I wasn't eating, I should have been making good use of my time by replaying Henry Buzzo's lecture to myself, or diligently ploughing through some relevant background material. After a few minutes contemplating this prospect, I got up and walked around to take a look at the work-in-progress.

The picture was an impressionistic snapshot of the square. Or partly impressionistic; the 'palms' and the grass looked like patches of green light caught reflected on an uneven window-pane, through which the rest of the scene was viewed – but the buildings and pavement were rendered as soberly as they would have been by any architect's computer. The whole thing was executed on Transition – a material which changed colour under the influence of an electric stylus. Different voltages and frequencies made each type of embedded metal ion migrate towards the surface of the white polymer at a different rate; it looked almost like oil paint appearing from nowhere – and I'd heard that creating a desired colour could be as much of an art as mixing oils. Erasure was easy, though; reversing the voltage drove all the pigments back out of sight.

Without pausing to glance at me, the artist said, 'Five hundred dollars.' He had a rural Australian accent.

I said, 'If I'm going to get ripped off, I think I'll wait for a local to do it.'

He gave me a mock-wounded glare. 'And ten years doesn't qualify me? What do you want? *Citizenship records*?'

'Ten years? I apologise.' Ten years meant he was practically a pioneer; Stateless had been seeded in 2032, but it had taken almost a decade to become habitable and self-sustaining. I was surprised; the founders, and most of the earliest settlers, had come from the US.

I said, 'My name's Andrew Worth. I'm here for the Einstein Conference.'

'Bill Munroe. Here for the light.' He didn't offer his hand.

'I can't afford the picture. But I'll buy you lunch, if you're interested.'

He looked at me sourly. 'You're a journalist.'

'I'm covering the conference. Nothing else. But I'm curious about . . . the island.'

'Then read about it. It's all on the nets.'

'Yes, and it all contradicts itself. I can't decide what's propaganda and what isn't.'

'So what makes you think anything I might tell you would be any more reliable?'

'Face to face, I'll know.'

He sighed. 'Why me?' He put down his stylus. 'All right. Lunch and anarchy. This way.' He started to walk across the square.

I hung back. 'You're not going to leave this.' He kept walking, so I caught up with him. 'Five hundred dollars – plus the easel and the stylus – and you're willing to trust people to leave it untouched?'

He glanced at me irritably, then turned and waved his notepad at the easel; it emitted a brief ear-splitting squeal. A few people turned to stare. 'Don't you have alarm tags where you come from?' I felt my face redden.

Munroe chose a cheap-looking open-air café, and ordered a

steaming white concoction from the instant-serve display counter. It smelled nauseatingly fishy – although here that didn't necessarily imply that it had once been the flesh of any vertebrate. Still, I lost whatever faint hint of an appetite I might have been working up.

As I thumbed approval of the payment for the meal, he said, 'Don't tell me: you're deeply perplexed by our use of international credit as a means of exchange, the existence of free-enterprise eating establishments, my shameless attachment to private property, and all the other trappings of capitalism which you see around you.'

'You've done this before. So what's the stock answer to the stock question?' Munroe carried his plate out to a table which gave him a clear view of his easel.

He said, 'Stateless *is* a capitalist democracy. And a liberal socialist democracy. And a union of collectives. And several hundred other things for which I have no name.'

'You mean . . . people here choose to act as they would in those kinds of society?'

'Yes, but it goes deeper than that. Most people join syndicates which effectively *are* those kinds of society. People want freedom of choice, but they also want a degree of stability. So they enter into agreements which give them a framework in which to organise their lives – agreements which allow for release, of course . . . but then, most democracies permit emigration. If sixty thousand people in one syndicate agree to pay a portion of their income – subject to audit – into a fund used for health, education and welfare, disbursed according to policies fleshed out in detail by committees of elected delegates . . . they may not have a parliament or a head of state, but that still sounds like a socialist democracy to me.'

I said, 'So freely chosen "government" isn't forbidden. But – overall – are you anarchists, or not? Aren't there universal laws here, which everyone is forced to obey?'

'There are a handful of principles endorsed by a large

majority of residents. Basic ideas about freedom from violence and coercion. They're widely promulgated and anyone who disagrees with them would be better off not coming here. I won't split hairs, though, they might as well be laws.

'So are we anarchists, or not?' Munroe mimed indifference. '*Anarchy* means "no ruler", not "no laws" . . . but no one on Stateless loses any sleep contemplating ancient Greek semantics – or the writings of Bakunin, or Proudhon, or Godwin. Sorry, I retract that: about the same percentage of the population as you'd find in Beijing or Paris cares passionately about each of those subjects. But you'll have to interview one of them, if you want their opinion.

'Personally, I think the word carries too much historical baggage to be salvaged. No great loss. Most of the nineteenth- and twentieth-century anarchist movements were bogged down, as much as the Marxists, by the question of seizing power from the ruling class. On Stateless that issue was dealt with very simply. In 2025, six employees of a Californian biotech company called EnGeneUity absconded with all the information they needed to make the seed. Much of which was their own work, if not their own property. They also took some engineered cells from various cultures, but too few to be missed. By the time anyone knew that Stateless was growing, there were a few hundred people living here in shifts, and it would have been bad PR to summarily sterilise the place.

'That was our "revolution". Beats measuring out your life in Molotov cocktails.'

'Except that the theft means you're saddled with the boycott.'

Munroe shrugged. 'The boycott is a great pain. But Stateless under the boycott is still better than the alternative: a company island, every square metre privately owned. It's bad enough when every decent food crop on the planet is licensed. Imagine the ground beneath your feet being the same.'

I said, 'Okay. So the technology gave you a short cut to a

new society; all the old models were irrelevant. No invasion and genocide, no bloody uprising, no glacial democratic reforms. But getting there's the easy part. I still don't understand what holds the place together.'

'Small invertebrate organisms.'

'I meant politically.'

Munroe looked baffled. 'Holds the place together against *what*? The onset of anarchy?'

'Violence. Looting. Mob rule.'

'Why bother travelling to the middle of the Pacific for something you can do in any city in the world? Or do you think we went to all this trouble just for a chance to play *Lord of the Flies*?'

'Not intentionally. But when it happens in Sydney, they send in the riot squad. When it happens in Los Angeles, they send in the National Guard.'

'We have a trained militia, who have near-universal consent to use reasonable force to protect people and vital resources in an emergency.' He grinned. ' "Vital resources". "Emergency powers". Sounds just like home, doesn't it? Except that the emergency has never arisen.'

'Okay. *But why hasn't it?*'

Munroe massaged his forehead, and regarded me as if I were an overpersistent child. 'Good will? Intelligence? Some other bizarre alien force?'

'Be serious.'

'There are some obvious things. People turn up here with a slightly higher than average level of idealism. They *want* Stateless to work, or they wouldn't have come – give or take the occasional tedious *agent provocateur*. They're prepared to cooperate. I don't mean living in dormitories, pretending everyone's your extended family, and going on work parties singing uplifting communal anthems – though there's some of that about. But they're willing to be more flexible and tolerant

144

than the average person who chooses to live elsewhere . . . because that's the whole point.

'There's less concentration of wealth, and of power. Maybe that's only a matter of time – but with so much power so heavily decentralised, it's very hard to *buy*. And yes, we have private property, but the island, the reefs, and the waters are a commons. Syndicates which collect and process food trade their products for money, but they have no monopoly; there are plenty of people who feed themselves directly from the sea.'

I looked around the square, frustrated. 'Okay. You're not all slaughtering each other or rioting in the streets, because no one's starving, and no one's obscenely rich – yet. But do you honestly think it's going to last? The next generation won't be here by choice. What are you going to do – indoctrinate them all with tolerance, and hope for the best? It's never worked before. Every other experiment like this has ended in violence, been conquered or absorbed . . . or given up and turned into a nation state.'

Munroe said, 'Of course we're trying to pass on our own values to our children, like everyone else on the planet. And with about as much success. But at least most children here are taught sociobiology from an early age.'

'*Sociobiology?*'

He grinned. 'More use than Bakunin, believe me. People will never agree on the details of how society should be organised – and why should they? But unless you're an Edenite who believes there's some "natural", Gaia-given Utopian condition to which we should all return, then adopting *any* form of civilisation means choosing some kind of cultural response – other than passive acceptance – to the fact that we *are* animals with certain innate behavioural drives. And whether that response involves the most subtle compromise, or the most vehement opposition, it helps to know exactly *what it is* you're trying to accommodate, or oppose.

145

'If people understand the biological forces acting on themselves and everyone around them then at least they have a chance of adopting intelligent strategies for getting what they want with a minimum of conflict . . . instead of blundering around with nothing but romantic myths and wishful thinking, courtesy of some dead political philosopher.'

I let that sink in. I'd come across no end of detailed prescriptions for ludicrous 'scientific' Utopias, and blueprints for societies organised on allegedly 'rational' grounds . . . but this was the first time I'd heard anyone advocate *diversity* in the same breath as acknowledging *biological forces*. Instead of exploiting sociobiology to try to justify some rigid political doctrine to be imposed from above – from Marxism to the nuclear family, from racial purity to gender separatism – 'we *must* live this way, because *human nature* requires it' . . . Munroe was suggesting that people could use the self-knowledge of the species to make better decisions for themselves.

Informed anarchy. It was an appealing notion – but I still felt obliged to be sceptical. 'Not everyone's going to let their children learn sociobiology; there must be a few cultural and religious fundamentalists, even here, who'd find it too threatening. And . . . what about adult migrants? If someone's twenty years old when they arrive on Stateless, they'll still be around for another sixty years. Plenty of time to lose their idealism. Do you really think the whole thing can hold together while the first generation grow old and disillusioned?'

Munroe was bemused. 'Does it matter what I think? If you really care one way or the other: explore the island, talk to people, make up your own mind.'

'You're right.' I wasn't here to explore the island, though, or to form an opinion on its political future. I glanced at my watch; it was after one. I stood up.

Munroe said,' There's something going on right now which you might like to see. Or even . . . try. Are you in a hurry?'

I hesitated. 'That depends.'

'I suppose you could call this the closest thing we have to a ceremony for new residents.' I must have looked less than thrilled; Munroe laughed. 'No anthems, no oaths, no gilded scrolls, I promise. And no, it's not *compulsory* – it just seems to have become the fashion for new arrivals. Mere tourists are welcome, too, though.'

'Are you going to tell me, or do I have to guess?'

'I can tell you that it's called inland diving. But you really have to see it to know what that means.'

Munroe packed up his easel and accompanied me; I suspected he was secretly enjoying playing veteran radical tour guide. We stood in the doorway to catch the breeze, as the tram headed out towards the northern arm of the island. The track ahead was barely visible: two parallel trenches carved in the rock, the grey ribbon of superconductor running down the middle all but hidden beneath a layer of fine chalky dust.

By the time we'd travelled about fifteen kilometres, we were the only passengers left. I said, 'Who pays for the maintenance of these things?'

'Fares cover some of it. The syndicates pay the rest.'

'So what happens if a syndicate decides not to pay? To freeload?'

'Then everyone knows.'

'Okay, but what if they genuinely can't afford to contribute. What if they're poor?'

'Most syndicate finances are public knowledge. By choice, but it's viewed as odd if they're kept secret. Anyone on Stateless can pick up their notepad and find out if the wealth of the island is being concentrated in one syndicate or being siphoned off-shore, or whatever. And act on that knowledge as they see fit.'

We were clear of the built-up centre now. There were buildings which looked like factories and warehouses scattered around the tram line, but more and more of the view was

147

becoming bare reef-rock, flat but slightly uneven. The limestone appeared in all the hues I'd seen in the city, zebra-striping the landscape in distinctly ungeological patterns, governed by the diffusion of different subspecies of litho-philic bacteria. The ground here wouldn't be amenable to rock farming, though; the inner core of the island was too dry and hard, too devascularised. Further out, the rock was much more porous, and suffused with calcium-rich water and the engineered organisms needed to replenish it. The tram lines didn't run to the coast because the ground became too soft to bear the weight of the vehicles.

I invoked **Witness** and started recording; at this rate I'd have more private travelogue footage than material for the documentary, but I couldn't resist.

I said, 'Did you really come here for the light?'

Munroe shook his head. 'Hardly. I just had to get away.'

'From what?'

'All the noise. All the cant. All the *Professional Australians*.'

'Ah.' I'd first heard that term when I was studying film history; it had been coined to describe the mainstream directors of the 1970s and 80s. As one historian had put it: 'They possessed no distinguishing features except for their nationality; they had nothing to say, and nothing to do except foist a claustrophobic vocabulary of tired nationalist myths and icons on to their audience, while loudly proclaiming themselves to be "defining the national character", and to represent, in person, "a nation finding its voice".' I'd thought this was probably a harsh judgement – until I'd seen some of the films. Most of them were stultifying horse operas – rural colonial melodramas – or sentimentalised war stories. The nadir of the period, though, was probably an attempted comedy in which Albert Einstein was portrayed as an Australian apple farmer's son, who 'splits beer atoms' and falls in love with Marie Curie.

I said, 'I always thought the visual arts had grown out of that long ago. Especially in your mode.'

Munroe scowled. 'I'm not talking about *art*. I'm talking about the entire dominant culture.'

'Come on! There is no "dominant culture" anymore. The filter is mightier than the broadcaster.' At least, that was the net-swoon line; I still wasn't sure I'd bought it.

Munroe hadn't. 'Very Zen. Try exporting Australian medical biotech to Stateless, and you'll soon find out exactly who's in control.'

I had no answer to that.

He said, 'Don't you ever get tired of living in a society which talks about itself, relentlessly – and usually lies? Which defines everything worthwhile – tolerance, honesty, loyalty, fairness – as "uniquely Australian"? Which pretends to encourage diversity – but can't ever stop babbling about its "national identity"? Don't you ever get sick of the endless parade of buffoons who claim the authority to speak on your behalf: politicians, intellectuals, celebrities, commentators – defining and characterising you in every detail . . . from your "distinctive Australian sense of humour" right down to your fucking "collective subconscious iconography" . . . who are all, simply, liars and thieves?'

I was taken aback for a moment, but on reflection this was a recognisable description of the mainstream political and academic culture. Or if not the mainstream, at least the loudest. I shrugged. 'Every country has some level of parochial bullshit like that going on, somewhere. The US is almost as bad. But I hardly notice it anymore, least of all at home. I suppose I've just learnt to tune it out, most of the time.'

'I envy you, then. I never could.'

The tram slid on, displaced dust hissing softly. Munroe had a point: nationalists – political and cultural – who claimed to be the voice of their nation could disenfranchise those they 'represented' just as effectively as sexists who claimed to be the voice of their sex. A handful of people pretending to speak for forty million – or five billion – would always wield disproportionate power, merely by virtue of making the claim.

So what was the solution? *Move to Stateless? Become asex?* Or just stick your head in a Balkanised corner of the net, and try to believe that none of it mattered?

Munroe said, 'I would have thought that the flight from Sydney was enough to make anyone want to leave for good. Physical proof of the absurdity of nations.'

I laughed drily. 'Almost. Being petty and vindictive with the East Timorese is understandable; imagine dirtying the bayonets of our business partners for all those years, and then having the temerity to turn around and take us to court. What the problem is with Stateless, though, I have no idea. None of the EnGeneUity patents were Australian-owned, were they?'

'No.'

'So what's the big deal? Even Washington doesn't go out of its way to punish Stateless quite so . . . comprehensively.'

Munroe said, 'I do have one theory.'

'Yeah?'

'Think about it. What's the biggest lie the political and cultural ruling class tells itself? Where's the greatest disparity between image and truth? What are the attributes which any self-respecting Professional Australian boasts about the most – and possesses the least?'

'If this is a cheap Freudian joke, I'm going to be very disappointed.'

'Suspicion of authority. Independence of spirit. Nonconformity. So what could they possibly find more threatening than an island full of anarchists?'

13

We walked north from the terminus, across a plane of marbled grey-green, in places still imprinted with faint hints of stubby branched tubing: coral from the shores of a decade ago, incompletely digested. Knowing the time-scale made the sight curiously shocking; it was a bit like stumbling across fossils of distinctive forties artifacts – clunky old-model notepads, quaint shoes which had been alpha fashion in living memory – converted into nothing but mineralised outlines. I thought I could feel the rock yielding beneath my feet more than the dense, cured paving of the city, but we left no visible imprints behind us. I paused and crouched to touch the ground, wondering if it would be palpably moist; it wasn't, but there was probably a plasticised skin beneath the surface to limit evaporation.

In the distance, a group of twenty or so people were gathered around a gantry several metres high, with a large motorised winch beside it. Nearby was a small green bus with big, balloon-tyred wheels. The gantry sprouted half a dozen bright orange awnings, and I could hear them snapping in the breeze. Orange cable stretched from the winch to a pulley suspended from the gantry, then dropped straight down – presumably into a hole in the ground, concealed by the circle of spectators.

I said, 'They're being lowered into some kind of maintenance shaft?'

'That's right.'

'What a charming custom. Welcome to Stateless, tired and hungry traveller . . . now check out our sewers.'

Munroe snorted. 'Wrong.'

As we drew nearer, I could see that everyone in the group was gazing intently at the hole beneath the gantry. A couple of people glanced our way briefly, and one woman raised a hand in a tentative greeting. I returned the gesture, and she smiled nervously, then turned back to the hidden entrance.

I whispered (though we were barely within earshot), 'They look like they're at a mine disaster. Waiting to identify the bodies as they're raised to the surface.'

'It's always tense. But . . . be patient.'

From a distance, I'd thought people were just randomly, casually dressed, but close-up it was clear that they were mostly in swimming costumes, though some wore T-shirts as well. A few were in short-limbed wetsuits. Some peoples' hair looked distinctly dishevelled; one man's was visibly still wet.

'So what are they diving into? The water supply?' Ocean water was desalinated in specialised pools out on the reefs, and the fresh water pumped inland to supplement recycled waste.

Munroe said, 'That'd be a challenge. None of the water arteries is thicker than a human arm.'

I stopped a respectful distance from the group, feeling very much an intruder. Munroe went ahead and gently squeezed his way into the outer circle; no one seemed to mind, or to pay either of us much attention. It finally struck me that the awnings overhead were flapping and shuddering out of all proportion to the gentle wind from the east. I moved closer and caught the edge of a strong, cool breeze emerging from the tunnel itself, carrying a stale damp mineral odour.

Peering over people's shoulders, I could see that the mouth of the tunnel was capped with a knee-high structure like a small well, built of dark reef-rock or heavy-duty biopolymer, with an iris seal which had been wrenched open. The winch, a few metres away, seemed monstrous now – far too large and industrial-looking to be involved in any light-hearted sport. The cable was thicker than I'd expected; I thought of trying to estimate its total length, but the sides of the drum concealed the number of layers wrapped around it. The motor itself was silent except for the hiss of air across magnetic bearings, but the cable squeaked against itself as it spooled on to the drum, and the gantry creaked as the cable slid over the pulley.

No one spoke. It didn't seem like the time to start asking questions.

Suddenly I heard a gasping sound, almost a sobbing. There was a buzz of excitement, and everyone craned forward expectantly. A woman emerged from the tunnel, clinging tightly to the cable, scuba tanks strapped to her back, face mask pulled up on to her forehead. She was wet, but not dripping – so the water had to be some way down.

The winch stopped. The woman unhooked a safety line linking the scuba harness to the cable; people reached out to help her on to the lip of the well, and then the ground. I stepped forward, and saw a small circular platform – a coarse grid of plastic tubes – on which she'd been standing. There was also a twin-beam lantern fixed to the cable, about a metre and a half above the platform.

The woman seemed dazed. She walked some distance away from the group, almost staggering, then sat down on the rock and stared up at the sky, still breathless. Then she removed the tanks and mask, slowly and methodically, and lay down on her back. She closed her eyes and stretched out her arms, palms down, spreading her fingers on the ground.

A man and two teenage girls had separated from the others; they stood nearby, watching the woman anxiously. I was beginning to wonder if she needed medical attention – and I was on the verge of discreetly asking **Sisyphus** to refresh my memory on heart attack symptoms and emergency first aid – when she sprung to her feet, smiling radiantly. She began to speak excitedly to her family, in what I took to be a Polynesian language; I didn't understand a word she said, but she sounded elated.

The tension vanished, and everyone began laughing and talking. Munroe turned to me. 'There are eight people in the queue ahead of you – but it's worth waiting for, I promise.'

'I don't know. Whatever's down there, my insurance doesn't cover it.'

'I doubt your insurance covers a tram ride, on Stateless.'

A thin young man in bright floral shorts was putting on the scuba gear the woman had discarded. I introduced myself; he seemed nervous, but he didn't mind talking. His name was Kumar Rajendra, an Indian-Fijian civil engineering student; he'd been on Stateless less than a week. I took a button camera from my wallet and explained what I wanted. He glanced over at the people gathered around the hole – as if wondering if he needed to ask permission of someone – but then he agreed to take it down. Fixing the camera to the top of the scuba mask, where it sat like a third eye, I noticed a faint chalky residue on the faceplate's transparent plastic.

An elderly woman in a wetsuit came over and checked that the scuba gear was fitted properly, then went through emergency procedures with Rajendra. He listened solemnly. I backed away and checked the reception on my notepad. The camera transmitted in ultrasound, radio and IR – and if all those signals failed to get through, it had a forty-minute memory.

Munroe approached me, exasperated. 'You're crazy, you know. It won't be the same. Why record someone else's dive, when you could do it yourself?'

Just my luck. Even on Stateless, I'd found someone who wanted me to *shut up and do what I was told*. I said, 'Maybe I will. This way I get to see exactly what I'd be letting myself in for. Then again . . . I'm just a tourist, aren't I? So my

154

experience of a ceremony for new residents would hardly be authentic.'

Munroe rolled his eyes. '*Authentic*? Make up your mind: are you covering the Einstein Conference, or making *Coming of Age on Stateless*?'

'That remains to be seen. If I end up with two programs for the price of one . . . all the better.'

Rajendra climbed on to the edge of the well, took hold of the cable, then stepped on to the platform; it tilted precariously until he managed to centre himself. The breeze ballooned his shorts and sent his hair streaming comically upwards, but the sight was more vertiginous than amusing; it made him look like a skydiver *sans* parachute, or some lunatic balanced on the wing of a plane. He finally attached the safety line – but the impression of free-fall remained.

I was surprised that Munroe was so enthusiastic about what looked to me like just one more bonding-through-bravery ritual, one more initiation-by-ordeal. Even if there was no real pressure to take part, and even if the dangers were minimal . . . so much for the island of radical nonconformists.

Someone started the winch unwinding. Rajendra's friends, standing – and then kneeling – on the lip of the well, reached out and patted his shoulders as he descended, cheering him on; he grinned nervously as he disappeared from sight. I squeezed forward myself, and leant over with the notepad to maintain line-of-sight communication. The button camera's memory would probably be more than enough, but it was impossible to resist the lure of real-time. I wasn't alone; people jostled to get a view of the screen.

Munroe called out from behind the crush, 'So much for *authenticity*. You realise you're changing the experience for everyone?'

'Not for the diver.'

'Oh, right, that's all that matters. Capture the last glimpse of the real thing – before destroying it forever. You ethnovandal.' He added, half seriously, 'Anyway, you're wrong. It changes things for the diver, too.'

The tunnel was about two metres wide, the walls about as cylindrical as the surface rock was flat – too good to be the product of any geological process, but too rough to have been machined. The morphogenesis of Stateless was a complex process which I'd never investigated in detail, but I did know that explicit human intervention had been required for many of the fine points. Still, whether this tunnel had formed unbidden at the intersection of certain levels of marker-chemical gradients, because lithophilic bacteria had noticed the cue and switched on all the right genes – or whether they'd had to be told more forcefully, by a person tipping a bucketload of primer on to the surface – it beat attacking the rock for a month or two with a diamond-coated drill.

I watched the twin reflections of the lantern beams slowly shrinking into the darkness, and the point-of-view image of pebbled grey-green rock sliding by. There were more hints of ancestral coral, and fleeting glimpses of the bones of fish trapped in the compacting of the reefs – and again, I felt an eerie sense of the compressed time scale of the island. The idea that subterranean depths belonged to inconceivably remote eons was so ingrained that it required a constant effort to remain prepared for soft drink bottles or car tyres – predating Stateless, but perfectly likely to have drifted into the mix when this rock was being formed.

The decorative trace minerals began to fade, not to be wasted at a depth where they'd rarely be seen. Rajendra's breathing accelerated, and he glanced up towards the surface; some of the people watching the screen called down to him and waved, their arms skinny silhouettes half eaten by the glare from the dazzling circle of sky. He looked away, and then directly down; the grid of the platform was no real obstruction, but neither lantern beams nor sunlight penetrated far. He seemed to grow calm again. I'd considered asking him to provide a running commentary, but I was glad now that I hadn't; it would have been an unfair burden.

The wall of the tunnel grew visibly moist; Rajendra reached out and trailed his fingers through the chalky fluid. Water and nutrients penetrated every part of the island (even the centre, although the dry, hard surface layer was thickest there). It didn't matter that the rock here would never be mined – and the fact that the tunnel remained 'unhealed' showed that this region had been explicitly programmed against regrowth. The lithophiles were still indispensable; the heart-rock could never be allowed to die.

I began to make out tiny bubbles forming in the fluid clinging to the wall – and then, deeper still, visible effervescence. Beyond the edges of the guyot, Stateless was unsupported from below – and a solid limestone overhang forty kilometres long, strengthened by biopolymers or not, would have snapped in an instant. The guyot was a useful anchor, and it bore some of the load, but most of the island simply had to *float*. Stateless was three-quarters air; the heartrock was a fine, mineralised foam, lighter than water.

The air in the foam was under pressure, though; from the rock above, and – below sea level – from the surrounding water trying to force its way in. Air was constantly being lost to diffusion through the rock; the wind blasting out of this tunnel was the accumulated leakage from hundreds of square metres, but the same thing was happening, less dramatically, everywhere.

The lithophiles prevented Stateless from collapsing like a punctured lung, and sinking like a drowned sponge. Plenty of natural organisms were proficient at making gas but they tended to excrete products you wouldn't want wafting out of the ground in vast amounts, like methane or hydrogen sulphide. The lithophiles consumed water and carbon dioxide (mostly dissolved) to make carbohydrates and oxygen (mostly undissolved) – and because they manufactured 'oxygen-deficient' carbohydrates (like deoxyribose), they released more oxygen than they took in carbon dioxide, adding to the net increase in pressure.

All of this required energy as well as raw materials; the lithophiles, living in darkness, needed to be fed. The nutrients they consumed, and the products they excreted, were part of a cycle which stretched out to the reefs and beyond; ultimately, sunlight on distant water powered everything they did.

Soon the surface was frothing and boiling, spraying calcareous droplets towards the camera like spittle. And it finally dawned on me that I'd been utterly mistaken: the dive had nothing to do with Edenite notions of 'modern tribalism'. Whatever courage it required was incidental; that wasn't being valued for its own sake. The point was to descend through the palpable exhalation of the rock, and to see with your own eyes what Stateless *was*: to understand the hidden machinery which kept the island afloat.

Rajendra's hand appeared at the border of the image as he fitted the mouthpiece and switched on the air supply. Of course: all this seeping liquid would build up at the bottom of the tunnel. He glanced down once, at what looked like a dark, sulphureous pool, boiling with volcanic heat; in fact, it was probably chilly and almost odourless. Munroe had been right about one thing: you really had to be there. What's more . . . the tunnel wind would be weaker at this depth than at the surface, because much of the leaking rock contributing to the total airflow was now overhead. Rajendra would have no trouble noticing the difference – but the view, alone, of gas escaping at ever greater pressure, suggested exactly the opposite.

As the camera plunged beneath the surface, the image flickered and then switched to lower resolution. Even through the turbulent, cloudy water, I could still catch occasional glimpses of the tunnel wall – or at least the wall of bubbles streaming out of the rock. It was a weird, disorienting sight –

it almost looked as if the water was so acidic that it was dissolving the limestone right before my eyes . . . but once again, that impression would have been instantly untenable if I'd been down there in person, swimming in the stuff.

The resolution dropped again, and then the frame rate fell; the picture became a series of stills in rapid succession as the camera struggled to maintain contact. Sound came through clearly enough, though I probably wouldn't have recognised distortion in the noise of bubbles breaking against a scuba mask. Rajendra glanced down; the view showed ten thousand pearls of oxygen streaming up through opalescent water – and nothing more distant than his knees. I thought I heard him inhaling sharply, tensing himself in preparation for touching the bottom – and then I almost sent the notepad tumbling down after him.

One still showed a startled, bright red fish staring straight into the camera. In the next image, it was gone.

I turned to the woman beside me. 'Did you see—?' She had – but she didn't seem at all surprised. The skin tingled all over my body. *How thick was the rock we were standing on? How long was the cable?*

When Rajendra emerged from the underside of the island, he made a noise which might have expressed anything from exuberance to terror; with a plastic tube in his mouth, and all the other acoustic complications, all I could discern was a muffled choking sound. As he descended through the subterranean ocean, the water around him gradually became clearer. I saw a whole school of tiny, pale fish cross the lantern beam in the distance, followed by a grey manta ray at least a metre wide, mouth stretched open in a permanent, plankton-straining grin. I glanced up from the screen, shaken. *This couldn't be happening beneath my feet.*

The winch halted. Rajendra looked up, back towards Stateless, tilting the lantern on its pivot, swinging it back and forth.

159

Milky water roiled in a layer that clung to the underside. Fine particles of limestone? I was confused; why didn't they simply fall? Even from strobed stills, I could see that this haze was in constant motion, surging rhythmically towards the hidden rock. I could also make out bubbles of gas, dragged down a few metres in some kind of undertow, before finally escaping back into the haze. Rajendra played the beam back and forth, improving his control; the lantern was obviously difficult to manipulate accurately, and I could sense his frustration – but after a few minutes his persistence paid off.

A stronger-than-average surge mixed an updraught of clear water into the milky layer above, parting the curtain for an instant. Beam and camera transfixed the event, exposing lumpy rock sparsely populated with barnacles and pale, frond-mouthed anemones. In the next frame, the image was blurred – not yet obscured by the haze of white particles, but crinkled, distorted by refraction. At first, we'd seen the rock through pure water; now we saw it through water and air.

There was a thin layer of air constantly trapped against the underside, maintained by the steady stream of oxygen escaping from the foamed rock.

This air gave the water a surface which could carry waves. Every wave which crashed on the distant reefs would send a twin diving beneath the island.

No wonder the water was cloudy. The underside of Stateless was being constantly scraped by a vast, wet, jagged file. Waves eroded the shoreline – but at least that stopped at the high-tide mark. This assault was going on beneath dry land, all the way to the rim of the guyot.

I turned again to the woman beside me, one of Rajendra's friends. 'The limestone detritus, tiny particles like that, must lose all their oxygen, all their buoyancy. Why don't they just . . . fall?'

'They do. The white comes from engineered diatoms. They scavenge calcium from the water, mineralise it – then migrate up and paste themselves into the rock when the waves dash them against it. Coral polyps can't grow in the darkness, so the diatoms are the only repair mechanism.' She smiled, hyperlucid; she'd been there to see for herself. 'That's what holds the island up: just a fine mist of calcium, fading away into the depths, and a few trillion microscopic creatures whose genes tell them what to do with it.'

The winch started rewinding. No one was near it; there must have been a control button for the diver, which I'd missed – or maybe it was preprogrammed, the whole dive calculated in advance to limit the risk of decompression sickness. Rajendra put his hand in front of his face and waved to us. People laughed and joked as he began his ascent; it was nothing like the mood when I'd arrived.

I asked the woman, 'Do you have a notepad?'

'In the bus.'

'Do you want the communications software? You could keep the camera . . .'

She nodded enthusiastically. 'Good idea. Thanks!' She went to fetch the notepad.

The camera had only cost me ten dollars, but the copy fee for the software turned out to be two hundred; I could hardly retract the offer, though. When she returned, I approved the transaction and the machines conversed in infrared. She'd have to pay for any more duplicates, but the program could be moved and erased for free, passed on to other groups of divers.

When Rajendra emerged he started whooping with joy. As soon as he was free of the safety line, he sprinted away across the plain, still carrying the scuba tanks, before doubling back and collapsing in a breathless heap. I didn't know if he was hamming it up or not – he hadn't seemed the type – but as he took off the diving gear, he was grinning like a madman in love, exhilarated, trembling.

Adrenaline, yes, but he'd been diving for more than the

thrill of it. He was back on solid ground . . . but it would never be the same, now that he'd seen exactly what lay beneath it: now that he'd swum *right through* the island's tenuous foundations.

This was what the people of Stateless had in common: not merely the island itself, but the firsthand knowledge that they stood on rock which the founders had crystallised out of the ocean – and which was forever dissolving again, only enduring through a process of constant repair. Beneficent nature had nothing to do with it; conscious human effort, and cooperation, had built Stateless – and even the engineered life which maintained it couldn't be treated as God-given, infallible; the balance could be disturbed in a thousand ways: mutants could arise, competitors could move in, phages could wipe out bacteria, climate change could shift vital equilibria. All the elaborate machinery had to be monitored, had to be understood.

In the long run, discord could literally sink the place. If it was no guarantee of harmony that nobody on Stateless *wanted* their society to disintegrate . . . maybe it helped focus the attention to realise that the land beneath their feet might do the same.

And if it was naive to think of this understanding as any kind of panacea, it had one undeniable advantage over all the contrived mythology of *nationhood*.

It was true.

I copied everything from the camera's memory, to give me the scene in high resolution. When Rajendra had calmed down slightly, I asked for his permission to use the footage for broadcast; he agreed. I had no definite plans, but at the very least I could always smuggle it into the interactive version of *Violet Mosala*.

Munroe came with me, still shouldering his folded easel and rolled-up canvas, as I headed back for the terminus.

I said sheepishly, 'I might try it myself once the conference is over. Right now, it looks too . . . intense. I just don't want to be distracted. I have a job to do.'

He faked bewilderment. 'It's entirely your decision. You don't have to justify anything to anyone, here.'

'Yeah, sure. And I've died and gone to heaven.'

At the terminus, I hit the call button; the box predicted a ten-minute wait.

Munroe fell silent for a while. Then he said, 'I suppose you have all the inside information about everyone attending the conference?'

I laughed. 'Not exactly. But I'm sure I'm not missing out on much. Soap operas starring physicists are just as dull as any other kind. I really don't care who's screwing whom, or who's stealing whose brilliant ideas.'

He frowned amiably. 'Well, neither do I – but I wouldn't mind knowing if the rumour about Violet Mosala has any substance.'

I hesitated. 'Which rumour did you have in mind? There are so many.' It sounded pitiful even as I said it; I might as well have come right out and admitted that I had no idea what he was talking about.

'There's only one serious question, isn't there?'

I shrugged. Munroe looked irritated, as if he believed I was being disingenuous, and not just trying to conceal my ignorance.

I said candidly, 'Violet Mosala and I aren't exactly swapping intimate secrets. The way things are going, if I make it through to the end of the conference with decent coverage of all her public appearances, I'll count myself lucky. Even if I have to spend the next six months chasing her between appointments in Cape Town, trying to flesh things out.'

Munroe nodded with grim satisfaction, like a cynic whose opinions had just been confirmed. 'Cape Town? Right. Thanks.'

'For what?'

He said, 'I never believed it – I just wanted to hear it put to rest by someone in a position to be sure. Violet Mosala – Nobel-prize-winning physicist, inspiration to millions, twenty-first-century Einstein, architect of the TOE most likely to succeed . . . "abandons" her home country – just when the peace in Natal is starting to look more solid than ever – not for Caltech, not for Bombay, not for CERN, not for Osaka . . . but to join the rabble on *Stateless*?

'Not in a million years.'

14

Back at the hotel, climbing the stairs to my room, I asked
Sisyphus: 'Can you name a group of political activists – with
the initials AC – who might have taken an interest in Violet
Mosala emigrating to Stateless?'

'No.'

'Come on! A is for anarchy . . . ?'

'There are two thousand and seventy-three organisations
with "anarchy" or a related word in their title, but they all
contain more than two words.'

'Okay.' Maybe AC itself was shorthand, like US for USA.
But then, if Munroe was to be believed, no serious anarchist
would ever use the A-word.

I tried a different angle. 'What about A for African, C for
culture . . . with any number of other letters?'

'There are two hundred and seven matches.'

I scrolled through the list; AC didn't seem like a plausible
abbreviation for any of them. One name was familiar, though;
I replayed a section of the audio log from the morning's press
conference:

'William Savimbi, Proteus Information. You speak approvingly of a convergence of ideas which has no respect
for ancestral cultures – as if your own heritage were of no
importance to you at all. Is it true that you received death
threats from the Pan-African Cultural Defence Front, after
you publicly stated that you didn't consider yourself to *be* an
African woman?'

Mosala had put the quote in context – but she hadn't

answerd the question. If a comment like that *had been* enough to result in death threats, what might rumours of 'defection' – baseless or not – bring down on her?

I had no idea; I knew even less about South African cultural politics than I knew about ATMs. Mosala would hardly be the first prominent scientist to leave the country, but she would be one of the most celebrated – and the first to emigrate to Stateless. Chasing money and prestige at a world-class institution was one thing, but it would be hard to read a move to Stateless (which could offer neither) as anything but a deliberate renunciation of her nationality.

I paused on the landing, and stared at my useless electronic teat. 'AC? Mainstream AC?' **Sisyphus** was silent. *Whoever they were, Sarah Knight had managed to find them.* I was beginning to feel an ache in the pit of my stomach every time I thought about what I'd done to her. It was clear that she'd prepared for this job meticulously, researching every issue surrounding Mosala – and coming from politics, where nothing on the nets was true, she'd probably gone out and talked to everyone in the flesh. Someone must have told her about the rumours, and put her on the trail which led to Kuwale – all off the record, of course. I'd stolen the project, walked in cold, and now I couldn't even tell whether I was making a documentary about an emigrant anarcho-physicist in fear of her life . . . or whether I was jumping at shadows, and the only threat anyone on Stateless faced was being goaded into giving Janet Walsh some long overdue career advice.

I had **Hermes** call every hotel on the island, and inquire about a guest called Akili Kuwale.

No luck.

In my room, I turned up the windows' sound insulation, and tried to psych myself into doing some work. The next morning I was scheduled to film a lecture by Helen Wu, chief advocate of the view that Mosala's methodology verged on circular logic. Before letting Munroe talk me into filming the inland divers, I'd been planning to spend the whole afternoon reading Wu's previous papers; I had a lot of catching up to do.

First, though . . .

I scanned the relevant databases (eschewing help from **Sisyphus**, and taking three times as long). The Pan-African Cultural Defence Front turned out to be a loose affiliation of fifty-seven radical traditionalist groups from twenty-three nations, with a council of representatives which met each year to decide strategies and issue proclamations. PACDF itself was twenty years old; it had appeared in the wake of a resurgence of the traditionalist debate in the early-thirties, when a number of academics and activists, mostly in central Africa, had begun to speak of the need to 're-establish continuity' with the pre-colonial past. Political and cultural movements of the previous century – from Senghor's *négritude* to Mobutu's 'authenticity' to Black Consciousness in all its forms – were dismissed as corrupt, assimilationist, or overly concerned with responding to colonialism and Westernisation. The correct response to colonialism – according to the most vocal of the new traditionalists – was to excise it from history completely: to aim to behave, in its aftermath, as if it had never happened.

PACDF was the most extreme manifestation of this philosophy, taking an uncompromising and far from populist line. They decried Islam as an invader religion, as much as Christianity or Syncretism. They opposed vaccination, bioengineered crops, electronic communications. And if there was more to the group than a catalogue of the foreign (or local, but insufficiently ancient) influences they explicitly renounced, they might have found it hard to differentiate themselves without such a hit-list. Many of the policies they advocated – wider official use of local languages, greater support for traditional cultural forms – were already high on the agenda of most governments, or were being lobbied for from other quarters. PACDF's *raison d'être* seemed to consist of being greater purists than anyone else. When the most effective anti-malarial vaccine on the planet was manufactured in Nairobi – based on research carried out in that well-known imperialist superpower, Colombia – condemning its use as 'a criminal betrayal of traditional healing practices' sounded like sheer fundamentalist perversity to me.

If Violet Mosala had chosen to emigrate to Stateless, I would have thought they'd be glad to be rid of her. She might have been a hero on half the continent, but to PACDF she could never have been anything but a traitor. And I could find no report of a death threat, so maybe Savimbi's claim had been pure hype; the reality might have involved nothing more than an anonymous call to his news desk.

I ploughed on, regardless. Maybe Kuwale's mysterious faction had revealed themselves by taking part in the other side of the debate? There was certainly no shortage of vocal opposition to PACDF – from more moderate traditionalists, from numerous professional bodies, from pluralist organisations, and from self-described *technolibérateurs*.

Mismatched initials aside, I couldn't quite see a member of the African Union for the Advancement of Science collaring journalists in airports and asking them to play unofficial bodyguard to a world-renowned physicist. And while the African Pluralists League organised worldwide student exchange programs, theatre and dance tours, physical and net-based art exhibitions, and lobbied aggressively against cultural isolationism and discriminatory treatment of ethnic, religious and sexual minorities . . . I doubted they had time on their hands to fret about Violet Mosala.

The late Muteba Kazadi had coined the term *techno-libération*, to mean both the empowerment of people through technology, and the 'liberation' of the technology itself from restrictive hands. Muteba had been a communications engineer, poet, science writer – and Minister for Development in Zaire in the late-30s. I viewed some of his speeches, impassioned pleas for 'the use of knowledge in the service of freedom'; he'd called for an end to the patenting of engineered crops, public ownership of communications resources, and a universal right of access to scientific information. As well as championing the obvious pragmatism of 'liberation biology' (though Zaire had never gone renegade and used unlicensed crops), he'd spoken of the long-term need for African nations to participate in pure research in every area of basic science – an extraordinary stand at a time when such activities were deeply unpopular in the wealthiest countries on the planet, and unthinkable in terms of his own government's immediate priorities.

Muteba had had his eccentricities, his three biographers concurred, with a leaning towards Nietzschean metaphysics, fringe cosmology, and dramatic conspiracy theories – including the old one that 'El Nido de Ladrones', the bioengineered haven built by drug runners on the Peruvian-Colombian border, had been H-bombed in 2035 not because the modified forest was out of control and threatening to overrun the whole Amazon basin, but because some kind of 'dangerously liberating' neuroactive virus had been invented there. The act had been an obscenity, thousands of people had died – and the public outrage it attracted had quite possibly helped to save Stateless from a similar fate – but I thought the more prosaic explanation was far more likely to be true.

Learned commentators from every part of the continent stated that Muteba's legacy lived on, and that proud *technolibérateurs* were active across the face of Africa, and beyond. I found it difficult to pin down his direct intellectual descendants, though; hundreds of academic and political groups, and tens of thousands of individuals, cited Muteba as a source of inspiration – and many people who'd spoken out against PACDF in net debates had explicitly labelled themselves *technolibérateurs* – but each seemed to have adapted the philosophy to a slightly different agenda. I had no doubt that every one of them would have been horrified at the thought of Violet Mosala coming to harm – but I was no wiser as to who might have taken it upon themselves to watch over her.

Around seven, I headed downstairs. Sarah Knight still hadn't returned my call – and I could hardly blame her for snubbing me. I thought again about offering to hand back the project, but I told myself that I'd left it too late, and she'd probably committed herself to another assignment. The truth was, the more the complications surrounding Mosala mocked the fantasy I'd held of retreating into the 'inconsequential' abstractions of TOEs, the harder it became to imagine walking away. If this was the reality behind the mirage, I had an obligation to face it.

I was heading towards the main restaurant when I spotted Indrani Lee coming down one of the corridors which led into the lobby. She was with a small group, but they were splitting up – with volleys of rejoinders and afterthoughts, as if they'd just emerged from a long, hectic meeting and couldn't bear each other's company any longer, but couldn't quite bring themselves to end the discussion, either. I approached; she saw me and raised a hand in greeting.

I said, 'I missed you on the connecting flight. How are you settling in?'

'Fine, fine!' She seemed happy and excited; the conference was obviously living up to her expectations. 'But you don't look at all well.'

I laughed. 'As a student, did you ever find yourself sitting for an exam where all the questions on the paper, and all the questions you'd stayed up until dawn preparing to answer . . . had so little in common that they might as well have come from two completely different subjects?'

'Several times. But what's brought on the *déjà vu*? Is all the mathematics going over your head?'

'Well, yes, but that's not the problem.' I glanced around the lobby; no one was likely to overhear us, but I didn't want to add to the rumours about Mosala if I could help it. I said, 'You looked like you were in a hurry. Maybe I'll bore you with all my tribulations on the flight back to Phnom Penh.'

'In a hurry? No, I was just going out for some air. If you're not busy yourself, you're welcome to join me.'

I accepted gratefully. I'd been planning to eat, but I still had no real appetite – and it occurred to me that Lee might have some professional insights into *technolibération* which she'd be willing to share.

As we stepped through the doors, though, I could see what she'd really meant by 'going out for some air': Mystical Renaissance had decided to show themselves, crowding the street outside the hotel. Banners read: TO EXPLAIN IS TO DESTROY! REVERE THE NUMEN! SAY NO TO TOE! T-shirts displayed Carl Jung, Pierre Teilhard de Chardin, Joseph Campbell, Fritjof Capra, the cult's late founder Günter Kleiner, event artist Sky Alchemy – and even Einstein, poking out his tongue.

No one was chanting slogans; after Janet Walsh's confrontationist salvo, Mystical Renaissance had opted for a carnival atmosphere, all mime artists and fire-jugglers, palmists and tarot-card readers. Tumbling firesticks cast oscillating deep-blue shadows everywhere, giving the street an oceanic cast. Bemused locals threaded their way through this obstacle course with expressions of weary resignation; they hadn't asked to have a circus shoved down their throats. So far as I could see, it was only a few badge-wearing conference members who were availing themselves of the free entertainment, or giving money to the buskers and fortune-tellers.

One of the cultists who'd stolen Albert was singing 'Puff, the Magic Dragon', accompanying himself on a keyboard – a common brand, like his T-shirt; both had IR programming ports. I paused in front of him, smiling appreciatively, while I invoked some notepad software I'd written several years before, and quietly typed instructions. As we walked away, his keyboard fell silent – every volume level set to zero – and Einstein sprouted a thought balloon which read: 'Our experience hitherto justifies us in believing that nature is the realisation of the simplest conceivable mathematical ideas.'

Lee gave me an admonishing look. I said, 'Come on! He was begging for it.'

Further down the street, a small theatre group were in the middle of a compressed version of *The Iceman Cometh*, rewritten in contemporary MR vernacular. A woman in a clown costume tore at her hair and declaimed: 'I've failed to be psychically attuned! Everyone in my net-clan would have remained closer to the healing numen, if only I'd respected their need to continue to be nourished by their imagination-driven self-narratives!' Images of tears flowed down her cheeks.

I turned to Lee. 'Well, I'm convinced. I'm joining up tomorrow. And to think: I used to take the fragile beauty of the sunset and reduce it to ugly technical jargon.'

'If you think this is painful, you should hear their five-minute *Mahabharata*-as-Jungian-psychobabble.' She shuddered. 'But the original remains intact, doesn't it? And they have a right to their own . . . *interpretation* . . . as much as anyone.' She didn't sound entirely convinced.

I said wearily, 'I don't know what these people hoped to gain by coming here. Even if they disrupted the conference, all the research has already taken place; it's all going to be posted on the nets, regardless. And if the whole idea of a TOE offends them so deeply . . . they can just close their eyes to it, can't they? They've closed their eyes to every other scientific discovery which has failed to meet their stringent *spiritual requirements*.'

Lee shook her head. 'It's a matter of territorial defence. You must see that. A TOE effectively claims sovereignty over the universe, and everyone in it. If a conference of lawyers in

New York set themselves up as rulers of the cosmos, wouldn't you be tempted to go and thumb your nose at them, at the very least?'

I groaned. 'Physics doesn't claim *sovereignty*. Least of all here, where the whole aim is to find the one thing about the universe which physicists and technologists will *never* have the power to change. Using crude political metaphors like "sovereignty" or "imperialism" is just empty rhetoric; no one at this conference is sending troops to annex the weak force to the strong force. Unification isn't being *legislated* or *enforced*. It's being *mapped*.'

Lee said portentously, 'Ah, the power of *maps*.'

'Oh, stop it, you know exactly what I mean! As in a map of the sky, not a map of . . . Kurdistan. And with no constellations drawn in . . . or stars named.' Lee smirked, as if she had a much, much longer list of culturally charged attributes in mind, and wasn't going to let me off the hook until I'd ruled out every one of them. I said, 'All right, forget the whole metaphor! But the fact is: exactly the same TOE underlies the universe – and keeps these cultists alive, juggling, and spouting gibberish – whether the evil reductionist physicists are allowed to discover it, or not.'

'Not according to the Anthrocosmologists, it doesn't.' Lee offered a conciliatory smile. 'But of course, yes, the laws of physics *are* whatever they are – and half of Mystical Renaissance would concede as much, in suitably evasive and conditional jargon. Most of them accept that the universe rules itself in some . . . *systematic* fashion. But they still feel deeply affronted by an explicit, mathematical formulation of that system.

'You say they should be satisfied with personal ignorance, rather than trying to keep the TOE out of human hands entirely. And of course, they'll go on believing whatever they like, even if a successful TOE is announced; they've never let scientific orthodoxy stand in their way before. But the very beliefs they've chosen to hold dictate that they *can't* ignore the fact that physicists – and geneticists, and neurobiologists – are tunnelling ever deeper beneath *everybody's* feet, and dragging to the surface whatever they find there . . . and what they find *will* influence every culture on Earth, in the long run.'

'And that's reason enough to come here and intimidate innocent people with the mutilated corpse of Eugene O'Neill?'

'Be fair: if you're conceding them the right to believe what they like, that has to include the right to feel threatened.'

The play was coming to a close; one of the actors was delivering a monologue on the need to show only compassion to poor scientists who'd lost touch with the soul of Gaia.

I said, 'So what do you call claiming to know *the divine will of the Earth itself* – if not an equally global land grab, couched in warmer and fuzzier terms?'

Lee gave me a puzzled frown. 'But of course. MR are like everyone else; they want to define the world on their own terms. *They* want to set the parameters, *they* want to make all the rules. Naturally, they've evolved an elaborate strategy to try to mask that fact – such as describing themselves with words like "generous", "open" and "inclusive" – but I'm certainly not suggesting that they're any more humble, virtuous or tolerant than the most fanatical rationalist. I'm just trying to explain their beliefs to you as an outsider, as best I can.'

'With your own universal explanatory scheme?'

'Exactly. That's my arduous duty: expert guide and interpreter to every subculture on Earth. The sociologist's burden. But then, who else could shoulder it?' She smiled solemnly. 'I am, after all, the only objective person on the planet.'

We walked on through the warm night, passing right out of the carnival. After a minute or two, I turned and looked back. From a distance, it was an odd sight, compacted by perspective and framed by the surrounding buildings: a flamboyant sideshow embedded in the middle of a city – going about its ordinary life – which had built itself out of the ocean, molecule by molecule, *and knew it*. The adjacent streets certainly looked mundane and colourless in comparison – full of ordinary pedestrians: no one dressed as harlequins, no one juggling fire or swallowing swords – but the memory of the afternoon's dive, and what it had revealed about the island, was enough to make all of the cult's self-conscious exotica and desperately cheerful busyness fade into insignificance.

I suddenly recalled what Angelo had said, the night before I left Sydney. *We sanctify what we're stuck with*. Maybe that was the heart of it, for Mystical Renaissance. Most of the universe *had* been inexplicable, for most of human history – and MR had inherited the strand of the culture which had doggedly made a virtue out of that necessity. They'd stripped away – or fed through a cultural blender, in a kind of mock-pluralism – the historical baggage of most of the specific religions and other belief systems which had done the same, in their day . . . and then inflated what remained into the essence of Big-H itself. *To sanctify mystery is to be 'fully human'. Fail to do so, and you're something less: 'soulless', 'left-brained', 'reductionist' . . . and in need of being 'healed'.*

James Rourke should have been here. The Battle for the H-words was in full swing.

As we started back towards the hotel, I realised I'd meant to ask Lee a question which had almost slipped my mind.

I said, 'Who are the Anthrocosmologists?' The term sounded as if it should have meant something to me, but – vague etymological inferences aside – it didn't.

Lee was hesitant. 'I doubt you really want to know. If Mystical Renaissance raise your ire . . .'

'They're an Ignorance Cult? I've never heard of them.'

'They're not an Ignorance Cult. And the word "cult", of course, is terribly value-laden and pejorative; although I use it in the vernacular sense like everyone else, I really shouldn't.'

'Why don't you just tell me what these people believe, and

then I'll make up my own mind exactly how intolerant and condescending to be towards them?'

She smiled, but looked genuinely pained, as if I was asking her to betray a confidence. 'The ACs are extremely sensitive about . . . the way they're represented. It was hard enough persuading them to talk to me at all, and they still won't let me publish anything about them.'

The ACs! I feigned indignation, trying to mask my jubilation. 'What do you mean, "let"?'

Lee said, 'I agreed in advance to certain conditions, and I have to keep my word if I want their cooperation to continue. They've promised there'll be a time when I can put everything on the nets – but until then, I'm on indefinite probation. Disclosing information to a journalist would destroy the whole relationship in an instant.'

'I don't want to publicise anything about them. This is purely off the record, I swear. I'm just curious.'

'Then it won't do you any harm to wait a few years, will it?'

A few years? I said, 'All right, I'm more than curious.'

'Why?'

I thought it over: I could tell her about Kuwale – and ask her to swear to keep it to herself, to avoid embroiling Mosala in any more unwelcome speculation. Except that . . . how could I ask her to betray one confidence while begging her to respect another? It would be pure hypocrisy – and if she *was* willing to swap secrets with me, what would her promise be worth?

I said, 'What have they got against journalists, anyway? Most cults are dying to recruit new members. What sort of ethos—?'

Lee eyed me suspiciously. 'I'm not going to be tricked into any more indiscretions. It's my fault entirely that the name slipped out, but the topic is now closed. The Anthrocosmologists are a non-subject.'

I laughed. 'Oh, come on! This is absurd! You're one of them, aren't you? No secret handshakes; your notepad is sending out coded infrared: *I am Indrani Lee, High Priestess of the Revered and Sacred Order*—'

She took a swat at me with the back of her hand; I pulled back just in time. She said, 'They certainly don't have *priestesses*.'

'You mean they're sexist? All male?'

She scowled. '*Or* priests. And I'm not saying anything more.'

We walked on in silence. I took out my notepad and gave **Sisyphus** several meaningful glances. The full word had unlocked no Aladdin's cave of data, though; every search on 'Anthrocosmologists' came up blank.

I said, 'I apologise. No more questions, no more provocation. What if I really do need to get in touch with them, though, but I just can't tell you why?'

Lee was unmoved. 'That sounds unlikely.'

I hesitated. 'Someone called Kuwale has been trying to contact me. Ve's been sending me cryptic messages for days. But ve failed to turn up at an arranged meeting last night, so I just want to find out what's going on.' Almost none of this was true, but I wasn't going to admit that I'd screwed up a perfect opportunity to discover for myself what AC was about. In any case, Lee remained impassive; if she'd heard the name before, she showed no sign of it.

I said, 'Can't you pass on the message that I want to speak to them? Give them the right to choose for themselves whether or not to turn me down?'

She stopped walking. A cultist on stilts reached down and thrust a stack of edible pamphlets in her face, MR's own Einstein Conference Newsletter in the non-electronic edition. Lee waved the woman away irritably. 'You're asking a lot. If they take offence, and I lose five years' work . . .'

I thought: You wouldn't *lose* five years' work; you'd finally be free to publish. But it didn't seem diplomatic to put it that way.

I said, 'I first heard the term *Anthrocosmologists* from Kuwale, not you. So you don't even have to tell them that you admitted knowing anything. Just say I asked you more or less at random, that I've been asking everyone at the conference, and I just happened to include you.'

She hesitated. I said, 'Kuwale was dropping hints about . . . violence. So what am I supposed to do? Just forget about ver? Or start trying to navigate my way through whatever bizarre apparatus Stateless employs for dealing with *suspicious disappearances*?'

Lee gave me a look which seemed to imply that she hadn't been taken in by any of this – but then she said begrudgingly, 'If I tell them you've been blundering around shooting your mouth off, I suppose they can't hold that against me.'

'Thank you.'

She didn't look happy. '*Violence*? Against whom?'

I shook my head. 'Ve didn't say. I mean, it may all come to nothing, but I still have to follow it up.'

'I want to hear everything, when you do.'

'You will, I promise.'

We'd arrived back at the theatre group, who were now acting out a laborious fable about a child with cancer . . . whose life could only be saved if he was kept from hearing the – stressful, immunosuppressant – truth. Look, Ma, real science! Except that the effects of stress on the immune system had been amenable to pharmacological control for the last thirty years.

I stood and watched for a while, playing devil's advocate against my own first impressions, trying to convince myself that there might be some real insight hidden in the story: some eternal verity which transcended the outdated medical contingencies.

If there was, I honestly couldn't find it. The earnest clowns might as well have been envoys from another planet, for all that they conveyed to me about the world we supposedly shared.

And if I was wrong, and they were right? If everything I saw as specious contrivance was, in fact, luminous with wisdom? If this clumsy, sentimental fairy tale spoke the deepest truth about the world?

Then I was more than *wrong*. I was utterly deluded. I was lost beyond redemption – a foundling from another cosmology, another logic entirely, with no place in this one at all.

There was no possibility of compromise, no question of building bridges. We couldn't both be 'half-right'. Mystical Renaissance endlessly proclaimed that they'd found 'the perfect balance' between mysticism and rationality – as if the universe had been waiting for this cosy detente before deciding how to conduct itself, and was, frankly, relieved that the conflicting parties had been able to reach an amicable settlement which would respect everyone's delicate cultural sensibilities and give due weight to everyone's views. Except, of course, the view that the human ideals of balance and compromise, however laudable in political and social spheres, had absolutely nothing to do with the way the universe itself behaved.

Humble Science! could denounce as 'tyrants of scientism' anyone who expressed this opinion, Mystical Renaissance could call them 'victims of psychic numbing' who needed to be 'healed' . . . but even if the cults were right, *the principle itself* could not be diluted, reconciled with its opposites, brought into the fold. It was either true or false – or truth and falsehood were meaningless, and the universe was an incomprehensible blur.

I thought: *Empathy at last.* If any of this was mutual – if MR felt half as alienated and dispossessed by the prospect of a TOE, as I did at the thought of *their* lunatic ideas shaping the ground beneath *my* feet – then I finally understood why they'd come here.

The actors bowed. A few people, mainly other cultists in fancy dress, applauded. I suspected there'd been a happy ending; I'd stopped paying attention. I took out my notepad and transferred twenty dollars to the one they'd placed before them on the ground. Even Jungians in clown costumes had to eat: First Law of Thermodynamics.

I turned to Indrani Lee. 'Tell me, honestly: are you really the one person who can step outside every culture, every belief system, every source of bias and confusion, and see the truth?'

She nodded unassumingly. 'Of course I am. Aren't you?'

Back in my room, I stared blankly at the first page of Helen Wu's most controversial *Physical Review* article – and tried to piece together how Sarah Knight could have stumbled on the Anthrocosmologists in the course of her research for *Violet Mosala*. Maybe Kuwale had heard about the project and approached her, just as ve'd approached me.

Heard about it how?

Sarah had come out of politics – but she'd already completed one science documentary for SeeNet. I checked the schedules. The title was *Holding Up the Sky* . . . and the subject was fringe cosmology. It wasn't due to be broadcast until June, but it was sitting in SeeNet's private library – to which I had full access.

I viewed the whole thing. It ranged from near-orthodox (but probably untestable) theories: quantum parallel universes (diverging from a single Big Bang), multiple Big Bangs freezing out of pre-space with different physical constants, universes 'reproducing' via black holes and passing on 'mutated' physics to their offspring . . . through to more exotic and fanciful concepts: the cosmos as a cellular automaton, as the coincidental by-product of disembodied Platonic mathematics, as a 'cloud' of random numbers which only possessed form by virtue of the fact that one possible form happened to include conscious observers.

There was no mention of the Anthrocosmologists, but maybe Sarah had been saving them for a later project – by which time she hoped to have won their confidence and secured their cooperation? Or maybe she'd been saving them for *Violet Mosala*, if there was a substantial connection between the two – if it was more than a coincidence that Kuwale was a devotee of both.

I sent **Sisyphus** exploring the nooks and crannies of the interactive version of *Holding Up the Sky*, but there were no buried references, no hints of more to come. And no public database on the planet contained a single entry on the ACs. Every cult employed image managers to try to keep the right spin on their media representations . . . but total invisibility suggested extraordinary discipline, not expensive PR.

The cult of Anthrocosmology. Meaning: *Human knowledge of the universe*? It was not an instantly transparent label. At least Mystical Renaissance, Humble Science! and Culture First didn't leave you guessing about their priorities.

It did contain the H-word, though. No wonder they had opposing factions – a mainstream and a fringe.

I closed my eyes. I thought I could hear the island breathing, ceaselessly exhaling – and the subterranean ocean, scouring the rock beneath me.

I opened my eyes. This close to the centre, I was still above the guyot. Underneath the reef-rock was solid basalt and granite, all the way down to the ocean floor.

Sleep reached up and took me, regardless.

15

I arrived early for Helen Wu's lecture. The auditorium was almost empty – but Mosala was there, studying something on her notepad intently. I took a seat one space removed from her. She didn't look up.

'Good morning.'

She glanced at me, and replied coldly, 'Good morning,' then went back to whatever she was viewing. If I kept filming her like this, the audience would conclude that the whole documentary had been made at gunpoint.

Body language could always be edited.

That wasn't the point, though.

I said, 'How does this sound? I promise not to use anything you said about the cults yesterday – if you agree to give me something more considered later on.'

She thought it over, without lifting her eyes from the screen.

'All right. That's fair.' She glanced at me again, adding, 'I don't mean to be rude, but I really do have to finish this.' She showed me her notepad: she was half-way through one of Wu's papers, a *Physical Review* article about six months old.

I didn't say anything, but I must have looked momentarily scandalised. Mosala said defensively, 'There are only twenty-four hours in a day. Of course I should have read this months ago, but . . .' She gestured impatiently.

'Can I film you reading it?'

She was horrified. 'And let everyone know?'

I said, ' "Nobel laureate catches up on homework." It

would show that you have something in common with us mortals.' I almost added: 'It's what we call *humanisation*.'

Mosala said firmly, 'You can start filming when the lecture begins. That's what it says on the schedule we agreed to. Right?'

'Right.'

She carried on reading – now truly ignoring me; all the self-consciousness and hostility had vanished. I felt a wave of relief wash over me: between us, we'd probably just saved the documentary. Her reaction to the cults *had to be* dealt with, but she had a right to express it more diplomatically. It was a simple, obvious compromise; I only wished I'd thought of it sooner.

I peeked at Mosala's notepad while she read (without recording). She invoked some kind of software assistant every time she came to an equation: windows blossomed on the screen, full of algebraic cross-checking and detailed analysis of the links between the steps in Wu's argument. I wondered if I would have been able to make better sense of Wu's papers myself, with this kind of help. Probably not: some of the notation in the 'explanatory' windows looked even more cryptic to me than that of the original text.

I could follow, in the broadest qualitative terms, most of the issues being discussed at the conference – but Mosala, with a little computerised help, could clearly penetrate right down to the level where the mathematics either survived rigorous scrutiny, or fell apart. No seductive rhetoric, no persuasive metaphors, no appeals to intuition: just a sequence of equations where each one *did* or *did not* lead inexorably to the next. Passing this inspection wasn't proof of anything, of course; an immaculate chain of reasoning led to nothing but an elegant fantasy, if the premises were, physically, wrong. It was crucial to be able to test the connections themselves, though, to check every strand in the web of logic which bound two possibilities together.

The way I saw it, every theory and its logical consequences – every set of general laws, and the specific possibilities they dictated – formed an indivisible whole. Newton's universal laws of motion and gravity, Kepler's idealised elliptical orbits, and any number of particular (pre-Einsteinian) models of the solar system, were all part of the same fabric of ideas, the same tightly knit layer of reasoning. None of which had turned out to be entirely correct, so the whole layer of Newtonian cosmology had been peeled away (fingernails slipped under the unravelling corner where velocities approached the speed of light) in search of something deeper . . . and the same thing had happened half a dozen times since. The trick was to know precisely what constituted each layer, to prise away each interlinked set of falsified ideas and failed predictions, no more and no less . . . until a layer was reached which was seamless, self-consistent – and which fit every available observation of the real world.

That was what set Violet Mosala apart (from half her colleagues, no doubt, as well as third-rate science journalists – and which no amount of *humanisation* would ever change): if a proposed TOE was inconsistent with experimental data, or unravelled under its own contradictions, *she* had the ability to follow the logic as far as it went, and peel away the whole beautiful failure, like a perfect sheet of dead skin.

And if it wasn't a beautiful failure? *If the TOE in question turned out to be flawless?* Watching her parse Wu's elaborate mathematical arguments as if they were written in the most transparent prose, I could picture her, when that day came – whether the TOE was her own or not – patiently mapping out the theory's consequences at every scale, every energy, every level of complexity, doing her best to weave the universe into an indivisible whole.

The auditorium began to fill. Mosala finished the paper just as Wu arrived at the podium. I whispered, 'What's the verdict?'

Mosala was pensive. 'I think she's largely correct. She hasn't quite proved what she's set out to prove – not yet. But I'm almost certain that she's on the right track.'

I was startled. 'But doesn't that worry—?'

She raised a finger to her lips. 'Be patient. Let's hear her out.'

Helen Wu lived in Malaysia, but had worked for the University of Bombay for the last thirty years. She'd co-authored at least a dozen seminal papers, including two with Buzzo and one with Mosala, but somehow she'd never reached the same quasi-celebrity status. She was probably every bit as ingenious and imaginative as Buzzo, and maybe even as rigorous and thorough as Mosala – but she seemed to have been slower to move straight to the frontiers of the field (always really visible only in retrospect), and not as lucky in choosing problems which had yielded spectacular general results.

Much of the lecture was simply beyond me. I covered every word, every graphic, scrupulously, but my thoughts wandered to the question of how I could paraphrase the message without the technicalities. With an interactive dialogue, maybe?

Pick a number between ten and a thousand. Don't tell me what it is.
    [Thinks . . . 575]
Add the digits together.
    [17]
Add them again.
    [8]
Add 3.
    [11]
Subtract this from the original number.
    [564]
Add the digits together.
    [15]

Find the remainder left when you divide by nine.
    [6]
Square it.
    [36]
Add 6.
    [42]
The number in your head now is . . . 42?
[Yes!]
Now try it once again . . .

The end result, of course, was guaranteed to be the same every time; all the elaborate steps of this cheap party trick were just a long-winded way of saying that X minus X would always equal zero.

Wu was suggesting that Mosala's whole approach to building a TOE amounted to much the same thing: all the mathematics simply cancelled itself out. On a grander scale, and in a far less obvious manner – but in the end, a tautology was still a tautology.

Wu spoke quietly as equations flowed across the display screen behind her. To spell out these connections, to short-circuit one part of Mosala's work with another, Wu had had to prove half a dozen new theorems in pure mathematics – difficult results, all of them, and useful in their own right. (This was not my own uneducated opinion; I'd checked the databases for citations of her earlier work, which had prepared the ground for this presentation.) And *that* was the extraordinary thing, for me: that such a rich and complex restatement of 'X minus X equals zero' was even possible. It was as if an elaborately twisted length of rope, weaving in and out of its own detours a few hundred thousand times, had turned out not to be *knotted* at all, but just a simple loop – ornately arranged, but ultimately able to be completely untangled. Maybe that would make a better metaphor – and in the interactive, viewers with force gloves could reach in and prove for themselves that the 'knot' really *was* just a loop in disguise . . .

You couldn't grab hold of a couple of Mosala's tensor equations and simply *tug*, though, to find out how they were joined. You had to unpick the false knot in your mind's eye (with help from software – but it couldn't do everything). Subtle mistakes were always possible. The details were everything.

Wu finished, and began taking questions. The audience was subdued; there were only a couple of tentative requests for clarification, expressing no hint of acceptance or rejection.

I turned to Mosala. 'Do you still think she's on the right track?'

She hesitated. 'Yes, I do.'

The auditorium was emptying around us. In the corner of my eye, I could see people's gaze lingering on Mosala as they made their way past us. It was all very civilised – no swooning teenagers begging for autographs – but there were unmistakable flashes of infatuation, reverence, adoration. I recognised some members of the fan club whose support had been so evident at the press conference – but I still hadn't so much as glimpsed Kuwale anywhere in the building. If ve was so concerned about Mosala, why wasn't ve here?

I said, 'What does that mean for your TOE? If Wu is correct?'

Mosala smiled. 'Maybe that strengthens my position.'

'Why? I don't understand.'

She glanced at her notepad. 'It's a complicated issue. Maybe we could go into it tomorrow?'

Wednesday afternoon: our first interview session.

'Of course.'

We began to walk out together. Mosala clearly had another appointment; it was now or never. I said, 'There's something I've been meaning to tell you. I don't know if it's important, but . . .'

She seemed distracted, but she said, 'Go on.'

'When I arrived, I was met at the airport by someone called Akili Kuwale.' She didn't react to the name, so I continued. 'Ve said ve was a "mainstream Anthrocosmologist", and—'

Mosala groaned softly, closed her eyes, and stopped dead. Then she turned on me. 'Let me make this *absolutely clear*. If you so much as mention the Anthrocosmologists in this documentary, I'll—'

I broke in hurriedly, 'I have no intention of doing that.'

She stared at me angrily, disbelieving.

I added, 'Do you think they'd *let me*, even if I wanted to?'

She wasn't mollified. 'I never know what they might do. What did this person want from you, if it wasn't coverage for their lunatic views?'

I said carefully, 'Ve seemed to feel you might be in some kind of danger.' I contemplated raising the question of emigration to Stateless, but Mosala was already so close to flashpoint that I didn't think it was worth the risk.

She said acidly, 'Well, that's the Anthrocosmologists for you, and their concern is very touching, but I'm not in any *danger*, am I?' She gestured at the empty auditorium, as if to point out the absence of lurking assassins. 'So they can relax, and you can forget about them, and we can both get on with our jobs. Right?'

I nodded dumbly. She started to walk away; I caught up with her. I said, 'Look, I didn't seek these people out. I was approached straight off the plane by this mysterious person making cryptic remarks about your safety. I thought you had a right to hear about it; it's as simple as that. I didn't know ve was a member of your least favourite cult. And if the whole subject's taboo . . . fine. I'll never speak their name in your presence again.'

Mosala stopped, her expression softening. She said, 'I apologise. I didn't mean to chew your head off. But if you knew the kind of *pernicious nonsense*—' She broke off. 'Never mind. You say the subject's closed? You have no interest in them?' She smiled sweetly. 'Then there's nothing to argue about, is there?' She walked to the doorway, then turned and called back, 'So – I'll see you tomorrow afternoon. We can finally have a talk about some things that matter. I'm looking forward to *that*.'

I watched her walk away, then I retreated back into the empty room and sat down in a front-row seat, wondering how I'd ever talked myself into believing that I could 'explain' Violet Mosala to the world. I hadn't even known what my own lover was thinking, living with her week after week, so what kind of ludicrous misjudgements would I make with this highly strung, mercurial stranger . . . whose life revolved around mathematics I could barely comprehend?

My notepad beeped urgently. I took it from my pocket; **Hermes** had deduced that the lecture was over, and audible signalling was now acceptable. There was a message for me from Indrani Lee.

'Andrew, you may not fully appreciate what kind of coup this is, but a representative of the people we discussed last night has agreed to speak with you. Off the record, of course. 27 Chomsky Avenue. Nine o'clock tonight.'

I clutched my stomach, and tried not to laugh.

I said, 'I'm not going. I'm not risking it. What if Mosala finds out? Of course I'm curious – but it's just not worth it.'

After a few seconds, **Hermes** asked, 'Is that a reply to the sender?'

I shook my head. 'No. And it's not even the truth, either.'

The address Lee had given me was a short walk from the north-east tram line, through what looked – almost – like a patch of middle-class suburbia back home . . . except that there was no vegetation, ostentatious or otherwise, just relatively large paved courtyards and occasional kitsch statuary. No obviously electrified fences, either. The air was chilly;

autumn was making itself felt here, after all. The dazzling coral of Stateless gave the wrong impression entirely; the natural cousins of its engineered polyps would not have thrived, this far from the tropics.

I thought: Sarah Knight had been in touch with the Anthrocosmologists, and Mosala never got to hear of it. She would hardly have spoken about Sarah in such glowing terms if she'd known there'd been some kind of deal between her and Kuwale. *That* was pure supposition, but it made sense: research for *Holding Up the Sky* must have led Sarah to the ACs, who were at least part of the reason why she'd worked so hard to get the contract for *Violet Mosala*. And maybe the Anthrocosmologists had now decided to offer the same deal to me. *Help us keep watch over Violet Mosala, and we'll give you a world exclusive: the first media coverage of the planet's most secretive cult.*

Why did they feel it was their duty to guard Mosala, though? What role did TOE specialists play in the Anthrocosmologists' scheme of things? Revered gurus? Unworldly holy fools who needed to be protected from their enemies by a secret cadre of devoted followers? Sanctifying physicists would make a change from sanctifying ignorance – but I could imagine Mosala finding it even more galling to be told that she was some kind of precious (but ultimately, naive and helpless) conduit for mystical insights, than to be told she was in need of being *humbled*, or *healed*.

Number 27 was a single-storey house of silver-grey granite-like reef-rock. It was large, but no mansion; four or five bedrooms, maybe. It made sense for the reclusive ACs to lease themselves something out in the suburbs; it was certainly more discreet than booking themselves rooms in a hotel swarming with journalists. Warm yellow light showed through windows set to opalescent, a deliberately welcoming configuration. I walked through the unlocked gate, crossed the empty courtyard, steeled myself, and rang the bell. If Mystical Renaissance could don clown costumes and talk about 'imagination-driven self-narratives' out on the street for all the world to see, I wasn't sure I was ready for a cult whose practices had to take place behind closed doors.

My notepad emitted a brief, soft squeal, like a children's toy impaled on a knife. I took it from my pocket; the screen was blank – the first time ever I'd seen it that way. The door opened, and an elegantly dressed woman smiled at me and extended a hand, saying, 'You must be Andrew Worth. I'm Amanda Conroy.'

'Pleased to meet you.'

Still clutching my notepad, I shook her hand. She glanced at the dead machine. 'It won't be damaged – but you understand, this *is* off the record.' She had a West Coast US accent, and unashamedly unnatural milk-white skin, smooth as polished marble. She might have been any age from thirty to sixty.

I followed her into the house, down a plushly carpeted hallway, and into the living room. There were half a dozen wall-hangings: large, abstract and colourful. They looked to me like Brazilian Mock Primitive – the work of a school of fashionable Irish artists – but I had no way of knowing whether or not they were the 'genuine' article: self-consciously exploitative 'remixes' of 20s Sao Paulo ghetto art, currently valued at a hundred thousand times the price of the real thing from Brazil. The four-metre wall-screen certainly wasn't cheap, though, and nor was the hidden device which had turned my notepad into a brick. I didn't even contemplate trying to invoke **Witness**; I was just glad I'd transmitted the morning's footage to my editing console at home, before leaving the hotel.

We seemed to be alone in the house. Conroy said, 'Take a seat, please. Can I offer you anything?' She moved towards a small beverage dispenser in a corner of the room. I glanced at the machine, and declined. It was a twenty-thousand-dollar synthesiser model – essentially a scaled-up pharm; it could have served anything from orange juice to a cocktail of neuro-active amines. Its presence on Stateless surprised me – I hadn't been allowed to bring my own out-of-date pharm here – but not having memorised the schedules to the UN resolution, I wasn't sure what technology was prohibited universally, and what was banned only from Australian exports.

Conroy sat opposite me, composed but thoughtful for a moment. Then she said, 'Akili Kuwale is a very dear friend of mine, and a wonderful person, but ve's something of a loose cannon.' She smiled disarmingly. 'I can't imagine what impression you have of us, after ve led you on with all that cloak-and-dagger nonsense.' She glanced at my notepad again, meaningfully. 'I suppose our insistence on strict privacy doesn't help matters, either – but there's nothing sinister about that, I assure you. You must appreciate the power of the media to take a group of people, and their ideas, and distort the representation of both to suit . . . any number of agendas.' I started to reply – to concede the point, actually – but she cut me off. 'I'm not trying to libel your profession, but we've seen it happen so many times, to other groups, that you shouldn't be surprised if we treat it as an inevitable consequence of going public.

'So we've made the difficult choice, for the sake of auto-nomy, to refuse to be represented by outsiders at all. We don't wish to be portrayed to the world at large: fairly or unfairly, sympathetically or otherwise. And if we have no public image whatsoever, the problem of distortion vanishes. We are who we are.'

I said, 'And yet, you've asked me here.'

Conroy nodded, regretfully. 'Wasting your time, and risk-ing making things even worse. But what choice did we have? Akili stirred your curiosity, and we could hardly expect you to let the matter drop. So . . . I'm willing to discuss our ideas with you directly rather than leaving you to track down and piece together a lot of unreliable hearsay from third parties. But it must all be off the record.'

I shifted in my seat. 'You don't want me drawing any more attention to you by asking questions of the wrong people – so you'll answer them yourself, just to shut me up?'

I'd expected this blunt appraisal to be met with wounded denials and a barrage of euphemisms but Conroy replied calmly, 'That's right.'

Indrani Lee must have taken my suggestion at face value: *Just say I asked you more or less at random – that I've been asking everyone at the conference, and I just happened to include you.* If the ACs thought my hastily improvised story for Lee about the 'vanishing informant' Kuwale was in the process of being repeated to every last journalist and physicist on Stateless, no wonder they'd wasted no time in calling me in.

I said, 'Why are you willing to trust me? What's to stop me from using everything you say?'

Conroy spread her hands. 'Nothing. But why would you want to do that? I've viewed your previous work; it's clear that quasi-scientific groups like us don't interest you. You're here to cover Violet Mosala at the Einstein Conference – which must be a challenging enough subject, without any detours and distractions. It may be impossible to leave Mystical Renaissance or Humble Science! out of the picture – they're forcing themselves into the frame at every opportunity. But we're not. And with no images of us – unless you care to fake them – what would you put in your documentary? A five-minute interview with yourself, recounting this meeting?'

I didn't know what to say; she was right on every count. And on top of all that was Mosala's antipathy, and the risk I ran of losing her cooperation if I was caught straying into this territory at all.

What's more, I couldn't help but sympathise a little with the ACs' stand. It seemed that almost everyone I'd encountered in the last few years – from gender migrants fleeing other people's definitions of sexual politics, to refugees from nationalist cant like Bill Munroe – was weary of having someone else claim the authority to portray them. Even the Ignorance cults and TOE specialists resented each other for similar reasons, although they were ultimately contesting the definition of something infinitely larger than their own identities.

I said cautiously, 'I can hardly offer you a vow of unconditional secrecy. But I'll try to respect your wishes.'

This seemed to be enough for Conroy. Perhaps she'd weighed up everything before we'd even met and decided that a quiet briefing had to be the lesser of two evils, even if she could extract no guarantees.

She said, 'Anthrocosmology is really just the modern form of an ancient idea. I won't waste your time, though, listing what we do and don't have in common with various philosophers of classical Greece, the early Islamic world, seventeenth-century France, or eighteenth-century Germany . . . you can mine all the distant history yourself, if you really care. I'll start with a man I'm sure you've heard of: a twentieth-century physicist called John Wheeler.' I nodded recognition, although all I could recall immediately was that he'd played a seminal role in the theory of black holes.

Conroy continued, 'Wheeler was a great advocate of the idea of a participatory universe: a universe shaped by the inhabitants who observe and explain it. He had a favourite metaphor for this concept . . . do you know the old game of twenty questions: One person thinks of an object, and the other keeps asking yes-or-no questions, to try to find out what it is.

'There's another way to play the game, though. You don't choose any object at all, to start with. You just answer the questions "yes" or "no", more or less at random – but constrained by the need to be consistent with what you've already said. If you've said that "it" is blue all over, you can't change your mind later and say that it's red . . . even though you still have no precise idea what "it" really is. But as more and more questions are asked, what "it" might be becomes narrower and narrower.

'Wheeler suggested that *the universe itself* behaved like that undefined object – only coming into being as something specific through a similar process of interrogation. We make observations, we carry out experiments – we ask questions about "it". We get back answers – some of them more or less random – but they're never absolute contradictions. And the more questions we ask . . . the more precisely the universe takes shape.'

I said, 'You mean like . . . making measurements on microscopic objects? Some properties of subatomic particles don't exist until they're measured – and the measurement you get has a random component – but if you measure the same thing a second time, you get the same result?' This was old, old ground, well established and uncontroversial. 'Surely that's the kind of thing Wheeler would have meant?'

Conroy agreed. 'That's the definitive example. Which dates back to Neils Bohr, of course, whom Wheeler studied under in Copenhagen, in the 1930s. Quantum measurement was certainly the inspiration for the whole model. Wheeler and his successors took it further, though.

'Quantum measurement is about individual, microscopic events which do or don't happen – at random, but according to probabilities determined by a set of *pre-existing* laws. About . . . individual heads and tails, not the shape of the coin, or the overall odds when it's thrown repeatedly. It's easy enough to see that a coin is neither "heads" nor "tails" while it's still up in the air, spinning – but what if it's not even *any particular coin*? What if there really *are no* pre-existing laws governing the system you're about to measure . . . any more than there are pre-existing answers to any of those measurements?'

I said warily, 'You tell me.' I'd come here expecting a serve

195

of the usual florid cult-speak from the very start: gibberish about archetypal warlocks and witches, or the urgent need to rediscover the lost wisdom of the alchemists. The strategy of taking quantum mechanics and distorting the boundaries of its counter-intuitive weirdness in whatever direction suited the cult philosophy was far harder to track. In the hands of a smooth-talking charlatan, QM could be blurred into just about anything – from a 'scientific' basis for telepathy, to a 'proof' of Zen Buddhism. Still, if I couldn't gauge the precise moment when Conroy moved from established science to Anthrocosmological fantasy, that hardly mattered; I could map it all out later, when I had my electronic teat back, giving me access to some expert guidance.

Conroy smiled at my edginess – and continued in the language of science. 'What happened, historically, was that physics merged with *information theory*. Or at least, a lot of people explored the union, for a while. They tried to discover whether it made sense to talk about building, not just a space-time of individual microscopic events, but all of the underlying quantum mechanics, and all of the various – then, non-unified – field equations . . . out of nothing but a stream of yes-and-no answers. Reality from information, from an accumulation of knowledge. As Wheeler put it, "an it from a bit".'

I said, 'Sounds like one of those nice ideas that just didn't pan out. No one at the conference is talking about anything of the kind.'

Conroy conceded, 'Information physics pretty much vanished from serious contention when the Standard Unified Field Theory rose from the ashes of superstrings. What did the geometry of ten-dimensional total space have to do with sequences of bits? Very little. Geometry took over. And it's been the most productive approach ever since.'

'So where do the Anthrocosmologists fit in? Do you have your own rival TOEs from "information physics", which the establishment won't take seriously?'

Conroy laughed. 'Hardly! We couldn't begin to compete in that arena, and we have no wish to do so. Buzzo, Mosala and Nishide can fight it out between themselves. One of them *will* come up with a flawless TOE in the end, I'm certain of that.'

'Then—?'

'Go back to the old Wheeler model of the universe. Laws of physics emerge from patterns – consistencies – in random data. But if an event doesn't take place unless it's observed . . . then a law doesn't exist unless it's understood. But that begs the question, doesn't it: *understood by whom?* Who decides what "consistent" means? Who decides what form a "law" can take – or what constitutes an "explanation"?

'If the universe instantly succumbed to any human explanation whatsoever . . . we'd be living in a world where Stone Age cosmology was literally true. Or . . . it would be like the old satires of the afterlife – a separate heaven for every conflicting faith – even before we died. But the world just isn't like that. However much people disagree, we still find ourselves together, arguing about the nature of reality. We don't float off into individual universes where our own private explanations are the ultimate truth.'

'Well, no.' I had a vivid image of the Mystical Renaissance theatre troupe following Carl Jung – dressed in a Pied Piper costume – down a psychedelic wormhole into another cosmos entirely, where no rationalists could follow.

I said, 'Doesn't that suggest to you that the universe might not be participatory after all? That the laws just might be fixed principles, independent of the people who understand them?'

'No.' Conroy smiled gently, as if this suggestion struck her as quaintly naive. 'Everything in relativity and quantum mechanics cries out against any absolute backdrop: absolute time, absolute history . . . absolute laws. But I think it does suggest that the whole idea of *participation* needs to be formulated rigorously in the mathematics of information theory, and different possibilities analysed with great care.'

It was hard to argue with that. 'To what end, though? If you're not competing for the discovery of a successful TOE . . . ?'

'The point is to understand the means by which TOE science can *give rise to* an active TOE. How knowledge of the equations can fix the reality they describe firmly in place – so firmly that we can't even hope to see behind them, to glimpse the process which holds them there.'

I laughed. 'If you admit we can't hope to do that, you've just crossed right over into metaphysics.'

Conroy was unfazed. 'Certainly. But we believe it can still be done in the spirit of science: applying logic, using appropriate mathematical tools. That's what Anthrocosmology is: the old information-theoretic approach, revived as something external to physics. It may not be needed to discover the TOE itself – but I believe it can make sense of the fact that there is a TOE at all.'

I leant forward – I think I was smiling, almost unwillingly – fascinated in spite of my scepticism. As cult pseudoscience went, at least this was high-class bullshit.

'*How, exactly*? Which of these possibilities you've "analysed with great care" can give a theory any kind of power which wasn't already there in nature?'

Conroy said, 'Imagine this cosmology: forget about starting the universe with just the right finely tuned Big Bang needed to create stars, planets, intelligent life . . . and a culture capable of making sense of it all. Instead, take as your "starting point" the fact that there's a living human being who can explain an entire universe, in terms of a single theory. Turn everything around, and *take it as the only thing given* that this one person exists.'

I said irritably, 'How can it be *the only thing*? You can't have a living human being . . . and nothing else. And if it's *given* that this person can explain the universe, then there has to be a universe *to explain*.'

'Exactly.'

Conroy smiled, calmly and sanely, but the hairs stood up on the back of my neck, and I suddenly knew what she was going to say next.

'From this person, the universe "grows out" of the power to explain it: out in all directions, and forwards and backwards in time. Instead of being blasted out of pre-space – instead of being "caused" inexplicably at the beginning of time – it crystallises quietly around a single human being.

'That's why the universe obeys *a single law* – a Theory of Everything. It's all explained by a single person. We call this one person the Keystone. Everyone, and everything, exists because the Keystone exists. The Big Bang model of cosmology can lead to anything at all: a universe of cold dust, a universe of black holes, a universe of dead planets. But the Keystone *needs* everything which the universe actually contains – stars, planets, life – in order to explain ver own existence. And not only needs them: the Keystone can *account for* all of them, make sense of all of them, without gaps, without flaws, without contradictions.

'That's why it's possible for billions of people to be *wrong*. That's why we're not living with Stone Age cosmology or even Newtonian physics. Most explanations just aren't powerful, rich or coherent enough to bring a whole universe into being – and to explain a mind capable of holding such an explanation.'

I sat and stared at Conroy, not wishing to insult her, but at a loss for anything polite to say. This was pure cult-speak at last: she might as well have been telling me that Violet Mosala and Henry Buzzo were the incarnations of a pair of warring Hindu deities, or that Atlantis would rise from the ocean and the stars would fall from the sky when the Final Equation was written.

Except that, if she had, I doubt I would have felt the same uneasy tingling down my back and across my forearms. She'd steered close enough to the shores of science, for enough of the way, to disarm me a little.

She continued, 'We can't watch the universe emerge; we're part of it, we're trapped inside the space-time created by the act of explanation. All we can hope to witness, in the progression of time, is one person become the first to hold the TOE in ver mind, and grasp its consequences, and – invisibly, imperceptibly – *understand us all into being*.'

She laughed suddenly, breaking the spell. 'It's only a theory. The mathematics behind it makes perfect sense – but the reality is untestable, by its very nature. So, of course, we could be wrong.

'But now, can you understand why someone like Akili – who believes, perhaps too passionately, that we could be right – wishes to be certain that Violet Mosala will come to no harm?'

I walked further south than I needed to, heading for a tram stop some way down the line from the point where I'd disembarked. I needed to be out under the stars for a while, to come back down to Earth. Even if Stateless didn't exactly qualify as solid ground.

I was greatly relieved by the night's revelations: they seemed to wrap up everything, to make sense, finally, of all the distractions which had been keeping me from doing my job.

The ACs were harmless cranks – and, entertaining as it might be to give them a footnote in *Violet Mosala*, it would hardly undermine the integrity of the whole documentary to leave them out – as they wished, as Mosala wished. Why offend both parties in the name of fearless journalism – in reality, just to raise a brief smirk with SeeNet's target audience?

And Kuwale was – understandably, if not justifiably – thoroughly paranoid. The life of a potential Keystone was not a matter to be taken lightly. It wasn't a question of the universe crumbling; if you died before 'explaining everything into being', then obviously someone else would have to do it, and you simply weren't the one. That didn't exclude a great deal of reverence, though, for the, as yet, mere candidate creators – and the rumours of Mosala's emigration must have been enough to start Kuwale seeing enemies crawling out of the reef-rock.

I waited for the tram on a deserted street, gazing up through the clear, cold air at a dazzling richness of stars – and satellites – Conroy's perversely elegant fantasy still running through my head. I thought: If Mosala *is* the Keystone, it's a good thing that she treats the ACs with such contempt. If her explanation of the universe included a conventional TOE, and nothing else, then all was fine. If she'd taken Anthrocosmology seriously, though . . . surely *that* would have plucked her right out of the tight web of explanation she was supposed to be spinning for us all? A Theory of Everything wasn't a Theory of Everything if there was another level, a deeper layer of truth.

And it seemed a sufficiently tall order to have to grow your own universe to wrap yourself in: your own ancestors (needed to explain your own existence), your own billions of human cousins (an unavoidable logical consequence – as would be more distant relatives, animal and plant), your own world to stand on, sun to orbit – and other planets, suns, and galaxies, not obviously essential for survival . . . but possibly allowing a relatively simple TOE (which could fit in one mind) to be traded for a trickier version which was more economical with cosmic real estate. Explaining all that into existence would be hard enough; you wouldn't want to be obliged to *create the power to create it*, as well – to have to explain into being the Anthrocosmology which allowed you to explain things into being.

A wise separation of powers. Leave the metaphysics to someone else.

I boarded the tram. A couple of the passengers smiled and greeted me, and chatted for a while – without anyone drawing a weapon and demanding money.

Walking up the street towards the hotel, I scrolled through a few documents on my notepad, just to check that nothing had been lost in the blackout. I'd made a list of the questions I'd planned to ask the Anthrocosmologists; I checked through them, to see how I'd done. I'd only missed one point; not bad for someone used to a permanent electronic crutch, but it was still an irritation.

Kuwale had said that ve was 'mainstream AC'. So if all of the wild metaphysics which Conroy had just fed me was the *mainstream* of Anthrocosmology . . . what did they believe out on the fringe?

My complacency was beginning to unravel. All I'd heard was one version of the ACs' doctrine. Conroy had taken it upon herself to speak for all of them – but that didn't prove that they all agreed. At the very least, I needed to speak to Kuwale again . . . but I had better things to do than stake out the house in the hope that ve would turn up there.

Back in my room, I had **Hermes** scan the world's communications directories. There were over seven thousand Kuwales listed, with primary addresses in a dozen countries – but no Akili. Which meant it was probably a nickname, a diminutive, or an unofficial nom de asex. Without even knowing what country ve came from, it was going to be impossible to narrow the search.

I hadn't filmed my conversation with Kuwale – but I closed my eyes and invoked **Witness**, and played with the identikit option until I had vis face clearly in front of me – in digital form in my gut memory, as well as in my mind's eye. I plugged in the umbilical fibre and moved the image into my notepad, then searched the global news databases for a match to either name or face. Not everyone had their fifteen minutes of fame, but with nine million non-profit netzines on top of all the commercial media, you didn't exactly have to be a celebrity to make it into the archives. Win an agrotech competition in rural Angola, score the winning goal for even the most obscure Jamaican soccer team, and—

No such luck. The electronic teat fails again – at a cost of three hundred dollars.

So where was I meant to look for ver, if not on the nets? Out in the world. But I couldn't scour the streets of Stateless.

I invoked **Witness** again, and flagged the identikit image for continuous real-time search. If Kuwale so much as appeared in the corner of my eye – whether or not I was recording, and whether or not I noticed – **Witness** would let me know.

16

Karin De Groot led me into Violet Mosala's suite. Despite the difference in scale, it had the same sunny-but-spartan feel as my own single room. A skylight added to the sense of space and light, but even this touch failed to create the impression of opulence which it might have done in another building, in another place. Nothing on Stateless appeared lavish to me, however grand, but I couldn't decide to what extent this judgement was the product of the architecture itself, and how much was due to an awareness of the politics and biotechnology which lay behind every surface.

De Groot said, 'Violet won't be long. Take a seat. She's talking to her mother, but I've already reminded her about the interview. Twice.'

It was three in the morning in South Africa. 'Has something happened? I can come back later.' I didn't want to intrude in the middle of a family crisis.

De Groot reassured me, 'Everything's fine. Wendy keeps strange hours, that's all.'

I sat in one of the armchairs arranged in a cluster near the middle of the room; they looked like they might have been left that way after a meeting. Some kind of late-night brainstorming session . . . between Mosala, Helen Wu, and a few other colleagues? *Whoever it was, I should have been there, filming.* I was going to have to push harder for access, or Mosala would keep me at a distance to the end. But I was going to have to win her confidence somehow, or *pushing* would only get me shut out even more. Mosala clearly had no particular desire for publicity – let alone the desperate need of a politician or a hack. The only thing I could offer her was the chance to communicate her work.

De Groot remained standing, one hand on the back of a chair. I said, 'So how did you get to meet her?'

'I answered an advertisement. I didn't know Violet, personally, before I took the job.'

'You have a science background too, though?'

She smiled. '*Too*. My background's probably more like yours than like Violet's – I have a degree in science and journalism.'

'Did you ever work as a journalist?'

'I was science correspondent for Proteus, for six years. The charming Mr Savimbi is my successor.'

'I see.' I strained my ears; I could just make out Mosala in the adjoining room, still talking. I said quietly, 'What Savimbi said on Monday, about *death threats* – was there anything in that?'

De Groot eyed me warily. 'Don't bring that up. Please. Do you really want to make everything as difficult as you possibly can for her?'

I protested, 'No, but put yourself in my position. Would you ignore the whole issue? I don't want to inflame the situation – but if some cultural purity group is issuing death sentences against Africa's top scientists, don't you think that's worthy of serious discussion?'

De Groot said impatiently, 'But they're not. For a start, the Stockholm quote was picked up and mangled by a Volksfront netzine – running the bizarre line that Violet was saying that the Nobel wasn't hers, wasn't "Africa's", but really belonged to "white intellectual culture" – for which she was only a politically expedient figurehead. That "story" got taken up and echoed in other places – but nobody except the original audience would have believed for a second that it was anything but ludicrous propaganda. As for PACDF, they've never so much as acknowledged Violet's existence.'

'Okay. Then what made Savimbi leap to the wrong conclusion?'

De Groot glanced towards the doorway. 'Garbled fifth-hand reports.'

'Of what? Not just the netzine propaganda itself. He could hardly be that naive.'

De Groot leaned towards me with an anguished expression, torn between discretion and the desire to set me straight. 'She had a break-in. All right? A few weeks ago. A burglar. A teenage boy with a gun.'

'Yeah? What happened? Was she hurt?'

'No, she was lucky. Her alarm went off – he'd disabled one, but she had a backup – and there was a patrol car nearby at the time. The burglar told the police he'd been paid to frighten her. But he couldn't name names, of course. It was just a pathetic excuse.'

'Then why should Savimbi take it seriously? And why "fifth-hand reports"? Surely he would have read the whole story?'

'Violet dropped the charges. She's an idiot, but that's the kind of thing she does. So there was no court appearance, no official version of events. But someone in the police must have leaked—'

Mosala entered the room, and we exchanged greetings. She glanced curiously at De Groot, who was still so close to me that it must have been obvious that we'd been doing our best to avoid being overheard.

I moved to fill the silence. 'How's your mother?'

'She's fine. She's in the middle of negotiating a major deal with Thought Craft, though, so she's not getting much sleep.' Wendy Mosala ran one of Africa's largest software houses; she'd built it up herself over thirty years, from a one-person operation. 'She's bidding for a licence for the **Kaspar** clonelets, two years in advance of release, and if it all pans out . . .' She caught herself. 'All of which is strictly confidential, okay?'

'Of course.' **Kaspar** was the next generation of pseudo-intelligent software, currently being coaxed out of a prolonged infancy in Toronto. Unlike **Sisyphus** and its numerous cousins – which had been created fully-fledged, instantly 'adult' by design – **Kaspar** was going through a learning phase, more anthropomorphically styled than anything previously attempted. Personally, I found it a little disquieting . . . and I wasn't sure that I wanted a clonelet – a pared-down copy of the original – sitting in my notepad, enslaved to some menial task, if the full software had spent a year singing nursery rhymes and playing with blocks.

De Groot left us. Mosala slumped into a chair opposite me, spot-lit by the sunshine flooding through the pane above. The call from home seemed to have lifted her spirits, but in the harsh light she looked tired.

I said, 'Are you ready to start?'

She nodded, and smiled half-heartedly. 'The sooner we start, the sooner it's over.'

I invoked **Witness**. The shaft of sunlight would drift visibly in the course of the interview, but at the editing stage everything could be stripped back to reflectance values, and recomputed with a fixed set of rather more flattering light sources.

I said, 'Was it your mother who first inspired you to take an interest in science?'

Mosala scowled, and said in disgusted tones, 'I don't know! Was it *your* mother who inspired *you* to come up with that kind of pathetic—' She broke off, managing to look contrite and resentful at the same time. 'I'm sorry. Can we start again?'

'No need. Don't worry about continuity; it's not your problem. Just keep on talking. And if you're halfway through an answer and you change your mind – just stop, and start afresh.'

'Okay.' She closed her eyes, and tilted her face wearily into the sunlight. 'My mother. My childhood. My *role models*.' She opened her eyes and pleaded, 'Can't we just take all that bullshit as read, and get on to the TOE?'

I said patiently, '*I* know it's bullshit, *you* know it's bullshit – but if the network executives don't see the required quota of *formative childhood influences* . . . they'll screen you at 3 a.m. after a last-minute program change, having promoted the timeslot as a special on drug-resistant skin diseases.' SeeNet (who claimed the right to speak for all their viewers, of course) had a strict checklist for profiles: so many minutes on childhood, so many on politics, so many on current relationships, etcetera – a slick paint-by-numbers guide to commodifying human beings . . . as well as a template for deluding yourself into thinking that you'd explained them. A sort of externalised version of Lamont's area.

Mosala said, '3a.m.? You're serious, aren't you?' She thought it over. 'Okay. If that's what it comes down to . . . I can play along.'

'So tell me about your mother.' I resisted the urge to say: *Feel free to answer more or less at random, so long as you don't contradict yourself.*

She improvised fluently, churning out *my life as a soundbite* without a trace of detectable irony. 'My mother gave me an education. By which I don't mean *school*. She plugged me into the nets, she had me using an adult's knowledge miner by the time I was seven or eight. She opened up . . . the whole planet to me. I was lucky: we could afford it, and she knew exactly what she was doing. But she didn't *steer me* towards science. She gave me the keys to this giant playground, and let me loose. I might just as easily have headed towards music, art, history . . . anything. I wasn't pushed in any direction. I was just set free.'

'And your father?'

'My father was in the police force. He was killed when I was four.'

'That must have been traumatic. But do you think that early loss might have given you the drive, the independence . . . ?'

Mosala flashed me a look more of pity than anger. '*My father* was shot in the head by a sniper at a political rally, where he was helping to protect twenty thousand people whose views he found completely repugnant. And – this is now off the record, by the way, whatever it means for your *timeslot* – he was someone I loved, and whom I still love; he was not an assembly of missing gears in my psychodynamic clockwork. He was not *an absence to be compensated for*.'

I felt myself flush with shame. I glanced down at my notepad, and skipped over several equally fatuous questions. I could always pad out the interview material with reminiscences from childhood friends . . . stock footage of Cape Town schools in the 30s . . . whatever.

'You've said elsewhere that you were hooked on physics by the time you were ten: you knew it was what you wanted to do for the rest of your life – for purely personal reasons, to satisfy your own curiosity. But when do you think you began to consider the wider arena in which science operates? When did you start to become aware of the economic, social, and political factors?'

Mosala responded calmly, perfectly composed again. 'About two years later, I suppose. That was when I started reading Muteba Kazadi.'

She hadn't mentioned this in any of the earlier interviews I'd seen – and it was lucky I'd stumbled on the name when researching PACDF, or I would have looked extremely foolish at this point. *Muteba who?*

'So you were influenced by *technolibération*?'

'Of course.' She frowned slightly, bemused – as if I'd just asked her if she'd ever heard of Albert Einstein. I wasn't even sure if she was being honest, or whether she was still just helpfully, cynically, trying to accommodate SeeNet's demand for clichés – but then, that was the price I paid for asking her to play the game.

She said, 'Muteba spelt out the role of science more clearly than anyone else at the time. And in a couple of sentences, he could . . . *incinerate* any doubts I might have had about ransacking the entire planetary storehouse of culture and science, and taking exactly what I wanted.' She hesitated, then recited:

> 'When Leopold the Second rises from the grave
> Saying, "My conscience plagues me, take back
> This un-Belgian ivory and rubber and gold!"
> Then I will renounce my ill-gotten un-African gains
> And piously abandon the calculus and all its offspring
> To . . . I know not whom, for Newton and Leibniz both
> Died childless.'

I laughed. Mosala said soberly, 'You've no idea what it was like, though, to have that *one sane voice* cutting through all the noise. The anti-science, traditionalist backlash didn't really hit South Africa until the 40s – but when it did, so many people in public life who'd spoken perfect sense until then seemed to cave in, one way or another . . . until science was somehow either the rightful "property" of "the West" – which Africa didn't need or want anyway – or it was nothing but a weapon of cultural assimilation and genocide.'

'It has been used as exactly that.'

Mosala eyed me balefully. 'No shit. Science has been abused for every conceivable purpose under the sun. Which is all the more reason to deliver the power it grants to as many people as possible, as rapidly as possible, instead of leaving it in the hands of a few. It is *not* a reason to retreat into fantasy – to declare: knowledge is a cultural artifact, nothing is universally true, only mysticism and obfuscation and ignorance

210

will save us.' She reached out and mimed taking hold of a handful of space, saying, 'There is no *male* or *female* vacuum. There is no *Belgian* or *Zairean* space-time. Inhabiting this universe is not a cultural prerogative, or a lifestyle decision. And I don't have to forgive or forget a single act of enslavement, theft, imperialism, or patriarchy, in order to be a physicist – or to approach the subject with whatever intellectual tools I need. Every scientist sees further by standing on a pile of corpses – and frankly, I don't care what kind of genitals they had, what language they spoke, or what the colour of their skin was.'

I tried not to smile; this was all highly usable. I had no idea which of these slogans were sincere, and which were conscious theatrics – where the telegenic sugar-coating I'd asked for ended, and Mosala's real passions began – but then, she may not have been entirely clear about the borders, herself.

I hesitated. My next note read: *Emigration rumours?* Now was the logical time to raise the issue – but that progression could be reconstructed during editing. I wasn't going to risk blowing the interview until I had a lot more material safely in the can.

I skipped ahead to safer ground. 'I know you don't want to reveal the full details of your TOE before your lecture on the eighteenth – but maybe you could give me a rough sketch of the theory, in terms of what's already been published?'

Mosala relaxed visibly. 'Of course. Though the main reason I can't give you all the details is that I don't even know them myself.' She explained, 'I've chosen the complete mathematical framework. All the general equations are fixed. But getting the specific results I need involves a lot of supercomputer calculations, which are in progress even as we speak. They should be completed a few days before the eighteenth, though – barring unforeseen disasters.'

'Okay. So tell me about the framework.'

'That part is extremely simple. Unlike Henry Buzzo and

Yasuko Nishide, I'm not looking for a way to make "our" Big Bang seem like less of a "coincidence". Buzzo and Nishide both take the view that an infinite number of universes must have arisen out of pre-space – freezing out of that perfect symmetry with different sets of physical laws. And they both aim to re-evaluate the probability of a universe "more-or-less like our own" being included in that infinite set. It's relatively easy to find a TOE in which our universe is possible, but freakishly unlikely. Buzzo and Nishide define a successful TOE as one which guarantees that there are *so many* universes similar to our own that we're not unlikely at all – that we're not some kind of miraculous, perfect bull's-eye on a meta-cosmic dartboard, but just one unexceptional point on a much larger target.'

I said, 'A bit like proving – from basic astrophysical principles – that thousands of planets in the galaxy should have carbon-and-water-based life, and not just Earth.'

'Yes and no. Because . . . yes, the probability of other Earth-like planets can be computed from theory alone – but it can also be validated by observation. We can *observe* billions of stars, we've already deduced the existence of a few thousand extrasolar planets – and eventually, we'll visit some of them, and *find* other carbon-and-water-based life. But, although there are no end of elegant frameworks for assigning probabilities to hypothetical *other universes*, there is no prospect of observing or visiting them, no conceivable method for checking the theory. So I don't believe we *should* choose a TOE on that basis.

'The whole point of moving beyond the Standard Unified Field Theory is that, one, it's an ugly mess, and two, you have to feed ten completely arbitrary parameters into the equations to make them work. Melting total space into pre-space – moving to an All-Topologies Model – gets rid of the ugliness and the arbitrary nature of the SUFT. But following that step by tinkering with the way you integrate across all the topologies of pre-space – excluding certain topologies for no good reason, throwing out one measure and adopting a new one whenever you don't like the answers you're getting – seems like a retrograde step to me. And instead of "setting the dials" of the SUFT machine to ten arbitrary numbers, you now have a sleek black box with no visible controls, apparently self-contained – but in reality, you're just opening it up and tearing out every internal component which offends you, to much the same effect.'

'Okay. So how do you get around that?'

Mosala said, 'I believe we have to take a difficult stand and declare: the probabilities just don't matter. Forget the hypothetical ensemble of other universes. Forget the need to fine-tune the Big Bang. This universe *does* exist. The probability of our being here is *one hundred per cent*. We have to take that as given, instead of bending over backwards trying to contrive assumptions which do their best to conceal the fact of that certainty.'

Forget fine-tuning the Big Bang. Take our own existence as given. The parallels with Conroy's spiel the night before were striking, but I should hardly have been surprised. The whole *modus operandi* of pseudoscience was to cling as closely as possible to the language and ideas of the orthodoxy of the day – to adopt appropriate camouflage. The ACs would have read every paper Mosala had published – but a similar ring to their words hardly granted their ideas the same legitimacy. And if they clearly shared her vehement distaste for the fantasy that every culture could somehow inhabit a cosmology of its own choosing, I didn't doubt for a moment that Mosala was infinitely more repelled by their alternative, in which a lone TOE specialist played absolute monarch. Worse than a Belgian or Zairean space-time: a Buzzo, Mosala, or Nishide cosmos.

I said, 'So you take the universe for granted. You're against twisting the mathematics to conform to a perceived need to prove that what we see around us is "likely". But you don't exactly go back to setting the dials on the SUFT machine, either.'

'No. I feed in complete descriptions of experiments, instead.'

'You choose the most general All-Topologies Model possible – but you break the perfect symmetry by giving a one hundred per cent probability to the existence of various setups of experimental apparatus?'

'Yes. Can I just—?' She rose from her chair and went into the bedroom, then returned with her notepad. She held up the screen for me. 'Here's one example. It's a simple accelerator experiment: a beam of protons and antiprotons collide at a certain energy, and a detector is used to pick up any positrons emitted from the point of collision at a certain angle with a certain range of energies. The experiment itself has been carried out, in one form or another, for eighty or ninety years.'

The animation showed an architectural schematic of a full-size accelerator ring, and zoomed in towards one of several points where counter-rotating particle beams crossed, and spilt their debris into elaborate detectors.

'Now, I don't even try to model this entire set-up – a piece of apparatus ten kilometres wide – on a subatomic level, atom by atom, as if I needed to start with a kind of blank, "naive" TOE which would somehow succeed in telling me that all the superconducting magnets would produce certain fields with certain measurable effects, and the walls of the tunnel would deform in certain ways due to the stresses imposed on them, and the protons and antiprotons would circle in opposite directions. *I already know* all of those things. So I assign them a probability of one hundred per cent. I take these established facts as a kind of *anchor* . . . and then reach down to the level of the TOE, down to the level of infinite sums over all topologies. I calculate what the consequences of my assumptions are . . . and then I follow them all the way back up again to the macroscopic level, to predict the ultimate results of the experiment: how many times a second will the positron detector register an event.'

The graphics responded to her narration, zooming in from a schematic of the detector array criss-crossed with particle tracks, down into the froth of the vacuum itself, thirty-five powers of ten beyond the reach of vision, into the chaos of writhing wormholes and higher-dimensional deformations – colour-coded by topological classification, a thrashing nest of brightly hued snakes blurring into whiteness at the centre of the screen, where they moved and changed too rapidly to follow. But these otherwise perfectly symmetrical convulsions were forced to take heed of the certain existence of accelerator, magnets, and detector – a process hinted at by the panchromatic whiteness acquiring a specific blue tinge . . . and then the view pulled back, zooming out to an ordinary human scale again, to show the imprint of this submicroscopic bias on the detector circuitry's final, visible behaviour.

The animation, of course, was ninety per cent metaphor, a colourful splash of poetic licence – but a supercomputer somewhere was crunching away at the serious, unmetaphoric calculations which made these pictures more than stylish whimsy.

And after all my hasty skimming of incomprehensible scientific papers, and all my agonising over the near-impenetrable mathematics of ATMs, I thought I finally had a handle on Mosala's philosophy.

I said tentatively, 'So instead of thinking of pre-space as something from which the whole universe can be derived in one stroke . . . you see it more as *a link* between the kind of events we can observe with our raw senses. Something which . . . glues together the particular set of macroscopic things we find in the world. A star full of fusing hydrogen, and a human eye full of cold protein molecules, are bridged across distances and energies . . . are able to co-exist, and affect each other . . . because at the deepest level, they both break the symmetry of pre-space in the same way.'

Mosala seemed pleased with this description. 'A link, a bridge. Exactly.' She leant forward, reached over and took my hand; I glanced down, thinking: I'm in shot now, so this is unusable.

She said, 'Without pre-space to mediate between us – without an infinite mixture of topologies able to represent us all with a single flicker of asymmetry – nobody could even *touch*.

'That's what the TOE *is*. And even if I'm wrong in every detail – and Buzzo is wrong, and Nishide is wrong, and nothing is resolved for a thousand years – I still know it's down there, waiting to be found. Because there has to be *something* which lets us touch.'

We broke off for a while, and Mosala called room service. After three days on the island, I still had no appetite, but I ate a few of the snacks she offered me from the tray which emerged from the service chute, just to be polite. My stomach began protesting – loudly – as soon as I swallowed the first mouthful, rather defeating the point.

Mosala said, 'Did you know that Yasuko hasn't arrived yet? I don't suppose you've heard what's holding him up?'

'I'm afraid not. I've left three messages with his secretary in Kyoto, trying to schedule an interview, and all I've got back are promises that he'll be in touch with me "very soon".'

'It's odd.' She pursed her lips, obviously concerned, but trying not to plunge the conversation into gloom. 'I hope he's all right. I heard he'd been sick for a while, early in the year – but he assured the convenors he'd be here, so he must have expected to be well enough to travel.'

I said, 'Travel to Stateless is more than . . . travel.'

'That's a point. He should have pretended to belong to

Humble Science! and stolen a ride on one of their charter flights.'

'He might have had better luck with Mystical Renaissance. He's a self-described Buddhist, so they almost forgive him for working on TOEs. So long as he didn't remind them that he once wrote that *The Tao of Physics* was to Zen what a Creation Science biology text was to Christianity.'

Mosala reached up and started massaging the back of her neck, as if talk of the journey was rekindling its symptoms. 'I would have brought Pinda, if the flight had been shorter. She would have loved it here. Left me to my boring lectures, and dragged her father off to explore the reefs.'

'How old is she?'

'Three and a bit.' She glanced at her watch and complained wistfully, 'It's still only four in the morning, back home. Not much chance of a call from *her*, for two or three hours.'

It was another opportunity to raise the emigration rumours – but I held off, yet again.

We resumed the interview. The beam from the skylight had shifted to the east, leaving Mosala almost silhouetted against the window and a dazzling blue sky. When I invoked **Witness** again, it reached up into my retinas and made some adjustments, enabling me to register the fine details of her face in spite of the back-lighting.

I moved on to the question of Helen Wu's analysis.

Mosala explained, 'My TOE predicts the outcome of various experiments, given a detailed description of the apparatus involved: details which "betray" clues about all the less-fundamental physics which – some people insist – a TOE is meant to pull out of thin air, all by itself. But unravelling those clues certainly isn't trivial. You or I can't just glance at an idle particle accelerator and predict, instantly, the outcome of any experiment which might be performed with the machine.'

'But a supercomputer, programmed with your TOE, can.

217

So is that good, bad, or indifferent . . . are you guilty of circular logic, or not?'

Mosala seemed unsure of the verdict, herself. 'Helen and I have been talking it over, trying to thrash out exactly what it means. I have to confess that I started out resenting what she was doing – and then ignoring most of her later work. Now, though . . . I'm beginning to find it very exciting.'

'Why?'

She hesitated. It was clear that her ideas on this were too new, too unformed; she really didn't want to say anything more. But I waited patiently, without prompting her, and she finally relented.

'Ask yourself this: if Buzzo or Nishide can come up with a TOE in which the whole universe is more or less implicit in a detailed description of the Big Bang – details deduced, *right here and now*, from observations of helium abundance, galactic clustering, the cosmic background radiation, and so on – no one accuses *them* of circular logic. Feeding in the results of any number of "telescope experiments" is fine, apparently. So why is it any more "circular" to have a TOE in which the universe is implicit in the details of ten contemporary particle physics experiments?'

I said, 'Okay. But isn't Helen Wu saying that your equations have virtually no *physical content* at all? I mean, no amount of pure mathematics could ever produce Newton's law of gravity – because there's no purely mathematical reason why the inverse square law couldn't be replaced by something different. The whole basis for it lies in the way the universe happens to work. Isn't Wu trying to show that your TOE doesn't rely on *anything* out there in the world – that it collapses into a lot of statements about numbers, which simply have to be true?'

Mosala replied, frustrated, 'Yes! But even if she's right . . . when those "statements which have to be true" are coupled with real, tangible experiments – which are *very much* "out

218

there in the world" – the theory ceases to be pure mathematics . . . in the same way that the pure symmetry of pre-space ceases to be symmetrical.

'Newton came up with the inverse square law by analysing *existing astronomical observations*. By treating the solar system in the way I treat a particle accelerator: saying, "This much we know for a fact." Later, the law was used to make predictions, and those predictions turned out to be correct. Okay . . . but where exactly does the *physical content* reside, in that whole process? With the inverse-square law itself . . . or with the observed motions of the planets, from which that equation was deduced in the first place? Because if you stop treating Newton's law as something given, standing outside the whole show as an eternal truth, and look at . . . *the link, the bridge* . . . between all the different planets orbiting different stars, coexisting in the same universe, having to be consistent with each other . . . what you're doing starts to become much more like pure mathematics.'

I thought I had an inkling of what she was suggesting. 'It's a bit like saying that . . . the general principle that "people form net clans with other people with whom they have something in common" has nothing to do with *what* those common interests happen to be. Exactly the same process brings together . . . fans of Jane Austen, or students of the genetics of wasps, or whatever.'

'Right. Jane Austen "belongs" to all the people who read her – not to the sociological principle which suggests that they'll get together to discuss her books. And the law of gravity "belongs" to all the systems which obey it – not to a TOE which predicts that they'll get together to form a universe.

'And maybe the Theory of Everything *should* collapse into nothing but "statements about numbers which have to be true". Maybe pre-space itself has to melt into nothing but

219

simple arithmetic, simple logic – leaving us with no choices to make about its structure at all.'

I laughed. 'I think even SeeNet's audience might have some trouble wrapping their minds around *that*.' I certainly did. 'Look, maybe it's going to take a while for you and Helen Wu to make sense of all this. We can always do an update on it, back in Cape Town, if it turns out to be an important development.'

Mosala agreed, relieved. Throwing ideas around was one thing, but she clearly didn't want to take a position on this, officially. Not yet.

Before I could lose my nerve, I said, 'Do you think you'll still be living in Cape Town, in six months' time?'

I'd braced myself for the kind of outburst the word *Anthro-cosmologist* had produced – but Mosala simply observed drily, 'Well, I didn't think it could remain a secret for long. I suppose the whole conference is talking about it.'

'Not exactly. I heard it from a local.'

She nodded, unsurprised. 'I've been having discussions with the academic syndicates here, for months. So it's probably all over the island by now.' She flashed a wry smile. 'Not much into *confidentiality*, these anarchists. But what can you expect from patent violators and intellectual property thieves?'

I said, 'So what's the attraction?'

She stood. 'Can you stop recording, please?' I complied. 'When all the details have been worked out, I'll make a public statement – but I don't want some off-the-cuff remark on the subject coming out first.'

'I understand.'

She said, 'What's the attraction of patent violators and intellectual property thieves? That very fact. Stateless is renegade, they flout the biotech licensing laws.' She turned towards the window, and stretched out her arms. 'And look at them! They're not the wealthiest people on the planet – but no one here is starving. *No one.* That's not true in Europe, Japan,

Australia – let alone in Angola, Malawi . . .' She trailed off, and studied me for a moment, as if trying to decide if I really had stopped filming. If she really should trust me at all.

I waited. She continued.

'What's that got to do with me? My own country's doing well enough. I'm not exactly in danger of malnutrition, am I?' She closed her eyes and groaned. 'This is very hard for me to say. But . . . like it or not, the Nobel prize has given me a certain kind of power. If I move to Stateless – and state the reasons why – it will make news. It *will* make an impact, in certain places.'

She hesitated again.

I said, 'I can keep my mouth shut.'

Mosala smiled faintly. 'I know that. I think.'

'So what kind of impact do you want to make?'

She walked over to the window. I said, 'Is this some kind of political gesture – against traditionalists like PACDF?'

She laughed. 'No, no, no! Well . . . maybe it will be that as well, coincidentally. But that's not the point.' She steeled herself. 'I've had assurances. From a number of highly placed people. I've been promised that if I move to Stateless . . . not because I matter, but *because it will make news*, and create a pretext . . . the South African government will unilaterally drop all sanctions against the island, within six months.'

I had goose bumps. One country might make no difference – except that South Africa was the major trading partner of about thirty other African nations.

Mosala said quietly, 'The voting patterns in the UN don't show it but the fact is, the anti-sanctions faction is *not* a tiny minority. At present, there's all kinds of bloc solidarity and surface agreement, because everyone believes they can't win, and they don't want to cause offence.'

'But if someone gave the right little push, they might start an avalanche?'

'Maybe.' She laughed, embarrassed. 'Talk about delusions

221

of grandeur. The truth is, I get sick to the core every time I think about it – and I don't actually believe anything dramatic is going to happen.'

'One person to break the symmetry. Why not?'

She shook her head firmly. 'There've been other attempts to shift the vote, which have all fallen through. Anything's worth trying, but I have to keep my feet on the ground.'

Several things were running through my mind at once – though what might happen if the biotech patent laws ever really collapsed, globally, was almost too distant a prospect to contemplate. But the fact remained that Mosala had more *use* for the documentary than I'd ever imagined – and she'd told me all this to let me know as much, to give me the leverage she wanted me to employ, to ensure that her emigration *did* cause a stir.

It was also clear that the whole endeavour – however quixotic – would be extremely unpopular in certain quarters.

Was that what Kuwale had had in mind? Not the Ignorance Cults, not PACDF fundamentalists, not even pro-science South African nationalists outraged by Mosala's 'desertion' – but powerful defenders of the biotech status quo? *And if the teenaged burglar 'paid to frighten her' hadn't been lying, after all . . .*

Mosala walked over to a side table and poured herself a glass of water. 'Now you know all my deepest secrets, so I declare this interview over.' She raised the glass and declaimed self-mockingly, '*Vive la technolibération!*'

'*Vive.*'

She said seriously, 'Okay: there are rumours. Maybe half of Stateless knows exactly what's going on – but I still don't want those rumours confirmed until certain arrangements, certain agreements, are much more solid.'

'I understand.' And I realised, with a kind of astonishment, that somewhere along the way I'd won some measure of trust from her. Of course she was using me – but she must have believed that my heart was in the right place, that I'd let myself be used.

I said, 'Next time you're arguing circularity with Helen Wu deep into the night, do you think I could . . .?'

'Sit in? And record it?' She seemed to find the prospect dubious, but she said, 'All right. Just so long as you promise not to fall asleep before we do.'

She walked me to the door, and we shook hands. I said, 'Be careful.'

She smiled serenely, slightly amused at my concern, as if she didn't have an enemy in the world.

'Don't worry. I will.'

17

I was woken by a call just after four, the ringing growing louder and more shrill until it reached into my melatonin dreams and turned the darkness of my skull inside-out. For an instant, the mere fact of consciousness was shocking, unspeakable; I was outraged as a newborn child. Then I stretched out an arm and groped around on the bedside table for my notepad. I squinted at the screen, blinded for a moment by its brightness.

The call was from Lydia. I almost refused to take it, assuming that she'd somehow miscalculated the time zones, but then I woke sufficiently to realise that it was the middle of the night for her, too. Sydney was only two hours behind Stateless. Geographically, if not politically.

She said, 'Andrew, I'm sorry to disturb you, but I thought you had a right to hear this in real-time.' She looked uncharacteristically grim, and though I was still too groggy even to speculate about what was coming next, it was obvious that it wasn't going to be pleasant.

I said hoarsely, 'That's okay. Go ahead.' I tried not to imagine what I looked like, gaping bleary-eyed at the camera. Lydia seemed to be in a darkened room, herself, her face lit only by the image on the screen . . . of me, lit only by the image of her. *Was that possible?* I suddenly realised I had a pounding headache.

'*Junk DNA* is going to have to be re-edited, with the Landers story removed. If you had time, of course I'd ask you to do it yourself, but I'm assuming that's not possible. So I'll give it to Paul Kostas; he used to be one of our news room editors, but he's freelance now. I'll send you his final cut, and if you strongly disagree with anything, you'll have an opportunity to change it. Just remember that it's being screened in less than a fortnight.'

I said, 'That's fine, that's all . . . fine.' I knew Kostas; he wouldn't mutilate the program. 'Why, though? Was there some legal glitch? Don't tell me Landers is suing?'

'No. Events have overtaken us. I won't try to explain; I've sent you a trailer from the San Francisco bureau – it'll all be public by morning, but . . .' She was too tired to elaborate, but I understood; she didn't want me to learn about this as just another viewer. A quarter of *Junk DNA*, and some three months' work on my part, had just been rendered obsolete, but Lydia was doing her best to salvage some vestige of my professional dignity. This way, at least I'd stay a few hours ahead of the masses.

I said, 'I appreciate that. Thank you.'

We bade each other goodnight, and I viewed the 'trailer' – a hastily assembled package of footage and text, alerting other news rooms to the story, and giving them the choice either to wait for the polished item soon to follow, or to edit the raw material themselves and put out their own version. It consisted mainly of FBI news releases, plus some archival background material.

Ned Landers, his two chief geneticists, and three of his executives, had just been arrested in Portland. Nine other people – working for an entirely separate corporation – had been arrested in Chapel Hill, North Carolina. Laboratory equipment, biochemical samples, and computer records had been taken from both sites in pre-dawn raids. All fifteen people had been charged with violating federal biotechnology safety laws – but not because of Landers' highly publicised neo-DNA and symbiont research. At the Chapel Hill laboratory, according to the charges, workers had been manipulating infectious, natural-RNA viruses – in secret, without permission. Landers had been footing the bills, circuitously.

The purpose of these viruses remained unknown; the data and samples were yet to be analysed.

There were no statements from the accused; their lawyers were counselling silence. There were some external shots of the Chapel Hill laboratory, sealed off behind police barricades. All the footage of Landers himself was relatively old material; the latest was cannibalised from my interview with him (not completely wasted, after all).

The lack of detail was frustrating, but the implications already seemed clear. Landers and his collaborators had been constructing perfect viral immunity for themselves, beyond the specific powers of any one vaccine or drug, beyond the fear of mutant strains out-evolving their defences . . . while engineering new viruses capable of infecting the rest of us. I stared at the screen, which was frozen on the last frame of the report: Landers, as I'd seen him in the flesh, myself, smiling at the vision of his brand new kingdom. And though I baulked at accepting the obvious conclusion . . . what possible use could he have had for a novel human virus, except for some kind of *thinning*?

I sprinted to the bathroom, and brought up the meagre contents of my stomach. Then I knelt by the bowl, shivering and sweating – lapsing into microsleeps, almost losing my balance. The melatonin wanted me back, but I was having trouble convincing myself that I was through vomiting. Pampered hypochondriac that I was, I would have consulted my pharm at once if I'd had it, for a precise diagnosis and an instant, optimal solution. With visions of choking to death in my sleep, I contemplated tearing off my shoulder patch – but the symbolic attempt to surrender to natural circadian forces would have taken hours to produce any effect at all – and then it would have rendered me, at best, a zombie for the rest of the conference.

226

I retched, voluntarily, for a minute or two, and nothing more emerged, so I staggered back to bed.

Ned Landers had gone further than any gender migrant, any anarchist, any Voluntary Autist. *No man is an island? Just watch me.* And yet, apparently, it still hadn't been far enough. He'd still felt crowded, threatened, encroached-upon. A biological kingdom wasn't enough; he'd aspired to more elbow room than even that unbridgeable genetic gulf could provide.

And he'd almost attained it. That was what *species self-knowledge* had given him: a precise, molecular definition of the H-word . . . which he could personally transcend, before turning it against everyone who remained in its embrace.

Vive la technolibération! Why not have a million Ned Landers? Why not let every solipsistic lunatic and paranoid, self-appointed ethnic-group-saviour on the planet wield the same power? Paradise for yourself and your clan – and apocalypse for everyone else.

That was the fruit of perfect understanding.

What's wrong, don't you like the taste?

I clutched my stomach and slid my knees towards my chin; it changed the character of the nausea, if not exactly removing it. The room tipped, my limbs grew numb, I strived for absolute blankness.

And if I'd dug deeper, done my job properly, I might have been the one to find him out, to stop him . . .

Gina touched my cheek, and kissed me tenderly. We were in Manchester, at the imaging lab. I was naked, she was clothed.

She said, 'Climb inside the scanner. You can do that for me, can't you? I want us to be much, much closer, Andrew. So I need to see what's going on inside your brain.'

I started to comply – but then I hesitated, suddenly afraid of what she'd discover.

She kissed me again. 'No more arguments. If you love me, you'll shut up and do what you're told.'

She forced me down, and closed the hatch of the machine. I saw my body from above. The scanner was more than a scanner – it raked me with ultraviolet lasers. I felt no pain, but the beams prised away layer after layer of living tissue with merciless precision. All the skin, all the flesh, which concealed my secrets dissolved into a red mist around me, and then the mist began to part . . .

I dreamt that I woke up screaming.

At seven-thirty, I interviewed Henry Buzzo in one of the hotel meeting rooms. He was charming and articulate, a natural performer, but he didn't really want to talk about Violet Mosala; he wanted to recount anecdotes about famous dead people. 'Of course Steve Weinberg tried to prove that I was wrong about the gravitino, but I soon straightened *him* out . . .' SeeNet alone had devoted three full-length documentaries to Buzzo, over the years, but it seemed that there were still more names he desperately needed to drop, on camera, before dying.

I wasn't in a charitable mood; the three hours' sleep I'd had after Lydia's call had been about as refreshing as a blow to the head. I went through the motions, feigning fascination, and trying half-heartedly to steer the interview in a direction which might produce some material I could actually use.

'What kind of place in history do you think the discoverer of the TOE will attain? Wouldn't that be the ultimate form of scientific immortality?'

Buzzo became self-deprecating. 'There's no such thing as immortality, for a scientist. Not even for the greatest. Newton and Einstein are still famous today – but for how long? Shakespeare will probably outlast them both . . . and maybe even Hitler will, too.'

I didn't have the heart to break the news to him that none of these were exactly household names anymore.

I said, 'Newton's and Einstein's theories have been swallowed whole, though. Absorbed into larger schemes. I know, you've already carved your name on one TOE which turned out to be provisional – but all of the SUFT's architects said at the time that it was just a stepping stone. Don't you think the next TOE will be the real thing: the final theory which lasts forever?'

Buzzo had given the question a lot more thought than I had. He said, 'It *might*. It certainly might. I can imagine a universe in which we can probe no further, in which deeper explanations are literally, physically, impossible. But . . .'

'Your own TOE describes such a universe, doesn't it?'

'Yes. But it could be right about everything else, and wrong about that. The same is true of Mosala's and Nishide's.'

I said sourly, 'So when will we know, one way or the other? When will we be sure that we've struck bottom?'

'Well . . . if *I'm* right, then you'll never be sure that I'm right. My TOE doesn't allow itself to be proved final and complete – even if it *is* final and complete.' Buzzo grinned, delighted at the prospect of such a perverse legacy. 'The only kind of TOE which could leave any less room for doubt would be one which *required* its own finality – which made that fact absolutely central.

'Newton was swallowed up and digested, Einstein was swallowed up and digested . . . and the old SUFT will go the same way, in a matter of days. They were all closed systems, they were all vulnerable. The only TOE which could be *guaranteed* immune to the process would be one which actively defended itself – which turned its gaze outwards to describe, not just the universe, but also *every conceivable alternative theory* which could somehow supersede it – and then rendered them all demonstrably false, at a single blow.'

He shook his head gleefully. 'But there's nothing like that

on offer here. If you want absolute certainty, you've come to the wrong side of town.'

The other side of town was still just outside the hotel's main entrance; the Mystical Renaissance carnival hadn't gone away. I headed out on to the street, anyway; I urgently needed a dose of fresh air if I was going to be more than half-conscious for the lecture on ATM software techniques which Mosala was due to attend at nine. The sky was dazzling, and the air was already warm; Stateless seemed unable to decide whether to surrender to a temperate autumn, or hold out for an Indian summer. The sunshine lifted my spirits, slightly, but I still felt crippled, beaten, overwhelmed.

I weaved my way past the stalls and small tents, dodging goldfish-bowl-jugglers and hand-stilt-walkers – impressive acts, mostly; it was only the droning songs of the buskers which really made me feel that I was running a gauntlet. While members of Humble Science! had been showing up at every press conference and doing their best to repeat the tone of Walsh's encounter with Mosala, MR had remained endearingly innocuous by comparison. I was beginning to suspect that it was a deliberate strategy: a good cult/bad cult game, to widen their combined appeal. Humble Science! had nothing to lose by extremism; those few members who left in disgust at Walsh's tactics (to join MR, most likely) would be more than compensated for by an influx from groups like Celtic Wisdom and Saxon Light – northern Europe's equivalents of PACDF, only more influential.

I recalled a scene from one of the Muteba Kazadi biographies I'd skimmed: when asked in reproving tones by a BBC journalist why he'd declined an invitation to take part in a traditional Lunda fertility ceremony, he'd politely suggested that she go home and berate a few cabinet minsters for failing to celebrate the solstice at Stonehenge. Ten years later, there were half a dozen MPs who seemed to have taken the suggestion at face value. No cabinet ministers, though. So far.

I paused to watch the MR theatre troupe, ready to play spot-the-mutilated-classic. After a few baffling lines of garbled biotech-speak – unplaceable, but weirdly familiar – hairs stood up on the back of my neck. They'd seized on the news of Landers and his viruses, and were acting out their own hastily scripted version of the story. What's more, most of their descriptions of Landers' modified personal biochemistry came straight out of the narration to *Junk DNA*; SeeNet's news editors must have mined the discarded segment of the documentary for some instant technical background when they put together their final release.

I shouldn't have been surprised by any of this – but the speed with which events thousands of kilometres away had been recycled as an instant parable was unsettling enough; hearing my own words echoed back at me as part of the feedback loop verged on the surreal.

An actor playing one of the FBI agents sent to gather Landers' computer files turned to the audience (all three of us) and proclaimed, 'This knowledge could destroy us all! We must avert our gaze!' His companion replied mournfully, 'Yes – but this is only one man's folly! The same sacred mysteries are spelt out in ten million other machines! Until every one of those files is erased . . . none of us will ever sleep safely!'

My head throbbed and my throat tightened. I couldn't deny that in the dead of night, confused and in pain, I'd shared this sentiment entirely.

And now?

I walked on. I had no time to waste on Landers, or MR; keeping up with Violet Mosala was already proving near enough to impossible. The whole documentary kept being transmuted into something new before my eyes – and however gloriously unworldly her arcane physics, Mosala was

231

entangled in so many political complications that I was beginning to lose count.

Had Sarah Knight known about Mosala's plans to emigrate to Stateless? If she had, it would have made the project a thousand times more attractive to her than any deal with the Anthrocosmologists. *Would she have kept a selling point like that from SeeNet, though?* Maybe, if she'd wanted to take it to another network – but in that case, why wasn't she here, shouldering me aside, making *Violet Mosala: Technolibérateur?* Or maybe Mosala had sworn her to secrecy and she'd honoured that promise, even though it had meant losing the job?

It was driving me insane: even in her absence, Sarah seemed to be one step ahead of me all the way. At the very least, I should have asked her to collaborate; it would have been worth splitting my fee with her, and giving her a co-director's credit, just to find out what she knew.

A bright red graphic flashed up over my visual field, a small circle at the centre of a larger one with cross-hairs. I froze, confused. As I shifted my gaze, the target clung to a face in the crowd. It was a person in a clown suit, handing out MR literature.

Akili Kuwale?

Witness thought it was.

The clown wore a mask of active make-up, currently a chequer-board of green and white. From this distance, ve might have been any gender, including asex; ve was about the right build and height – and vis features weren't dissimilar, so far as I could tell with squares painted all over them. It wasn't impossible – but I wasn't convinced.

I approached. The clown called out, 'Get your *Daily Archetype*! Get the truth about the dangers of frankenscience!' The accent, even if I couldn't place it geographically, was unmistakable – and this hawker's cry sounded every bit as ironic as Kuwale's observations about Janet Walsh.

I walked up to the clown; ve regarded me impassively. I said, 'How much?'

'The truth costs nothing . . . but a dollar would help the cause.'

'Which cause is that? MR or AC?'

Ve said quietly, 'We all have our roles to play. I'm pretending to be MR. You're pretending to be a journalist.'

That stung. I said, 'Fair enough. I admit I still don't know half as much as Sarah Knight . . . but I'm getting there. And I'd get there faster with your help.'

Kuwale regarded me with undisguised mistrust. The chequerboard on vis face suddenly melted into blue and red diamonds – a disorienting sight, though vis fixed stare throughout the transition only made vis contempt shine through all the more clearly.

Ve said, 'Why don't you just take a pamphlet and fuck off?' Ve held one out to me. 'Read it and eat it.'

'I've swallowed enough bad news today. And the Keystone—'

Ve grinned sardonically. 'Ah, Amanda Conroy summons you to her *hearthside*, and you think you know it all.'

'If I thought I knew it all, why would I be pleading with you to tell me what I've missed?'

Ve hesitated. I said, 'On Sunday night, you asked me to keep my eyes open. Tell me why, and tell me what I'm looking for – and I'll do it. I don't want to see Mosala hurt, any more than you do. But I need to know exactly what's going on.'

Kuwale thought it over, still suspicious but clearly tempted. Short of Mosala's colleagues, or Karin De Groot – all highly unlikely to co-operate – I was probably the closest ve could ever hope to get to vis idol.

Ve mused, 'If you were working for the other side, why would you pretend to be so incompetent?'

I took the insult in my stride. 'I'm not even sure that I know who *the other side* is.'

233

Kuwale caved in. 'Meet me outside this building in half an hour.' Ve took my hand and wrote an address on my palm; it wasn't the house where I'd met Conroy. In half an hour, I was supposed to be filming Mosala at yet another lecture – but the documentary would survive with a few less reaction shots to choose from, and Mosala would probably be relieved to be left in peace for a change.

Kuwale thrust a rolled-up pamphlet into my open hand before I turned away. I almost discarded it, but then I changed my mind. Ned Landers was on the cover, bolts protruding from the side of his neck, while an Escher-rip-off effect had him reaching out of the portrait and painting it himself. The headline read: THE MYTH OF A SELF-MADE MAN – which was, at least, wittier than anything the murdochs would come up with. When I flicked through the article within, though . . . there was no talk of monitoring or restricting access to human genome data, no discussion of US and Chinese resistance to international inspections of sites with DNA synthesis equipment, no practical suggestions whatsoever for preventing another Chapel Hill. Beyond a call for all human DNA maps to be 'erased and undiscovered' – about as useful as imploring the people of the world to forget the true shape of the planet – there was nothing but cult-speak: the danger of meddling with quintessential mysteries, the 'human need' for an ineffable secret to life, the techno-rape of the collective soul.

If Mystical Renaissance really wanted to speak for all humanity, define the fit and proper boundaries of knowledge, and dictate – or censor – the deepest truths of the universe . . . they were going to have to do better than this.

I closed my eyes, and laughed with relief and gratitude. Now that it had passed, I could admit it: for a while, I'd almost believed that they might have claimed me. I'd almost imagined that I might have ended up crawling into their recruitment tent on my hands and knees, head bowed with appropriate humility (at last), proclaiming: 'I was blind, but now I see! I was psychically numbed, but now I'm attuned! I was all Yang and no Yin – left-brained, linear, and hierarchical – but now I'm ready to embrace the Alchemical Balance between the Rational and the Mystical! Only say the word . . . and I will be Healed!'

The address Kuwale had given me was a baker's shop. Imported luxuries aside, all the food on Stateless came from the sea – but the proteins and starches in the nodules of the engineered seaweeds which flourished at the borders of the reefs were all but identical to those in any grain of wheat, and so was the smell they produced on baking. The familiar aroma made me light-headed with hunger, but the thought of swallowing a single mouthful of fresh bread was enough to make me nauseous. I should have known, by then, that there was something physically wrong with me – beyond the after-effect of the flight, beyond broken melatonin sleep, beyond my sadness over losing Gina, beyond the stress of finding myself in at the deep end of a story which showed no sign of bottoming out. But I didn't have my pharm to pronounce the illness real, I didn't trust the local doctors, I didn't have time to be sick. So I told myself that it was all in my head – and the only possible cure was to try to ignore it.

Kuwale appeared, sans clown suit, just in time to save me from either passing out or throwing up. Ve walked past without even glancing at me, radiating nervous energy; I followed – and started recording – resisting the urge to shout out vis name and deflate the implied cloak-and-dagger solemnity.

I caught up, and walked alongside ver. 'What does "mainstream AC" mean, anyway?'

Kuwale glanced at me sideways, edgy and irritated, but ve deigned to answer. 'We don't know who the Keystone is. We accept that we may never know, for certain. But we respect all the people who seem to be likely candidates.'

That all sounded obscenely moderate and reasonable. 'Respect, or revere?'

Ve rolled vis eyes. 'The Keystone is just another person. The first to grasp the TOE completely – but there's no reason why a billion others can't do the same, after ver. Someone has to be first – it's as simple as that. The Keystone is not – remotely – a "god"; the Keystone need not even know that ve's created the universe. All ve has to do is *explain* it.'

'While people like you stand back and explain that act of creation?'

Kuwale made a dismissive gesture, as if ve had no time to waste on metaphysical nit-picking.

I said, 'So why are you so concerned about Violet Mosala, if she's nothing so cosmically special after all?'

Ve was bemused. 'Does a person have to be some kind of supernatural being, to deserve not to be killed? Do I have to get down on my knees and worship the woman as Mother Goddess of the universe, in order to care whether she lives or dies?'

'Call her *Mother Goddess of the Universe* to her face, and you'd soon wish you were dead, yourself.'

Kuwale grinned. 'And rightly so.' Ve added stoically, 'But I know she thinks AC is even lower than the Ignorance Cults; the very fact that we desist from god-talk only makes us more insidious, in her eyes. She thinks we're parasites feeding off science: following the work of TOE theorists, stealing it, abusing it . . . and not even having the honesty to speak the language of the anti-rationalists.' Ve shrugged lightly. 'She despises us. I still respect her, though. And whether she's the Keystone or not . . . she's one of the greatest physicists of her generation, she's a powerful force for *technolibération* . . . why should I need to deify her, to value her life?'

'Okay.' This whole laid-back attitude seemed far too good to be true – but it wasn't inconsistent with anything I'd heard from Conroy. 'That's mainstream AC. Now tell me about the heretics.'

Kuwale groaned. 'The permutations are . . . endless. Imagine any variation you like, and there's sure to be someone on the planet who embraces it as the truth. We don't have a patent on Anthrocosmology. There are ten billion people out there, and they're all capable of believing anything they want to, however close to us in metaphysics, however far away in spirit.'

This was pure evasion, but I didn't get a chance to press the point. Kuwale saw a tram ahead, beginning to move away from its stop, and ve started running for it. I struggled to keep up; we both made it, but I took a while to get my breath back. We were headed west, out towards the coast.

The tram was only half-full, but Kuwale remained standing in the doorway, gripping a hand rail and leaning out into the wind. Ve said, 'If I show you the people you need to recognise, will you let me know if you see them? I'll give you a contact number, and an encryption algorithm, and all you have to do is—'

I said, 'Slow down. Who are these people?'

'They're a danger to Violet Mosala.'

'You mean, you suspect they're a danger.'

'I know it.'

'Okay. So who are they?'

'What difference would it make if I told you their names? It wouldn't mean anything to you.'

'No, but you can tell me who they're working for. Which government, which biotech company . . . ?'

Vis face hardened. 'I told Sarah Knight too much. I'm not repeating that mistake.'

'Too much for what? Did she betray you? To . . . SeeNet?'

'No!' Kuwale scowled; I was missing the point. 'Sarah told me what happened with SeeNet. You pulled a few strings . . . and all the work she'd done counted for nothing. She was angry, but she wasn't surprised. She said that's what the networks are like. And she bore you no real grudge; she said she was ready to pass on everything she knew, if you agreed to refund her costs out of your research budget, and maintain confidentiality.'

I said, 'What are you talking about?'

'I gave her the okay to tell you everything she knew about AC. Why do you think I made such a fool of myself, at the airport? If I'd known you were still in the dark, do you think I would have approached you like that?'

'No.' That much, at least, made sense. 'But why would she tell you she was going to brief me, and then change her mind? I haven't heard a word from her. She doesn't answer my calls—'

Kuwale fixed vis eyes on me, sad and ashamed, but suddenly, painfully, honest.

'And she doesn't answer mine.'

We left the tram, at a stop on the outskirts of a small industrial complex, then walked south-east. If we were under professional surveillance, all of this incessant motion would change nothing – but if Kuwale believed it made it safe for us to talk more freely, I was willing to tag along.

I didn't accept for a moment that anything had happened to Sarah; she had every reason to wish both of us out of her life – a wish which a few words to her communications software could have granted. She might have had a brief, magnanimous fantasy about putting me in the picture, in spite of what I'd done to her, out of sheer journalistic solidarity – all of us pulling together for the sake of Mosala's history-making story-which-must-be-told, ra ra – but then felt differently in the morning, once the chemical solace had worn off.

What's more, I was beginning to have second thoughts about the threat to Mosala herself.

I turned to Kuwale. 'If biotech interests ever *did* assassinate Violet Mosala, she'd be an instant martyr for *technolibération*. And as a corpse, she'd be just as good a mascot, just as good an excuse for the South African government to lead an anti-boycott revolt in the UN.'

'Maybe,' ve conceded. 'If the headlines told the right story.'

'How could the story fail to get out? Mosala's backers would hardly stay silent.'

Kuwale smiled grimly. 'Do you know who *owns* most of the media?'

'Yes, I do, so don't give me that paranoid bullshit. A hundred different groups, a thousand different people . . .'

'A hundred different groups – most of which also own large biotech concerns. A thousand different people – most of them on the boards of at least one major player, from AgroGenesis to VivoTech.'

'That's true, but there are other interests, with other agendas. It's not as simple as you make it sound.'

We were alone now, on a large stretch of flat but unpaved reef-rock, prepared but not yet built upon; some small-scale construction machinery was clustered in the distance, but it appeared to be idle. Munroe had told me that no one could own land on Stateless – any more than they could own air – but equally, there was nothing to stop people fencing off and monopolising vast tracts of it. That they *chose not to* made me distinctly uneasy; it seemed like an unnatural exercise of restraint – a delicately balanced consensus poised ready to collapse into a spate of land grabs, the creation of *de facto* titles, and an outraged – probably violent – backlash from those who hadn't got in first.

And yet . . . *Why come all the way out here, just to play Lord of the Flies?* No society chooses to destroy itself. And if an ignorant tourist was capable of imagining how disastrous a land rush would be, the residents of Stateless must have thought it through themselves, in a thousand times more detail.

I spread my arms to encompass the whole renegade island.

'If you really think the biotech companies can get away with murder, tell me why they haven't turned Stateless into a fireball?'

'Bombing El Nido made that solution unrepeatable. You need a government to do it for you – and no government, now, would risk the backlash.'

'Sabotaged it, then? If EnGeneUity can't come up with something to dissolve their own creation back into the sea, then the Beach Boys were lying.'

'The Beach Boys?'

' "Californian biotechnologists are the best in the world". Wasn't that one of theirs?'

Kuwale said, 'EnGeneUity are selling versions of Stateless all over the Pacific. Why would they sabotage their best demonstration model – their best advertisement, unauthorised or not? They might not have planned it this way, but the truth is, Stateless has cost them nothing – so long as no one else goes renegade.'

I wasn't convinced, but the argument was going nowhere. 'Do you want to show me your gallery of alleged corporate assassins? And then explain to me, very carefully, exactly what you plan to do if I tell you that I've sighted one of these people? Because if you think I'm entering into a conspiracy to murder – even in defence of the Keystone herself, even on Stateless—'

Kuwale cut me off. 'There's no question of violence. All we want to do is watch these people, gather the necessary intelligence, and tip off conference security as soon as we have something tangible.'

Vis notepad beeped. Ve halted, took it out of vis pocket and gazed at the screen for several seconds, then carefully paced a dozen metres south. I said, 'Do you mind if I ask what you're doing?'

Kuwale beamed proudly. 'My data security is linked to the Global Positioning System. The most crucial files can't be opened, even with the right passwords and voiceprint, unless you're standing on the right spot – which changes, hour by hour. And I'm the only one who knows exactly how it changes.'

I almost asked: Why not memorise a long list of passwords, instead of locations? Stupid question. The GPS was there, so it had to be used – and a more convoluted security scheme was better, not because it was any more secure, but because the complexity of the system was an end in itself. Technophilia was like any other aesthetic; there was no point asking *why?*

Kuwale was only half a generation younger than me, and we probably shared eighty per cent of our world views – but ve'd pushed all the things we both believed much further. Science and technology seemed to have given ver everything ve could ask for: an escape from the poisoned battleground of gender, a political movement worth fighting for, and even a quasi-religion – insane enough in its own way, but unlike most other science-friendly faiths, at least it wasn't a laboriously contrived synthesis of modern physics and some dog-eared historical relic: a mock truce like the fatuities of Quantum Buddhism, or the Church of the Revised Standard Judaeo-Christian Big Bang.

I watched ver tinkering with the software, waiting for some conjunction of satellites and atomic clocks, and wondered: *Would I have been happier, if I'd made the same decisions?* As an asex – saved from a dozen screwed-up relationships. As a *technolibérateur* – with ideological zeal to shield me from any doubts about Nagasaki or Ned Landers. As an Anthrocosmologist – with a final explanation for everything which put me one up on even the TOE theorists, and inoculated me against competing religions in my old age.

Would I have been happier?

Maybe. But then, happiness was overrated.

Kuwale's software chimed success. I walked over and

accepted the data ve'd unlocked, tight-beam infrared flowing between our notepads.

I said, 'I don't suppose you want to tell me how you know about these people? Or how I'm meant to verify what you say about them?'

'That's what Sarah Knight asked me.'

'I'm not surprised. And now *I'm* asking.'

Kuwale ignored me; the subject was closed. Ve gestured at my abdomen with vis notepad, and instructed me solemnly, 'Move everything in there, first chance you get. Perfect security. You're lucky.'

'Sure. While one EnGeneUity assassin is running around Stateless with your notepad, trying to find the right geographical coordinates, the others will be saving time by carving me open.'

Kuwale laughed. 'That's the spirit. You may not be much of a journalist, but we'll make a revolutionary martyr out of you yet.'

Ve pointed across the expanse of reef-rock, glistening green and silver in the morning sun. 'We should return to the city by separate routes. If you head that way, you'll hit the south-west tram line in twenty minutes.'

'Okay.' I didn't have the energy to argue. As ve turned to leave, though, I said, 'Before you vanish, will you answer one last question?'

Ve shrugged. 'No harm in asking.'

'Why are you doing this? I still don't understand. You say you really don't care whether Violet Mosala is the Keystone or not. But even if she's such a great human being that her death would be a global tragedy . . . what makes that your personal responsibility? She *knows* exactly what she's buying into, moving to Stateless. She's a grown woman, with resources of her own, and more political clout than you or I could ever hope for. She's not helpless, she's not stupid – and if she knew what you were doing, she'd probably strangle you with her bare hands. So . . . why can't you leave her to take care of herself?'

Kuwale hesitated, and cast vis eyes down. I seemed to have hit a nerve, at last; ve had the air of someone searching for the right words with which to unburden verself.

The silence stretched on, but I waited patiently. *Sarah Knight had extracted the whole story, hadn't she? There was no reason why I couldn't do the same.*

Kuwale looked up and replied casually, 'Like I said: no harm in asking.'

Ve turned and walked away.

18

I viewed the data Kuwale had given me while I waited for the
tram. Eighteen faces, but no names. The images were stan-
dardised 3D portraits: backgrounds removed, lighting homo-
genised, like police mug shots. There were twelve men and six
women, of diverse ages and ethnicities. It seemed a curiously
large number; Kuwale hadn't suggested that every one of them
was actually on Stateless – but how, exactly, could ve have got
hold of portraits of the *eighteen* corporate assassins most
likely to be sent to the island? What kind of source, what
kind of leak, what kind of data theft could have yielded
precisely this much, and no more?

In any case, I had no intention of letting the ACs know if I
spotted one of these faces in a crowd – less out of fear that I
might be putting myself at risk by siding with radical *technolibérateurs* against powerful vested interests, than out of a
lingering suspicion that Kuwale might yet prove to be entirely
off the planet – as paranoid a Mosala fan as I'd first imagined,
and more. Without any way of confirming vis story, I could
hardly unleash an unknown retribution on some total stranger
who happened to stray too close to Violet Mosala. For all I
knew, this was a gallery of innocent Ignorance Cultists,
snapped as they disembarked from a charter flight. The fact
that Mosala had no shortage of potential enemies didn't prove
that Kuwale knew who they were – or that ve'd told me the
truth about anything.

Even the version of Anthrocosmology I'd been fed sounded
far too reasonable and dispassionate to be true. *The Keystone*

is just another person, honestly – all our concern for Violet Mosala is due to her numerous other good points. Why go to the trouble of inventing a cult which elevates someone to the status of Prime Cause for Everything – and then treat that fact as all but insignificant? Kuwale had protested too much.

By the time I reached the hotel, the ATM software lecture was almost over, so I sat in the lobby to wait for Mosala to emerge.

The more I thought about it, the less I was prepared to trust anything Kuwale and Conroy had told me – but I knew it could take months to find out what the Anthrocosmologists were really about. Other than Indrani Lee, there was only one person who was likely to hold the answers – and I was sick of remaining ignorant out of sheer dumb pride.

I called Sarah. If she was in Australia, it was broad daylight on the east coast by now . . . but the same answering system responded as before.

I left another message for her. I couldn't bring myself to come right out and say it in plain English: *I abused my position with SeeNet. I stole the project from you, and I didn't deserve it. That was wrong, and I'm sorry.* Instead, I offered her participation in *Violet Mosala* in whatever role now suited her, on whatever terms we could agree were mutually fair.

I signed off, expecting to feel at least some small measure of relief from this belated attempt to make amends. Instead, a powerful sense of unease descended on me. I looked around the brightly lit lobby, staring at the dazzling patches of sunshine on the ornately patterned gold-and-white floor – Stateless-spartan as ever – as if hoping that the light itself might flood in through my eyes and clear the fog of panic from my brain.

It didn't.

I sat with my head in my hands, unable to make sense of the dread I felt. *Things weren't that desperate.* I was still in the dark about far too much – but less so than four days ago.

I was making progress, wasn't I?

I was staying afloat.

Barely.

The space around me seemed to expand. The lobby, the sunlit floor, retreated – an infinitesimal shift, but it was impossible to ignore. I glanced down at my notepad clock, light-headed with fear; Mosala's lecture was due to end in three minutes, but the time seemed to stretch out ahead of me, an uncrossable void. I had to make contact with someone, or something.

Before I could change my mind, I had **Hermes** call **Caliban**, a front end for a hacking consortium. An androgynous grinning face appeared – mutating and flowing, changing its features second-by-second as it spoke; only the whites of its eyes stayed constant, as if peering out from behind an infinitely malleable mask.

'Bad weather coming down, petitioner. There's ice on the signal wires.' Snow began to swirl around the faces; their skin tones favoured greys and blues. 'Nothing's clear, nothing's easy.'

'Spare me the hype.' I transmitted Sarah Knight's communications number. 'What can you tell me about that, for . . . one hundred dollars?'

Caliban leered. 'The Styx is frozen solid.' Frost formed on its various lips and eyelashes.

'A hundred and fifty.' **Caliban** seemed unimpressed – but **Hermes** flashed up a window showing a credit transfer request; I okayed it, reluctantly.

A screenful of green text, mockingly out-of-focus, appeared to illuminate the software faces. 'The number belongs to Sarah Alison Knight, Australian citizen, primary residence 17E Parade Avenue, Lindfield, Sydney. En-fem, date-of-birth 4 April, 2028.'

'I know all that, you useless shit. Where is she now – precisely? And when did she last accept a call, in person?'

The green text faded, and **Caliban** shivered. 'Wolves are howling on the steppes. Underground rivers are turning to glaciers.'

I restrained myself from wasting more invective. 'I'll give you fifty.'

'Veins of solid ice beneath the rock. Nothing moves, nothing changes.'

I gritted my teeth. 'A hundred.' My research budget was vanishing fast – and this had nothing to do with *Violet Mosala*. But I had to know.

Orange symbols danced across grey flesh. **Caliban** announced, 'Our Sarah last accepted a call – in person, on this number – in the central metropolitan footprint for Kyoto, Japan, at 10.23.14 Universal Time, on 26 March, 2055.'

'And where is she now?'

'No device has connected to the net under this ID since the stated call.' Meaning: she hadn't used her notepad to contact anyone, or to access any service. She hadn't so much as viewed a news bulletin, or downloaded a three-minute music video. Unless . . .

'Fifty bucks – take it or leave it – for her new communications number.'

Caliban took it, and smiled. 'Bad guess. She has no new number, no new account.'

I said numbly, 'That's all. Thank you.'

Caliban mimed astonishment at this unwarranted courtesy, and blew me a parting kiss. 'Call again. And remember, petitioner: data *wants* to be free!'

Why Kyoto? The only connection I could think of was Yasuko Nishide. Meaning what? She'd still planned to cover the Einstein Conference, after all – but with a rival profile of a rival theorist? And the only reason she wasn't yet on Stateless was Nishide's illness?

Why the communications blackout, though? Kuwale's grim unspoken conclusion made no sense. Why would biotech interests want to harm Sarah Knight, if she'd shown every sign of abandoning Violet Mosala for another – thoroughly apolitical – physicist?

People began to cross the lobby, talking excitedly. I looked up. The auditorium down the corridor was emptying. Mosala and Helen Wu emerged together; I met up with them.

Mosala was beaming. 'Andrew! You missed all the fun! Serge Bischoff just released a new algorithm which is going to save me *days* of computer time!'

Wu frowned and corrected her. 'Save *all of us* days, please!'

'Of course.' Mosala stage-whispered to me, 'Helen still doesn't realise that she's on my side, whether she likes it or not.' She added, 'I have a summary of the lecture, if you want to see it?'

I said tonelessly, 'No.' I realised how blunt that sounded, but I felt so spaced out, so disconnected, that I really didn't care. Mosala gave me a curious look, more concerned than angry.

Wu left us. I asked Mosala, 'Have you heard any more about Nishide?'

'Ah.' She became serious. 'It seems he's not going to make it to the conference, after all. His secretary contacted the organisers; he's had to be hospitalised. It's pneumonia again.' She added sadly, 'If this keeps up . . . I don't know. He may retire altogether.'

I closed my eyes; the floor began to tilt. A distant voice asked, 'Are you all right? Andrew?' I pictured my face, glowing white hot.

I opened my eyes. And I thought I finally understood what was happening.

I said, 'Can I talk to you? Please?'

'Of course.'

Sweat began running down my cheeks. 'Don't lose your temper. Just hear me out.'

Mosala leant forward, frowning. She hesitated, then put a

hand on my forehead. 'You're burning up. You need to see a doctor, straight away.'

I screamed at her hoarsely. 'Just listen! *Listen to me!*'

People around us were staring. Mosala opened her mouth, outraged, ready to put me in my place – but then she changed her mind. 'Go ahead. I'm listening.'

'You need blood tests, a full . . . micropathology report . . . everything. You're asymptomatic, now, but . . . however you feel . . . *do it* . . . there's no way of knowing what the incubation period might be.' I was dripping sweat, and swaying on my feet; every breath felt like a lungful of fire. 'What did you think they were going to do? Send in a hit squad with machine guns? I doubt . . . I was meant to get sick . . . at all . . . but the thing must have mutated on the way. Keyed to your genome . . . but the lock fell off, en route.' I laughed. 'In my blood. In my brain.'

I sagged, and dropped to my knees. A convulsion passed through my whole body, like a peristaltic spasm trying to squeeze the flesh right out of my skin. People around me were shouting, but I couldn't make out what they were saying. I struggled to lift my head – but when I succeeded, briefly, black and purple bruises flowered across my vision.

I stopped fighting it. I closed my eyes and lay down on the cool, welcoming tiles.

In the hospital ward, for a long time, I paid no attention to my surroundings. I thrashed about in a knot of sweat-soaked sheets, and let the world remain mercifully out of focus. I sought no information from the people around me; in my delirium, I believed I had all the answers.

Ned Landers was behind everything. When we met, he'd infected me with one of his secret viruses. And now, because I'd travelled so far to escape it . . . although Helen Wu had proved that the whole world was nothing but a loop, and everything led back to the same point . . . now I was coming down with Landers' secret weapon against Violet Mosala, Andrew Worth, and all his other enemies.

I was coming down with Distress.

A tall Fijian man dressed in white poked a drip into my elbow. I tried to shake it out; he held me still. I muttered triumphantly, 'Don't you know there's no point? There's no cure!' Distress was nowhere near as bad as I'd imagined. I wasn't screaming like the woman in Miami, was I? I was nauseous and feverish – but I felt sure that I was headed for some form of beautiful, painless oblivion. I smiled up at the man. 'I'm gone forever now! I've gone away!'

He said, 'I don't think so. I think you've been there, and you're coming back.'

I shook my head defiantly, but then cried out in surprise and pain. My bowels had gone into spasm, and I was emptying them, uncontrollably, into a pan I hadn't even noticed beneath me. I tried to stop. I couldn't. But it wasn't the incontinence that horrified me, as much as the consistency. This wasn't diarrhoea; it was water.

The motion stopped eventually, but I kept shuddering.

I pleaded for an explanation. 'What's happening to me?'

'You have cholera. Drug-resistant cholera. We can control the fever, and keep you hydrated – but the disease is going to have to run its course. So you're in for a long haul.'

19

As the first wave of delirium subsided, I tried to assess my position dispassionately, to arm myself with the facts. I was not an infant, I was not old. I was not suffering from malnutrition, parasite infestation, an impaired immune system, or any other complicating factor. I was in the care of qualified people. My condition was being monitored constantly by sophisticated machines.

I told myself that I was not going to die.

Fever and nausea, absent in 'classical' cholera, meant that I had the Mexico City biotype – first seen in the aftermath of the quake of '15, long since distributed globally. It entered the bloodstream as well as the gut, producing a wider range of symptoms, a greater risk to health. Nevertheless, millions of people survived it every year – often in much worse circumstances: without antipyritics to control the fever, without intravenous electrolytes, without any antibiotics at all – making drug resistance academic. In the largest metropolitan hospitals, in Santiago or Bombay, the particular strain of *Vibrio cholerae* could be sequenced completely, and a *de novo* drug designed and synthesised in a matter of hours. Most people who contracted the disease, though, had no prospect whatsoever of receiving this luxurious miracle cure. They simply lived through the rise and fall of the bacterial empire inside them. They rode it out.

I could do the same.

There was only one small flaw in this clear-eyed, optimistic scenario: most people had no reason to suspect that their guts were full of a genetic weapon which had detonated one step short of its target. Engineered to mimic a natural strain of cholera as closely as possible – but engineered to push the envelope of plausible symptoms far enough to kill a healthy, twenty-seven-year-old woman, receiving the best care that Stateless could provide.

The ward was clean, bright, spacious, quiet. I spent most of my time screened off from the other patients, but the white translucent partitions let the daylight through – and even when my skin was on fire, the faint touch of radiant warmth reaching my body was strangely comforting, like a familiar embrace.

By late afternoon on the first day, the antipyritics seemed to be working. I watched the graph on the bedside monitor; my temperature was still pathological, but the immediate risk of brain damage had passed. I tried to swallow liquids, but nothing stayed down – so I moistened my parched lips and throat, and let the intravenous drip do the rest.

Nothing could stop the cramps and the bowel spasms. When they came, it was like demonic possession, like being ridden by a voodoo god: an obscene bear-hug by something powerful and alien constricting inside my flesh. I couldn't believe that any muscle in my own rag-doll body could still be so strong. I tried to stay calm – to accept each brutal convulsion as inevitable, to keep my mind fixed on the sure and certain knowledge that *this too would pass* – but every time, the surge of nausea swept away my laboriously composed stoicism like a house of matchsticks beneath a tidal wave, and left me shuddering and sobbing, convinced that I was finally dying, and half believing that that was what I wanted more than anything else: instant release.

My melatonin patch had been removed; the abyssal sleep it generated was too dangerous, now. But I couldn't begin to tell the difference between the erratic rhythms of melatonin withdrawal, and my otherwise natural state: long stretches of half-sensate paralytic stupor, broken up by brief, violent dreams – and moments of panic-stricken clarity each time I believed my intestines were about to rupture and wash out of me in a red and grey tide.

I told myself that I was stronger and more patient than the disease. Generations of bacteria could come and go; all I had to do was hang on. All I had to do was outlive them.

On the morning of the second day, Mosala and De Groot came to visit. They seemed like time travellers to me; my previous life on Stateless had already receded into the distant past.

Mosala seemed shocked by my appearance. She said gently, 'I've taken your advice; I've been examined thoroughly. I'm not infected, Andrew. I've spoken to your doctor, and he thinks you must have caught this from food on the plane.'

I croaked, 'Has anyone else, on the same flight—?'

'No. But one sealed package might have missed being irradiated, and ended up imperfectly sterilised. It can happen.'

I didn't have the strength to argue. And this theory made a certain amount of sense: a random glitch had breached the technological barrier between Third World and First, momentarily scrambling the impeccable free-market logic of employing the cheapest caterers on the planet and then blasting away the risks with an equally cheap burst of gamma rays.

That evening, my temperature began rising again. Michael – the Fijian man who'd greeted me when I first woke, and who'd since explained that he was 'both doctor and nurse, if you insist on using those archaic foreign words here' – sat by my bed for most of the night . . . or at least, he was there in the flesh during every brief window of lucidity I experienced; the rest of the time, for all I knew, I hallucinated his presence.

I slept three straight hours from dawn to mid-morning – long enough for my first coherent dream. Clawing my way up towards consciousness, I clung defiantly to the happy ending: *The disease had run its course, it had burned itself out. My symptoms had vanished. Gina had even flown in overnight – to take me back, to take me home.*

I'd been woken by an intense cramp. I was soon expelling grey water full of intestinal mucus, gasping obscenities, wanting to die.

In the late afternoon, with the sunlit ward behind the screens as vague and luminous as heaven – re-enacting the same convulsions for the thousandth time, shitting out, yet again, every last drop of fluid the drip had fed into me – I found myself emitting a keening noise, baring my teeth and shivering, like a dog, like a sick hyena.

Early on the fourth day, my fever almost vanished. Everything which had come before seemed like an anaesthetised nightmare, violent and frightening but inconsequential – a dream sequence shot through gauze.

A merciless grey solidity clung to everything in sight. The screens around me were caked with dust. The sheets were stained yellow from dried sweat. My skin was coated with slime. My lips, my tongue, my throat, were cracked and stinging, sloughing dead cells and seeping a thin discharge which tasted more like salt than blood. Every muscle from my diaphragm to my groin felt injured, useless, tortured beyond repair – but tensed like an animal flinching from a rain of blows, ready for more. The joints of my knees felt as if I'd been crouching for a week on cold, hard ground.

The cramps, the spasms, began again. I'd never been so lucid; they'd never been worse.

I had no patience left. All I wanted to do was rise to my feet and walk out of the hospital, leaving my body behind. Flesh and bacteria could fight it out between themselves; I'd lost interest.

I tried. I closed my eyes and pictured it. I willed it to

254

happen. I wasn't delirious – but walking away from this pointless, ugly confrontation seemed like such a sensible choice, such an obvious solution, that for a moment I suspended all disbelief.

And I finally understood, as I never had before – not through sex, not through food, not through the lost exuberant physicality of childhood, not from the pinpricks of a hundred petty injuries and instantly cured diseases – that this vision of escape was meaningless, a false arithmetic, an idiot dream.

This diseased body was my whole self. It was not a temporary shelter for some tiny, indestructible man-god living in the safe warm dark behind my eyes. From skull to putrid arsehole, this was the instrument of everything I'd ever do, ever feel, ever be.

I'd never believed otherwise—

—but I'd never really felt it, never really known it. I'd never before been forced to embrace the whole sordid, twitching, visceral truth.

Was this what Daniel Cavolini had learnt, when he tore away his blindfold? I stared up at the ceiling, tense and shivering, claustrophobic, all the nausea and pain spread across my abdomen hardening into rigid bands like metal embedded in the flesh.

By noon, my temperature started climbing again. I was glad: I wanted delirium, I wanted confusion. Sometimes the fever flayed every nerve, magnified and sharpened every sensation – but I still hoped it might erase this new understanding, which was worse than the pain.

It didn't.

Mosala visited again. I smiled and nodded, but said nothing, and I couldn't concentrate on her words. The two screens either side of the bed remained in place, but the third had been moved aside, and when I raised my head I could see the patient opposite me, a forlorn skinny boy with a drip, his parents beside him. His father was reading to him quietly; his mother held his hand. The whole tableau seemed impossibly distant, separated from me by an unbridgeable gulf; I couldn't imagine ever again having the power to climb to my feet and walk five metres.

Mosala left. I drifted.

Then I noticed someone standing near the foot of the bed, and an electric jolt ran through my body. A shock of transcendental awe.

Striding through unforgiving reality: an angel.

Janet Walsh turned, half towards me. I raised myself up on my elbows and called out to her, terrified, enraptured. 'I think I understand now. Why you do it. Not how . . . but why.'

She looked straight at me, mildly puzzled, but unperturbed.

I said, 'Please talk to me. I'm ready to listen.'

Walsh frowned slightly, tolerant but uncomprehending, her wings fluttering patiently.

'I know I've offended you. I'm sorry. Can't you forgive me? I want to hear everything now. I want to understand how you make it work.'

She regarded me in silence.

I said, 'How do you lie about the world? And how do you make yourself believe it? How can you see the whole truth, *know the whole truth* . . . and go on pretending that none of it matters? What's the secret? What's the trick? *What's the magic?*'

My face was already burning white hot, but I leant forward, hoping that her sheer radiance might infect me with her great transforming insight.

'I'm trying! You have to believe I'm trying!' I looked away, suddenly at a loss for words, struck dumb by the ineffable mystery of her presence. Then a cramp seized me; the thing I could no longer pretend was a demon snake constricted inside me.

I said, 'But when the truth, the underworld, *the TOE* . . . reaches up, takes you in its fist, and *squeezes* . . .' I raised my own hand, meaning to demonstrate, but it was already clenched tight involuntarily. 'How do you ignore it? How do you deny it? How do you go on fooling yourself that you've ever stood above it, ever pulled the strings, ever run the show?'

Sweat was running into my eyes, blinding me. I brushed it away with my clenched fist, laughing. 'When every cell, every fucking *atom* in your body, burns the message into your skin: everything you value, everything you cherish, everything you live for . . . is just the scum on the surface of a vacuum thirty-five powers of ten deep – how do you go on lying? How do you close your eyes to *that*?'

I waited for her answer. Solace, redemption, were within my grasp. I held my arms out towards her in supplication.

Walsh smiled faintly, then walked on without saying a word.

I woke in the early hours of the morning. Burning up again, drenched in sweat.

Michael was sitting on the chair beside me, reading from his notepad. The whole ward was lit softly from above, but the light of the words shone up more brightly.

I whispered, 'Today I tried to become . . . everything I despise. But I couldn't even manage that.'

He put the notepad down, and waited for me to continue.

'I'm lost. I really am lost.'

Michael glanced at the bedside monitor, and shook his head. 'You're going to live through this. In a week, you won't even be able to imagine how you feel right now.'

'I'm not talking about the cholera. I'm having—' I laughed; it hurt. 'I'm having what Mystical Renaissance would call a *spiritual crisis*. And I have nowhere to turn to for comfort. Nowhere to turn to for strength. No lover, no family, no nation. No religion, no ideology. Nothing.'

Michael said calmly, 'Then you're lucky. I envy you.'

I gaped at him, appalled by this heartlessness.

He said, 'Nowhere to bury your head. Like an ostrich on reef-rock. I envy you. You might learn something.'

I had no reply to that. I started shivering; I was sweating and aching, but icy cold. 'I take back what I said about the cholera. It's fifty-fifty. I'm being equally fucked by both.'

Michael put his hands behind his neck and stretched, then re-arranged himself on the chair. 'You're a journalist. Do you want to hear a story?'

'Don't you have some vital medical work to do?'

'I'm doing it.'

Waves of nausea began sweeping up from my bowels. 'Okay, I'll listen. If you'll let me record. What's this story about?'

He grinned. 'My own *spiritual crisis*, of course.'

'I should have guessed.' I closed my eyes and invoked **Witness**. The whole action was instinctive, and it was over in half a second – but when it was done, I was shocked. I felt like I was on the verge of disintegrating . . . but this machinery – as much a part of me as anything organic – still worked perfectly.

He began, 'When I was a child, my parents used to take me to the most beautiful church in the world.'

'I've heard that line before.'

'This time it's true. The Reformed Methodist Church in Suva. It was a huge, white building. It looked plain from the outside – austere as a barn. But it had a row of stained-glass windows, showing scenes from the scriptures, carved by a computer in sky blue, rose and gold. Every wall was lined with a hundred kinds of flowers – hibiscus, orchids, lilies – piled up to the roof. And the pews were always crammed with people; everyone wore their finest, brightest clothes, everyone sang, everyone smiled. It was like stepping straight into heaven. Even the sermons were beautiful: no hell-fire, only comfort and joy. No ranting about sin and damnation: just some modest suggestions about kindness, charity, love.'

I said, 'Sounds perfect. What happened? Did God send a Greenhouse storm to put an end to all this blasphemous happiness and moderation?'

'Nothing happened to the church. It's still there.'

'But you parted company? Why?'

'I took the scriptures too literally. They said put away childish things. So I did.'

'Now you're being facetious.'

He hesitated. 'If you really want to know the precise escape route . . . it all started with just one parable. Have you heard the story of the widow's mite?'

'Yes.'

'For years, as a schoolboy, I turned it over and over in my head. The poor widow's small gift was more precious than the rich man's large one. Okay. Fine. I understood the message. I could see the dignity it gave to every act of charity. But I could see a whole lot more encoded in that parable, and those other things wouldn't go away.

'I could see a religion which cared more about feeling good than doing good. A religion which valued the pleasure of giving – or the pain – more than any tangible effect. A religion which put . . . *saving your own soul through good works* far above their worldly consequences.

'Maybe I was reading too much into one story. But if it hadn't started there, it would have started somewhere else. My religion was beautiful – but I needed more than that. I demanded more. It had to be true. And it wasn't.'

He smiled sadly, and raised his hands, let them fall. I thought I could see the loss in his eyes, I thought I understood.

He said, 'Growing up with faith is like growing up with crutches.'

'But you threw away your crutches and walked?'

'No. I threw away my crutches and fell flat on my face. All the strength had gone into the crutches – I had none of my own. I was nineteen when it finally all fell apart for me. The end of adolescence is the perfect age for an existential crisis, don't you think? You've left yours awfully late.'

My face burned with humiliation. Michael reached over and touched my shoulder. He said, 'I've had a long shift, my judgement's slipping. I'm not trying to be cruel.' He laughed. 'Listen to me, spouting "season for everything" bullshit – like the Edenites meet Il Duce: *Get those emotional trains running on time!*' He leant back, and ran a hand through his hair. 'But I *was* nineteen, there's no getting around it. And I'd lost God. What can I say? I read Sartre, I read Camus, I read Nietzsche—'

I winced. Michael was puzzled. 'You have a problem with *Friedrich*?'

The cramp tightened. I replied through gritted teeth, 'Not at all. All the best European philosophers went mad and committed suicide.'

'Exactly. And I read them all.'

'And?'

He shook his head, smiling, embarrassed. 'For a year or so . . . I really believed it: *Here I am, staring into the abyss with Nietzsche.* Here I am, on the brink of insanity, entropy, meaninglessness: the Enlightenment's unspeakable godless rational damnation. One wrong step, and I'll go spiralling down.'

He hesitated. I watched him closely, suddenly suspicious. *Was he making this up as he went along? A little improvised Care-for-the-Whole Patient routine?* And even if he wasn't . . . we'd had different lives, different histories. What use was any of this to me?

I listened, though.

'But I didn't go spiralling down. Because there is no *abyss*. There *is no* yawning chasm waiting to swallow us up, when we learn that there is no god, that we're animals like any other animal, that the universe has no purpose, that our souls are made of the same stuff as water and sand.'

I said,' There are two thousand cultists on this island who believe otherwise.'

Michael shrugged. 'What do you expect from moral flat-Earthers, if not fear of falling? If you desperately, passionately want to plummet into the abyss, of course it's possible – but only if you work hard. Only if you will the entire thing into being. Only if you manufacture every last centimetre of it, on your way down.

'I don't believe that honesty leads to madness. I don't believe we need delusions to stay sane. I don't believe the truth is strewn with booby-traps, waiting to swallow up anyone who *thinks too much*. There is nowhere to fall – not unless you stand there digging the hole.'

I said, 'You fell, didn't you? When you lost your faith.'

'Yes – but how far? What have I become? A serial killer? A torturer?'

'I sincerely hope not. But you lost a lot more than "childish things", didn't you? What about all those stirring sermons on kindness, charity and love?'

Michael laughed softly. 'And the least of these is *faith*. What makes you think I've lost anything? I've stopped pretending that the things I value are locked up in some magical vault called "God" – outside the universe, outside time, outside myself. That's all. I don't need beautiful lies anymore, just to make the decisions I want to make, to try to live a life I think is good. If the truth *had* taken those things away . . . I could never really have had them in the first place.

'And I still clean up your shit, don't I? I still tell you stories at three in the morning. If you want greater miracles than that, you're out of luck.'

Whether it was genuine autobiography, or just a slick piece of *ad hoc* therapy, Michael's story began to undermine my panic and claustrophobia. His arguments made too much sense to me; they sliced through my self-pity like a hot wire. If the universe itself wasn't a cultural construct, the grey terror I felt from seeing myself as a part of it certainly was. I'd never had the honesty to embrace the molecular nature of my own existence – but then, the whole society I'd inhabited had been equally coy. The reality had always been glossed over, censored, ignored. I'd spent thirty-six years in a world still infested with lingering dualism, with tacit dumb spirituality, where every movie, every song, still wailed about the immortal soul . . . while everyone swallowed designer drugs predicated on pure materialism. No wonder the truth had come as a shock.

The abyss – like everything else – was understandable. I lost interest in digging myself a hole.

Vibrio cholerae declined to follow my example.

I lay curled on my side, my notepad propped up against an extra pillow, while **Sisyphus** showed me what was happening inside me.

'The B subunit of the choleragen molecule binds to the surface of the intestinal mucosal cell; the A subunit detaches and traverses the membrane. This catalyses increased adenylate cyclase activity, which in turn raises the level of cyclic AMP, stimulating the secretion of sodium ions. The ordinary concentration gradient is reversed, and fluid is pumped in the wrong direction: out into the intestinal space.'

I watched the molecules interlocking, I watched the merciless random dance. *This was what I was* – whether it gave me any comfort to understand it or not. The same physics which had kept me alive for thirty-six years might or might not casually destroy me – but if I couldn't accept that simple, obvious truth, I had no business explaining the world to anyone. Solace and redemption could screw themselves. I'd been tempted by the Ignorance Cults – and maybe I half understood what drove them, now – but what did they have to offer, in the end? Alienation from reality. The universe as an unspeakable horror to be endlessly denied, shrouded in saccharine artificial mysteries, every truth subjugated to doublethink and fairy tales.

Fuck that. I was sick from too little honesty, not too much. Too many myths about the H-word, not too few. I would have been better prepared for the whole ordeal by a lifetime spent calmly facing the truth, than a lifetime spent rehearsing the most seductive denials.

I watched a schematic of the worst-case scenario. 'If anti-biotic-resistant, Mexico City *V. cholerae* succeed in crossing the blood-brain barrier, immunosuppressants can limit the fever – but bacterial toxins themselves are likely to cause irreversible damage.'

Mutant choleragen molecules fused with neural membranes. The cells collapsed like punctured balloons.

I still feared death as much as ever – but the truth had lost its sting. If the TOE had taken me in its fist and squeezed . . . at least it had proved that there was solid ground beneath me: the final law, the simplest pattern, holding up the world in all its strangeness.

I'd hit bottom. Once you'd touched the bedrock of the underworld, the foundations of the universe, there was nowhere else to fall.

I said, 'That's enough. Now find something to cheer me up.'

'How about the Beat poets?'

I smiled. 'Perfect.'

Sisyphus ransacked the libraries, and played them reading their own works. Ginsberg howling 'Moloch! Moloch!' Burroughs rasping 'A Junkie's Christmas' – all severed limbs in suitcases, and scoring the immaculate fix.

And best of all, Kerouac himself, wild and melodic, stoned and innocent: 'What If The Three Stooges Were Real?'

Afternoon sunlight slanted across the ward and brushed the side of my face, bridging distance, energy, scale, complexity.

This was not a reason for terror. It was not a reason for awe. It was the most ordinary thing imaginable.

I was as ready as I'd ever be. I closed my eyes.

Someone prodded my shoulder, and said for the fourth or fifth time, 'Wake up, please.'

I'd lost all choice in the matter. I opened my eyes.

A young woman stood beside me, no one I'd seen before. She had serious, dark brown eyes. Olive skin, long black hair. She spoke with a German accent.

'Drink this.' She held out a small vial of clear liquid.

'I can't keep anything down. Didn't they tell you?'

'This, you will.'

I was past caring; vomiting was as natural to me as breathing. I took the vial and tipped the contents down my throat. My oesophagus spasmed, and acid hit the roof of my mouth – but nothing more.

I coughed. 'Why didn't someone offer me that sooner?'

'It only just arrived.'

'From where?'

'You don't want to know.'

I blinked at her. My head cleared slightly. 'Arrived? What kind of drug wouldn't be in stock already?'

'What do you think?'

The flesh at the base of my spine went cold. 'Am I dreaming? Or am I dead?'

'Akili had samples of your blood smuggled out to . . . a certain country, and analysed by friends. You just swallowed a set of magic bullets for every stage of the weapon. You'll be on your feet in a matter of hours.'

My head throbbed. *The weapon.* My worst fear had just been confirmed and banished in the same sentence; it was disorienting. 'Every *stage*? What would have come next? What have I missed out on?'

'You don't want to know.'

'I think you're right.' I still wasn't convinced that any of this was happening. 'Why? Why did Akili go to all that trouble just to save me?'

'We had to find out exactly what you were carrying. Violet Mosala might still be at risk, even though she's showing no symptoms. We had to have a cure for her, ready, here on the island.'

I absorbed that. At least she hadn't said: *We don't care who is or isn't the Keystone. We're all prepared to risk our lives to protect just about anyone.*

'So what was I carrying? And why did it detonate prematurely?'

The young AC frowned solemnly. 'We still haven't worked out all the details – but the timing fell apart. It looks like the bacteria generated confused internal signals, due to a disparity between intracellular molecular clocks and the host's biochemical cues. The melatonin receptors were choked, saturated—' She stopped, alarmed. 'I don't understand. Why are you laughing?'

By the time I left the hospital, on Tuesday morning, I had my strength back – and I was enraged. The conference was half over, but TOEs were no longer the story – and if Sarah Knight, for whatever unfathomable reasons, had abandoned the war over Mosala to sit by Yasuko Nishide's bedside, incommunicado . . . I'd finally have to start unravelling the whole complicated truth for myself.

Back in my hotel room, I plugged in my umbilical fibre, passed Kuwale's eighteen mug shots to **Witness**, and flagged them for constant real-time search.

I called Lydia. 'I need five thousand dollars extra for research: database access and hacking fees. More is going on here than I can begin to describe. And if you don't agree that it's worth every cent in a week's time, I'll refund it all.'

We argued for fifteen minutes. I improvised; I dropped

misleading hints about PACDF and an impending political storm, but I said nothing about Mosala's planned emigration. In the end, Lydia caved in. I was astonished.

I used the software Kuwale had given me to send ver a deep-encrypted message. 'No, I haven't spotted one of your goons. But if you expect any more help from me – beyond acting as a living culture medium – you're going to have to give me all the details: who these people are, who employed them, your analysis of the weapon . . . everything. Take it or leave it. Meet me at the same place as last time, in an hour.'

I sat back and took stock of what I knew, what I believed. *Biotech weapons, biotech interests?* Whether or not that was true, the boycott itself had almost killed me. I'd always seen both sides of the gene patent laws, I'd always been equally suspicious of the corporations and the renegades – but now the symmetry was broken. I had a long history of apathy and ambivalence – and I was ashamed to admit that it had taken so much to politicise me – but now I was ready to embrace *technolibération*, I was ready to do everything I could to expose Mosala's enemies and help her cause.

The Beach Boys never lied, though. I couldn't believe that a weapon from EnGeneUity and their allies would have failed because of anything as simple as my distorted melatonin cycle. That sounded more like the work of brilliant, resourceful amateurs making do with limited knowledge, limited tools.

PACDF? The Ignorance Cults? Hardly.

Other *technolibérateurs*, who'd decided that Mosala's original scheme would benefit greatly from a Nobel-prize-winning martyr? Unaware that they were pitted against people who largely shared their goals – but who weren't merely averse to treating people as expendable, but had elevated the sacrificial celebrity in question to the status of creator of the universe?

There was an irony there, somewhere: the cool, pragmatic

realpolitik faction of *technolibération* seemed to be infinitely more fanatical than the quasi-religious Anthrocosmologists.

An irony, or a misunderstanding.

Kuwale's reply arrived while I was in the shower, scouring away the dead skin and the sour odour I'd been unable to remove in the hospital bathroom.

'The data you insist on seeing can't be unlocked at the place you've specified. Meet me at these coordinates.'

I checked a map of the island. There was no point arguing.

I dressed, and set out for the northern reefs.

PART THREE

20

The easiest way to travel beyond the tram lines turned out to be hitching a ride on one of the balloon-tyred trucks used to carry produce inland. The trucks were automated, and followed predetermined routes; people seemed to treat them as public transport, although the sea farmers effectively controlled the schedule by the delays they imposed, loading and unloading them. The bed of each truck was divided crosswise by a dozen low barriers, forming spaces into which crates were slotted, and doubling as benches for the passengers.

There was no sign of Kuwale; ve seemed to have found another route, or left for the rendezvous point much earlier. I sat with about twenty other people on the ride north-east from the terminus, resisting the urge to ask the woman beside me what would happen if one of the farmers insisted on loading so many crates that there was no room for anyone to return – or what discouraged passengers from looting the food. The harmony of Stateless still seemed precarious to me, but I was growing increasingly reluctant to give voice to questions which amounted to asking: Why don't you people all run amok, and make your own lives as miserable as possible?

I didn't believe for a moment that the rest of the planet could ever function like this – or that anyone on Stateless would particularly want it to – but I was beginning to understand Monroe's cautious optimism. If I lived here, myself, would I try to tear the place down? No. Would I bring about riots and massacres inadvertently, in pursuit of some short-term gain? Hopefully not. So, what ludicrous vanity allowed me to imagine that I was so much more reasonable or intelligent than the average resident of the island? If I could recognise the precariousness of their society, so could they – and act accordingly. It was an active balance, flying by wire, survival through self-awareness.

A tarpaulin sheltered the bed of the truck, but the sides were open. As we drew nearer to the coast, the terrain began to change: incursions of partly compacted coral appeared, moist and granular, glistening in the sun like rivers choked with powdery grey-and-silver snow. Entropy should have favoured the solid reef-rock banks dissolving into this sludge and washing away – but it favoured more strongly the flow of energy from the sun into the lithophilic bacteria infesting the coral debris, which laboured to stitch the loose aggregate of limestone into the denser polymer-mineral matrix around it. Cool, efficient biological pathways, catalysed by perfectly shaped enzymes like molecule-sized injection moulds, had always mocked the high-temperature-and-pressure industrial chemistry of the nineteenth and twentieth centuries. Here, they mocked geology itself. The conveyor belt of subduction, feeding ocean sediments deep into the earth to be crushed and metamorphised over eons, was as obsolete on Stateless as the Bessemer process for steel, the Haber process for ammonia.

The truck moved between two broad streams of crushed coral. In the distance, other streams widened and merged, the fingers of reef-rock between them narrowing then vanishing, until the land around us was more than half sludge. The part-digested coral grew coarser, the surface of the channels less even; glistening pools of water began to appear. I noticed occasional streaks of colour surviving within the bleached limestone – not the muted trace minerals of the city's masonry, but vivid, startling reds and oranges, greens and blues. The truck already stank of the ocean, but soon the breeze – which had been carrying the scent away – began to compound it.

Within minutes, the landscape was transformed. Vast

banks of living coral, inundated with ocean water, surrounded narrow, winding causeways. The reefs were dazzling, polychromatic; the algal symbionts living within the various species of coral-building polyps employed a rainbow of distinct photosynthetic pigments – and even from a distance I could make out wild variations of morphology between the mineralised skeletons of each colony: pebbled aggregates, riots of thick branched tubing, delicate fernlike structures – no doubt a pragmatic exercise in diversity for the sake of ecological robustness, as well as a deliberately opulent display of bioengineering virtuosity.

The truck stopped, and everyone else clambered off – except for the two people I'd seen shifting crates on to a freight tram back at the terminus. I hesitated, then followed the crowd; I had further to go, but I didn't want to attract attention.

The truck moved on. Most of the other passengers were carrying masks, snorkels, flippers; I wasn't sure if they were tourists or locals, but they all headed straight for the reefs. I wandered along with them, and stood for a while, watching, as they stepped gingerly out on to the half-protruding coral, heading for deeper water. Then I turned and strolled north along the shoreline, away from the divers.

I caught my first glimpse of the open ocean, still hundreds of metres ahead. There were a dozen small boats moored in the harbour – one of the six armpits of the giant starfish. The view from the air came back to me, fragile and exotic. *What exactly was I standing on? An artificial island? An ocean-going machine? A bioengineered sea monster?* The distinctions blurred into meaninglessness.

I caught up with the truck at the harbour; the two workers loading it glanced at me curiously, but didn't ask what I was doing here. My idleness made me feel like a trespasser; everyone else in sight was shifting crates or sorting seafood. There was machinery, but most of it was very low-tech: electric forklifts, but no giant cranes, no vast conveyor belts feeding processing plants; the reef-rock was probably too soft to support anything heavy. They could have built a floating platform out on the harbour to take the weight of a crane, but apparently no one felt it was worth the investment. Or maybe the farmers simply preferred it this way.

There was still no sign of Kuwale. I moved away from the loading bay and wandered closer to the water's edge. Biochemical signals diffusing out from the rock kept the harbour free from coral, and plankton transported sediment to the reefs where it was needed; the water here looked bottomless, deep blue-green. Amidst the froth of the gently breaking swell, I thought I could discern an unnatural effervescence; bubbles were rising up everywhere. The outgassing from the pressurised rock, which I'd seen – second hand – on the underside of Stateless, was escaping here to the surface.

Out on the harbour, farmers were winching aboard what might have been a fishing net bursting with produce. Gelatinous tendrils embracing the bounty glistened in the sun. One worker stretched up and touched the top of the 'net' with something on the end of a long pole, and the contents abruptly spilt on to the deck, leaving the slack tendrils quivering; within seconds, when the last scraps had fallen, the translucent creature was almost invisible. I had to strain my eyes to follow it, as they lowered it back into the ocean.

Kuwale said, 'Do you know what non-renegades pay Ocean Logic for a harvester like that? All its genes were taken straight from existing species – all the company ever did was patent them, and rearrange them.'

I turned. 'Spare me the propaganda. I'm on your side – if you'll give me some straight answers.'

Kuwale looked troubled, but said nothing. I spread my arms in a gesture of frustration. 'What do I have to do to convince you to trust me – as much as you trusted Sarah Knight? Do I have to die for the cause first?'

'I'm sorry you were infected. The wild type's bad enough; I know, I've had it.' Ve was wearing the same black T-shirt I'd seen ver in at the airport, flickering with random points of brightness. It suddenly struck me again just how young ve was: little more than half my age – and in at the deep end.

I said, begrudgingly, 'That wasn't your fault. And I'm grateful for what you did.' Even if saving my life wasn't the point.

Kuwale looked distinctly uncomfortable, as if I'd just showered ver with undeserved praise. I hesitated. 'It wasn't your fault, was it?'

'Not directly.'

'What's that supposed to mean? The weapon was yours?'

'No!' Ve looked away, and said bitterly, 'But I still have to take some responsibility for everything they do.'

'*Why?* Because they're not working for the biotech companies? Because they're *technolibérateurs*, like you?' Ve wouldn't meet my eyes; I felt a small surge of triumph. I'd finally got something right.

Kuwale replied impatiently, 'Of course they're *technolibérateurs*.' As if to say: Isn't everyone? 'But that's not why they're trying to kill Mosala.'

A man was walking towards us with a crate on his shoulder. As I glanced in his direction, red lines flashed up across my vision. He kept his face half-turned away from us, and a wide-brimmed hat concealed half of the rest, but **Witness** – reconstructing the hidden parts by symmetry and anatomical extrapolation rules – saw enough to be convinced.

I fell silent. Kuwale waited until the man was out of earshot, then said urgently, 'Who was it?'

'Don't ask me. You wouldn't give me any names to go with the faces, remember?' But I relented, and checked with the software. 'Number seven in your list, if that means anything to you.'

'What kind of swimmer are you?'

'Very mediocre. Why?'

Kuwale turned and dived into the harbour. I crouched by the edge of the water, and waited for ver to surface.

I called out, 'What are you doing, you lunatic? He's gone.'

'Don't follow me in yet.'

'I have no intention—'

Kuwale swam towards me. 'Wait until it's clear which one of us is doing better.' Ve held up vis right hand; I reached down and took it, and began to haul ver up; ve shook vis head impatiently. 'Leave me in, unless I start to falter.' Ve trod water. 'Immediate irrigation is the best way to remove some transdermal toxins – but for others, it's the worst thing you can do: it can drive the hydrophobic spearheads into the skin much faster.' Ve submerged completely, dragging me in up to the elbow, almost dislocating my shoulder.

When ve surfaced again, I said, 'What if it's a mixture of both?'

'Then we're fucked.'

I glanced towards the loading bay. 'I could go and get help.' In spite of everything I'd just been through – no doubt thanks to a passing stranger with an aerosol – part of me still flatly refused to believe in *invisible weapons*. Or maybe I just imagined that some principle of double jeopardy meant that the molecular world had no more power over me, no right to a second attempt to claim me. Our presumed assailant was walking calmly off into the distance; it was impossible to feel threatened.

Kuwale watched me anxiously. 'How are you feeling?'

'Fine. Except you're breaking my arm. This is insane.' My skin began to tingle. Kuwale groaned, a worst-expectations-come-true sound. 'You're turning blue. Get in.'

My face was growing numb, my limbs felt heavy. 'And drown? I don't think so.' My speech sounded slurred; I'd lost all feeling in my tongue.

'I'll hold you up.'

'*No*. Climb out and get help.'

'You don't have time.' Ve yelled towards the loading bay; vis cry sounded weak to me – either my hearing was fading, or ve'd inhaled enough of the toxin to affect vis voice. I tried turning my head to see if there was any response; I couldn't.

Cursing my stubborness, Kuwale raised verself up and dragged me over the edge.

I sank. I was paralysed and numb, unsure if we were still connected. The water would have been transparent if not for the air bubbles; it was like falling through flawed crystal. I desperately hoped that I wasn't inhaling – it seemed impossible to tell.

Bubbles drifted past my face in contradictory wavering streams, refusing to define the vertical. I tried to orient myself by the gradient of light, but the cues were ambiguous. All I could hear was my heart pounding – slowly, as if the toxin was blocking the pathways that should have had it racing in agitation. I had a weird sense of *déjà vu*; with no feeling in my skin, I felt no wetter than when I'd stood on dry land watching the image from the tunnel diver's camera. I was having a vicarious experience of my own body.

The bubbles suddenly blurred, accelerated. The turbulence around me grew brighter, then without warning my face emerged into the air, and all I could see was blue sky.

Kuwale shouted in my ear, 'Are you okay? I've got you now. Try to relax.' Ve sounded distant; all I could manage was an indignant grunt. 'A couple of minutes, and we should be safe. My lungs are affected, but I think that's passing.' I stared up into the unfathomable sky, drowning in reverse.

Kuwale splashed water over my face. I was improving; at least I could tell that I was swallowing most of it. I coughed angrily. My teeth started chattering; the water was colder than I'd imagined. 'Your friends are pathetic. One amateur burglar, caught out by a backup alarm. Cholera that gets confused by a melatonin patch. Toxins that wash off in seawater. Violet Mosala has nothing to fear.'

Someone grabbed my foot and dragged me under.

I counted five figures in wetsuits and scuba gear; they were all clad in polymer from ankles to wrists, and all wore gloves and hoods as well. *No skin exposed. Why?* I struggled weakly, but two divers held me tight, trying to thrust some kind of metal device into my face. I pushed it away.

The harvester emerged from the translucent distance, barely visible against the sunlit water, and I felt my first real shock of visceral fear. If they'd poisoned the tentacles – restored the natural gene to the engineered species – we were dead. I broke free long enough to turn and see the other three divers thrashing around Kuwale, trying to hold ver still.

One of my captors waved the device in front of me again. It was a regulator, attached to an air hose. I turned to stare at her; I could barely make out her expression through the faceplate, though **Witness** instantly recognised another target. The air hose led to a second tank on her back. I had no way of knowing what the tank contained – but if it was harmful, I was only minutes away from drowning anyway.

The diver's eyes seemed to say: *It's your decision. Take it or leave it.*

I looked around again. Kuwale's arms were tied behind vis back, and ve'd given in and accepted the unknown gas. I was still weak from the toxin, and short of breath. I had no chance of escaping.

I let them bind my hands together, then I opened my mouth and bit hard on the regulator tube. I sucked in air gratefully, reeling between panic and relief. If they'd wanted us dead, they would have run a fishing knife through our ribs by now – but I still wasn't ready for the alternative.

The harvester approached, and the divers swam forward to meet it, dragging us along. I wanted to shield my face with my hands, but I couldn't. The medusa's knot of transparent tentacles opened up around us, writhing like the pathological topologies of pre-space, like the vacuum come to life.

Then the net closed tight.

21

The harvester's toxins were enervating, but not painful. If anything, they made the ride more bearable: relaxing muscles tensed in revulsion and claustrophobia, dulling the sense of being eaten alive. The creature was probably just a commercial species, not the privately engineered weapon I'd imagined. Belatedly, I started recording; my eyes stung from the salt, but closing them gave me vertigo. I could see Kuwale and the divers guarding ver, blurred as if through frosted glass. Pacified by the toxins, cocooned in translucent jelly, we moved through the bright water.

I pictured us being winched into the air and dropped unceremoniously on to the deck, like the catch I'd seen disgorged earlier. Instead, someone relaxed the harvester with a hormonal wand while we were still in the water, and the divers hauled us up over the side, climbing rope ladders. On deck, **Witness** matched three more faces. No one spoke to us, and I was still too spaced out to compose an intelligent question. The woman who'd offered me the regulator bound my feet together, then tied my hands, already joined, to Kuwale's, linking us back-to-back. Another of the divers took away our notepads, wrapped a length of (non-living) fishing net around us – threading it under our arms – then hooked it to the winch and lowered us into an empty hold. When they closed the hatch, we were in total darkness.

I felt my biochemical stupor lifting; the odour of decaying seaweed seemed to help. I waited for Kuwale to volunteer an assessment of our situation; after several minutes of silence, I said, 'You know all their faces; they know all your communications codes. Now tell me who's winning the intelligence war.'

Ve shifted irritably. 'I'll tell you this much: I don't think they'll harm us. They're moderates; they just want us out of the way.'

'While they do what?'

'Kill Mosala.'

My head swam from the stench; the smelling-salts effect had outlived its usefulness and gone into reverse. 'If moderates want to kill Mosala, what do the extremists have in mind?'

Kuwale didn't answer.

I stared out into the blackness. Back on the docks, ve'd insisted that the threat to Mosala had nothing to do with *technolibération*. I said, 'Do you want to clear up one small point of Anthrocosmological doctrine for me?'

'No.'

'If Mosala dies before becoming the Keystone . . . nothing happens, nothing changes. Right? Someone else will take her place – eventually – or we wouldn't even be here to talk about it.'

No reply.

'Yet you still feel responsible for keeping her safe? *Why?*' I cursed myself silently; the answer had been staring me in the face ever since I'd spoken to Amanda Conroy. 'These people are *not* the political enemies of someone who just happens to be a potential Keystone, are they? They're a walking affront to every mainstream Anthrocosmologist – because they've stolen your ideas, and pushed them to their logical conclusion. They're AC, just like you, except that they've decided they don't *want* Violet Mosala as creator of the universe.'

Kuwale responded venomously, 'It's no "logical conclusion". Trying to choose the Keystone is insanity. The universe exists because the Keystone is *given*. Would you try to change the Big Bang?'

'No. But this act of creation still hasn't happened, has it?'

'That makes no difference. Time is a part of what is created. The universe exists – now – because the Keystone *will create it*.'

I persisted, 'But there's still room left to change things, isn't there? No one knows yet exactly which TOE is true.'

Kuwale shifted again; I could feel vis body grow rigid with anger. 'That's the wrong way to look at it! The Keystone is given! The TOE is fixed!'

I said, 'Don't waste your breath defending the mainstream to me. I think you're all equally braindead; I'm just trying to come to grips with the more dangerous version. Don't you think I have a right to know what we're up against?'

I could hear ver breathing slowly, trying to calm verself. Then ve explained, reluctantly: 'They believe that the identity of the Keystone is determined, preordained . . . along with everything else in history, including the killing of any "rivals". But determinism doesn't take away the illusion of power – have you ever known an Islamic fatalist to be passive? It's not as if the hand of God is going to reach out of the sky and make sure that they spare the Keystone – or some improbable conspiracy of fate will frustrate them, if they go after the wrong physicist. There's no need for supernatural intervention, when the whole universe and everyone in it is just a conspiracy to explain the Keystone's existence. Whoever they murder, for whatever reason, they can't *get it wrong*.

'So . . . if they kill all the rivals of the theorist with the TOE they favour, then *that TOE* must be the one that brings the universe into being. And whether they've really chosen anything or not, the result is the same. The TOE they want, and the TOE they get, end up being identical.'

It hit me, belatedly. 'And they're in Kyoto, too? You think they got to Nishide – that's why he's sick? And they got to Sarah, before she could expose them?'

'Most likely.'

'Have you told the Kyoto police? Do you have people, there—?' I stopped; ve could hardly discuss countermeasures, when we were almost certainly being monitored. I said wearily, 'What's so wonderful about Buzzo's TOE, anyway?'

Kuwale was derisive. 'They think it leaves open a chance of access to other universes, seeded from pre-space by other Big Bangs. Mosala and Nishide both rule that out completely; other universes might still exist, but they're unreachable. Black holes, wormholes, in their TOEs, all lead back to this one cosmos.'

'And they're willing to kill Mosala and Nishide – because one *universe* isn't enough for them?'

Kuwale protested sardonically, 'Think of the infinite riches we'd be throwing away if we chose a self-contained cosmos. Take a long-term perspective. Where would we flee to, when the Big Crunch came? One or two lives is a small price to pay for the future of all humanity, isn't it?'

I thought of Ned Landers again, trying to step outside the human race, in order to take control of it. You couldn't *step outside* the universe – but out-explaining every TOE theorist with Anthrocosmology, and then playing choose-your-own-creator, came close.

Kuwale said despondently, 'Maybe Mosala is right to despise us, if this is where our ideas have led.'

I wasn't going to argue. 'Does she know? That there are ACs who want to kill her?'

'She does and she doesn't.'

'Meaning what?'

'We've tried to warn her. But she loathes even the mainstream so passionately that she won't take the threat seriously. I think she thinks . . . bad ideas can't touch her. If Anthrocosmology is nothing but superstition, it has no power to harm her.'

'Tell that to Giordano Bruno.' My eyes were adapting to

the darkness; I could see a faint strip of light on the floor of the hold in the distance.

I said, 'Have I missed something – or have we been talking all this time about the people you call *moderates*?' Kuwale didn't reply, but I felt ver move – slumping forward, as if in a final surrender to shame. 'What do the extremists believe? Break it to me gently, but break it to me now. I don't want any more surprises.'

Kuwale confessed miserably, 'You might say they . . . hybridised with the Ignorance Cults. They're still ACs, in the broadest sense: they believe that the universe is *explained into being*. But they believe it's possible – and desirable – to have a universe without any TOE at all: without a final equation, a unifying pattern. No deepest level, no definitive laws, no unbreakable proscriptions. No end to the possibility of *transcendence*.

'But the only way to guarantee that . . . is to slaughter everyone who might become the Keystone.'

My clothes seemed to reach an equilibrium with the hold's moist air at the most uncomfortable level of dampness possible. I needed to urinate, but I held off for the sake of dignity – hoping that I'd be able to judge correctly when the problem became life-threatening. I thought of the astronomer Tycho Brahe, who'd died after rupturing his bladder during a banquet, because he was too embarrassed to ask to be excused.

The strip of light on the floor didn't move, but it grew slowly brighter, and then dim again, as the hours wore on. The sounds reaching the hold meant little to me; random creaking and clanking, muffled voices and footsteps. There were distant hums and throbbing noises, some constant, some intermittent; no doubt the most casual boating enthusiast could have discerned the signature of an MHD engine, propelling a jet of seawater backwards with superconducting magnets – but I couldn't have picked the difference between maximum thrust and a crew member taking a shower.

I said, 'How does anyone ever become an Anthrocosmologist, when no one knows you exist?'

Kuwale didn't answer; I nudged ver with my shoulder.

'I'm awake.' Ve sounded more dispirited than I was.

'Then talk to me, I'm going out of my mind. How do you find new members?'

'There are net discussion groups, dealing with related ideas: fringe cosmology, information metaphysics. We take part – without revealing too much – but we approach people individually if they seem sympathetic and trustworthy. Someone, somewhere, re-invents Anthrocosmology two or three times a year. We don't try to persuade anyone that it's true – but if they reach the same conclusions for themselves, we let them know that there are others.'

'And the non-mainstream do the same? Pluck people off the nets?'

'No. They're all defectors. They all used to be with the rest of us.'

'Ah.' No wonder the mainstream felt such a strong obligation to protect Mosala. Mainstream Anthrocosmologists had literally recruited her would-be murderers.

Kuwale said quietly, 'It's sad. Some of them really do see themselves as the ultimate *technolibérateurs*: taking science into their own hands, refusing to be steam-rollered by someone else's theory – refusing to have no say in the matter.'

'Yeah, very democratic. Have they ever thought of holding an election for the Keystone, instead of killing off all the rival candidates to their own pretender?'

'And give up all that power, themselves? I don't think so. Muteba Kazadi had a "democratic" version of Anthrocosmology which didn't involve murdering anyone. No one could understand it, though. And I don't think he ever got the mathematics to work.'

I laughed, astonished. '*Muteba Kazadi* was AC?'

'Of course.'

'I don't think Violet Mosala knows that.'

'I don't think *Violet Mosala* knows anything she doesn't want to.'

'Hey, show some respect for your deity.'

The boat lurched slightly. 'Are we moving? Or did we just stop?' Kuwale shrugged. Adaptive ballast smoothed the ride so thoroughly that it was almost impossible to judge what was going on; I'd felt no wave motion in all the time we'd been on board, let alone the subtle accelerations of the journey.

I said, 'Do you know any of these people, personally?'

'No. They all left the mainstream before I joined.'

'So you can't really be sure how *moderate* they are?'

'I'm sure of the faction they belong to. And if they were going to kill us, we'd be dead.'

'There must be good and bad places for disposing of corpses. Points where illegal discharge is least likely to wash ashore – computable by any half-decent piece of marine navigation software.'

The boat lurched again, then something struck the hull; it resonated all around us, setting my teeth on edge. I waited, tensed. The sound died down, and nothing followed.

I struggled to fill the silence. 'Where are you from? I still can't place the accent.'

Kuwale laughed wearily. 'You'd be wrong if you could. I was born in Malawi, but I left when I was eighteen months old. My parents are diplomats – trade officials; we travelled all over Africa, South America, the Caribbean.'

'Do they know you're on Stateless?'

'No. We parted company. Five years ago. When I migrated.'

To asex. 'Five years ago? How old were you?'

'Sixteen.'

'Isn't that too young for surgery?' I was still only guessing, but it would take more than superficial androgyny to split up most families.

'Not in Brazil.'

'And they took it badly?'

Ve said bitterly, 'They didn't understand. *Technolibéra-tion*, asex – everything that mattered to me – none of it made sense to them. Once I had a mind of my own, they started treating me like some kind of . . . alien foundling. They were highly educated, highly paid, sophisticated, cosmopolitan . . . traditionalists. They were still tied to Malawi – and to one social stratum, and all its values and prejudices – wherever they went. I had no homeland. I was free.' Ve laughed. 'Travel shows up the invariants: the same hypocrisies repeating them-selves, over and over. By the time I was fourteen, I'd lived in thirty different cultures – and I'd figured out that *sex* was for dumb conformists.'

That almost shut me up. I asked tentatively, 'You mean gender – or intercourse?'

'Both.'

I said, 'Some people need both. Not just biologically – I know, you can switch that off. But . . . for identity. For self-esteem.'

Kuwale snorted, highly amused. '*Self-esteem* is a com-modity invented by twentieth-century personal growth cults. If you want *self-esteem* – or *an emotional centre* – go to Los Angeles and buy it.' Ve added, more sympathetically, 'What *is* it with you Westerners? Sometimes it sounds to me like all the pre-scientific psychology of Freud and Jung – and all its market-driven US regurgitations – has hijacked your language and culture so completely that you can't even *think about yourselves* anymore, except in cult-speak. And it's so in-grained now, you don't even know when you're doing it.'

'Maybe you're right.' I was beginning to feel unspeakably old and traditionalist myself. If Kuwale was the future, the generation after ver was going to be entirely beyond my comprehension. Which was probably no bad thing, but it was still a painful realisation. 'But what do you put in place of Western psychobabble? Asex and *technolibération* I can almost understand – but what's the great attraction of Anthrocosmology? If you want a dose of cosmic reassurance, why not at least choose a religion with an afterlife?'

'You should join the murderers up on deck, if you think you can choose what's true and what isn't.'

I stared out across the dark hold. The faint strip of light was fading rapidly; it looked like we were going to spend a freezing night here. My bladder felt close to bursting but I was having trouble forcing myself to let go. Every time I thought I'd finally accepted my body and all it could do to me, the underworld tugged the leash again. I'd accepted nothing. I'd had one brief glimpse beneath the surface, and now I wanted to bury everything I'd learnt, to carry on as if nothing had changed.

I said, 'The truth is whatever you can get away with.'

'No, that's journalism. The truth is whatever you can't escape.'

I was woken by torchlight in my face, and someone jagging an enzyme-coated knife through the polymer net which bound me to Kuwale. It was so cold it had to be early morning. I blinked and shivered, blinded by the glare. I couldn't see how many people there were, let alone what weapons they carried, but I sat perfectly still while they cut me free, working on the assumption that anything less could earn me a bullet through the brain.

I was winched up in a crude sling, then left suspended in midair while three people clambered out of the hold on a rope ladder, leaving Kuwale behind. I looked around at the moonlit deck and – so far as I could see – open ocean. The thought of leaving Stateless behind chilled my blood; if there was any chance of help, it was surely back on the island.

They slammed the hatch closed, lowered me and untied my feet, then started hustling me towards a cabin at the far end of the boat. After some pleading, I was allowed to stop and piss over the side; for several seconds afterwards, I was so overcome with gratitude that I would have been willing to despatch Violet Mosala personally with my bare hands, if anyone had asked.

The cabin was packed with display screens and electronic equipment. I'd never been on a fishing boat before in my life, but this looked distinctly like overkill, when the average fleet could probably be run by a single microchip.

I was tied to a chair in the middle of the cabin. There were four people present; **Witness** had already matched two of them – numbered three and five in Kuwale's gallery – but it came up blank on the others, two women about my age. I captured and filed their faces; nineteen and twenty.

I said, to no one in particular, 'What was all the noise, before? I thought we'd run aground.'

Three said, 'We were rammed. You missed all the excitement.' He was a Caucasian umale, heavily muscled, with Chinese characters tattooed on both forearms.

'Rammed by who?' He ignored the question, a little too coolly; he'd already said too much.

Twenty had waited in the cabin while the others fetched me; now she took charge. 'I don't know what fantasies Kuwale's been feeding you. Portraying us as rabid fanatics, no doubt.' She was a tall, slender black woman with a Francophone accent.

'No, ve told me you were moderates. Weren't you listening?'

She shook her head innocently, bemused, as if it were self-evident that eavesdropping was beneath her dignity. She had an air of calm authority which unnerved me; I could imagine her instructing the others to do just about anything, while retaining a demeanour of absolute reasonableness. '"Moderate" – but still "heretical", of course.'

I said wearily, 'What do you expect other ACs to call you?'

'Forget other ACs. You should make your own judgement – once you've heard all the facts.'

'I think you blew any chance of a favourable opinion when you infected me with your home-brewed cholera.'

'That wasn't us.'

'No? Who was it, then?'

'The same people who infected Yasuko Nishide with a virulent natural strain of pneumococcus.'

A chill ran through me. I didn't know if I believed her, but it fit with Kuwale's description of the extremists.

Nineteen said, 'Are you recording now?'

'No.' It was the truth; although I'd captured their faces, I'd stopped continuous filming hours before, back in the hold.

'Then start. Please.' Nineteen looked and sounded Scandinavian; it seemed every faction of AC was relentlessly internationalist. Those cynics who claimed that people who forged transglobal friendships on the nets never came together in the flesh were wrong, of course. All it required was a good enough reason.

'Why?'

'You're here to make a documentary about Violet Mosala, aren't you? Don't you want to tell the whole story? Right to the end?'

Twenty explained, 'When Mosala's dead, there'll be an uproar, naturally, and we'll have to go into hiding. And we're not interested in martyrdom – but we're not afraid of being identified, once the mission's over. We're not ashamed of what we're doing here; we have no reason to be. And we want someone objective, non-partisan, trustworthy, to carry our side of the story to the world.'

I stared at her. She sounded perfectly sincere – and even

formally apologetic, as if she was asking for a slightly inconvenient favour.

I glanced at the others. Three regarded me with studied nonchalance. Five was tinkering with the electronics. Nineteen stared back, unwavering in her solidarity.

I said, 'Forget it. I don't do snuff movies.' It was a nice line; if I hadn't recalled Daniel Cavolini's interrogation the moment the words were out, I might have had a warm inner glow for hours.

Twenty put me straight, politely. 'No one expects you to film Mosala's death. That would be impractical, as well as tasteless. We only want you to be in a position to explain to your viewers *why* her death was necessary.'

My grasp on reality was slipping. In the hold, I'd anticipated torture. I'd imagined, in detail, the process of being made to look like a plausible victim of a shark attack.

But not this.

I forced myself to speak evenly. 'I'm not interested in an exclusive interview with my subject's murderers.' The thought crossed my mind that half of SeeNet's executives would never forgive those words, if they ever found out that I'd uttered them. 'Why don't you take out a paid spot on TechnoLalia? I'm sure their viewers would give you an unqualified vote of support – if you pointed out that it was necessary to kill Mosala in order to preserve the possibility of *wormhole travel to other universes*.'

Twenty frowned, unjustly slandered. 'I knew Kuwale was feeding you poisonous lies. Is that what ve told you?'

I was growing light-headed, disbelieving; her obsessive concern with exactly the wrong proprieties was surreal. I shouted, 'It doesn't matter what the fucking *reason* is!' I tried to stretch my hands out, to implore her to see sense; they were tied firmly to the back of the chair. I said numbly, 'I don't know . . . maybe you just think Henry Buzzo has more gravitas, more presidential style. A suitably Jehovian manner.

Or maybe you think he has more elegant equations.' I very nearly told them what Mosala had told me: Buzzo's methodology was fatally flawed; their favourite contender could never be the Keystone. I caught myself in time. 'I don't care. It's still murder.'

'But it's not. It's self-defence.'

I turned. The voice had come from the doorway of the cabin.

Helen Wu met my eyes, and explained sadly, 'Wormholes have nothing to do with it. Buzzo has nothing to do with it. But if we don't intervene, Violet will soon have the power to kill us all.'

22

After Helen Wu entered the cabin, I recorded everything.

Not for SeeNet. For Interpol.

'I've done all I can to try to steer her on to safer ground,' Wu insisted solemnly. 'I thought, if she understood where she was heading, she'd change her methods – for conventional scientific reasons. For the sake of a theory with *physical content* – which is what most of her peers expect of a TOE.' She raised her hands in a gesture of despair. 'Nothing stops Violet! You know that. She absorbed every criticism I offered – and turned it into a virtue. I've only made things worse.'

Twenty said, 'I don't expect Amanda Conroy even began to convey a true picture of the richness of *information cosmology*. What did she describe to you? One model only: a Keystone creating a perfect, seamless universe – with no observable effects, ever, violating the TOE? No prospect of seeing through to the metaphysics beneath?'

'That's right.' I'd given up expressing outrage; the best strategy I could think of was to play along, let them incriminate themselves as much as they wanted, and cling to the hope that I might still have a chance to warn Mosala.

'That's only one possibility, among millions. And it's about as simplistic as the earliest cosmological models of General Relativity from the 1920s: perfectly homogenous universes, bland and empty as giant toy balloons. They were only studied because anything more plausible was too difficult to analyse, mathematically. Nobody ever believed that they described reality.'

Wu took up the thread. 'Conroy and her friends are not scientists; they're enthusiastic dilettantes. They seized hold of the very first solution that came along, and decided it was everything they wanted.' I didn't know about the others, but Wu had a career, a comfortable life, which she was tearing to shreds before my eyes. Maybe the intellectual energy she'd devoted to Anthrocosmology had already cost her any success she might have had with ATMs – but now she was sacrificing everything.

'That kind of perfect, stable cosmos isn't impossible – but it depends entirely on the structure of the theory. The observable physics, and the information metaphysics underlying it, can only be guaranteed independent and separable under certain rigorous constraints. Mosala's work shows every sign of violating those constraints in the most dangerous manner possible.'

Wu stared at me for a moment longer, as if trying to judge whether or not she'd hammered home the gravity of the situation. Nothing in her manner betrayed any hint of paranoia or fanaticism; however mistaken she was, she seemed as sober to me as a Manhattan Project scientist, terrified that the first A-bomb test might set off an atmospheric chain reaction which would engulf the world.

I must have looked suitably dismayed; she turned to Five, and said, 'Show him.' Then she left the room.

My heart sank. I said, 'Where's she going?' *Back to Stateless, in another boat?* No one here had a better chance of getting close to Mosala than Wu. I remembered the two of them walking through the hotel lobby, laughing, almost arm in arm.

'Helen already knows too much about Mosala's TOE – and too much information cosmology,' Nineteen explained. 'Pushing that any further could make a dangerous combination, so she no longer attends sessions where we discuss new results. There's no point taking risks.'

I absorbed that in silence. The ACs' obsessive secrecy went far beyond Conroy's fear of media ridicule, or the need to plot assassinations unobserved. They really did believe that their ideas alone were as perilous as any physical weapon.

I could hear the ocean moving gently around us, but the windows only mirrored the scene within. My reflection looked like someone else: hair sticking out oddly, eyes sunken, context all wrong. I pictured the boat perfectly becalmed, the cabin a tiny island of light fixed in the darkness. I forced my wrists apart experimentally, gauging the strength of the polymer, the topology of the knot. There was no give, no slippage. Since I'd been woken and hauled above the deck, I'd been sick with dread, wired and ragged – but for a moment I felt something like the clarity of the hospital ward returning. The world lost all pretence of meaning: no comfort, no mystery, no threat.

Five – a middle-aged Italian man – finished tinkering with the electronics. He addressed me as self-consciously as if I was pointing a thousand-watt floodlight and a 1950s movie camera in his face.

'This is our latest supercomputer run, based on everything Mosala has published so far. We've deliberately avoided trying to extrapolate to a TOE, for obvious reasons – but it's still possible to approximate the effects which might result if the work was ever completed.'

The largest display screen in the cabin, some five metres wide and three high, suddenly lit up. The image it showed resembled an elaborately interwoven mass of fine, multicoloured thread. I'd seen nothing like it at the conference; this wasn't the writhing, anarchic foam of the quantum vacuum. It looked more like a compact ball of neon-luminous twine, which had been wound by Escher and Mandelbrot in turn, with exquisite care, over several centuries. There were symmetries within symmetries, knots within knots, details and patterns which seized the eye, but were too intricate and convoluted to follow to any kind of closure.

I said, 'That's not pre-space, is it?'

'Hardly.' Five regarded me dubiously, as if he suspected that my ignorance would prove insurmountable. 'It's a very crude map of information space, at the instant the Keystone "becomes" the Keystone. We call this initial configuration "Aleph", for short.' I didn't respond, so he added with distaste, as if forced to resort to baby-talk, 'Think of it as a snapshot of *the Explanatory Big Bang*.'

'This is the starting point of . . . everything? The premise for an entire universe?'

'Yes. Why are you surprised? The physical, primordial Big Bang is orders of magnitude simpler; it can be characterised by just ten numbers. Aleph contains a hundred million times more information; the idea of creating galaxies and DNA out of *this* is far less outlandish.'

That remained a matter of opinion. 'If this is meant to be the contents of Violet Mosala's skull, it doesn't look like any kind of brain map I've ever seen.'

Five said drily, 'I should hope not. It's not an *anatomical scan* – or a functional neural map, or even a cognitive symbolic network. The Keystone's neurons – let alone vis skull – don't even exist, "yet". This is the pure information which logically precedes the existence of *all* physical objects. The Keystone's "knowledge" and "memory" come first. The brain which encodes them follows.'

He gestured at the screen, and the ball of twine exploded, sending brilliant loops arching out into the darkness in all directions. 'The Keystone is, at the very least, armed with a TOE, and aware of both vis own existence, and a canonical body of observations of experimental results – whether vis own, or "second hand" – which need to be accounted for. If ve lacked either the information density or the organisational schema to explain vis own existence self-consistently, the whole event would be sub-critical: there'd be no universe implied. But given a sufficiently rich Aleph, the process won't stop until an entire physical cosmos is created.

'Of course, the process never "starts" or "stops" in the conventional sense – it doesn't take place in time at all. Successive frames in this simulation simply correspond to increments in logical extension – like steps in a mathematical proof, adding successive layers of consequences to an initial set of premises. The history of the universe is embedded in those consequences like . . . the sequence of a murder, pieced together by pure deduction from evidence at the scene of the crime.'

As he spoke, the patterns I'd glimpsed on the surface of 'Aleph' were woven and re-woven in the surrounding 'information vacuum'. It was like watching a dazzling new tapestry being created every second from the one beneath – threads picked loose enough to drag a little further, and then re-combined by a million invisible hands. A thousand subtle variations echoed the original canon, but there were also startling new themes emerging, apparently from nowhere. Intermeshing fractal islands, red and white, drifted apart and recombined, struggled to engulf each other, then melted into an archipelago of hybrids. Hurricanes within hurricanes, violet and gold, spun the thread ever tighter – and then the tiniest vortices counter-rotated, and the whole hierarchy dissolved. Tiny jagged shards of crystalline silver slowly diffused through all the chaos and regularity, infiltrating and interacting with everything.

I said, 'This is beautiful technoporn – but what exactly is it meant to be showing?'

Five hesitated, but then condescended to point out a few features. 'This is the age of the Earth, being refined towards a definite value, as various geophysical and biological conclusions feed into it. This is the commonality of the genetic code, on the way towards giving rise to a sharp set of possibilities for the origins of life. Here, the underlying regularity in the chemistry of the elements—'

'And you expect Violet Mosala to fall into some kind of trance, and think all these things through, right after her moment of apotheosis?'

He scowled. 'No! All of this follows *logically* from the Keystone's information content at the Aleph moment – it's not a prediction of the Keystone's *thought processes*. Do you imagine that the Keystone has to count from one to a trillion – out loud – to create all the numbers in between, before arithmetic can make use of them? No. Zero, one, and addition are enough to *imply* all of them, and more. The universe is no different. It just grows out of a different seed.'

I glanced at the others. They were watching the screen with uneasy fascination, but no sign of anything remotely like religious terror. They might have been observing a runaway Greenhouse climate model, or a simulation of a meteor strike. Secrecy had insulated these people from any serious challenges to their ideas, but they still clung to some semblance of rationality. They hadn't plucked the supposed need to kill Mosala out of thin air, and then invented Anthrocosmology after the fact, to justify it. They really did believe that they'd been forced to this unpalatable conclusion by reason alone.

And maybe the same relentless logic could still be used to change their minds. I was an ignorant outsider, but they'd invited my scrutiny for the sake of explaining their actions to the world. They'd brought me up here so they could argue their case for posterity, but if I accepted their terms as given, and argued back at them in their own language . . . maybe there was still a small chance that I could inject enough doubt to persuade them to spare Mosala.

I said carefully, 'All right. Logical implication is enough; the Keystone doesn't have to think through every last microscopic detail. But wouldn't ve still have to sit down, eventually, and at least . . . map out the full extent of whatever vis

TOE implies? And satisfy verself that there were no loose ends? That would still be a lifetime's work. Maybe the race to complete the TOE is only the first step in the race to become the Keystone. How can anything be explained into being, until the Keystone *knows* that it's been explained?'

Five cut me off impatiently. 'A Keystone with a TOE is inexplicable without all of human history, and all prior human knowledge. And just as every biological ancestor or cousin requires their own quota of space and time to inhabit and observe – their own body, their own food and air, their own patch of ground to stand on – every intellectual predecessor or contemporary requires their own partial explanation of the universe. It all fits together, in a mosaic reaching back to the Big Bang. If it didn't, we wouldn't be here.

'But the Keystone's burden is to occupy the point where all explanations converge into a kernel concise enough to be apprehended by *a single mind*. Not to recapitulate all of science and history – merely to encode it.'

This was futile. I couldn't beat them at their own game; they'd had years in which to ponder all the obvious objections, and convince themselves that they'd answered them. And if mainstream ACs, sharing almost the same mindset, hadn't been able to sway them, what hope did I have?

I tried another angle. 'And you're happy to believe that you're nothing but a bit player in some jumped-up TOE theorist's dream? Dragged into the plot to save ver from having to invent a way for intelligence to evolve in a species with only one member?'

Five regarded me with pity. 'Now you're talking in oxy-morons. The universe is not *a dream*. The Keystone is not the avatar of some slumbering god-computer in a higher reality, threatening to wake and forget us. The Keystone anchors the universe *from within*. There's nowhere else to do it.

'A cosmos can have no more solid foundation than a single observer's coherent explanation. What would you consider less ethereal than that? A TOE which is simply true – for no reason? And what would we be, then? A dream of inanimate pre-space? Figments of the vacuum's imagination? No. Because everything is exactly what it seems to be, whatever underlies it. And whoever the Keystone is, *I'm* still alive, *I'm* still conscious' – he kicked the leg of my chair – 'the world I inhabit is solid. The only thing that matters to me is *keeping it that way*.'

I turned to the others. Three was gazing at the floor; he seemed embarrassed by the whole unnecessary business of trying to justify anything to an ungrateful world. Nineteen and Twenty regarded me hopefully, as if expecting that the stupidity of my reluctance to embrace their ideas would dawn on me at any moment.

How could I argue with these people? I no longer knew what was reasonable. It was three in the morning; I was damp, freezing cold, captive, isolated, and outnumbered. They had all the insider jargon, all the computing power, all the slick graphics, all the condescending rhetoric. Anthrocosmology possessed all the intimidating weapons it could possibly need – according to Culture First – to *be* a science, as good or bad as any other.

I said, 'Name one single experiment you can do, to distinguish all this *information cosmology* from a TOE which is "true for no reason".'

Twenty said quietly, 'Here's an experiment for you. Here's an empirical test. We can leave Violet Mosala to finish her work, unmolested. And if you're right, nothing will happen. Ten billion people will live through the eighteenth of April – most of them not even knowing that a Theory of Everything has been completed, and proclaimed to the world.'

Five said, 'If you're wrong, though . . .' He gestured at the screen, and the animation accelerated. 'Logically, the process has to reach right back to the physical Big Bang, to set the ten parameters of the Standard Unified Field Theory, to explain the entire history of the Keystone. That's why it takes so long to compute the simulation. In real-time, though, the *observable consequences* will begin within seconds of the Aleph moment – and locally at least, they should only last a matter of minutes.'

'Locally? You mean, on Stateless—?'

'I mean the Solar System. Which itself should only last a matter of minutes.'

As he spoke, a small dark patch on the outermost layer of the information tapestry began to grow. Around it, the thread of explanation was unwinding, knots which weren't really knots were unravelling. I had a sickening, giddy sense of *déjà vu*; my fanciful metaphor for Wu's complaints about Mosala's circular logic was being paraded in front of me as supporting evidence for a death sentence.

Five said, 'Conroy and the "mainstream" take it for granted that every information cosmology must be time-symmetric, with the same physics holding true after the Aleph moment as before. *But they're wrong.* After Aleph, Mosala's TOE would begin to undermine all of the physics it first implied. It goes through all the labour of creating a past – only to reach the conclusion that it has no future.'

The darkness on the screen spread faster, as if on cue. I said, 'This isn't proof of anything. Nothing behind this so-called "simulation" has ever been tested, has it? You're just grinding away at a set of equations from information theory, with no way of knowing whether or not they describe the truth.'

Five agreed. 'There is no way of knowing. But suppose it happens, unproven?'

I pleaded, '*Why should it?* If Mosala is the Keystone, she doesn't need *this*' – I tugged at my hands, wishing I could point at the travesty – 'to explain her own existence! Her TOE doesn't predict it, *doesn't allow it!*'

'No, it doesn't. But her TOE can't survive its own

expression. It can make her the Keystone. It can grant her a seamless past. It can manufacture twenty billion years of cosmology. But once it's been stated explicitly, it will resolve itself into pure mathematics, pure logic.' He joined his hands together, fingers interlocked – and then dragged them slowly apart. 'You can't hold a universe together with a system which spells out its own lack of physical content. There's no . . . *friction* anymore. No fire in the equations.'

Behind him, the tapestry was coming apart; all the ornate dazzling patterns of knowledge were disintegrating. Not devoured by entropy, or halted and reversed like the galaxies' flight; the process was simply pushing on, relentlessly, towards a conclusion which had been implicit from the start. Every possible rearrangement of meaning had been extracted from the Aleph 'knot' – except the very last. It wasn't a knot at all: it was a simple loop, leading nowhere. The colours of a thousand different explanatory threads had encoded only the lack of awareness of their hidden connections. And the universe which had bootstrapped itself into existence by spinning those explanations into a billion tangled hierarchies of ever-increasing complexity . . . was finally unwinding into a naked statement of its own tautology.

A plain white circle spun in the darkness for a second, and then the screen switched off.

The demonstration was over. Three began to untie me from the chair.

I said, 'There's something I have to tell you. I've kept it from everyone – SeeNet, Conroy, Kuwale. Sarah Knight never found out. No one else knows, except me and Mosala. But you really need to hear it.'

Twenty said, 'We're listening.' She stood by the blank display screen, watching me patiently, the model of polite interest.

This was the last chance I had to change their minds. I struggled to concentrate, to put myself in their place. *Would it make any difference to their plans if they knew that Buzzo was wrong?* Probably not. With or without other candidates to take her place, Mosala would be equally dangerous. If Nishide died, his intellectual legacy could still be pursued – and they'd simply race to protect his successors, and to slaughter Mosala's.

I said, 'Violet Mosala completed her TOE back in Cape Town. The computing she's doing now is all just cross-checking; the real work was finished months ago. So . . . *she's already become the Keystone.* And nothing's happened, the sky isn't falling, we're all still here.' I tried to laugh. 'The experiment you think is too dangerous to risk is already over. And we've survived.'

Twenty continued to watch me, with no change of expression. A wave of intense self-consciousness swept over me. I was suddenly aware of every muscle in my face, the angle of my head, the stoop of my shoulders, the direction of my gaze. I felt like a barely man-shaped lump of clay, which would need to be moulded, painstakingly, into a convincing likeness of a human being speaking the truth.

And I knew that every bone, every pore, every cell in my body was betraying the effort I was making to fake it.

Rule number one: Never let on that there are any rules at all.

Twenty nodded at Three, and he untied me from the chair. I was taken back to the hold, lowered in with the winch, and bound to Kuwale again.

As the others began to climb out on the rope ladder, Three hesitated. He crouched down beside me and whispered, like a good friend offering painful but essential advice: 'I don't blame you for trying, man. But hasn't anyone ever told you that you're the worst liar in the world?'

23

When I'd finished my account of the killers' media presentation, Kuwale said flatly, 'Don't kid yourself that you ever had a chance. No one could have talked them out of it.'

'No?' I didn't believe ver. They'd talked themselves into it, systematically enough. There had to be a way to unravel their own supposedly watertight logic before their eyes, to force them to confront its absurdity.

I hadn't been able to find it, though. I hadn't been able to get inside their heads.

I checked the time with **Witness**. It was almost dawn. I couldn't stop shivering; the slick of algae on the floor felt damper than ever, and the hard polymer beneath had grown cold as steel.

'Mosala will be under close protection.' Kuwale had been despondent when I left ver, but in my absence ve seemed to have recovered a streak of defiant optimism. 'I sent a copy of your mutant cholera genome to conference security, so they know the kind of risk she's facing – even if she won't acknowledge it herself. And there are plenty of other mainstream AC back on Stateless.'

'No one back on Stateless knows that Wu is involved, do they? And anyway . . . Wu could have infected Mosala with a bioweapon days ago. Do you think they would have confessed everything on camera, if the assassination wasn't already a *fait accompli*? They wanted to ensure that they'd receive due credit, they had to get in early and avoid the rush, before everyone from PACDF to EnGeneUity comes under suspicion.

But it would have to be the last thing they'd do, before confirming that she's dead, and fleeing Stateless.' Meaning that nothing I'd said above deck could have made the slightest difference? Not quite. They might still have furnished an antidote, their own pre-existing magic bullet.

Kuwale fell silent. I listened for distant voices or footsteps, but there was nothing: the creaking of the hull, the white noise of a thousand waves.

So much for my grandiose visions of rebirth through adversity as a fearless champion of *technolibération*. All I'd done was stumble into a vicious game betwen rival lunatic god-makers – and been cut back down to my proper station in life: conveyor of someone else's messages.

Kuwale said, 'Do you think they're monitoring us, right now? Up on deck?'

'Who knows?' I looked around the dark hold; I wasn't even sure if the faint grey light which might have been the far wall was real, or just retinal static and imagination. I laughed. 'What do they think we're going to do? Jump six metres into the air, punch a hole in the hatch, and then swim a hundred kilometres – all dressed as Siamese twins?'

I felt a sudden sharp tug on the rope around my hands. Irritated, I almost protested aloud – but I stopped myself in time. It seemed Kuwale had made good use of an hour without vis wrists jammed between our backs. Working some slack into vis own bonds and then hiding the loop between vis hands . . . which in turn might have helped ver keep them slightly apart, when we were tied together again? Whatever houdini ve'd used, after a few more minutes of painstaking manipulation the tension on the rope vanished. Kuwale pulled vis arms free of the space between us, and stretched them wide.

I couldn't help feeling a rush of pure, dumb elation – but I waited for the inevitable sound of boots on the deck. IR cameras in the hold, monitored non-stop by software, would have registered this transgression easily.

The silence stretched on. Grabbing us must have been a spur-of-the-moment decision when they intercepted my call to Kuwale. If they'd planned it in advance, they would have had handcuffs, at the very least. Maybe their surveillance technology, at short notice, was as down-market as their ropes and nets.

Kuwale shuddered with relief – I envied ver; my own shoulders were painfully cramped – then squeezed vis hands back into the gap.

The polymer rope was slippery and knotted tight, and Kuwale's fingernails were cut short (they ended up in my flesh several times). When my hands were finally untied, it was an anticlimax; the surge of elation had long faded, I knew we didn't have the slightest chance of escape. But anything was better than sitting in the dark and waiting for the honour of announcing Mosala's death to the world.

The net was made from a smart plastic which adhered selectively to its own opposite surface – presumably for ease of repair – and the join was as strong as the stuff itself. We'd been wrapped tight with our arms behind us, though; now that they were free, there was some slack – four or five centimetres. We rose to our feet awkwardly, shoes slipping on the algal slime. I exhaled and flattened my stomach, glad of my recent fast.

The first dozen attempts failed. In the dark, it took ten or fifteen minutes of tortuous repositioning to find a way of standing which minimised our combined girth all the way down. It seemed like the kind of arduous, inane activity contestants would have to go through on game shows in Hell. By the time the net touched the floor, I'd lost all feeling in my calves; I took a few steps across the hold and almost keeled over. I could hear the faint click of fingernails slipping over plastic; Kuwale was already working on the rope around vis feet. No one had bothered to bind my legs, the second time. I paced a few metres in the darkness, working out the kinks, making the most of the visceral illusion of freedom while it lasted.

I walked back to where Kuwale was sitting, and bent down until I could make out the whites of vis eyes; ve reached up and pressed a vertical finger to my lips. I nodded assent. So far, it seemed we'd been lucky – no IR camera – but there might still be audio surveillance, and there was no way of knowing how smart the listening software might be.

Kuwale stood up, turned and vanished; vis T-shirt had gone dead, deprived of sunlight for so long. I heard occasional squeaks from the wet soles of vis shoes; ve seemed to be slowly circumnavigating the hold. I had no idea what ve was hoping to find – some unlikely breach in the structure itself? I stood and waited. The faint line of light on the floor was visible again, just barely. Dawn was breaking, and daylight could only mean more people awake on deck.

I heard Kuwale approach; ve tapped my arm, then took my elbow. I followed ver to a corner of the hold. Ve pressed my hand to the wall, about a metre up. Ve'd found some kind of utilities panel, guarded by a protective cover, a small spring-loaded door flush with the wall. I hadn't noticed it when we were being lowered in, but the walls were heavily stained and spattered, an effective camouflage pattern.

I explored the exposed panel with my fingertips. There was a low voltage DC power socket. Two threaded metal fittings, each a couple of centimetres wide, with flow-control levers beneath them. Whatever they supplied – or whatever they were meant to pump out – they didn't strike me as much of an asset. Unless Kuwale had visions of flooding the hold, so we could float up to the hatch?

I almost missed it. At the far right of the panel, there was a shallow-rimmed circular aperture, just five or six millimetres wide.

An optical interface port.

Connected to what? The boat's main computer? If the vessel's original design had allowed for carrying cargo, maybe a crew member with a portable terminal would have fed in inventory data from here. In a fishing boat leased to Anthrocosmologists, I didn't have high hopes that it was configured to do anything at all.

I unbuttoned my shirt, while invoking **Witness**. The software had a crude 'virtual terminal' option which would let me view any incoming data, and mime-type as if on a keyboard. I unsealed the interface port in my navel, and stood pressed against the wall, trying to align the two connectors. It was awkward – but after wriggling out of the fishing net, this seemed like no challenge at all.

The best I could get was a brief surge of random text and then an error message from the software itself. It was picking up an answering signal but the data was scrambled beyond recognition. Both ports were sockets, designed to be joined to an umbilical's connector. Their identical protective rims kept them too far apart – their photodetectors a millimetre beyond the plane of focus of each other's signal lasers.

I stepped back, trying not to vent my frustration audibly. Kuwale touched my arm, enquiringly. I put vis hand to my face, shook my head, then guided vis finger to my artificial navel. Ve clapped me on the shoulder: *I understand. Okay. We tried.*

I stood slumped against the wall beside the panel. It occurred to me that if I buried the ACs' confession, EnGeneUity might still get the blame. If Helen Wu and friends, in hiding, tried claiming responsibility after the fact, they were more than likely to be written off as obscure cranks. No one had ever heard of Anthrocosmologists. Mosala's martyrdom could, still, break the boycott wide open.

I could already hear myself reciting the comforting

rationalisation over and over in my head: *It would have been what she wanted.*

I took off my belt and forced the prong of the buckle into the flesh around my metal navel. There was a thin layer of bioengineered connective tissue around the surgical steel, sealing the permanent wound against infection; the sound of tearing collagen set my teeth on edge, but there were no nerve endings to register the damage. A couple of centimetres down, though, I hit the metal flange which anchored the port in place. I levered the flesh away from the tube, and managed to force the prong past the edge of the flange.

It had seemed like a small enough piece of DIY surgery: enlarging the existing hole in the abdominal wall by seven or eight millimetres. My body disagreed. I persisted, digging around under the flange and trying to twist it free, while conflicting waves of chemical messengers flooded out from the site, delivering razor-sharp rebukes and analgesic comfort in turn. Kuwale came over and helped me, pulling the aperture open. As vis warm fingers brushed the scars where I'd slashed myself in front of Gina, I found I had an erection; it was the wrong response for so many reasons that I almost burst out laughing. Sweat ran into my eyes, blood trickled down towards my groin – and my body kept on blindly signalling desire. And the truth was, if ve'd been willing, I would have happily lain down on the floor and made love in any way possible. Just to feel more of vis skin against my skin. Just to believe that we'd made some kind of connection.

The buried steel tube emerged, trailing a short length of blood-slick optical fibre. I turned away and spat out a mouthful of acid. Mercifully, nothing followed.

I waited for my fingers to stop shaking, then wiped everything clean on my shirt, and unscrewed the whole end assembly, leaving the windowed port naked, unencumbered. More like circumcision than phalloplasty – and a lot of trouble to go through for a millimetre of penetration. I pocketed the metal foreskin, then found the wall socket and tried again.

Large, cheerful, blue-on-white letters appeared in front of me – unable to dazzle, but no less of a shock.

> **Mitsubishi Shanghai Marine**
> **Model Number LMHDV–12–5600**
> **Emergency Options:**
> **F – launch Flares**
> **B – activate radio Beacon**

I hit all the possible escape codes in the hope of finding some wider menu – but this was it, the complete list of choices. All the glorious fantasies I hadn't dared entertain had involved reaching the ship's main computer, gaining instant access to the net, and archiving the ACs' pre-recorded confession in twenty safe places, while simultaneously sending copies to everyone at the Einstein Conference. This was nothing but a vestigial emergency system, probably built into the design as a minimum statutory requirement, and then ignored when the ship was fitted out by a third party with proper communications and navigation equipment.

Ignored – or disconnected?

I mimed typing **B**.

The text of a simple mayday broadcast flowed across the virtual screen. It gave the ship's model number, serial number, latitude and longitude – if I remembered the map of Stateless correctly, we were closer to the island than I'd thought – and stated that 'survivors' were located in the 'main cargo hold'. I suddenly had a strong suspicion that if we'd bothered to search the rest of the hold, we might have found another panel, hiding two fist-sized red buttons labelled BEACON and FLARES – but I didn't want to think about that.

Somewhere up on deck, a siren started screaming.

Kuwale was dismayed. 'What did you do? Trigger a fire alarm?'

'I broadcast a mayday. I thought flares might get us into trouble.' I closed the panel and started rebuttoning my bloody shirt, as if hiding the evidence might help.

I heard someone heavy running across the deck. A few seconds later, the siren shut off. Then the hatch was wound halfway open, and Three peered down at us. He was holding a gun, almost absent-mindedly. 'What good do you think that's going to do you? We're sending out the false-alarm code already; no one's going to take any notice.' He seemed more bemused than angry. 'All you have to do is sit tight and stop fucking about, and you'll be free soon enough. So how about some cooperation?'

He unfurled the ladder and came down, alone. I stared up at the strip of pale dawn sky behind him; I could see a fading satellite, but I had no way to reach it. Three picked up two pieces of discarded rope and tossed them at us. 'Sit down and tie your feet together. Do it properly and you might get breakfast.' He yawned widely, then turned and yelled, 'Giorgio! Anna! Give me a hand!'

Kuwale rushed him, faster than I'd seen anyone move in my life. Three raised the gun and shot ver in the thigh. Kuwale staggered, pirouetting, still moving forward. Three kept the gun aimed squarely on ver, as vis knees buckled and vis head sagged. As the shot's reverb faded from my skull, I could hear ver gasping for breath.

I stood and shouted abuse at him, barely conscious of what I was saying. I'd lost it: I wanted to take the hold, the ship, the ocean, and wipe them all away like cobwebs. I stepped forward, waving my arms wildly, screaming obscenities. Three glanced at me, perplexed, as if he couldn't imagine what all the fuss was about. I took another step, and he aimed the gun at me.

Kuwale sprang forward and knocked him off his feet. Before he could rise, ve leapt on him and pinned his arms, slamming his right hand against the floor. I was paralysed for

311

a second, convinced that the struggle was futile, but then I ran to help.

Three must have looked like an indulgent father playing with two belligerent five year olds. I tugged at the gun barrel protruding from his huge fist; the weapon might as well have been set in stone. He seemed ready to climb to his feet as soon as he caught his breath, with or without Kuwale's slender frame attached.

I kicked him in the head. He protested, outraged. I attacked the same spot repeatedly, fighting down my revulsion. The skin above his eye split open; I ground my heel hard into the wound, crouching down and pulling on the gun. He cried out in pain and let it slip free – and then half sat up, throwing Kuwale to one side. I fired the gun into the floor behind me, hoping to discourage him from making me use it. Another shot rang out, above. I looked up. Nineteen – Anna? – was lying on her stomach at the edge of the hold.

I aimed the gun at Three, stepping back a few paces. He stared at me, bloodied and angry – but still curious, trying to fathom my senseless actions.

'You want it, don't you? The unravelling. You want Mosala to take the world apart.' He laughed and shook his head. 'You're too late.'

Anna called out, 'There's no need for any of this. Please. Put the gun down, and you'll be back on Stateless in an hour. No one wants to harm you.'

I shouted back, 'Bring me a working notepad. *Fast*. You have two minutes before I blow his brains out.' I meant it – if only for as long as it took to get the words out.

Anna crawled back from the edge; I heard a murmur of angry low voices as she consulted with the others.

Kuwale limped over to me. Vis wound was bleeding steadily; the bullet had clearly missed the femoral artery, but vis breathing was ragged, ve needed help. Ve said, 'They're not going to do it. They'll just keep stalling. Put yourself in their place—'

Three said calmly, 'Ve's right. Whatever value anyone puts on my life . . . if Mosala becomes the Keystone, we all die anyway. If you're trying to save her, you've got nothing to trade – because whatever you threaten, it's forfeit either way.'

I glanced up towards the deck; I could still hear them arguing. But if they had enough faith in their cosmology to kill Mosala – and to trash their own lives and become self-righteous fugitives, hiding out in rural Mongolia or Turkistan without so much as a share of the media rights . . . the threat of one more death was not going to dent their conviction.

I said, 'I think your work is in urgent need of peer review.'

I handed Kuwale the gun, then took off my shirt and tied it around the top of vis leg. I'd stopped bleeding, myself; the ruptured sealant tissue was oozing a colourless balm of anti-biotics and coagulants.

I returned to the utilities panel and plugged myself in again. Independent of the main computer, the emergency system couldn't be shut down; I repeated the mayday, then fired the flares. I heard three loud hisses of expanding gas – and then a merciless actinic glare began to spread down the far wall, displacing the soft dawn light. The brown patina of algal stains had never been clearer – but it lost its camouflage value completely: the edges of another recessed compartment appeared, the gap around the protective cover starkly etched in black. I looked inside; there were two large buttons, just as I'd suspected, and an emergency air supply as well. On close inspection, the faintest hint of a cryptic logo – incomprehensible across all languages and cultures – showed through the stains on the compartment's door.

The conversation above had fallen silent. I was just hoping they wouldn't panic, and rush us.

Three seemed tempted to say something disparaging, but he kept his mouth shut. He eyed Kuwale nervously; maybe he'd decided that ve was the real fanatic who wanted the unravelling, and I'd merely been duped into helping ver.

The flare rose towards the zenith, its light filling the hold. I said, 'I don't understand. How do you get to the point where you're ready to kill an innocent woman just because some computer tells you she can bring on Armageddon?' Three mimed indifference in the presence of fools. I said, 'So you found a theory that could swallow any TOE. A system that could out-explain any kind of physics. But don't kid yourself: it's not science. You might as well have stumbled on some way to add up the gematria numbers of "Mosala" to get 666.'

Three said mildly, 'Ask Kuwale if it's all cabalistic gibberish. Ask ver about Kinshasa in '43.'

'What?'

'That's just . . . apocryphal bullshit.' Kuwale was drenched in sweat, and showing signs of going into shock. I took the gun, and ve went to sit against the wall.

Three persisted, 'Ask ver how Muteba Kazadi died.'

I said, 'He was seventy-eight years old.' I struggled to recall what his biographers had said about his death; given his age, I hadn't paid much attention. 'I think the words you're looking for are "cerebral haemorrhage".'

Three laughed, disbelieving, and a chill ran through me. Of course they had more than pure information theory behind their beliefs: they also had at least one mythical *death by forbidden knowledge* – to validate everything, to convince them that the abstractions had teeth.

I said, 'Okay. But if Muteba didn't bring down the universe when he went . . . why should Mosala?'

'Muteba wasn't a TOE theorist; he couldn't have become the Keystone. No one knows exactly what he was doing, all his notes have been lost. But some of us think he found a way to mix with information – and when it happened, the shock was too much for him.'

Kuwale snorted derisively.

I said, 'What's "mix with information" supposed to mean?'

Three said, 'Every physical structure encodes information – but normally it's the laws of physics alone which control how the structure behaves.' He grinned. 'Drop a Bible and a copy of the *Principia* together, and they'll fall side-by-side all the way. The fact that the laws of physics are themselves *information* is invisible, irrelevant. They're as absolute as Newtonian space-time – a fixed backdrop, not a player.

'But nothing's pure, nothing's independent. Time and space mix at high velocities. Macroscopic possibilities mix at the quantum level. The four forces mix at high temperatures. And *physics and information* mix . . . by an unknown process. The symmetry group isn't clear, let alone the detailed dynamics. But it could just as easily be triggered by pure knowledge – knowledge of information cosmology itself, encoded in a human brain – as by any physical extreme.'

'To what effect?'

'Hard to predict.' The blood on his face resembled a black caul in the flare's light. 'Maybe . . . exposing the deepest unification: revealing precisely how physics is created by explanation – and vice versa. Spinning the vector, rotating all the hidden machinery into view.'

'Yeah? If Muteba had such a great cosmic revelation, how do you know it didn't turn him into the Keystone the instant before he died?' I knew I was probably wasting my breath, but I couldn't stop trying to get Mosala off the hook.

Three smirked at my ignorance. 'I don't think so. I've seen models of an information cosmos with a Keystone who *mixed*. And I know we don't live in that universe.'

'Why?'

'Because after the Aleph moment, everyone else would get dragged along. Exponential growth: one person mixing, then two, four, eight . . . if that had happened in '43, we'd all have followed Muteba Kazadi by now. We'd all know, firsthand, exactly what killed him.'

The flare descended out of sight, plunging the hold into greyness again. I invoked **Witness**, adapting my eyes to the ambient light again instantly.

Kuwale said, 'Andrew! Listen!'

There was a deep rhythmic pulsing sound coming through the hull, growing steadily louder. I'd finally learnt to recognise an MHD engine – and this one wasn't ours.

I waited, sick with uncertainty. My hands were beginning to shake as badly as Kuwale's. After a few minutes, there was shouting in the distance. I couldn't make out the words, but there were new voices, with Polynesian accents.

Three said quietly, 'You keep your mouth shut, or they'll all have to die. Or is Violet Mosala worth a dozen farmers to you?'

I stared at him, light-headed. *Would the rest of the ACs think like that?* How many real deaths would they have to confront, before they admitted that they might be mistaken? Or had they surrendered completely to a moral calculus where even the smallest chance of *the unravelling* outweighed any crime, any atrocity?

The voices grew nearer, then the engine stopped; it sounded as if the fishing boat had pulled up right beside us. But I could already hear another one in the distance.

I caught snatches of a conversation: 'But I leased you this boat, so it's my responsibility. The emergency system should not have malfunctioned.' It was a deep voice, a woman's, puzzled, reasonable, persistent. I glanced at Kuwale; vis eyes were shut, vis teeth clenched tight. The sight of ver in pain cut me up badly; I didn't trust what I was beginning to feel for ver, but that wasn't the point. Ve needed treatment, we had to get away.

But if I called out . . . how many people would I endanger?

I heard a third ship approaching. Mayday . . . false-alarm code . . . mayday . . . flares. The whole local fleet seemed to think that was strange enough to be worth looking into. Even if all these people were unarmed, the ACs were now completely outnumbered.

I raised my head and bellowed, 'In here!'

Three tensed, as if preparing to move. I fired the gun into the floor near his head, and he froze. A wave of vertigo swept over me and I waited for a barrage of automatic fire. *I was insane – what had I done?*

There were heavy footfalls on the deck, more shouting.

Twenty and a tall Polynesian woman in blue overalls approached the edge of the hold.

The farmer glanced down at us, frowning. She said, 'If they've threatened violence, gather your evidence and take it to an adjudicator back on the island. But whatever's gone on here, don't you think both sides would be better off separated?'

Twenty faked outrage. 'They hide on board, they intimidate us with firearms, they take a man hostage! And you expect us to hand them over to you, so you can let them go free!'

The farmer looked straight at me. I couldn't speak, but I met her gaze, and I let my right hand drop to my side. She addressed Twenty again, deadpan. 'I'm happy to testify for you, about what I've seen here. So if they're willing to give up their hostage and come with us, you have my word, justice won't be compromised.'

Four other farmers appeared at the edge of the hold. Kuwale, still sitting by the wall, raised a hand in greeting, and called out something in a Polynesian language. One of the farmers laughed raucously, and replied. I felt a surge of hope. The ship was swarming with people – and when it came down to the prospect of a massacre, face-to-face, the ACs had buckled.

I put the gun in my back pocket. I shouted up, 'He's free to go!'

Three rose to his feet, looking surly. I said quietly, 'She's dead anyway. You said so yourself. You're already saviour of the universe.' I tapped my stomach. 'Think of your place in history. Don't tarnish your image now.' He exchanged glances with Twenty, then started climbing the rope ladder.

I threw the gun into a corner of the hold, then went to help Kuwale. Ve took the ladder slowly; I followed close behind, hoping I'd be able to catch ver if ve lost vis grip.

There must have been thirty farmers on deck – and eight ACs, most of them with guns, who seemed far more tense than the unarmed anarchists. I felt a reprise of horror at the thought of what might have happened. I looked around for Helen Wu, but she was nowhere in sight. Had she returned to the island during the night, to oversee Mosala's death? I'd heard no boat . . . but she might have donned scuba gear, and ridden the harvester.

As we started making our way towards the edge of the deck, where a concertina bridge linked the two ships, Twenty called out, 'Don't think you're going to walk away with stolen property.'

The farmer was losing patience; she turned to me. 'Do you want to empty out your pockets, and save us all some time? Your friend needs a doctor.'

'I know.'

Twenty approached me. She looked around the deck, meaningfully, and my blood froze. *It wasn't over yet.* They hoped that whatever they'd done to Mosala was irreversible by now . . . but they weren't certain, and they were ready to start shooting rather than turn me loose with footage which proved that the danger was real.

They knew Mosala too well. I had no idea how I'd convince her, without it; she already believed that I'd cried wolf, once.

I had no choice, though. I invoked **Witness**, and wiped everything. 'Okay. It's done. It's erased.'

'I don't believe you.'

I gestured at the protruding fibre. 'Plug in a notepad, do an inventory. See for yourself.'

'That's no proof. You could fake that.'

'Then . . . what do you want? Do you want to put me in a tuned microwave field, and fry all the RAM?'

She shook her head solemnly. 'We don't have that kind of equipment here.'

I glanced at the bridge, which was sighing with the shifting pressure as the boats bobbed and swayed in the gentle swell. 'Okay. Let Kuwale go. I'll stay.'

Kuwale groaned. '*Don't*. You can't trust—'

Twenty cut ver off. 'It's the only way. And you have my word that you'll be returned to Stateless, unharmed, once this is over.'

She gazed at me calmly; so far as I could tell, she was perfectly sincere. Once Mosala was dead, I'd be free.

But if she survived, and completed her TOE – proving that these people were nothing but failed homicidal conspirators – how would they feel about their chosen messenger then?

I sank to my knees. I thought, among other things: *The sooner I start, the sooner it's over.*

I wrapped the fibre around my hand and started hauling the memory chips out of my gut. The wound left by the optical port was too small – but the chips' capsule-shaped protective casings forced it open, and they emerged into the light one by one, like the gleaming segments of some strange cybernetic parasite which was fighting hard to stay inside its host. The farmers backed away, alarmed and confused. The louder I bellowed, the more it dulled the pain.

The processor emerged last, the buried head of the worm, trailing a fine gold cable which led to my spinal cord, and the nerve taps in my brain. I snapped it off where it vanished into the chip, then rose to my feet, bent double, a fist pressed against the ragged hole.

I pushed the bloody offering towards Twenty with my foot. I couldn't stand up straight enough to look her in the eye.

'You can go.' She sounded shaken, but unrepentant. I wondered what kind of death she'd chosen for Mosala. Clean and painless, no doubt: straight into a fairytale coma, without a speck of blood or shit or vomit.

I said, 'Mail it back to me, once you're finished with it. Or you'll be hearing from my bank manager.'

24

In the cramped sick bay, a scan of Kuwale's leg revealed ruptured blood vessels and broken ligaments, a trail of damage like an aircraft's crash path leading to the bullet buried at the back of vis thigh. Ve watched the screen with grim amusement, sweat dripping from vis face as the ancient software ground away at a detailed assessment; the final line read: **Probable gunshot injury.** 'Oh, I *was* hit!' One of the farmers, Prasad Jwala, cleaned and dressed our wounds, and pumped us full of (off-the-shelf) drugs to limit bleeding, infection, and shock. The only strong painkillers on board were crude synthetic opiates which left me so high that I couldn't have given a coherent account of the ACs' plans to anyone if the fate of the universe had depended on it. Kuwale lost consciousness completely; I sat beside ver, fantasising about gathering my thoughts.

It was just as well that my stomach was tightly bandaged; I had a strong urge to reach through the portal I'd made and probe the machinery which remained inside me: the tight smooth coil of the intestines, the demon snake which Kuwale's magic bullet had tamed; the warm, blood-drenched liver, ten billion microscopic enzyme factories plugged straight into the circulation, a bootleg pharm dispensing whatever its chemical intuition desired. I wanted to drag every dark mysterious organ out into the daylight one by one, and arrange them all in front of me in their proper positions, until I was nothing but a shell of skin and muscle, face-to-face at last with my inner twin.

After about fifteen minutes, the same enzyme factories finally began degrading the opiates in my blood, and I clawed my way down from marshmallow heaven. I begged for a notepad; Jwala obliged, then left to help out on deck.

I managed to get through to Karin De Groot immediately. I stuck to the essentials. De Groot heard me out in silence; my appearance must have given the story a degree of credibility. 'You have to talk Violet into heading back to civilisation. Even if she's not convinced of the danger, what has she got to lose? She can always deliver her final paper from Cape Town.'

De Groot said, 'Believe me, she'll take every word of this seriously. Yasuko Nishide died last night. It was pneumonia – and he was very frail – but Violet's still badly shaken. And she's seen the cholera genome analysis, which was done by a reputable Bombay lab. But—'

'So you'll fly out with her?' Nishide's death saddened me, but Mosala's loss of complacency was pure good news. 'I know, it's a risk, she might get sick on the plane, but—'

De Groot cut me off. '*Listen*. There've been some problems here while you were away. No one's flying anywhere.'

'Why? What kind of problems?'

'A boatload of . . . mercenaries, I don't know . . . arrived on the island overnight. They've occupied the airport.'

Jwala had come back to check on Kuwale; he caught the last part of the conversation, and interjected derisively, '*Agents provocateurs*. Every few years a different pack of apes in designer camouflage show up, try to make trouble . . . fail, and go away.' He sounded about as concerned as someone from an ordinary democracy, complaining about the periodic irritation of election campaigns. 'I saw them last night, landing in the harbour. They were heavily armed, we had to let them pass.' He grinned. 'But they're in for some surprises. I'll give them six months, at the most.'

'Six months?'

He shrugged. 'It's never been longer.'

A boatload of mercenaries, trying to make trouble – the boat which had rammed the ACs? In any case, Twenty and her colleagues must have known by morning that the airport had been seized – and that my testimony would make little difference to Mosala's chances.

The timing could not have been worse, but it was hardly surprising. The Einstein Conference was already lending Stateless too much respectability, and Mosala's planned migration would be an even greater embarrassment. But EnGeneUity and their allies wouldn't try to assassinate her, creating an instant martyr. Nor would they dissolve the island back into the ocean, and risk scaring off legitimate customers worth billions of dollars. All they could do was try, one last time, to bring the social order of Stateless crashing down – proving to the world that the whole naive experiment had been doomed from the start.

I said, 'Where's Violet now?'

'Talking to Henry Buzzo. She's trying to convince him to go with her to the hospital.'

'Good idea.' Immersed in the schemes of the 'moderates', I'd almost forgotten that Buzzo was also in danger – and Mosala was at risk on two fronts. The extremists had already triumphed in Kyoto – and whoever had infected me with the cholera, *en route* from Sydney, was probably on Stateless right now, looking for a chance to make up for the botched first attempt.

De Groot said, 'I'll show them this conversation immediately.'

'And give a copy to security.'

'Right. For what that's worth.' She seemed to be holding up under the pressure far better than I was; she added wryly, 'No sign of Helen Wu in flippers, so far. But I'll keep you posted.'

We arranged to meet at the hospital. I signed off and closed my eyes, fighting the temptation to sink back into the lingering opiate fog.

323

It had taken the mainstream ACs five days to smuggle in a cure for me, even with the airport open. After everything I'd been through, I wasn't ready to swallow the fact that Mosala was now a walking corpse – but short of a counter-invasion by African *technolibérateurs*, over a distance of tens of thousands of kilometres, in the next day or two, at the latest . . . I could see no hope of her surviving.

As the boat approached the northern harbour, I sat watching over Akili. I badly wanted to take vis hand, but I was afraid it would only make things worse. *How could I have fallen for someone who'd surgically excised even the possibility of desire?*

Easily enough, apparently: a shared trauma, an intense experience, the confusing absence of gender cues . . . it was no great mystery. People became infatuated with asex all the time. And no doubt it would pass, soon enough – once I accepted the simple fact that nothing I felt could ever be reciprocated.

After a while, I found I could no longer bear to look at vis face; it hurt too much. So I watched the glowing traces on the bedside monitor, and listened for each shallow exhalation, and tried to understand why the ache I felt would not go away.

The trams were reportedly still running, but one of the farmers offered to drive us all the way to the city. 'Quicker than waiting for an ambulance,' she explained. 'There are only ten on the island.' She was a young Fijian named Adelle Vuni-bobo; I remembered seeing her looking down into the hold on the ACs' boat.

Kuwale sat between us in the cab of the truck, half awake but still stupefied. I watched the vivid coral inlets shrinking around us, like a fast-motion view of the reefs' slow compaction.

I said, 'You risked your life back there.'

'Maydays at sea are taken very seriously.' Her tone was

gently mocking, as if she was trying to puncture my deferential manner.

'Lucky we weren't on land.' I persisted, 'But you could see that the boat wasn't in danger. The crew told you to clear off and mind your own business. Underlining the suggestions with guns.'

She glanced at me curiously. 'So you think it was reckless? Foolish? There's no police force here. Who else would have helped you?'

'No one,' I admitted.

She fixed her eyes on the uneven terrain ahead. 'I was in a fishing boat that capsized, five years ago. We were caught in a storm. My parents, and my sister. My parents were knocked unconscious, they drowned straight away. My sister and I spent ten hours in the ocean, treading water, taking turns holding each other up.'

'I'm sorry. The Greenhouse Storms have claimed so many people—'

She groaned. 'I don't want your sympathy. I'm just trying to explain.'

I waited in silence. After a while, she said, 'Ten hours. I still dream about it. I grew up on a fishing boat – and I'd seen storms sweep away whole villages. I thought I already knew exactly how I felt about the ocean. But that time in the water with my sister changed everything.'

'In what way? Do you have more respect, more fear?'

Vunibobo shook her head impatiently. 'More lifejackets, actually, but that's not what I'm talking about.' She grimaced, frustrated, but then she said, 'Would you do something for me? Close your eyes, and try to picture the world. All ten billion people at once. I know it's impossible – but try.'

I was baffled, but I obliged. 'Okay.'

'Now describe what you see.'

'A view of the Earth from space. It's more like a sketch than a photograph, though. North is up. The Indian Ocean is in the centre – but the view stretches from West Africa to New Zealand, from Ireland to Japan. There are crowds of people – not to scale – standing on all the continents and islands. Don't ask me to count them, but I'd guess there are about a hundred, in all.'

I opened my eyes. I'd left her old and new homes right off the map, but I had a feeling this wasn't a consciousness-raising exercise in the marginalising force of geographical representations.

She said, 'I used to see something like that, myself. But since the accident, it's changed. When I close my eyes and imagine the world, now . . . I see the same map, the same continents . . . but the land isn't land at all. What looks like solid ground is really a solid mass of people; there is no dry land, there *is* nowhere to stand. We're all in the ocean, treading water, holding each other up. That's how we're born, that's how we die. Struggling to keep each other's heads above the waves.' She laughed, suddenly selfconscious, but then she said defiantly, 'Well, you asked for an explanation.'

'I did.'

The dazzling coral inlets had turned to rivers of bleached limestone sludge, but the reef-rock around us now shimmered with delicate greens and silver-greys. I wondered what the other farmers would have told me, if I'd asked them the same question. A dozen different answers, probably; Stateless seemed to run on the principle of people agreeing to do the same thing for entirely different reasons. It was a sum over mutually contradictory topologies which left the calculus of pre-space for dead; no imposed politics, philosophy, religion, no idiot cheer-squad worship of flags or symbols – but order emerged nonetheless.

And I still couldn't decide if that was miraculous, or utterly unmysterious. Order only arose and survived anywhere because enough people desired it. Every democracy was a kind of anarchy in slow motion: any statute, any constitution could be changed, given time; any social contract, written or unwritten, could be dishonoured. The ultimate safety nets were inertia, apathy and obfuscation. On Stateless, they'd had the – possibly insane – courage to unravel the whole political knot into its simplest form, to gaze at the undecorated structures of power and responsibility, tolerance and consensus.

I said, 'You kept me from drowning. So how do I repay you?'

Vunibobo glanced at me, measuring my seriousness. 'Swim harder. Help us all to stay afloat.'

'I'll try. If I ever have the chance.'

She smiled at this crudely hedged half-promise, and reminded me, 'We're heading straight into a storm, right now. I think you'll get your chance.'

I'd expected at least deserted streets in the centre of the island, but at first sight little seemed to have changed. There were no signs of panic – no queues of hoarders, no boarded-up shopfronts. When we passed the hotel, though, I saw that the Mystical Renaissance carnival had gone to ground; I wasn't the only tourist who was suffering from a sudden desire to be invisible. Back on the boat, I'd heard that one woman had been injured slightly when the airport was captured, but most of the staff had simply walked away. Munroe had spoken of a militia on the island, and no doubt they outnumbered the invaders – but how their equipment, training and discipline compared, I had no idea. The mercenaries seemed content, so far, to dig themselves in at the airport – but if the ultimate aim was not to take power, but to bring 'anarchy' to Stateless, I had a queasy suspicion that there'd be something a lot less palatable than the bloodless seizure of strategic assets, very soon.

The atmosphere at the hospital was calm. Vunibobo helped me get Kuwale into the building; ve smiled dreamily and tried to limp forward, but it took the two of us to keep ver from falling flat on vis face. Prasad Jwala had sent the scan of Kuwale's bullet wound ahead, and an operating theatre was already prepared. I watched ver being wheeled in, trying to convince myself that I felt nothing but the same anxiety that I would have felt for anyone else. Vunibobo bid me farewell.

After waiting my turn in casualty, I was sewn up under local anaesthetic. I'd managed to kill the bioengineered graft – which would have accelerated healing and formed a good seal – but the medic who treated me packed the wound with a spongy antibacterial carbo-hydrate polymer, which would slowly degrade in the presence of the growth factors secreted by the surrounding flesh. She asked what had made the hole. I told her the truth, and she seemed greatly relieved. 'I was beginning to wonder if something had eaten its way out.'

I stood up carefully, numb at the centre, but feeling the pinched absence of skin and muscle tug on every part of me. The medic said, 'Try to avoid strenuous bowel movements. And laughter.'

I found De Groot and Mosala in the anteroom to the Medical Imaging suite. Mosala looked drawn and nervous, but she greeted me warmly, shaking my hand, clasping my shoulder. 'Andrew, are you all right?'

'I'm fine. But the documentary may have a small gap in it.'

She managed to smile. 'Henry's being scanned right now. They're still processing my data; it could take a while. They're looking for foreign proteins, but there's some doubt as to whether the resolution's up to it. The machine's second-hand, twenty years old.' She hugged herself, and tried to laugh. 'Listen to me. If I'm planning to live here, I'd better get used to the facilities.'

De Groot said, 'No one I've spoken to has seen Helen Wu since early last night. Conference security checked out her room; it's empty.'

Mosala still seemed stunned by the revelation of Wu's

allegiance. 'Why would she get involved with the Anthrocos-mologists? She's a brilliant theorist in her own right – not some pseudoscientific hanger-on! I can understand how . . . a certain kind of person might think there's something mystical about working on TOEs, when they find they can't grasp the details themselves . . . but Helen understands my work almost better than I do!' I didn't think it was a good time to point out that that was half the problem. 'As for these other thugs, who you think killed Yasuko . . . I'll be giving a media conference this afternoon, outlining the problems with Henry Buzzo's choice of measure and what it means for his TOE. That should concentrate their tiny minds.' Her voice was almost calm – but she held her arms crossed in front of her, one hand clasped around the other wrist, trying to mask the faint tremor of rage. 'And when I announce my own TOE on Friday morning . . . they can kiss their *transcendence* goodbye.'

'Friday morning?'

'Serge Bischoff's algorithms are working wonders. All my calculations will be finished by tomorrow night.'

I said carefully, 'If it turns out that you've been infected with a bioweapon – and if you become too sick to work – is there anyone else who could interpret these results, and put the whole thing together?'

Mosala recoiled. 'What are you asking me to do? Anoint a successor to be targeted next?'

'No! But if your TOE is completed and announced, the moderates will have to admit that they've been proven wrong – and there's a chance they might hand over the antidote. I'm not asking you to publicise anyone's name! But if you can arrange for someone to put the finishing touches—'

Mosala said icily, 'I have nothing to prove to these people. And I'm not risking someone else's life, trying.'

Before I could pursue the argument any further, De Groot's notepad chimed. The head of security for the conference, Joe Kepa, had viewed the copy De Groot had sent him of my call from the fishing boat, and he wanted to talk to me. In person. Immediately.

In a small meeting room on the top floor of the hotel – with two large umale associates looking on – Kepa grilled me for almost three hours, questioning everything right back to the moment when I'd begged SeeNet to give me the documentary. He'd already seen reports from some of the farmers about events on the ACs' boat (they'd posted their accounts directly on to the local news nets), and he'd seen the cholera analysis – but he was still angry and suspicious, he still seemed to want to tear my story to pieces. I resented the hostile treatment, but I couldn't really blame him. Until the seizure of the airport, his biggest problem had been buskers in clown suits; now it was the threat of anything up to a full-scale military engagement around the hotel. Talk of information theorists armed with amateur bioweapons targeted at the conference's highest profile physicists must have sounded like either a sick hoax, or proof that he'd been singled out for divine punishment.

By the time Kepa told me the interview was over, though, I believed I'd convinced him. He was angrier than ever.

My testimony had been recorded to international judicial standards: each frame stamped with a centrally generated time code, and an encrypted copy lodged with Interpol. I was invited to scan through the file to verify that there'd been no tampering, before I electronically signed it. I checked a dozen points at random; I wasn't going to view the whole three hours.

I went to my room and took a shower, instinctively shielding the freshly bandaged wound although I knew there was no need to keep it dry. The luxury of hot water, the solidity of the plain elegant decor, seemed surreal. Twenty-four hours before, I'd planned to do everything I could to help Mosala smash the boycott, reshaping the documentary around the news of her emigration. But what could I do for *techno-libération* now? Buy an external camera, and proceed to

330

document her meaningless death – while Stateless collapsed in the background? Was that what I wanted? To claw back my delusions of objectivity, and calmly record whatever fate befell her?

I stared at myself in the mirror. *What use was I to anyone now?*

The room had a wallphone; I called the hospital. There'd been no problems with the operation, but Akili was still sleeping off the anaesthetic. I decided to visit ver anyway.

I walked through the hotel lobby just as the morning sessions were breaking up. The conference was still running on schedule – although screens announced a memorial for Yasuko Nishide later in the day – but the particpants were visibly nervous and subdued, talking quietly in small groups, or looking around furtively as if hoping to overhear some vital piece of news about the occupation, however unreliable.

I spotted a group of journalists, all people I knew slightly, and they let me join in as they swapped rumours. The consensus seemed to be that foreigners would be evacuated – by the US (or New Zealand, or Japanese) navy – within a matter of days, although no one could offer any firm evidence for this belief. David Connolly, Janet Walsh's photographer, said confidently, 'There are three US Nobel prize-winners here. Do you really think they're going to be left stranded indefinitely while Stateless goes to hell?'

The other consensus was that the airport had been taken by 'rival anarchists' – the infamous US gun law 'refugees'. Biotech interests didn't rate a mention, and if Mosala's plan to migrate was common knowledge on the island, nobody here had bothered to talk to the locals long enough to find out.

These people would be reporting everything that happened on Stateless to the world – and none of them had the slightest idea of what was really going on.

On my way to the hospital, I spotted an electrical retailer. I bought a new notepad and a small, shoulder-mounted camera.

I typed my personal code into the notepad, and the last satellite backup from the old machine flowed down from deep freeze and started catching up with real-time. The screen was a blur of activity for several seconds – and then **Sisyphus** announced, 'Reported cases of Distress have exceeded three thousand.'

'I do not wish to know that.' *Three thousand?* That was a sixfold increase in a fortnight. 'Show me a case map.' It looked more like the plot for a spontaneous cancer than any kind of infectious disease: a random scatter across the globe, ignoring every social and environmental factor, concentrated only by population density itself.

How could the numbers be increasing so rapidly – without any localised outbreaks? I'd heard that models based on airborne transmission, sexual contact, water supplies, parasites, had all failed to match the epidemiology.

'Any other news on this?'

'Not officially. But footage logged in SeeNet's library by your colleague John Reynolds includes the first reports of coherent speech by sufferers.'

'Some people are recovering?'

'No. But some new sufferers have shown an intermittent change in the pathology.'

'Change, or reduction?'

'The speech is coherent, but the subject matter is contextually inappropriate.'

'You mean they're psychotic? When they finally stop screaming, and calm down long enough to string two words together . . . it's only to pass on the news that they've gone insane?'

'That's a matter for expert opinion.'

I was almost at the hospital. I said, 'Okay, show me some of this *changed pathology*. Show me some of the joys I've missed out on.'

Sisyphus raided the library and brought me a clip. It was questionable etiquette to peek at other people's unfinished work, but if Reynolds had wanted the footage to be inaccessible to his colleagues, he would have encrypted it.

I watched the scene in the hospital elevator, alone – and I felt the blood draining from my face. *There was no explanation for this, no possible way to make sense of it.*

Reynolds had archived three other scenes of 'coherent speech' from Distress patients. I viewed them all, unwinding the notepad's headset so I could listen in private as I made my way along the busy corridors. The exact words the patients used were different in every case – but the implications were the same.

I suspended judgement. Maybe I was still in shock, or still affected by the drugs I'd been given on the boat. Maybe I was seeing connections which simply weren't there.

By the time I reached the ward, Akili was awake. Ve smiled ruefully when ve saw me – and I knew I had it bad. It wasn't just the fact that vis face seemed to have burned itself into my brain so deeply that I could no longer believe that I'd ever been attracted to anyone else. Beauty, after all, was the shallowest thing. But ver dark eyes showed a depth of passion, humour, and intelligence that no one else I'd known had ever possessed—

I caught myself. *This was ludicrous.* To a total asex, these were the sentiments of a hormone-driven wind-up toy, a pathetic biological robot. If ve ever found out how I felt . . . the most I could expect in return was to be *pitied*.

I said, 'Have you heard about the airport?'

Ve nodded, dismayed. 'And Nishide's death. How's Mosala taking all this?'

'She's not falling to pieces – but I'm not sure she's thinking straight.' *Not like me.*

I recounted my conversation with her. 'What do you think? If she can be kept alive until someone announces the TOE on

333

her behalf, would the moderates recant and hand over the cure?'

Kuwale didn't look hopeful. 'They might. If there was a clear proof that the TOE really had been completed, with no room for doubt. But they're on the run now, they can't *hand over* anything.'

'They could still transmit the molecule's structure.'

'Yeah. And then we just hope there's a machine on Stateless which can synthesise it in time.'

'If the whole universe is a conspiracy to explain the Keystone, don't you think she might get lucky?' I didn't believe a word of this, but it seemed like the right thing to say.

'Explaining the Aleph moment doesn't stretch to miraculous reprieves. Mosala doesn't have to be the Keystone – even with Nishide dead, and Buzzo's TOE refuted. If she survives, it will only be because the people who struggled to save her fought harder than those who struggled to kill her.' Ve laughed wearily. 'That's what a Theory of Everything means: there are no miracles, not even for the Keystone. Everyone lives and dies by exactly the same rules.'

'I understand.' I hesitated. 'There's something I have to show you. Some news that's just broken, about Distress.'

'Distress?'

'Humour me. Maybe it means nothing – but I need to know what you think.'

I had an obligation to Reynolds not to splash his unreleased footage around. The ward was full, but there were screens either side of us, and the man in a cast in the opposite bed appeared to be sleeping. I handed Kuwale my notepad, and had it replay one of the clips, with the volume down low.

A pale, dishevelled, middle-aged woman with long black hair, restrained in a hospital bed, faced the viewer squarely. She didn't look drugged, and she certainly wasn't exhibiting the syndrome's characteristic behaviour – but she regarded Reynolds with intense, horrified fascination.

She said, 'This pattern of information, this state of being conscious and possessing these perceptions, wraps itself in ever-growing layers of corollaries: neurons to encode the information, blood to nourish the neurons, a heart to pump the blood, intestines to enrich it, a mouth to supply the intestines, food to pass through it, fields of crops, earth, sunlight, a trillion stars.' Her gaze shifted slightly as she spoke, scanning back and forth across Reynolds' face. 'Neurons, heart, intestines, cells of proteins and ions and water wrapped in lipid membranes, tissues differentiated in development, genes switched on by intersecting marker hormone gradients, a million interlocking molecular shapes, tetravalent carbon, monovalent hydrogen, electrons shared in bonds between nuclei of protons, neutrons to balance electrostatic repulsion, quarks spinning in both to partner the leptons in a hierarchy of field excitations, a ten-dimensional manifold to support them . . . defining a broken symmetry on the space of all topologies.' Her voice quickened. 'Neurons, heart, intestines, morphogenesis converging back to a single cell, a fertilised egg in another body. Diploid chromosomes requiring a separate donor. Ancestry iterates. Mutations split species from earlier lineages, unicellular life, self-replicating fragments, nucleotides, sugars, amino acids, carbon dioxide, water, nitrogen. A condensing protostellar cloud – rich in heavy elements synthesised in other stars, flung throughout a gravitationally unstable cosmos which starts and ends in singularities.'

She fell silent, but her eyes kept moving; I could almost see the outline of Reynolds' face in the sweep of her gaze. And if he'd appeared to her, at first, as a bizarre apparition, flashes of intense comprehension now seemed to break through her astonishment – as if she was pushing her cosmological reasoning to its limits, and weaving this stranger, this logically necessary distant cousin, into the same unified scheme.

But then something happened to put an end to her brief

remission: an upwelling of horror and panic distorted her features. Distress had reclaimed her. I halted the replay before she could begin to thrash and scream.

I said, 'There are three other cases, more or less the same. So am I putting my own spin on this raving – or does it sound the same to you? Because . . . what kind of plague could make people believe that *they're the Keystone*?'

Kuwale put the notepad down on the bed and turned to face me. 'Andrew, if this is a hoax—'

'No! Why would I—?'

'To save Mosala. Because if it's a hoax, you'll never pull it off.'

I groaned. 'If I was going to invent a Keystone to get her off the hook, I would have simulated Yasuko Nishide on his deathbed having all the cosmic revelations – not some random psychiatric case.' I explained about Reynolds and the SeeNet documentary.

Ve searched my face, trying to decide if I was telling the truth. I gazed back at ver, too tired and confused now to conceal anything. There was a flicker of surprise, and then . . . amusement? I couldn't tell – and whatever ve felt, ve kept silent.

I said, 'Maybe some other mainstream ACs faked it, hacked into SeeNet . . .' I was grasping at straws, but I couldn't make sense of this any other way.

Kuwale said flatly, 'No. I would have heard.'

'Then—?'

'It's genuine.'

'How can it be?'

Ve met my eyes again, unashamed of vis fear. 'Because everything we thought was true, is true – but we got the details wrong. *Everyone got the details wrong.* The mainstream, the moderates, the extremists: we all made different assumptions – and we were all wrong.'

'I don't understand.'

'You will. We all will.'

I suddenly recalled the apocryphal story from the AC on the boat about Muteba Kazadi's death. 'You think Distress comes from . . . mixing with information?'

'Yes.'

'If the Keystone does it, everyone else gets dragged along? *Exponential growth*? Just like a plague?'

'Yes.'

'But – how? Who was the Keystone? Who started it? Muteba Kazadi, all those years ago?'

Kuwale laughed crazily. 'No!' The man in the opposite bed was awake now, and listening to every word, but I was past caring. 'Miller didn't get around to telling you the strangest thing about that cosmological model.'

Miller was the umale, the one I'd thought of as 'Three'.

'Which is?'

'If you follow through with the calculations . . . the effect reaches back in time. Not far: exponential growth forwards means exponential decay backwards. But the *absolute certainty* of the Keystone mixing at the Aleph moment implies a small probability of other people being "dragged along" at random, even before the event. It's a continuity condition; there's no such thing in any system as an instantaneous jump from zero to one.'

I shook my head, uncomprehending. I couldn't take this in.

Akili took my hand and squeezed it hard, unthinking, transmitting vis fear – and a vertiginous thrill of anticipation – straight into my body, from skin to skin.

'The Keystone isn't the Keystone yet. The Aleph moment hasn't even happened – but we're already feeling the shock.'

25

Kuwale borrowed my notepad and rapidly sketched out the details of the information flows which ve believed lay behind Distress. Ve even attempted to fit a crude computer model of the process to the epidemiological data – although ve ended up with a curve far less steep than the actual case figures (which had risen faster than exponential growth – 'probably distorted by early under-reporting'), and a predicted date for the Aleph moment somewhere between 7 February, 2055 . . . and 12 June, 3070. Undeterred, ve struggled to refine the model. Graphs, network diagrams, and equations flickered across the screen beneath vis fingertips; it looked as impressive as anything I'd seen Violet Mosala do – and I understood it about as well.

On one level, I couldn't help but be swept along with vis urgent logic – but as the initial shock of recognition faded, I began to wonder again if we weren't simply reading our own meaning into the four patients' bizarre soliloquies. Anthrocosmology had never before made a single testable prediction. I didn't doubt that it could provide an elegant mathematical underpinning to any TOE – but if the first distinct evidence for the theory itself consisted of the rantings of four people suffering from a new and exotic mental disease, that was a slender basis on which to throw out everything I believed about the universe.

And as for the prognosis, if Kuwale was right, of a world completely afflicted by Distress . . . that was a cataclysm as unthinkable as the moderates' *unravelling*.

I kept my doubts to myself, but by the time I left the ward – leaving Kuwale immersed in a conference with the other mainstream ACs – I had my feet back on the ground. All this talk of *echoes of the future Aleph moment* had to be ranked as less plausible than even the most far-fetched conventional alternatives.

Maybe a neuroactive military pathogen gone wrong, targeting a specific region of the brain, could induce the ordinary symptoms of Distress in most of its victims – plus these outbursts of manic-but-precise observations in four out of three thousand cases. *Reasoning* was the product of organic events in the brain, like every other mental process – and if a paranoid schizophrenic, injured by crude accidents of genetics and disease, could find personal significance in every advertising sign, every cloud, every tree . . . maybe the combination of the right scientific background with the highly focused damage wrought by this viral weapon could trigger an equally uncontrollable – but much more rigorous – avalanche of meaning. If the original aim of the weapon had been to impair analytical thought, it wasn't inconceivable that a wild version might end up overstimulating the very neural pathways it had been designed to destroy.

I went back to the electrical shop and bought myself another notepad. I called De Groot from the street; she seemed upset, but she didn't want to talk on the net.

We met at the hotel, in Mosala's suite. De Groot ushered me in, in silence. 'Is Violet—?' Dust motes swam beneath the skylight; when I spoke, the room sounded hollow.

'She's been admitted. I wanted to stay at the hospital, but she sent me away.' De Groot stood opposite me, hands clasped in front of her, eyes downcast. She said quietly, 'You know, we've had crank mail from just about everyone. Every cult, every lunatic on the planet wanted to let Violet in on their amazing cosmic revelations . . . or let her know that she was desecrating their precious mythology, and would burn in Hell for it . . . or drive away all the Buddha-nature . . . or crush the world's great civilisations into nihilistic rubble, with her male Western reductionist hubris. The Anthrocosmologists were just . . . one more voice shouting noise.' She looked at me squarely. 'Would you have picked them as the threat? Not the fundamentalists. Not the racists. Not the psychotics who gave detailed descriptions of what they planned to do to her corpse. People who sent us long dissertations on information theory – and P.S., we'd be happy to see you create the universe, but certain other parties may try to stop you.'

I said, 'No one could have picked them.'

De Groot ran a hand across her temple, then stood in silence, shielding her eyes.

'Are you all right?'

She nodded, and laughed humourlessly. 'Headache, that's all.' She inhaled deeply, visibly steeling herself to push on. 'They found traces of foreign proteins in her bloodstream, bone marrow, and lymph nodes. They can't resolve the molecular structures, though – and she's showing no symptoms, so far. So they've put her on a mixture of strong antiviral drugs – and until something happens, all they can do is watch her.'

'Is security—?'

'She's under guard. For what that's worth now.'

'And Buzzo?'

'Apparently his scan was clear.' De Groot snorted, angry and bewildered. 'He's unmoved by . . . all of this. He believes that Nishide simply died of natural causes, Violet has some harmless pollutant in her body, and your cholera analysis was some kind of forgery for the sake of a media beat-up. The only thing he seems worried about is how he's going to get home at the end of the conference if the airport is still closed.'

'But he has bodyguards—?'

'I don't know; you'd have to ask him that. Oh – and Violet

340

asked him to give a media conference himself, announcing the flaw in his TOE. The antiviral drugs are debilitating; she's so nauseous that she can barely speak. Buzzo made some vague promise to her – but then he muttered something to me about looking at the issues more closely before he retracted anything. So I don't know what he'll do.'

I felt a stab of anger and frustration, but I said, 'He's heard all the evidence, it's his decision.' I didn't much want to think about Buzzo's enemies, myself. Sarah Knight's body hadn't even been found yet – but the possibility that her killer was on Stateless unnerved me more than anything else. The moderates had let me walk free, once they'd reasoned that they could still get what they wanted. The extremists had nearly killed me, once already – and they hadn't even been trying.

I said, 'Even if this weapon is about to go off at any moment . . . there's nothing anyone can do on Stateless that couldn't be done in an air ambulance, right? And surely your government would be willing to send a fully equipped military hospital jet—'

De Groot gave a hollow laugh. 'Yeah? You make it sound so easy. Violet has some friends in high places – and some sworn enemies . . . but most of all, a lot of fucking pragmatists who'll happily use her in whatever way they see fit. It would take a small miracle for them to weigh up the pros and cons, take sides, battle it out, and make a decision, all in one day – even if Stateless was at peace, and the jet could land right at the airport.'

'Come on! The whole island's as flat as a runway! Okay, it's soft at the edges, but there must be a twenty-kilometre radius in which the ground is hard enough.'

'All within reach of a missile from the airport.'

'Yeah, but why should the mercenaries care about a medical evacuation? They must be expecting foreign navies to start moving in soon to take their nationals off the island. This is no different; it's just faster.'

De Groot shook her head sadly; she wanted to be convinced, but I wasn't making sense to her. 'Whatever you and I might think about the risks, it's just guesswork and wishful thinking. The government is still going to assess the situation from their own point of view – and they're not going to make a decision in thirty seconds. Tens of thousands of dollars for a mercy flight is one thing. A plane shot down over Stateless is another. And the last thing Violet – or any sane person – would want is three or four innocent people blown out of the sky for no reason.'

I turned away from her, and crossed to the window. From what I could see of the streets below, Stateless *was* still at peace. But whatever bloody havoc the mercenaries were planning, surely the last thing their employers wanted was a world-famous martyr for *technolibération*? That was why EnGeneUity had never really made sense as her would-be assassins: her death would be as bad for them as her highly publicised emigration.

It was a delicate proposition, though. What would they be admitting, if they made an exception for her? And which scenario would they consider most damaging to the anti-boycott push: the cautionary tale of Mosala's tragic death from a reckless flirtation with renegades – or the heart-warming story of survival when a mercy flight whisked her back into the fold (where every gene belonged to its rightful owner, and every disease had an instant cure)?

As yet, they probably didn't even know about the difficult choice they were facing. So it was up to whoever broke the news to sell them on the right decision.

I turned to De Groot. 'What if the mercenaries could be persuaded to guarantee safe passage for a rescue flight? To make a public statement to that effect? Do you think you could start things moving – on the chance of that?' I clenched my fists, fighting down panic. *Did I have any idea what I was saying?* Once I'd promised to do this, I couldn't back out.

But I'd already made a promise to *swim faster*.

De Groot looked torn. 'Violet hasn't even told Wendy or Makompo yet. And she's sworn me to silence. Wendy's on a business trip in Toronto—'

'If she can lobby from Cape Town, she can lobby from Toronto. And Violet's not thinking straight. Tell her mother everything. And her husband. Tell Marian Fox and the whole IUTP if you have to.'

De Groot hesitated, then nodded uncertainly. 'It's worth trying. Anything's worth trying. But how do you imagine we're going to get any kind of guarantee from the mercenaries?'

I said, 'Plan A is to hope very hard that they're answering the phones. Because I really don't want to have to walk into the airport and negotiate in person.'

Most of the island's centre still appeared untouched by the invasion – but four streets away from the airport, everything changed. There were no barricades, no warning signs – and no people at all. It was early evening, and the streets behind me were abuzz, with shops and restaurants open for business just five hundred metres from the occupied buildings – but once I'd crossed that invisible line, it was as if Stateless had suddenly given birth to its own Ruins, an imitation in miniature of the dead hearts of the net-slain cities.

There were no bullets flying, this was not a war zone, but I had no experience to guide me, no idea of what to expect. I'd kept away from battlefields; I'd chosen science journalism happy in the knowledge that I'd never be required to film anything more dangerous than a bioethics conference.

The entrance to the passenger terminal was a wide rectangle of blackness. The sliding doors lay ten metres away, in fragments. Windows had been broken, plants and statues scattered; the walls were strangely scarred, as if something mechanically clawed had scaled them. I'd hoped for a sentry, signs of order, evidence of a coherent command structure. This looked more like a gang of looters were waiting in the darkness for someone to wander in.

I thought: *Sarah Knight would have done this – for the story alone.*

Yeah. And Sarah Knight was dead.

I approached slowly, scanning the ground nervously, wishing I hadn't told **Sisyphus** fourteen years before to lose all junk mail from weapons manufacturers looking for technophile journalists to provide free publicity for their glamorous new anti-personnel mines. Then again . . . there'd probably been no helpful tips in those media releases for avoiding being on the receiving end – short of spending fifty thousand dollars on the matching sweepers.

The interior of the building was pitch black, but the floodlights outside bleached the reef-rock white. I squinted into the maw of the entrance, wishing I had **Witness** to rejig my retinas. The camera on my right shoulder was virtually weightless, but it still made me feel skewed and misshapen – about as comfortable, centred, and functional as if my genitals had migrated to one kneecap. And – irrationally or not – the invisible nerve taps and RAM had always made me feel shielded, protected. When my own eyes and ears had captured everything for the digital record, I'd been a privileged observer right up to the moment of being disembowelled or blinded. This machine could be brushed off like a speck of dandruff.

I'd never felt so naked in my life.

I stopped ten metres from the empty doorway, arms stretched out and hands raised. I yelled into the darkness: 'I'm a journalist! I want to talk!'

I waited. I could still hear the crowds of the city behind me, but the airport exuded silence. I shouted again. And waited. I was almost ready to give up fear for embarrassment; maybe the passenger terminal was abandoned, the mercenaries had set up camp on the farthest corner of the runway, and I was standing here making a fool of myself to no one.

Then I felt a gentle stirring of the humid air, and the blackness of the entrance disgorged a machine.

I flinched, but stood my ground; if it had wanted me dead, I would never have seen it coming. The thing betrayed a flickering succession of partial outlines as it moved – faint but consistent distortions of the light which the eye seized upon as edges – but once it halted, I was left staring at nothing but afterimages and guesswork. A six-legged robot, three metres high? Actively computing my view of its surroundings, and programming an optically active sheath to match luminosities? *No, more than that.* It stood protruding halfway into the floodlit forecourt, without even casting a shadow – which meant it was real-time holographing the blocked light sources, its polymer skin lasing out a perfectly matched substitute beam, wavefront by wavefront. I had a sudden, sickening realisation of what the people of Stateless were facing. This was alpha military tech, costing millions. EnGeneUity weren't messing around with cheap aggravation, this time. They wanted their intellectual property back, product reputation unscathed – and anything which stood above the reef-rock would be cut down if it got in the way.

The insect said, 'We've already chosen the journalists' pool, Andrew Worth. You're not on the invasion hit parade.' It spoke English, perfectly inflected right down to a hint of amusement, but with an unnerving geographical neutrality. Whether its speech was autonomous, or whether I was talking real-time to the mercenaries – or their PR people – I had no idea.

'I don't want to cover the war. I'm here to offer you a chance to avoid some . . . undesirable publicity.'

The insect scuttled forward angrily, delicate moiré patterns of interference fringes blossoming and fading on its camouflaged surface. I stayed rooted to the spot; my instinct was to flee, but my muscles felt like jelly. The thing came to a halt, two or three metres away – and vanished from sight again. I didn't doubt that, at the very least, it could have raised its forelegs and decapitated me in an instant.

I steadied myself, and addressed the solid air. 'There's a woman on this island who's going to die if she's not evacuated in a matter of hours. And if that happens . . . SeeNet are ready to broadcast a documentary called *Violet Mosala: Martyr to Technolibération*.' It was the truth – although Lydia had put up some resistance, at first. I'd sent her faked footage of Mosala talking about the reasons for her planned emigration – all more-or-less what had really been said, although I hadn't actually filmed it. Three SeeNet newsroom editors were hard at work incorporating that – and some of the genuine material I'd filed – into an up-to-date obituary. I'd neglected to include anything about the Anthrocosmologists, though. Mosala had been about to become the figurehead for a major challenge to the boycott – and now she was infected with a viral weapon, and Stateless was occupied. Lydia had drawn her own conclusions, and the editors would have been instructed accordingly.

The insect was silent for several long minutes. I remained frozen, my hands still in the air. I imagined the blackmail threat being passed up the chain of command. Maybe the biotech alliance were exploring the option of buying SeeNet and killing the story? But then they'd have to lean on other networks, too; they'd have to keep on paying to ensure the right spin. They could get what they wanted for free, if they let her live.

I said, 'If Mosala survives, you can stop her from returning. But if she dies here . . . she'll be linked in the public imagination to Stateless for the next hundred years.'

I felt a stinging sensation on my shoulder. I glanced down at the camera; it had been incinerated, and the ashes were tumbling away from a tiny charred patch on my shirt.

'The plane can land. And you can leave with her. Once she's out of danger, file a new story from Cape Town on her plans to emigrate – and what became of them.' It was the same voice as before – but the power behind the words came from far beyond the island.

There was no need to add: *If the spin is right, you'll be rewarded.*

I bowed my head in assent. 'I'll do that.'

The insect hesitated. 'Will you? I don't think so.' A searing pain slashed my abdomen; I cried out and sank to my knees. 'She'll return alone. You can stay on Stateless and document the fall.' I glanced up to see a faint hint of green and violet shimmering in the air as the thing retreated, like a glint of sunlight through half-closed eyes.

It took me a while to rise to my feet. The laser flash had burnt a horizontal welt right across my stomach – but the beam had lingered for whole microseconds on the existing wound; the carbohydrate polymer had been caramelised, and a brown watery fluid was leaking out of my navel. I muttered abuse at the empty doorway, then started hobbling away.

When I was back among the crowds, two teenagers approached me and asked if I needed help. I accepted gratefully. They held me up as I limped towards the hospital.

I called De Groot from casualty. I said, 'They were very civilised. We have clearance to land.'

De Groot looked haggard, but she beamed at me. 'That's fantastic!'

'Any news about the flight?'

'Nothing yet – but I spoke to Wendy a few minutes ago, and she was waiting for a call from the President, no less.' She hesitated. 'Violet's developed a fever. It's not dangerous yet, but . . .'

But the weapon had triggered. We'd be racing the virus every step of the way now. What had I expected, though? Another timing error? Or magical immunity for the Keystone?

'You're with her?'

'Yes.'

'I'll meet you there in half an hour.'

The same medic treated me as before. She'd had a long day; she said irritably, 'I don't want to hear your excuse this time. The last one was bad enough.'

I surveyed the pristine cubicle, the orderly cabinets of drugs and instruments, and I was gripped by despair. Even if Mosala was evacuated in time . . . there were one million people on Stateless, with nowhere to flee. I said, 'What will you do, when the war starts?'

'There won't be a war.'

I tried to imagine the machines being assembled, the fate being prepared for these people, deep inside the airport. I said gently, 'I don't think you're going to have a choice about that.'

The medic stopped applying cream to my burns, and glared at me as if I'd said something unforgivably offensive and belittling. 'You're a stranger here. You don't have the slightest idea what our choices are. What do you think? We've spent the last twenty years in some kind of blissful Utopian stupor, content in the knowledge that our positive karmic energy would repel all invaders?' She started dispensing the cream again, roughly.

I was bemused. 'No. I expect you're fully prepared to defend yourselves. But this time, I think you're going to be outgunned. Badly.'

She unrolled a length of bandage, eyeing me sharply. 'Listen, because I'm only going to say this once. When the time comes, you'd better trust us.'

'To do what?'

'To know better than you.'

I laughed grimly. 'That's not asking much.'

When I turned into the corridor which led to Mosala's room, I saw De Groot talking – in hushed tones, but with obvious excitement – to the two security guards. She spotted me and waved. I quickened my step.

When I reached them, De Groot silently held up her notepad and hit a key. A newsreader appeared.

'In the latest developments on the renegade island of Stateless, the violent anarchist splinter group occupying the airport have just acceded to a request from South African diplomats to allow the urgent evacuation of Violet Mosala, the twenty-seven-year-old Nobel laureate who has been attending the controversial Einstein Centenary Conference.' In the background, a stylised world globe spun beneath an image of Mosala, the view zooming in on Stateless, and then South Africa, on cue. 'With the primitive healthcare facilities on the island, local doctors have been unable to provide an accurate diagnosis, but Mosala's condition is believed to be life-threatening. Sources in Mandela say that President Ncha-baleng herself sent a personal appeal to the anarchists, and received their reply just minutes ago.'

I threw my arms around De Groot, lifted her off her feet and spun around until I was giddy with joy. The guards looked on, grinning like children. Maybe it was a microscopic victory in the face of the invasion – but it still seemed like the first good thing that had happened for a very long time.

De Groot said gently, 'That's enough.' I stopped, and we disengaged. She said, 'The plane lands at three a.m. Fifteen kilometres west of the airport.'

I caught my breath. 'Does she know?'

De Groot shook her head. 'I haven't told her anything yet. She's sleeping now; the fever's still high, but it's been stable for a while. The doctors can't say what the virus will do next, but they can carry a selection of drugs in the ambulance to cover the most likely emergencies.'

I said soberly, 'Only one thing really worries me now.'

'What?'

'Knowing Violet . . . when she finds out we've gone behind

her back, she'll probably refuse to leave – out of sheer stubborness.'

De Groot gave me an odd look, as if she was tryng to decide whether I was joking or not.

She said, 'If you really believe that, then you don't know Violet at all.'

26

I told De Groot I'd catch some sleep and be back by 2:30. I wanted to bid Mosala *bon voyage*.

I went looking for Akili to tell ver the good news, but ve'd been discharged. I sent ver a message, then returned to the hotel, washed my face, changed my laser-singed shirt. My burns were numb, absent; the local anaesthetic had magicked them away. I felt battered, but triumphant – and too wired to stand still, let alone sleep. It was almost eleven, but the shops were still open; I went out and bought myself another shoulder camera, then wandered the city, filming everything in sight. *The last night of peace on Stateless?* The mood on the streets was nothing like the atmosphere of siege among the physicists and journalists inside the hotel, but there was an edge of nervous anticipation, like Los Angeles during a quake risk alert (I'd been through one, a false alarm). When people met my gaze they seemed curious – even suspicious – but they showed no sign of hostility. It was as if they thought I might, conceivably, be a spy for the mercenaries – but if I was, that was merely an exotic trait which they had no intention of holding against me.

I stopped in the middle of a brightly lit square, and checked the news nets. Buzzo had given no press conference admitting his error, but with Mosala now showing symptoms, perhaps he'd take the risk of the extremists seriously, and reconsider. Coverage of the situation on Stateless stank, uniformly – but SeeNet would soon scoop everyone by announcing the real reasons for the occupation. And even with Mosala alive, the truth might come out badly for the pro-boycott alliance.

The air was humid, but cold. I stared up at the satellites which bridged the planet, and tried to make sense of the fact that I was standing on an artificial South Pacific island, on the eve of a war.

Was my whole life encoded in this moment – the memories I possessed, the circumstances I found myself in? Taking this much and no more as given . . . could I have reconstructed all the rest?

It didn't feel that way. My childhood in Sydney was unimaginable, as remote and hypothetical as the Big Bang – and even the time I'd spent in the hold on the fishing boat, and the encounter with the robot at the airport, had receded like fragments of a dream.

I'd never had cholera. I possessed no internal organs.

The stars glinted icily.

At one in the morning, the streets were still crowded, shops and restaurants still trading. Nobody seemed as sombre as they should have been; maybe they still believed that they were facing nothing more than the kind of harassment they'd survived before.

There was a group of young men standing around a fountain in the square, joking and laughing. I asked them if they thought the militia would attack the airport soon. I couldn't imagine why else they'd be in such high spirits; maybe they'd be taking part, and were psyching themselves up for it.

They stared at me in disbelief. 'Attack the airport? And get slaughtered?'

'It might be your only chance.'

They exchanged amused glances. One of them put a hand on my shoulder and said solicitously, 'Everything's going to be fine. Just keep an ear to the ground, and hang on tight.'

I wondered what kind of drugs they were on.

When I returned to the hospital, De Groot said, 'Violet's awake. She wants to talk to you.'

I went in alone. The room was dimly lit; a monitor near the head of the bed glowed with green and orange data. Mosala's voice was weak, but she was lucid.

'Will you ride in the ambulance with me?'

'If that's what you want.'

'I want you to record everything. Just make good use of it, if you have to.'

'I will.' I wasn't sure exactly what she meant — framing EnGeneUity for her death, if it came to that? I didn't press her for details; I was weary of the politics of martyrdom.

'Karin said you went to the airport and petitioned the mercenaries on my behalf.' She searched my face. 'Why?'

'I was returning a favour.'

She laughed softly. 'What did I ever do to deserve that?'

'It's a long story.' And I was no longer sure, myself, whether I'd been trying to repay Adelle Vunibobo, doing it all for *technolibération*, acting out of respect and admiration for Mosala, or hoping to impress Akili by 'saving the Keystone' — even if the role was beginning to sound less like a revered creator than a kind of information-theoretic Typhoid Mary.

De Groot came in with news of the flight; everything was on schedule, and it was time to leave. Two medics joined us. I stood back, filming with the shoulder camera as Mosala was moved to a trolley, monitor and drug pumps still attached.

In the garage, on the way to the ambulance, I saw half a dozen balloon-tyred vehicles being loaded with medical equipment, bandages, and drugs. Maybe they were moving supplies to other sites around the city, in case the hospital was captured. It was heartening to see that not everyone was taking the invasion lightly.

We rode through the city slowly, without the siren wailing.

More people were on the streets than I'd ever seen by daylight. Mosala asked De Groot for a notepad, then put it on the mattress beside her, and turned on to her side so she could type. Whatever she was doing seemed to demand intense concentration – but she spoke to me, without looking away from the screen.

'You suggested that I appoint a successor, Andrew. Some-one to make sure that the work was finished. Well, I'm arranging that now.'

I couldn't see the point anymore, but I didn't argue. A high-resolution scan in Cape Town would yield structures for all the viral proteins almost immediately, and precision drugs to block their actions could be designed and synthesised in a matter of hours. Proving the moderates wrong and then beg-ging them for the cure was no longer any kind of shortcut.

Mosala glanced up at me, and spoke for the camera. 'The software is working on ten canonical experiments. A full analysis of all of them, combined, will yield what used to be thought of as the ten parameters of total space – the details of the ten-dimensional geometry which underlies all the particles and forces. In modern terms . . . those ten experiments reveal, between them, exactly how the symmetry of pre-space is broken, for us. Exactly what it *is* that everything in this universe has in common.'

'I understand.'

She shook her head impatiently. 'Let me finish. What's running on the supercomputer network, right now, is just brute-force calculations. I wanted the software to leave the honours to me. Double-checking, pulling it all together . . . writing a paper which set out the results in a way which would make sense to anyone. But those things are trivial. I already know exactly what has to be done with the results, once they're available. And—' She executed a flurry of keystrokes, scrutinised the effects, then put the notepad aside. 'All of it has just been automated. My mother gave me a pre-release **Kaspar** clonelet last week – and it'll probably write up the results more smoothly than I ever could. So whether I'm alive, dead, or somewhere in between . . . by 6 a.m. on Friday, that paper *will* be written – and posted on the nets with toll-free, universal access. Copies will also be sent to every faculty member and every student of the Physics Departments of every university on the planet.' She flashed a smile of pure defiant glee. 'What are the Anthrocosmologists going to do, now? Kill every physicist on Earth?' I glanced up at De Groot, who was tight-lipped and ashen. Mosala groaned. 'Don't look so damned morbid, you two. I'm just covering all contingencies.'

She closed her eyes; her breathing was ragged, but she was still smiling. I turned to the monitor; her temperature was 40.9 degrees.

We'd left the city behind; the windows of the ambulance showed nothing but our reflections. The ride was smooth, the engine all but silent. After a while, I thought I could hear the reef-rock itself, exhaling through a distant borehole – but then I realised that it was the whine of the approaching jet.

Mosala had lost consciousness, and no one tried to rouse her. We reached the rendezvous point, and I climbed out quickly to cover the landing – more because of the promise I'd made than out of any real vestige of professionalism. The plane descended vertically, just forty or fifty metres away from us, grey fuselage lit by nothing but moonlight, the VTOL engines blasting a fine caustic dust of limestone out of the matrix of the rock. I wanted to savour this moment of victory – but the sight of the sleek military craft landing in darkness in the middle of nowhere made my heart sink. I imagined it would be the same with the naval evacuation: the outside world was going to tip-toe in, gather up its own people, and leave. The anarchists could take what was coming to them.

The two men who descended first wore officer's uniforms and side arms, but they might have been doctors. They took the medics aside and spoke in a huddle, their voices lost beneath the hum of the jets; air was still being forced through the stationary engines to keep them cool. Then a slender young man in rumpled civilian clothes emerged, looking haggard and disoriented. It took me a few seconds to recognise him; it was Mosala's husband, Makompo.

De Groot met him; they embraced silently. I stayed back as she led him to the ambulance. I turned and looked away across the grey-and-silver reef-rock; threads of scattered trace minerals caught the moonlight, shining like the foam on an impossibly tranquil ocean. When I turned back, the soldiers were carrying Mosala, bound to a stretcher, up into the plane. Makompo and De Groot followed. I suddenly felt very tired.

De Groot came down the steps and approached me, shouting, 'Are you coming with us? They say there's plenty of room.'

I stared back at her. What was there to keep me here? My contract with SeeNet was to make a profile of Mosala, not to record the fall of Stateless. The invisible insect had forbidden me to join the flight – but would the mercenaries have any way of knowing, if I did? Stupid question: outdoors, military satellites could just about fingerprint people and lip-read their conversations, all in infrared. But would they shoot down the plane – undermining the whole PR exercise, and inviting retribution – just to punish one obscure journalist? No.

I said, 'I wish I could. But there's someone here I can't leave behind.'

De Groot nodded, needing no further explanation, and shook my hand, smiling. 'Good luck to both of you, then. I hope we'll see you in Cape Town, soon.'

'So do I.'

The two medics were silent as we rode back to the hospital. I felt certain that they wanted to talk about the war – but not in front of a foreigner. I scanned through the footage I'd taken with the shoulder camera, not yet trusting the unfamiliar technology, then dispatched it to my console at home.

The city was more crowded than ever, though there were fewer people on their feet now. Most were camping out on the streets, with sleeping bags, folding chairs, portable stoves, and even some small tents. I didn't know whether to feel encouraged by this, or depressed at the pathetic optimism it implied. Maybe the anarchists were prepared to make the best of it, if the city's infrastructure was seized. And I'd still seen no evidence of panic, riots, or looting – so maybe Munroe was right, and their education in the origins and dynamics of these revered human cultural activities was enough to empower them with the ability to think through the consequences, and decline to take part.

But in the face of a billion dollars worth of military hardware, they were going to need a lot more than stoves, tents, and sociobiology to avoid being slaughtered.

27

I was woken by the shelling. The rumbling sounded distant but the bed was shaking. I dressed in seconds then stood in the middle of the room, paralysed by indecision. There were no basements here, no bomb shelters, so where was the safest place to be? Down on the ground floor? Or out on the street? I baulked at the prospect of exposure – but would four or five storeys over my head offer any real protection, or just a heavier pile of rubble?

It was just after six, barely light. I moved to the window cautiously, fighting down an absurd fear of snipers – as if anyone from either side would bother. Five columns of white smoke hung in the middle distance, funnelling out from hidden apexes like languid tornadoes. I asked **Sisyphus** to scan the local nets for close-up vision; dozens of people had posted footage. Reef-rock was resilient and non-flammable, but the shells must have been spiked with some chemical agent tailored to inflict damage beyond the reach of mere heat and percussion, because the results looked less like shattered buildings than mine tailings dumped on empty lots. I couldn't imagine anyone surviving inside – but the adjacent streets hadn't fared much better, buried metres deep in chalk dust.

The people camped outside the hotel showed no sign that they'd been taken by surprise; half of them were already packed and moving, the rest were taking down their tents, rolling up blankets and sleeping bags, disassembling stoves. I could hear young children crying, and the mood of the crowd was visibly tense – but no one was being trampled underfoot.

Yet. Looking further along the street, I could make out a slow, steady flow of people north, away from the heart of the city.

I'd been half expecting something deadly and silent – EnGeneUity were bioengineers, after all – but I should have known better. A rain of explosions, buildings reduced to dust, and a stream of refugees made far better pictures for *Anarchy Comes To Stateless*. The mercenaries weren't here to take control of the island with clinical efficiency; they were here to prove that all renegade societies were doomed to collapse into telegenic mayhem.

A shell went off somewhere east of the hotel, the closest yet. White powder rained down from the ceiling; one corner of the polymer window popped loose from its frame, and curled up like a dead leaf. I squatted on the floor, covering my head, cursing myself for not leaving with De Groot and Mosala – and cursing Akili for ignoring my messages. *Why couldn't I accept the fact that I meant nothing to ver?* I'd been of some use in the struggle to protect Mosala from the heretic ACs, and I'd brought ver the news which supposedly revealed the truth behind Distress . . . but now that the great information plague was coming, I was irrelevant.

The door swung open. An elderly Fijian woman stepped into the room; the hotel staff wore no uniforms, but I thought I'd seen her before, working in the building. She announced curtly, 'We're evacuating the city. Take what you can carry.' The floor had stopped moving, but I rose to my feet unsteadily, unsure if I'd heard her correctly.

I'd already packed my clothes. I grabbed my suitcase, and followed her out into the corridor. My room was just past the stairs, and she was heading for the next door along. I gestured at the other half of the corridor, some twenty rooms. 'Have you checked—?'

'No.' For a moment, she seemed reluctant to entrust me with the task, but then she relented. She held up her pass key and let my notepad clone its IR signature.

I left my suitcase by the stairs. The first four rooms were empty. More shells were exploding all the time now, most of them mercifully distant. I kept one eye on the screen as I waved my notepad at the locks; someone was collating all the damage reports and posting an annotated map of the city. So far, twenty-one buildings had been demolished – mainly apartment blocks. There was no question that if strategic targets had been chosen, they would have been hit; maybe the most valuable infrastructure was being spared – saved for the use of a puppet government to be installed by a second wave of invaders, who'd 'rescue' the island from 'anarchy'? Or maybe the aim was simply to level as many residential buildings as possible, in order to drive the greatest number of people out into the desert.

I found Lowell Parker – the Atlantica journalist I'd seen at Mosala's media conference – crouched on the floor, shaking . . . much as the woman from the hotel had found me. He recovered quickly, and seemed to accept the news of the evacuation gratefully – as if all he'd been waiting for was word of a definite plan, even if it came from someone else who didn't have a clue.

In the next ten or twelve rooms, I came across four more people – journalists or academics, probably, but no one I recognised – most of them already packed, just waiting to be told what to do. No one stopped to question the wisdom of the message I was passing on – and I badly wanted to get away from the bombing, myself – but the prospect of a million people pouring out of the city was beginning to fill me with dread. The greatest disasters of the last fifty years had all been among refugees fleeing war zones. Maybe it would be smarter to take my chances playing Russian roulette with the shells.

I knew the last room was a suite, the mirror image of Mosala and De Groot's; the architectural symmetry of the building demanded it. The cloned pass key signature unlocked the door – but there was a chain keeping it from opening more than a crack.

I called out, loudly. No one answered. I tried using my shoulder – and bruised myself badly, to no effect. Swearing, I kicked the door near the chain – which was twice as painful, almost splitting my stitches, but it worked.

Henry Buzzo was sprawled on the floor beneath the window, flat on his back. I approached, dismayed, doubting that there'd be much chance of getting help amid all the chaos. He was wearing a red velvet bathrobe, and his hair was wet, as if he'd just stepped out of the shower. A bioweapon from the extremists, finally taking hold? Or just a heart attack from the shock of the explosions?

Neither. The bathrobe was soaked with blood. A hole had been blasted in his chest. Not by a sniper; the window was intact. I squatted down and pressed two fingers against his carotid artery. He was dead, but still warm.

I closed my eyes and clenched my teeth, trying not to scream with frustration. After all it had taken to get Mosala off the island, Buzzo could have saved himself so easily. A few words admitting the flaw in his work, and he'd still be alive.

It wasn't *pride* that had killed him, though – screw that. He'd had a right to his stubborness, a right to defend his theory, flawed or not. He was dead for precisely one reason: some psychotic AC had sacrificed him to the mirage of *transcendence*.

I found two umale security guards in the second bedroom – one fully dressed; one had probably been sleeping. Both looked like they'd been shot in the face. I was in shock now – more dazed than sickened – but I finally had enough presence of mind to start filming. Maybe there'd be a trial, eventually, and if the hotel was about to be reduced to rubble, there'd be no other evidence. I surveyed the bodies in close-up, then walked from room to room, sweeping the camera around

361

indiscriminately, hoping to capture enough detail for a complete reconstruction.

The bathroom door was locked. I felt an idiotic surge of hope; maybe a fourth person had witnessed the crime, but had managed to hide here in safety. I rattled the handle, and I was on the verge of yelling out words of reassurance, when the meaning of the chained front door finally penetrated my stupor.

I stood frozen for several seconds, at first not quite believing it – and then afraid to move.

Because I could hear someone breathing. Soft and shallow – but not soft enough. Struggling for control. Centimetres away.

I couldn't let go of the handle; my fingers were clenched tight. I placed my left hand flat against the cool surface of the door, at the height where the killer's face would be – as if hoping to sense the contours, to gauge the distance from skin to skin by the resonant pitch of every screaming nerve end.

Who was it? Who was the extremists' assassin? Who had had the opportunity to infect me with the engineered cholera? Some stranger I'd passed in the Phnom Penh transit lounge, or the crowded bazaar of Dili airport? The Polynesian businessman who'd sat beside me, on the last leg of the flight? *Indrani Lee?*

I was shaking with horror, certain that a bullet would pierce my skull in a matter of seconds – but part of me still wanted, badly, to break open the door and *see*.

I could have broadcast the moment live on the net – and gone out in a blaze of revelation.

Another shell exploded nearby, the shock wave resonating through the building so powerfully that the frame almost flexed itself free of the lock.

I turned and fled.

The procession out of the city was an ordeal – but perhaps never more than it had to be. From my snail's-eye view of the crowd, everyone looked as terrified, as claustrophobic, as desperate for momentum as I was – but they remained stubbornly, defiantly patient, inching forward like novice tightrope walkers, calculating every movement, sweating from the tension between fear and restraint. Children wailed in the distance, but the adults around me spoke in guarded whispers between the ground-shaking detonations. I kept waiting for an apartment block to collapse in front of us, burying a hundred people and crushing a hundred more in the panic of retreat – but it failed to happen, again and again, and after twenty excruciating minutes we'd left the shelling behind.

The procession kept moving. For a long time, we remained jammed in a herd, shoulder-to-shoulder, with no choice but to keep step – but once we were out of the built-up suburbs and into the industrial areas, where the factories and warehouses were set in wide expanses of bare rock, there was suddenly space to move freely. As the opaque scrum around me melted into near transparency, I could see half a dozen quadcycles ahead in the distance, and even an electric truck keeping pace.

By then we'd been walking for almost two hours, but the sun was still low, and as the crowd spread out a welcome cool breeze moved in between us. My spirits were lifting, slightly. Despite the scale of the exodus, I'd witnessed no real violence; the worst I'd seen so far was an enraged couple screaming accusations of infidelity at each other as they trudged along, side by side, each holding up one end of a bundle of possessions wrapped in orange tent fabric.

It was clear that the whole evacuation had been rehearsed – or at least widely discussed, in great detail – long before the invasion. *Civil defence plan D: head for the coast.* And a planned evacuation, with tents, with blankets, with solar-rechargable stoves, didn't have to be the disaster, here, that it might have been almost anywhere else. We were moving closer to the reefs and the ocean farms – the source of all the island's food. The freshwater arteries in the rock could be tapped with relative ease, as could the sewage treatment conduits. If exposure, starvation, dehydration and disease were the greatest killers of modern warfare, the people of Stateless seemed to be uniquely equipped to resist them all.

The only thing that worried me was the certainty that the mercenaries understood all of this, perfectly. If their aim with the shelling had been to drive us out of the city, they must have known how relatively little misery it would cause. Maybe they believed that selective footage of the exodus would still be enough to confirm the political failure of Stateless in most people's eyes – and with or without scenes of dysentery and starvation, there was no doubt that the position of the anti-boycott nations had already been weakened. I had a queasy suspicion, though, that merely evicting a million people into tent villages wouldn't be enough for EnGeneUity.

I'd transmitted the footage from Buzzo's suite, along with a brief deposition putting it in context, to the FBI and to the security firm's head office in Suva. It had seemed the proper way to let the families of the three men hear of their deaths, and to set in motion as much of an investigation as was possible under the circumstances. I hadn't sent a copy to SeeNet – less out of respect for the bereaved relatives, than out of a reluctance to choose between admitting to Lydia that I'd concealed the facts about Mosala and the ACs . . . and compounding the crime, by pretending that I had no idea why Buzzo had been assassinated. Whatever I did, I was probably screwed in the long run, but I wanted to delay the inevitable for a few more days, if possible.

Some three hours' slow march from the city, I caught sight of a multicoloured blur in the distance, which soon resolved itself into a vast patchwork of vivid green and orange squares, scattered across the rock a few kilometres ahead. We'd just left the central plateau behind, and the ground now sloped gently down all the way to the coast; whether it was that modest gradient, or the end of the march coming into view, the going seemed suddenly easier. Thirty minutes later, the people around me stopped and began to pitch their own tents.

I sat on my suitcase and rested for a while, then dutifully commenced recording. Whether the evacuation had been rehearsed or not, the island itself collaborated with the refugees so fully as they set up camp that the process looked more like the smooth slotting into place of missing components in an elaborate machine – the logical completion of a function the bare rock had always implied – than any kind of desperate attempt to improvise in an emergency. One tear-sized droplet of signalling peptide was enough to start the cascade which instructed the lithophiles to open a shaft to a buried freshwater artery – and by the time I'd seen the third pump installed, I'd learnt to recognise the characteristic swirl of green-and-blue trace minerals which marked the sites where wells could be formed. Sewerage took a little longer – the shafts were wider and deeper, and the access points rarer.

This was the flipside of Ned Landers' mad, tyre-eating survivalist nightmare: autonomy-through-biotech, but without the extremism and paranoia. I only hoped that the founders and designers of Stateless – the Californian anarchists who'd worked for EnGeneUity all those decades ago – were still alive to see how well their invention was serving its purpose.

By noon, with royal blue marquees providing shade for the water pumps, bright red tents erected over the latrines, and even a rudimentary first-aid centre, I believed I understood what the medic had meant when she'd warned me not to think that I knew better than the locals. I checked the damage map of the city; it was no longer being updated, but at the last recorded count, over two hundred buildings – including the hotel – had been levelled.

Maybe *technolibération* could never transform the unforgiving rock of the continents into anything as hospitable as Stateless – but in a world accustomed to images of squalid refugee camps, choking on dust or drowning in mud . . . maybe the contrasting vision of the renegades' village could still symbolise the benefits of an end to the gene patent laws, more persuasively than the island at peace ever had.

I recorded everything, and dispatched the footage to See-Net's news room, with narration which I hoped would limit the perverse downside: the less dramatic the anarchists' plight, the less chance there was of any grassroots political backlash against the invasion. I didn't want to see Stateless discredited, with commentators tutting wisely that it had always been destined to slide into the abyss – but when it took a thousand corpses a day to raise a flicker of interest from the average viewer, if I painted too sanguine a picture the exodus would be a non-story.

The first truck from the coast which I sighted ran out of food long before it came near us. By 3 p.m., though, with the sixth delivery, two market tents had been set up near one of the water pumps and an ad hoc 'restaurant' was under construction. Forty minutes later, I sat on a folding chair in the shade of a photovoltaic awning, with a bowl of steaming sea urchin stew on my lap. There were a dozen other people eating out, forced to flee without their own cooking equipment; they eyed my camera suspiciously, but admitted that, of course, there'd been plans for leaving the city – first drafted long ago, but discussed and refined every year.

I felt more optimistic than ever – and more out of synch with the mood of the locals. They seemed to be taking the success of the exodus (a small miracle, in my eyes) for granted – but now that they'd come through it unscathed, as they'd always expected, and were waiting for the mercenaries to make the next move, everything had become less certain.

'What do you think will happen in the next twenty-four hours?' I asked one woman with a small boy on her lap. She wrapped her arms around the child protectively, and said nothing.

Outside, someone roared with pain. The restaurant emptied in seconds. I managed to penetrate the crowd which had formed in the narrow square between the markets and the restaurant – and then found myself forced back as they drew away in panic.

A young Fijian man had been lifted metres above the ground by invisible machinery; he was wide-eyed with terror, crying out for help. He was struggling pitifully – but his arms hung at his sides, bloody and ruined, white bone protruding through the flesh of one elbow. The thing which had taken him was too strong to be fought.

People were wailing and shouting – and trying to force their way out of the crowd. I resisted too long, transfixed with horror, and I was shoved to my knees. I covered my head and crouched down, but I was still an obstacle to the stampede. Someone heavy tripped on me, jabbing me with knees and elbows, then leaning on me to regain his balance, almost crushing my spine. I cowered on the ground as the buffeting continued, wishing I could rise to my feet, but certain that any attempt would only see me knocked flat on my back and trampled in the face. The man's desperate pleading was like a second rain of blows; I tucked my head deeper into my arms, trying to blot out the sound. Somewhere nearby, a tent wall collapsed gently to the ground.

Long seconds passed, and no one else collided with me. I raised my head; the square was deserted. The man was still alive, but his eyes were rolling up into his skull intermittently, his jaw working feebly. Both his legs had been shattered now. Blood trickled down on to his invisible torturer – each droplet halting in mid-fall and spreading out for a moment, hinting at a tangible surface before vanishing into the hidden carapace. I searched the ground for my camera, emitting soft angry choking noises. My throat was knotted, my chest constricted; every breath, every movement felt like a punishment. I found the camera and attached it, then rose shakily to my feet and began recording.

The man stared at me in disbelief. He looked me in the eye and said, 'Help me.'

I stretched a hand in his direction, impotently. The insect ignored me – and I knew I was in no danger, it wanted this to be seen – but I was giddy with rage and frustration, sweating cold stinking rivulets down my face and chest.

A delicate sheen of interference fringes raced over the robot's form as it raised the man higher. The camera followed my gaze upwards, until I knew it was framing only the broken body and the uncaring sky.

I heard myself bellowing, 'Where's the fucking militia now? Where are your weapons? Where are your bombs? *Do something!*'

The man's head lolled; I hoped he'd lost consciousness. Invisible pincers snapped his spine, then flung him aside. I heard the corpse thud against the marquee above the water pumps, then slide to the ground.

The whole camp of ten thousand seemed to be wailing in my skull, and I was screaming incoherently, but I kept my eyes locked on the place where the robot had to be.

There was a loud scrabbling sound from the space in front of me. A sickening hush descended in the alleys around the square. The insect played with the light, sketching its own outline for us, in reef-rock grey against the heavens, in sky blue against the rock. The body hanging from its six upturned-V legs was long and segmented; a blunt restless head at each end swivelled curiously, sniffing the air. Four lithe tentacles slithered in and out of sheaths in the carapace, tipped with sharp claws.

I stood swaying in the silence, waiting for something to happen – for someone with a jacket full of plastic explosives to burst out of an alley and run straight at the machine in the hope of a kamikaze embrace . . . though ve would not have come within ten metres before being blasted back into the crowd to incinerate a dozen friends, instead.

The thing arched its body and raised a pair of limbs, spreading them wide in a gesture of triumph.

Then it lurched towards a gap between the tents, sending people tripping into the walls and frantically clawing at the fabric, trying to tear a way out of its path.

It raced down the alley and disappeared, heading south, back towards the city.

Huddled on the ground behind the latrines, not ready to face the demoralised people of the camp, I dispatched the footage of the murder to SeeNet. I tried to compose some narration to go with it, but I was still in shock, I couldn't concentrate. I thought: War correspondents see much worse, day after day. How long will it be before I'm inured to this?

I scanned the international coverage. Everyone was still talking about 'rival anarchists' – including SeeNet, who'd broadcast nothing I'd sent them.

I spent five minutes trying to calm myself, then called Lydia. It took me half an hour to get through to her in person. All I could hear around me was people sobbing with grief. *What would it be like, after the tenth attack? The hundredth?* I closed my eyes and fantasised about Cape Town, Sydney, Manchester. Anywhere.

When Lydia answered, I said, 'I'm here, I'm covering this – so what's happening to my footage?' She was not in charge of news, but she was the only person likely to give me a straight answer.

But Lydia was stony-faced, cold with anger. 'Your "obituary" of Violet Mosala had a whole scene cooked up out of thin air. And it said nothing about the cult which killed Yasuko Nishide – and now Henry Buzzo. I've seen your deposition to the security firm, about the cholera, about the fishing boat. So what are you playing at?'

I clutched at excuses, trying to find the right ones, knowing that *Mosala would have died if I hadn't used you* was not good enough. I said, 'Everything I faked, she really said. Off the record. Ask her.'

Lydia was unmoved. 'It's still unacceptable, it still violates all the guidelines. And we can't *ask her* anything. She's comatose.'

I didn't want to hear that; if Mosala was brain-damaged, it had all been for nothing. I said, 'I couldn't tell you the rest . . . because I couldn't tip off the Anthrocosmologists by broadcasting everything.' I was ranting; the ACs had already known exactly how much I would have told the authorities.

Lydia's expression softened – as if I was clearly so far gone, now, that I deserved to be pitied, not rebuked. 'Look, I hope you find a way to get home safely. But the documentary's cancelled – you've broken the terms of the contract – and News isn't interested in your coverage of the political problems on the island.'

'*Political problems?* I'm in the middle of a war being funded by the biggest biotech company on the planet. I'm the only journalist on the island who seems to have a clue what's going on. And I'm SeeNet's only journalist, period. So how can they *not be interested*?'

'We're negotiating coverage from someone else.'

'Yeah? Who? *Janet Walsh?*'

'It's none of your business.'

'I don't believe you! EnGeneUity are *slaughtering people*, and—'

Lydia held up a hand to silence me. 'I don't want to hear any more of your . . . propaganda. Okay? I'm sorry you've been through so much unpleasantness. I'm sorry the anarchists are killing each other.' She spoke with genuine sadness, I think. 'But if you've taken sides, and you want to churn out polemics against the boycott and the patent laws, full of forged material . . . then that's your problem. I can't help you.

'Be careful, Andrew. Goodbye.'

As dusk fell, I wandered through the camp, filming, transmitting the signal in real-time to my console at home – guaranteeing a record of everything, for what it was worth.

The model refugee village was still intact, the pumps still working, the sanitation impeccable. Lights shone everywhere, haloed with orange and green through the fabric, and the aroma of cooking wafted out of every second doorway. The tents' stored photovolatic electricity would last for hours, yet. No great damage had been done – no source of physical comfort had been lost.

But the people I passed were tense, fearful, silent. The robot could return at any time, night or day, and kill one more person – or a thousand.

By sending the robots out of the city to strike at random, the mercenaries could rapidly undermine morale and drive people even further away, closer to the coast. Greenhouse refugees forced to cling to the shoreline, waiting for the next big storm – the fate they'd come to Stateless to avoid – might be ready to abandon the island altogether.

I couldn't imagine what had happened to the so-called militia – maybe they'd all been slaughtered already, in some brave idiotic stand back in the city. I scanned the local nets; there were bleak reports of dozens of attacks like the one I'd witnessed, but little else. I didn't expect the anarchists to broadcast all their military secrets on the nets, but I found the absence of blustering propaganda, of morale-boosting claims of imminent victory, strangely chilling. Maybe the silence meant something, but if it did, I couldn't decipher it.

It was growing cold. I was reluctant to ask for shelter in a stranger's tent – I wasn't afraid of being turned away, but I still felt too much like an outsider, despite all my feeble gestures of solidarity. These people were under siege, and they had no reason to trust me.

So I sat in the restaurant, drinking hot thin soup. The other customers talked among themselves, keeping their voices low, glancing at me more with measured caution than open hostility, but excluding me nonetheless.

I'd destroyed my career – for Mosala, for *technolibération* – but I'd achieved nothing. Mosala was in a coma. Stateless was on the verge of a long and bloody decline.

I felt numb, and paranoid, and useless.

Then a message arrived from Akili. Ve'd escaped the city unharmed, and was in another camp, less than a kilometre away.

28

'Sit down. Anywhere that looks comfortable.'

The tent contained nothing but a backpack and an unrolled sleeping bag; the transparent floor looked dry, despite the hint of dew outside, but almost thin enough for the grit beneath it to be felt through the plastic. A black patch on the wall radiated gentle heat, powered by the solar energy stored in the charge-displacement polymers which were woven into every strand of the tent's fabric.

I sat on one end of the sleeping bag. Akili sat cross-legged beside me. I looked around appreciatively; however humble, it was a vast improvement on bare rock. 'Where did you find this? I don't know if they shoot looters on Stateless . . . but I'd say it was worth the risk.'

Akili snorted. 'I didn't have to *steal it*. Where do you think I've been living for the past two weeks? We can't all afford the Ritz.'

We exchanged updates. Akili had heard most of my news already, from other sources: Buzzo's death; Mosala's evacuation, and uncertain condition. But not her joke on the ACs: the automatic dissemination of her TOE around the world.

Akili frowned intensely, silent for a long time. Something had changed in vis face since I'd seen ver in the hospital; the deep shock of recognition at the news of the supposed mixing plague had given way to a kind of expectant gaze – as if ve was prepared, now, to be taken by Distress at any moment and was almost eager to embrace the experience, despite the anguish and horror all its victims had displayed. Even the few who'd been briefly calm and lucid in their own strange way had swiftly relapsed; if I'd believed that the syndrome was everyone's fate, I would not have wished to go on living.

Akili confessed, 'We still can't fit our models to the data. No one I've been in contact with can work out what's going on.' Ve seemed resigned to the fact that the plague would elude precise analysis, in the short term – but still confident that vis basic explanation was correct. 'The new cases are appearing too rapidly, much faster than exponential growth.'

'Then maybe you're wrong about the mixing. You made a prediction of exponential growth – and now it's failed. So maybe you've been reading too much Anthrocosmology into four sick people's ranting.'

Ve shook vis head, calmly dismissing the possibility. 'Seventeen people, now. Your SeeNet colleague isn't the only one who's seen it; other journalists have begun to report the same phenomenon. And there's a way to explain the discrepancy in the case numbers.'

'How?'

'Multiple Keystones.'

I laughed wearily. 'What's the collective noun for that? Not an arch of Keystones, surely. A pantheon? One person, with one theory, explaining the universe into existence – isn't that the whole premise of Anthrocosmology?'

'One theory, yes. And *one person* always seemed the most likely scenario. We always knew that the TOE would be broadcast to the world – but we always assumed that every last detail would be worked out in full by its discoverer, first. But if the discoverer is lying in a coma when the complete TOE is despatched to tens of thousands of people, simultaneously . . . that's like nothing we ever contemplated. And nothing we can hope to model: the mathematics becomes intractable.' Ve spread vis hands in a gesture of acceptance. 'No matter. We'll all learn the truth, soon enough.'

My skin crawled. In Akili's presence, I didn't know what I

believed. I said, 'Learn it *how*? Mosala's TOE doesn't predict telepathy with the Keystone – or Keystones – any more than it predicts the universe unravelling. If she's right, you must be wrong.'

'It depends what she's right about.'

'Everything? As in Theory of?'

'*Everything* could unravel tonight – and most TOEs would have nothing to say about it, one way or another. The rules of chess can't tell you whether or not the board is strong enough to hold up every legal configuration of the pieces.'

'But every TOE has plenty to say about the human brain, doesn't it? It's a lump of ordinary matter, subject to all the ordinary laws of physics. It doesn't start "mixing with information" just because someone completes a Theory of Everything on the other side of the planet.'

Akili said, 'Two days ago, I would have agreed with you. But TOEs which fail to deal with their own basis in information are as incomplete as . . . General Relativity – which required the Big Bang to take place, but then broke down completely at that point. It took the unification of all four forces to smooth away the singularity. And it looks like it's going to take one more unification to understand the explanatory Big Bang.'

'But two days ago—?'

'I was wrong. The mainstream always assumed that an incomplete TOE was just the way things had to be. The Keystone would explain everything – except how a TOE could actually come into force. Anthrocosmology would answer that question – but that side of the equation would never be *visible*.' Akili held out both hands, palms pressed together horizontally. 'Physics and metaphysics: we believed they'd remain separate forever. They always had, in the past, so it seemed like a reasonable premise. Like the single Keystone.' Ve interlocked vis fingers and tipped vis hands to a forty-five-degree angle. 'It just happens to be wrong. Maybe because a TOE which unifies physics and information – which mixes the levels, and describes its own authority – is the very opposite of *unravelling*. It's more stable than any other possibility; it affirms itself, it tightens the knot.'

I suddenly recalled the night I'd visited Amanda Conroy, when I'd concluded, tongue-in-cheek, that the *separation of powers* between Mosala and the Anthrocosmologists was a good thing. And later, Henry Buzzo had jokingly postulated a theory which supported itself, defended itself, ruled out all competitors, refused to be swallowed.

I said, 'But whose theory is going to unify physics and information? Mosala's TOE makes no attempt to "describe its own authority".'

Akili saw no obstacle. 'She never intended it to. But either she failed to understand all the implications of her own work – or someone out on the net is going to get hold of her purely physical TOE, and extend it to embrace information theory. In a matter of days. Or hours.'

I stared at the ground, suddenly angry, all the mundane horrors of the day closing in on me. 'How can you sit here wrapped up in this bullshit? Whatever happened to *techno-libération*? Solidarity with the renegades? Smashing the boycott?' My own meagre skills and connections had already come to nothing in the face of the invasion but somehow I'd imagined Akili proving to be a thousand times more resourceful: taking a vital role at the hub of the resistance, orchestrating some brilliant counter-attack.

Ve said quietly, 'What do you expect me to do? I'm not a soldier; I don't know how to win the war for Stateless. There'll soon be more people with Distress than there are on this whole island – and if ACs don't try to analyse the mixing plague, no one else is going to do it.'

I laughed bitterly. 'And now you're ready to believe that *understanding everything* drives us insane? The Ignorance Cults were right? The TOE sends us screaming and kicking into the abyss? Just when I'd made up my mind that there was no such thing.'

Akili shifted uncomfortably. 'I don't know why people are taking it so hard.' For the first time there was a hint of fear in vis voice, breaking through the determined acceptance. 'But . . . mixing before the Aleph moment *must be* imperfect, distorted – because if it wasn't flawed in some way, the first victim of Distress would have explained everything, and become the Keystone. I don't know what the flaw is – what's missing, what makes the partial understanding so traumatic – but once the TOE is completed . . .' Ve trailed off. If the Aleph moment didn't put an end to Distress, the misery of a war on Stateless would be nothing. If the TOE could not be faced, all that lay ahead was universal madness.

We both fell silent. The camp was quiet, except for a few young children crying in the distance, and the faint clatter of cooking utensils in some of the nearby tents.

Akili said, 'Andrew?'

'Yes?'

'Look at me.'

I turned and faced ver squarely, for the first time since I'd arrived. Vis dark eyes appeared more luminous than ever: intelligent, searching, compasssionate. The unselfconscious beauty of vis face evoked a deep, astonished resonance inside me, a thrill of recognition which reverberated from the darkness in my skull to the base of my spine. My whole body ached at the sight of ver, every muscle fibre, every tendon. But it was welcome pain, as if I'd been beaten and left to die – and now found myself, impossibly, waking.

That was what Akili was: my last hope, my resurrection.

Ve said, 'What is it you want?'

'I don't know what you mean.'

'Come on. I'm not blind.' Ve searched my face, frowning slightly, puzzled but unaccusing. 'Have I done something? To lead you on? To give you the wrong idea?'

'No.' I wanted the ground to swallow me. And I wanted to touch ver more than I wanted to live.

'Neural asex can make people lose track of the messages they're sending. I thought I'd made everything clear, but if I've confused you—'

I cut ver off. 'You did. Make everything.' I heard my voice disintegrating; I waited a few seconds, forcing myself to breathe calmly, willing my throat to unknot, then said evenly, 'It's not your fault. I'm sorry I've offended you. I'll go.' I began to stand.

'No.' Akili placed a hand my shoulder, gently restraining me. 'You're my friend, and you're in pain, and we're going to work this out.'

Ve rose to vis feet – but then squatted down and began to unlace vis shoes.

'What are you doing?'

'Sometimes you think you know something, you think you've taken it in. But it's not real, until you've seen it with your own eyes.' Ve pulled vis loose T-shirt over vis head; vis torso was slender, lightly muscled, vis chest perfectly smooth – no breasts, no nipples, nothing. I looked away, and then climbed to my feet, determined to walk out – at that moment, prepared to abandon ver for no better reason than to preserve a desire which I'd always known led nowhere – but then I stood there paralysed, light-headed, vertiginous.

I said numbly, 'You don't have to do this.'

Akili walked up to me, stood beside me. I kept my eyes fixed straight ahead. Ve took my right hand and placed it against vis stomach, which was flat and soft and hairless, then forced my sweating fingers down between vis legs. There was nothing but smooth skin, cool and dry all the way – and then a tiny urethral opening.

I pulled free, burning with humiliation – swallowing a venomous barb about *African traditions* just in time. I retreated as far as the tent allowed, still refusing to face ver, and a wave of grief and anger swept over me.

'*Why?* How could you hate your body so much?'

'I never hated it. But I never worshipped it, either.' Ve spoke softly, striving for patience – but weary of the need to justify verself. 'I didn't pick you for an Edenite. The Ignorance Cults all worship the smallest cages they can find: the accidents of birth, of biology, of history and culture . . . and then rail against anyone who dares to show them the bars of a cage ten billion times larger. But my body is *not* a temple – or a dung-heap. Those are the choices of idiot mythology, not the choices of *technolibération*. The deepest truth about the body is that all that restrains it, in the end, is physics. We can reshape it into anything the TOE allows.'

This cool logic only made me recoil even more. I agreed with every word of it – but I clung to my instinctive horror like a lifeline. '*The deepest truth* would still have been true if you hadn't sacrificed—'

'I've sacrificed nothing. Except some ancient hardwired behavioural patterns buried in my limbic system, triggered by certain visual cues and pheromones . . . and the need to have small explosions of endogenous opiates go off in my brain.'

I turned and let myself look at ver. Ve stared back at me defiantly. The surgery had been well executed; ve did not look unbalanced, deformed. I had no right to grieve for a loss which existed only in my head. Nobody had mutilated ver by force; ve had made vis own decision with vis eyes wide open. I had no right to wish ver *healed*.

I was still shaken and angry, though. I still wanted to punish ver for what ve'd taken from me.

I asked sardonically, 'And where does that get you? Does hacking out your *base animal instincts* grant you some great, rarefied insight? Don't tell me: you can tune in to the lost wisdom of the celibate medieval saints?'

Akili grimaced, amused. 'Hardly. But sex grants no insight,

either – any more than shooting up heroin does – however much the cultists rant about *Tantric mysteries* and *the communion of souls*. Give an MR a magic mushroom or two, and they'll tell you, sincerely, that they've just fucked God. Because sex, drugs, and religion all hinge on the same kind of simple neurochemical events: addictive, euphoric, exhilirating – and all, equally, meaningless.'

It was a familiar truth – but at that moment it cut deep. Because I still wanted ver. And the drug I was hooked on did not exist.

Akili half raised vis hands, as if to offer a truce: ve'd had no wish to hurt me, only to defend vis own philosophy. 'If most people choose to remain addicted to orgasm, then that's their right. Not even the most radical asex would dream of forcing anyone to follow us. But I don't happen to want my own life to revolve around a few cheap biochemical tricks.'

'Not even to be made in the image of your beloved Keystone?'

'You still don't get it, do you?' Ve laughed wearily. 'The Keystone is not some . . . teleological endpoint, some cosmic ideal. In a thousand years' time, the Keystone's body will be the same obsolete joke as yours and mine.'

I'd run out of anger. I said simply, 'I don't care. Sex can still be much more than the release of endogenous opiates—'

'Of course it can. It can be a form of communication. But it can also be the very opposite – with all the same biology in play. And all I've given up is that which the best and the worst sex have in common. *Don't you see that?* All I've done is subtracted out the noise.'

These words made no sense to me. I looked away, defeated. And I knew that the pain I'd thought of as an *ache of longing* had never been more than the bruising I'd received from the crowd as they fled the robot, and the throbbing of the wound in my stomach, and the weight of failure.

I said, without hope, 'But don't you ever want some kind

of . . . physical solace? Some kind of contact? Don't you ever, still, just want to be *touched*?'

Akili walked towards me and said gently, 'Yes. That's what I've been trying to tell you.'

I was speechless. Ve placed one hand on my shoulder, and cupped the other against my face, raising my eyes to meet vis. 'If it's what you want, too – if it won't just be frustrating for you. And if you understand: this can't turn into any kind of sex, I don't—'

I said, 'I understand.'

I undressed quickly, before I could change my mind, trembling like a nervous adolescent – willing my erection to vanish, without success. Akili turned up the heating panel, and we lay on our sides on the sleeping bag, eyes locked, not quite touching. I reached over and tentatively stroked vis shoulder, the side of vis neck, vis back.

'Do you like that?'

'Yes.'

I hesitated. 'Can I kiss you?'

'Not a good idea, I think. Just relax.' Ve brushed my cheek with vis cool fingers, then ran the back of vis hand down the centre of my chest, towards my bandaged abdomen.

I was shivering. 'Does your leg still hurt?'

'Sometimes. *Relax*.' Ve kneaded my shoulders.

'Have you ever done this . . . with a non-asex before?'

'Yes.'

'Male or female?'

'Female.' Akili laughed softly. 'You should see your face. Look – if you come, it's not the end of the world. She did. So I'm not going to throw you out in disgust.' Ve slid a hand over my hip. 'It might be better if you did; you might loosen up.'

I shuddered at vis touch, but my erection was slowly subsiding. I stroked the smooth unmarked skin where a nipple might have been, searching for scar tissue with my fingertips,

381

finding nothing. Akili stretched lazily. I began massaging the side of vis neck again.

I said, 'I'm lost. I don't know what we're doing. I don't know where we're heading.'

'Nowhere. We can stop if you want to. We can always just talk. Or we can talk without stopping. It's called freedom – you'll get used to it, eventually.'

'This is very strange.' Our eyes remained locked together, and Akili seemed happy enough – but I still felt I should have been hunting for some way to make everything a thousand times more intense.

I said, 'I know why this feels wrong. Physical pleasure without sex—' I hesitated.

'Go on.'

'Physical pleasure without sex is generally classified as—'

'What?'

'You're not going to like this.'

Ve thumped me in the ribs. 'Spit it out.'

'*Infantile*.'

Akili sighed. 'Okay. Exorcism time. Repeat after me: Uncle Sigmund, I renounce you as a charlatan, a bully, and a fabricator of data. A corrupter of language, a destroyer of lives.'

I complied – then I wrapped my arms around ver tightly, and we lay there with our legs entwined, heads on each other's shoulders, gently stroking each other's backs. The whole futile sexual charge I'd felt since the fishing boat was finally lifting; all the pleasure came from the warmth of vis body, the unfamiliar contours of vis flesh, the texture of vis skin, the sense of vis presence.

And I still found ver as beautiful as ever. I still cared about ver as much as ever.

Was this what I'd always been looking for? Asexual love?

It was a disquieting notion – but I thought it through calmly.

382

Maybe all my life I'd unconsciously swallowed the Edenite lie: that everything in the perfect, harmonious modern emotional relationship somehow flowed magically out of beneficent nature. Monogamy, equality, honesty, respect, tenderness, selflessness – it was all pure instinct, pure sexual biology, taking its unfettered course – despite the fact that all those criteria of perfection had changed radically from century to century, from culture to culture. The Edenites proclaimed that anyone who fell short of the glowing ideal was either wilfully fighting Mother Gaia, or had been corrupted by a traumatic upbringing, media manipulation, or the deeply unnatural power structures of modern society.

In fact, the ancient reproductive drives had been hemmed in by civilising forces, inhibited by cultural strictures and pressed into service to create social cohesion in countless different ways – but they hadn't actually changed in tens of thousands of years, and they contradicted current mores, or were silent, just as often as they supported them. Gina's unfaithfulness had hardly been a crime against biology . . . and whatever I'd done to drive her away had been a failure of purely conscious effort – a lack of attentiveness that any Stone Age ancestor would have found second nature. Virtually everything which modern humans valued in relationships – over and above the act of sex itself, and some degree of protectiveness towards their partners and offspring – arose by a separate force of will. There was a massive shell of moral and social constructs wrapped around the tiny core of instinctive behaviour – and the pearl bore little resemblance to the grit.

I had no wish to abandon either – but if what I'd failed at so badly, again and again, had been *reconciling the two* . . .

If the choice came down to *biology* or *civilisation* . . .

I knew, now, which I valued the most.

And asex could still be close. Asex could still touch.

After a while, we climbed into the sleeping bag to keep warm. I was still numb with despair at the tragedy of Stateless,

Mosala's senseless half-murder, the ruins of my career. But Akili kissed me on the forehead, and tried vis best to unknot my aching back and shoulders – and I did the same for ver, in the hope that it might make vis fear of the great information plague, which I still did not believe was coming, in some small way easier to bear.

I woke, confused, to the sound of Akili breathing beside me. The tent was bathed in grey and blue light, shadowless as noon; I looked up and saw the disc of the moon overhead, a white spotlight penetrating the weave of the roof, rainbow-fringed by diffraction.

I thought: Akili met me outside the airport. Ve could have infected me with the engineered cholera then, knowing that I'd carry it to Mosala.

And when the weapon misfired, ve'd produced the antidote – to gain my trust, in the hope that ve could use me a second time . . . but then the moderates had unwittingly kidnapped us both, and there'd been no need to strike at Mosala again.

It was sheer paranoia. I closed my eyes. Why would an extremist pretend to believe in the information plague? And if the belief was genuine, why kill Buzzo when the Aleph moment had been proved inevitable? Either way, with Mosala back in Cape Town – and her work proceeding, with or without her – what use could I be to the extremists?

I disentangled myself, and climbed out of the sleeping bag. Akili woke while I was dressing, and muttered sleepily, 'The latrine tent glows red. You can't miss it.'

'I won't be long.'

I walked aimlessly, trying to clear my head. It was earlier than I'd imagined, barely after nine, but shockingly cold. Lights still showed from most of the tents, but the alleys between them were deserted.

Akili as an extremist assassin made no sense – why would ve have struggled to get us off the fishing boat? – but the doubt

I'd felt on waking still cast a shadow over everything, as if my mistrust itself was as much of a disaster as any possibility that I could be right. How could we have been through so much together – only for me to wake beside ver, wondering if it had all been a lie?

I reached the southern edge of the camp. These people must have been the last wave of refugees to head north, because there was nothing in sight but bare reef-rock, stretching to the horizon.

I hesitated, and almost turned back. But pacing the alleys made me feel like a spy – and I wasn't ready to return to Akili's tent, to the warmth of vis body, to the hope ve seemed to offer. Half an hour before, I'd seriously considered migrating to total asex – tearing out my genitals and several vital pieces of grey matter – as the panacea for all my woes. I needed to take a long walk, alone.

I headed out into the moonlit desert.

Whorls of trace minerals glittered everywhere; now that I'd seen a few of these hieroglyphs deciphered, the ground appeared transformed, dense with meaning – although for all I knew, most of the patterns could still have been nothing but random decoration.

The abandoned city was either in darkness, or hidden from view by the slope of the ground; I could see no hint of light on the southern horizon. I pictured a fresh swarm of the invisible insects scurrying out from their nest at the centre . . . but I knew I'd be no safer back in the camp – and the things only killed for the spectacle of it, for the panic they instilled. Alone, I was less of a target than ever.

I thought I felt the ground shudder – a tremor so slight that I doubted it immediately. Was there still shelling going on? I'd imagined everyone leaving the city to the mercenaries – but maybe a few dissenters had ignored the evacuation plan . . . or maybe the militia had remained, in hiding, and the real confrontation had finally begun. That was a dismal prospect; they didn't stand a chance.

It happened again. I couldn't judge the direction of the blast – I'd heard no sound at all, just felt the vibration. I turned a full circle, scanning the horizon for smoke. Maybe they were shelling the camps now. The white plumes over the city in the morning had been visible for kilometres – but shells meant for tents on bare rock would carry different charges, with different effects.

I kept walking south, hoping that the city would come into view, along with some sign that the pyrotechnic action was still confined there. And I tried to imagine myself living through the war, emerging unscathed, but cosily familiar with all the myriad technologies of death . . . offering – to the nets who didn't care what I'd faked – footage complete with my own now-expert commentary on 'the characteristic sound of a Chinese-made Vigilance missile meeting its target', or 'the unmistakable visual signature of a Peacetech forty-millimetre shell exploding over open ground'.

I felt a wave of resignation sweep over me. I'd swallowed too many dreams in the last three days: *technolibération*, an end to the gene patent laws, personal happiness, asexual bliss . . . It was time to wake up. The ordinary madness of the world had finally reached Stateless – so why not stand back, regain some perspective, and try to scrape some kind of a living out of it? The invasion was no greater tragedy than ten thousand other bloody conquests before it – and it had always been inevitable. War had come, one way or another, to every known human culture.

I whispered aloud, without much conviction, 'Screw every known human culture.'

The ground roared, and threw me.

The reef-rock was soft, but I hit it face-down, bloodying my nose, maybe breaking it. Winded and astonished, I raised myself on to my hands and knees, but the ground still hadn't stopped shaking, I didn't trust myself to stand. I looked around for some evidence of a nearby impact – but there was no glow, no smoke, no crater, nothing.

Was this the new terror? After invisible robots – invisible bombs?

I knelt, waited, then climbed to my feet unsteadily. The reef-rock was still reverberating; I paced in a drunken circle, searching the horizon, still refusing to believe that there could be no other sign of the blast.

The air had been silent, though. It was the rock which had carried the noise. An underground detonation?

Or undersea, beneath the island?

And no detonation at all—

The ground convulsed again. I landed badly, twisting one arm, but panic washed out everything, dulling the pain into insignificance. I clawed at the ground, trying to find the strength to deny every instinct which screamed at me to stay down, not to risk moving – when I knew that if I didn't stand – and then sprint faster across the shuddering dead coral than I'd ever moved in my life – I was lost.

The mercenaries had killed off the lithophiles which gave the reef-rock its buoyancy. That was why they'd driven us out of the city: only the centre of the island would hold. Beyond the support of the guyot, the overhang was sinking.

I turned to try to see what had happened to the camp. Blue and orange squares gazed back at me blankly; most of the tents were still standing. I could see no one moving out across the desert yet – it was too soon – but there was no question of going back to warn them. Not even Akili. Inland divers would surely understand what was happening, faster than I had. There was nothing I could do now but try to save myself.

I climbed to my feet and broke into a run. I covered about ten metres before the ground shifted, slamming me down. I got up, took three steps, twisted an ankle, fell again. There was a constant tortured cracking sound filling my head now, conducted through my body from reef-rock to bone, resonating from living mineral to living mineral – the underworld reaching up to me, sharing its disintegration.

I started crawling forward on my hands and knees, screaming wordlessly, almost paralysed by a vision of the ocean rushing over the sinking reefs, sweeping up bodies, propelling them inland, dashing them against the splintering ground. I glanced back and saw nothing but the placid tent village, still uselessly intact – but the whole island was roaring in my skull, the deluge could only be minutes away.

I stood again, ran for whole seconds despite the swaying stars, then landed heavily, splitting my stitches. Warm blood soaked the bandages. I rested, covering my ears, daring to wonder for the first time if it would be better to stop and wait to die. *How far was I from the guyot? How far would the ocean reach in, even if I made it to solid ground?* I groped at my notepad pocket, as if I could get a GPS fix, check a few maps, come to some kind of decision. I rolled on to my back and started laughing. The stars jittered into time-lapse trails.

I stood up, glanced over my shoulder – and saw someone running across the rock behind me. I dropped to my hands and knees, half voluntarily, but kept my eyes on the figure. Ve was dark-skinned and slender – but it wasn't Akili, the hair was too long. I strained my eyes. It was a teenage girl. Her face caught the moonlight, her eyes wide with fear, but her mouth set in determination. Then the ground heaved, and we both fell. I heard her cry out in pain.

I waited – but she didn't get up.

I started crawling back towards her. If she was injured, all I'd be able to do was sit with her until the ocean took us both – but I couldn't keep going and leave her.

When I reached her, she was lying on her side with her legs jack-knifed, massaging one calf, muttering angrily. I crouched beside her and shouted, 'Do you think you can stand?'

She shook her head. 'We'd better sit it out here! We'll be safe here!'

I stared at her. 'Don't you know what's happening? They've killed the lithophiles!'

'No! They've been reprogrammed – they're actively swallowing gas. Just killing them would be too slow – give too much warning!'

This was surreal. I couldn't focus on her; the ground was juddering too hard. 'We can't stay here! *Don't you under-stand?* We'll drown!'

She shook her head again. For an instant, contradictory blurs of motion cancelled; she was smiling up at me, as if I was a child afraid of a thunderstorm. 'Don't worry! We'll be fine!'

What did she think would happen, when the ocean came screaming in? We'd just . . . hold each other up? One million drowning refugees would all link hands and tread water together?

Stateless had driven its children insane.

A fine moist spray rained down on us. I crouched and covered my head, picturing deep water rushing into the depressurised rock, blasting fissures all the way to the surface. And when I looked up, there it was: in the distance, a geyser fountained straight into the sky, a terrible silver thread in the moonlight. It was some hundred metres away – to the south – meaning that the path to the guyot was already undermined, and there was no hope of escape.

I lay down heavily beside the girl. She shouted at me, 'Why were you running in the wrong direction? Did you lose your way?'

I reached over and gripped her shoulder, hoping to see her face more clearly. We gazed at each other in mutual incomprehension. She yelled, 'I was on scout duty. I should have stopped you at the edge of the camp, but I thought you'd just go a little way, I thought you just wanted a better view for your camera.'

The shoulder camera was still packed in my wallet; I hadn't even thought of using it, turning it back on the camp as it was flooded, broadcasting the genocide to the world.

The gentle rain grew heavier for a second or two – but then subsided. I looked south, and caught sight of the geyser collapsing.

Then, for the first time, I noticed my hands trembling.

The ground had quietened.

Meaning what? The stretch of rock we lay on had broken free of its surroundings, like an iceberg birthed screaming from a glacial sheet, and was floating in relative tranquillity now – before the water rushed in around the edges?

My ears rang, my body was quivering – but I glanced up at the sky, and the stars were rock-steady. Or vice versa.

And then the girl gave me a shaken, queasy, adrenaline-drunk grin, her eyes shining with tears of relief. *She believed that the ordeal was over. And I'd been warned not to think I knew better.* I stared back at her wonderingly, my heart still pounding with terror, my chest constricted with hope and disbelief. I found myself emitting long, gasping sobs.

When I'd regained my voice, I asked, 'Why aren't we dead? The overhang can't float without the lithophiles. Why aren't we drowning?'

She rose and sat cross-legged, massaging her bruised calf, distracted for a moment. Then she looked at me, took the measure of my misunderstanding, shook her head, and patiently explained.

'No one touched the lithophiles in the overhang. The militia sent divers to the edge of the guyot, and pumped in primer to make the lithophiles degass the reef-rock just above the basalt. Water flooded in – and the surface rock at the centre is heavier than water.'

She smiled sunnily. 'I look at it this way. We've lost a city. But we've gained a lagoon.'

PART FOUR

29

The camp was in jubilant disarray. There were thousands of people out in the moonlight, checking each other for injuries, raising collapsed tents, celebrating victory, mourning the city – or soberly reminding anyone who'd listen that the war might not be over. No one knew for certain what forces, what weapons, might have been concealed far from the city, safe from the devastation of the centre's collapse – or what might yet crawl out of the lagoon.

I found Akili, unharmed, helping with the marquee which had fallen on to the water pumps. We embraced. I was bruised all over, my face was caked with blood, and my thrice re-opened wound was sending out flashes of pain like electric arcs – but I'd never felt more intensely alive.

Akili pulled free of me gently. 'At 6 a.m., Mosala's TOE will be posted on the nets. Will you sit up with me and wait?' Ve looked me in the eye, hiding nothing – afraid of the plague, afraid of facing it alone.

I squeezed vis arm. 'Of course.'

I went to the latrines to clean up. Mercifully, the sewage conduits remained open, and the raw waste previously discharged hadn't been forced back up to the surface by the compression waves of the quake. I washed blood off my face, and then cautiously unbandaged my stomach.

The wound was still bleeding thinly. The cut from the insect's laser ran deeper than I'd realised; when I bent over the washbasin, I could feel the two walls of flesh on either side of the gash – some seven or eight centimetres long – slide

393

against each other, disconnected except at the ends. The burn had cauterised tissue all the way through the abdominal wall – and now the dead seam had split open.

I looked around; there was no one else in sight. I thought: *This is not a good idea*. But I'd already been pumped full of antibiotics against the risk of internal infection . . .

I closed my eyes and forced three fingers deep into the wound. I touched the small intestine, blood-warm not snake-cold, resilient, muscular and unslick beneath my fingertips. This was the part of me which had almost killed me – subverted by foreign enzymes, mercilessly wringing me dry. *But the body is not a traitor: it only obeys the laws it must obey in order to exist at all.*

Pain caught up with me, and I almost froze – I imagined spending my life as a Bonaparte, or a self-doubting Thomas – but I jerked my hand free and then leant against the plastic barrel of the washbasin, punching the side.

I wanted to stare into a mirror and proclaim: *This is it. I know who I am, now. And I accept, absolutely, my life as a machine driven by blood, as a creature of cells and molecules, as a prisoner of the TOE.*

There were no mirrors, though. Not in the latrines of a refugee camp, not even on Stateless.

And if I waited a few more hours, the words would carry more weight – because by dawn, I'd finally know the whole truth about the TOE which enabled me to speak them.

On my way back to meet Akili, I took out my notepad and scanned the international nets. The anarchists' strike against the mercenaries was being talked about, breathlessly, everywhere.

SeeNet's coverage was the best, though.

It started with a view of the lagoon itself, huge and eerily calm in the moonlight, almost a perfect circle – like some ancient flooded volcanic crater, an echo of the hidden guyot below. I felt, in spite of everything, a pang of sorrow at the death of the mercenaries whose faces I'd never seen, who'd been betrayed by solid rock, and had drowned in terror for nothing but money and the rights of EnGeneUity's shareholders.

The journalist spoke – a woman, out-of-shot, a professional with optic nerve taps. 'It may take decades to reveal exactly who funded the invasion of Stateless, and why. It's not even clear, as I speak, whether or not the desperate sacrifice the residents of this island have made will save them from the aggressors.

'But I do know this. Violet Mosala – the Nobel laureate who was evacuated from Stateless in a critical condition, less than twenty-four hours ago – had intended to make this island her new home. She had hoped to lend the renegades enough respectability to enable a group of nations opposed to the UN boycott to speak their minds at last. And if the invasion was an effort to silence those dissenting voices, it now seems doomed to failure. Violet Mosala is in a coma, fighting for her life after an attack by a violent cult – and the people of Stateless will be struggling harder than ever to survive the next few years, even if peace has come to them tonight – but the astonishing courage of both will not be easily forgotten.'

There was more, with some of my footage of Mosala at the conference, and this journalist's own coverage of the shelling, the dignified exodus from the city, the establishment of the camps, and an attack by one of the mercenaries' robots.

It was all immaculately shot and edited. It was powerful, but never exploitative. And from start to finish, it was unashamed – but absolutely honest – propaganda for the renegades.

I could not have done it half as well.

The best was yet to come, though.

As the view returned to the dark waters of the lagoon, the journalist signed off.

'This is Sarah Knight, for SeeNet News, on Stateless.'

As far as the personal com nets were concerned, Sarah Knight was still incommunicado in Kyoto. Lydia wouldn't take my call – but I found a SeeNet production assistant willing to pass on a message to Sarah. She called me half an hour later, and Akili and I dragged the story out of her.

'When Nishide became ill in Kyoto, I told the Japanese authorities exactly what I thought was happening – but his pneumococcus sequenced as an unengineered strain, and they refused to believe that it had been introduced by a trojan.' Trojans were bacteria which could reproduce themselves and their hidden pathogenic cargo – without symptoms or an immune response – for dozens of generations . . . and then self-destruct without a trace, leaving behind a massive but apparently natural infection to swamp the body's defences. 'After making so much of a stink – and no one believing me, not even Nishide's family – I thought it would be wise to keep a low profile.'

We weren't able to talk for long, Sarah had to get to an interview with one of the militia's divers, but just as she was about to break the connection, I said haltingly, 'The Mosala documentary. You deserved the commission. You should have got it.'

She made as if to dismiss the whole question laughingly as ancient history – but then she stopped herself, and said calmly: 'That's true. I spent six months making sure I was better prepared than anyone else – and you still came along and stole it in a day. Because you were Lydia's blue-eyed boy, and she wanted to keep you happy.'

I couldn't believe how hard it was to get the words out. The injustice was blindingly obvious – and I'd admitted it to myself a thousand times – but some splinter of pride and self-right-eousness resisted every step of the way.

I said, 'I abused my power. I'm sorry.'

Sarah nodded slowly, lips pursed. 'Okay. Apology accepted, Andrew. On one condition: you and Akili agree to be interviewed. The invasion is only half the story here – and I don't want the fuckers who put Violet in a coma to get away with anything. I want to hear exactly what happened on that boat.'

I turned to Akili. Ve said, 'Sure.'

We exchanged coordinates. Sarah was on the other side of the island, but she was working her way around to all of the camps, hitching rides with the militia.

'At 5 a.m.?' she suggested.

Akili laughed, flashing a conspiratorial glance at me. 'Why not? No one's sleeping tonight, on Stateless.'

The camp was full of the sounds of celebration. People streamed past the tent, laughing and shouting, shrunken silhouettes against the moonlight. Music from the satellites – from Tonga, from Berlin, from Kinshasa – blasted out of the main square, and someone, somehow, had found or made firecrackers. I was still intoxicated with adrenaline, but ragged with fatigue – I wasn't sure if I wanted to join the party, or curl up and hibernate for a fortnight. I'd promised to do neither.

Akili and I sat on the sleeping bag – warmly dressed, with the tent flap closed; the electricity was fading. We passed the hours talking, scanning the nets, lapsing into awkward silences. I longed to bring ver, somehow, inside the aura of invulnerability I felt, having survived my own imagined apocalypse. I wanted to comfort ver in any way I could. My judgement was paralysed, though; vis body language had become opaque to me, and I had no sense of how or when to touch ver. We'd lain together naked – but I couldn't keep that memory, that image, from signifying more to me than it could ever mean to ver. So we sat apart.

I asked why ve hadn't mentioned the mixing plague to Sarah.

'Because she might have taken it seriously enough to spread word, start a panic.'

'Don't you think people might panic less if they knew the cause?'

Akili snorted. '*You* don't believe what I've told you about the cause. Do you think people would react to the news with anything but incomprehension or hysteria? Anyway, after the Aleph moment, the "victims" will know far more than anyone who hasn't mixed could ever tell them. And there'll be no question of panic, then: Distress itself will have vanished.' Most of this was said with absolute conviction; it was only with the last pronouncement that ve seemed to waver.

I asked tentatively, 'So why did the moderates get it so wrong? They had their own supercomputers. They seemed to know as much about Anthrocosmology as anyone. If they could be mistaken about the unravelling . . .'

Akili gave me a long, hard look – still trying to judge how far ve could trust me. 'I don't *know* that they're mistaken about the unravelling. I hope they are, but I don't know it for sure.'

I thought that over. 'You mean the distortion in the mixing before the Aleph moment could be enough to have prevented the unravelling, so far – but once the TOE is completed . . . ?'

'That's right.'

I felt a chill, more of incomprehension than fear. 'And you still tried to protect Mosala? Believing there was a chance that she could end everything?'

Akili stared at the floor, trying to find the right words. 'If it does happen, we won't even have time to know it – but I still think it would have been wrong to kill her. Unless the unravelling was absolutely certain, and there was no other way to stop it. No one can deal with *an unknown chance of the end of the universe*. How many people can you kill, for a cause like that? One? A hundred? A million? It's like . . . trying to manipulate an infinitely heavy weight, on the end of an infinitely long lever. However fine your judgement is, you know it can't be good enough. All you can do is admit that, and walk away.'

Before I could reply, **Sisyphus** said, 'I think you'll want to see this.'

The fishing boat with the moderates had been intercepted off the coast of New Zealand. The news footage showed people in handcuffs being herded ashore from a patrol boat onto floodlit docks, eyes downcast. 'Five', Giorgio, who'd lectured me on the unravelling. 'Twenty', who'd refused to let me leave the boat with their confession in my gut. Others were missing, though.

Then sailors followed, carrying the bodies on stretchers. They were covered in sheets – but the umale, Three, was unmistakable. The journalist spoke of suicide pacts. Helen Wu was mentioned by name, dead from poison.

The first scenes of the arrest had filled me with a buzz of righteous euphoria at the prospect of these fanatics facing justice – but I felt nothing but enervating horror as I tried to understand what had gone on in their minds, in the last moments. Maybe they'd seen the reports of ranting Distress victims – and some had concluded that the unravelling was inevitable, others that it was now impossible. Or maybe the whole convoluted logic of their actions had simply unwound, leaving them staring at the unadorned truth of what they'd done.

I couldn't judge them. I didn't know how I could have clawed my way up, if I'd spiralled down into the nightmare of believing what they'd believed. I might have struggled hard to reason all of Anthrocosmology out of existence – but if I'd failed, would I have had the humility (or the genocidal irresponsibility) to walk away from the implications, to refuse to intervene?

Outside, people were roaring with laughter. In the square, someone turned the music up insanely loud for a second, distorting it into booming bass static, shaking the ground.

Akili held conference with the other mainstream ACs. Someone was hacking into a WHO computer, to get the unofficial latest figures for reported cases of Distress.

'Nine thousand and twenty.' Ve turned to me with a sharp intake of breath; I didn't know if it was panic, or the exhilaration of free fall. 'Tripled in two days. And you still think it's a virus?'

'No.' Even without this inexplicable burst of contagion, I knew my targeted neuroactive mutant bioweapon theory wouldn't stand up to any scrutiny at all. 'But we can still both be wrong, can't we?'

'Maybe.'

I hestitated. 'If it's this fast now, then after the Aleph moment . . . ?'

'I don't know. It could sweep the planet in a week. Or an hour. The faster the better – less suffering for the people who see it coming, but don't yet understand.' Akili closed vis eyes, began to put vis face in vis hands, stopped, clenched vis fists. 'When it comes, it better be good. The truth you can't escape had better be sweet.'

I moved closer and put my arm around ver, and swayed our bodies gently together from side to side.

Sarah arrived, barely a minute later than promised. She sat on my suitcase, and we talked for her camera eyes. Sometimes we had to shout to make ourselves heard – but software would bring the noise of the celebrations down to an atmospheric murmur.

Sarah and I had never been more than casual acquaintances – I'd only spoken to her in person a dozen times before – but for me, she came from the world beyond Stateless, the time before the conference; she was living proof of that era of sanity. And it only took one third party, there in the flesh, to anchor me to normality – to render me certain, again, that Akili was wrong. Distress was a mundane horror, no different from cholera. The universe was oblivious to human explanation. The laws of physics always had been and always would be solid – all the way down to the bedrock of the TOE – whether or not they were understood.

And – though we weren't going out in real-time – she'd brought her audience with her. Under the potential scrutiny of ten million people, what else could I do but think what they expected me to think, give in to their consensus, conform?

Akili, too, seemed to relax – but whether Sarah's presence anchored ver in the same way, or merely served as a welcome distraction, I couldn't tell.

Sarah guided us deftly through our roles in *Violet Mosala: Victim of Anthrocosmology*. The deposition I'd made for Joe Kepa had stuck to the legally pertinent facts; this interview pretended to probe the moral and philosophical depths of the ACs' conspiracy. But Akili and I both talked of the fishing boat, and the moderates' insane beliefs, as if we had no doubt that their whole world view – as much as their violent methods – deserved only contempt; as if nothing remotely similar could have crossed our own minds in a thousand years.

And it all became news. It all became history. Sarah was doing her job flawlessly – but for the record, the three of us willingly steam-rollered flat every unspoken fear, every qualm, every trace of doubt that the world could ever be different from the nets' pale imitation of it.

We were almost finished – I was on the verge of recounting the events in the ambulance – when my notepad chimed. It was a coded trill for a call to be taken only in private. If I answered, the communications software would shift to deepest encryption, automatically – but if the notepad sensed other people within earshot, it would refuse to maintain the connection.

I excused myself, and left the tent. The sky showed a faint wash of grey over the stars. Music and laughter still flooded out of the square behind the markets, and people were still roaming the camp, but I found a secluded spot nearby.

De Groot said, 'Andrew? Are you all right? Can you talk?' She looked haggard and tense.

'I'm fine. A little bruised by the quake, that's all.' I hesitated; I couldn't bring myself to ask the question.

'Violet died. About twenty minutes ago.' De Groot's voice faltered, but she steeled herself and pushed on wearily. 'No one knows exactly why, yet. Some kind of trap sprung by one of the anti-viral magic bullets – maybe an enzyme in concentrations too weak to detect, which converted it into a toxin.' She shook her head, disbelieving. 'They turned her body into a minefield. *What did she ever do to deserve that? She tried to find a few simple truths, a few simple patterns to the world.*'

I said, 'They've been caught. They'll stand trial. And Violet will be remembered . . . for centuries.' It was all hollow comfort, but I didn't know what else to say.

And I'd thought I'd been prepared for this news, ever since I'd heard she was in coma – but it still came like a sudden blow to the head . . . as if the anarchists' astonishing reversal of fortune, and Sarah's miraculous reappearance, had somehow rewritten the odds. I covered my eyes with my forearm for a moment, and saw her sitting in her hotel room beneath the skylight, raked by the sun, reaching out and taking my hand. *Even if I'm wrong . . . there has to be something down there. Or nobody could even touch.*

De Groot said, 'How soon can you get off the island?' She sounded more than a little concerned – which was touching, but strange. We'd hardly been that close.

I laughed dismissively. '*Why?* The anarchists have won, the worst is over. I'm sure of that.' De Groot did not look sure at all. 'Have you heard something? From . . . your political contacts?' There was a sudden chill in my bowels, like the disbelief I'd felt before each new spasm from the cholera: *It can't be happening again.*

'This isn't about the war. But – you're stuck, aren't you?'

'For now. Are you going to tell me what this—?'

'We had a message. Just after Violet died. A threat from the Anthrocosmologists.' Her face contorted with anger. 'Not the ones on the boat, obviously. So it must have come from the ones who killed Buzzo.'

'Saying what?'

'Shut down all of Violet's calculations. Present them with a verified audit trail for her supercomputer account, proving that all the records of her TOE work have been erased without being copied or read.'

I made a sound of derision. 'Yeah? Where do they think that will get them? All her methods and ideas have been published already. Someone else will duplicate everything . . . in a year at the most.'

De Groot seemed indifferent to the ACs' motives; she just wanted an end to the violence. 'I've shown the message to the police, here – but they say there's nothing anyone can do, with Stateless the way it is.' She caught herself; she still hadn't spelt it out. 'The threat is, we post the audit trail within an hour – or they kill you.'

'Right.' I could see the logic of it: De Groot, and Mosala's family, would all be too well guarded to threaten directly – but they'd hardly sit back and let the extremists kill me, after I'd helped get Violet off Stateless.

'The calculations were already completed when I logged on – lucky Violet programmed her net broadcast to wait until the hour.' De Groot laughed softly. 'Her idea of making it a formal occasion. We'll do what they've asked, of course. The police advised me not to call you – and I know the news does you no good – but I still thought you had a right to be told.'

I said, 'Don't do anything, don't erase a single file. I'll call you back, very soon.' I broke the connection.

I stood there in the alley for several seconds, listening to the wild music, chilled by the wind, thinking it through.

When I walked into the tent, Sarah and Akili were laughing. I'd meant to invent an excuse to get Sarah out quietly, so we could both just walk away – but it struck me at that moment that it would do me no good. Buzzo had been killed with a gunshot, but their favoured methods were biological. If I fled, the chances were that I'd be carrying the weapon inside me.

I reached down and grabbed Akili by the front of vis jacket and sent ver sprawling backwards on to the floor. Ve stared up at me, faking shock, anguish, bewilderment. I knelt down over ver and punched ver in the face, clumsily – surprised that I'd even got this far; I was no good at violence, and I'd expected ver to defend verself with all the agility ve'd demonstrated on the boat, long before I'd lain a finger on ver.

Sarah was outraged. 'What are you doing? *Andrew!*' Akili just stared at me – speechless, hurt, still playing dumb. I lifted ver half off the ground with one hand – ve barely resisted – then punched ver again.

I said evenly, 'I want the antidote. *Now*. Do you understand? No more threats to De Groot, no files destroyed, no negotiations – you're just going to hand it over.'

Akili searched my face, clinging to the charade, protesting innocence with vis eyes like some wrongfully accused lover. For a moment, I wanted to hurt ver badly; I had idiot visions of some bloody catharsis, washing the pain of betrayal away. But the thought of Sarah recording it all kept me in check; I never found out what I would have done, if we'd been alone.

And my rage slowly ebbed. Ve'd infected me with cholera, slaughtered three people, manipulated my pathetic emotional

404

needs, used me as a hostage . . . but ve hadn't, remotely, *betrayed me*. It had all been an act from the start; there'd never been anything between us to be sacrificed to the cause. And if the solace I thought we'd given each other had only been in my head, then so was the humiliation.

I'd live.

Sarah said sharply, 'Andrew!' I glanced at her over my shoulder; she was livid, she must have thought I'd gone insane. I explained impatiently, 'That call was from Karin De Groot. Violet's dead. And now the extremists have threatened to kill me if De Groot doesn't trash the TOE calculations.' Akili mimed grave consternation; I laughed in vis face.

'Okay. But what makes you think Akili's working for the extremists? It could be anyone in the camp—'

'Akili is the only person besides me and De Groot who knew about Mosala's joke on the ACs.'

'What *joke*?'

'In the ambulance.' I'd almost forgotten; I hadn't reached the end of the story for Sarah. 'Violet programmed software to write up the calculations, polish the TOE, and despatch it over the net. And the work's all completed; De Groot only caught it before it was sent.'

Sarah fell silent. I turned to her warily, still expecting Akili to make a move once my guard was down.

She had a gun in her hand. 'Stand up please, Andrew.'

I laughed wearily. 'You still don't believe me? You'd rather trust this piece of shit – just because ve was your source?'

'I know ve didn't send that message to De Groot.'

'Yeah? *How*?'

'Because I did. I sent it.' I stood up slowly, turning to face her, refusing to accept this ridiculous claim. The music from the square surged madly again, making the whole tent hum. She said, 'I knew there were calculations in progress, but I thought they still had days to run. I had no idea we'd cut it so fine.'

My ears were ringing. Sarah watched me calmly, aiming the gun with unwavering conviction. She must have made contact with the extremists when she'd been researching *Holding Up the Sky* – and no doubt she'd intended to expose them, once she had the whole story. But they would have realised how valuable she could be to them – and before resorting to killing her, they would have tried everything possible to bring her round to their point of view.

And they'd succeeded. In the end, they'd convinced her to swallow it all: *any TOE would be an atrocity, a crime against the human spirit, an unendurable cage for the soul.*

That was why she'd worked so hard to get *Violet Mosala* – and when she'd lost it, she'd had someone infect me with the cholera, modified to do the job indirectly. But they'd been sloppy with the timing provisions needed to accommodate the last-minute change of plan.

Nishide and Buzzo she'd dealt with in person.

And I'd just destroyed every chance of trust, every chance of friendship, every chance of love I might have found with Akili. I'd beaten it all into the ground. I covered my face with my hands, and stood there wrapped in the darkness of solitude, ignoring her commands. I didn't care what she did; I had no reason to go on.

Akili said, 'Andrew. Do as she says. It'll be okay.'

I looked at Sarah. She had the gun raised, and she was repeating angrily, 'Call De Groot!'

I took out my notepad and made the call. I swept the camera around, to illustrate the situation. Sarah gave detailed instructions to De Groot, a procedure for transferring authority over Mosala's supercomputer account.

De Groot seemed to be in shock at first, stunned to learn of Sarah's allegiance; she complied with barely a word. Then her anger boiled to the surface, and she interjected sardonically, 'All your resources and expertise, and you couldn't even have an *academic account* hacked open?'

Sarah was almost apologetic. 'Not for lack of trying. But Violet was paranoid, she had good protection.'

De Groot was incredulous. 'Better than Thought Craft's?' 'What?'

De Groot addressed me. 'They pulled a childish stunt, when Wendy was in Toronto. They hacked into **Kaspar** and had it spouting their stupid theories. All for the sake of what? *Intimidation?* The programmers had to shut it down and go to backups. Wendy didn't even know what it meant – until I had to tell her who was trying to kill her daughter.'

I heard Akili, still on the floor at my feet, inhale sharply. And then I understood, too.

Free fall.

Sarah frowned, irritated by the distraction. 'She's lying.' She took out her own notepad and checked something, still holding the gun on me. 'Break the connection, Andrew.' I did.

Akili said, 'Sarah? Have you been following Distress?'

'No. I've been busy.' She examined her notepad warily, as if it were a bomb that needed defusing. Mosala's work was all there in her hands now, and she had to be sure she destroyed it, thoroughly and irrevocably, without letting it taint her.

Akili persisted. 'You've lost, Sarah. The Aleph moment has passed.'

She glanced up from the screen at me. 'Would you shut ver up? I don't want to hurt ver, but—'

I said, 'Distress is a plague of mixing with information. I thought it was an organic virus – but **Kaspar** proves that it can't be.'

Sarah scowled. 'What are you saying? You think De Groot read the finished TOE paper, and became the Keystone?' She held up her notepad triumphantly, with an audit trail displayed. 'Nobody's read the paper. Nobody's accessed the final results.'

'Except the author. Wendy sent Violet a **Kaspar** clonelet. *It* wrote the paper, *it* pulled all the calculations together. And it's become the Keystone.'

Sarah was incredulous. 'A piece of *software*?'

Akili said, 'Scan the nets for lucid Distress victims. Hear what they have to say.'

'If this is some kind of ridiculous bluff, you're wasting—'

Sisyphus interrupted cheerfully, 'This pattern of information requires itself to be encoded in germanium phosphide crystals, in an artifact designed in collaboration with organic—'

Sarah screamed at me wordlessly, waving the gun above her head, casting wild belligerent shadows on the walls of the tent. I hit the MUTE button and killed the audio; the declaration continued silently, in text flowing across the screen. My mind was reeling at the implications – but I'd lost my death wish, and Sarah had my full attention.

Akili spoke calmly but urgently. 'Listen to me. Distress numbers must be exploding already. And with a software Keystone – a machine world view – the mixing's going to keep wrecking people's minds *until someone reads the TOE paper.*'

Sarah was unmoved. 'You're wrong. There is no *Keystone*. We've won: we've left the last question unanswered.' She smiled at me suddenly, radiantly, lost in some private apotheosis. 'It doesn't matter how small the loophole is, the residue of uncertainty; in the future, we'll know how to enlarge it. And we'll never be brute machines, we'll never be mere physical beings . . . so long as there's still that hope of *transcendence*.'

I kept my expression deadpan. The music swelled. The two tall Polynesian women – militia members? – creeping in behind her raised their truncheons and struck together; she went down cold.

One of them dropped to her knees to inspect Sarah; the other eyed me curiously. 'So what was her problem?'

'She was high on something.' Akili climbed to vis feet beside me.

I said, 'She came in here ranting, stole vis notepad. We couldn't get any sense out of her.'

'Is that true?'

Akili nodded meekly. The militia members looked suspicious. They took possession of the gun, with obvious distaste – but handed Akili the notepad. 'Okay. We'll take her to the first aid tent. Some people just don't know how to enjoy themselves.'

'We should restart Mosala's despatch procedure. Scatter the TOE over the net.' Akili sat beside me, tense with urgency, the notepad in one hand.

I struggled to focus my thoughts. The situation eclipsed everything which had happened between us – but I still couldn't look ver in the eye. Akili's knowledge miner had already counted more than a hundred new cases of Distress in five minutes – via media reports of people dropping in the streets.

I said, 'We can't scatter it. Not until we know if that would make things better, or worse. All your models, all your predictions, have failed. Maybe **Kaspar** proves that the mixing is real – but everything else is still guesswork. Do you want to send every TOE theorist on the planet insane?'

Akili turned on me angrily. 'It won't do that! This is the cure as well as the cause. It just needs one last step. It just needs a human interpretation.' But ve did not sound convinced. *Maybe the whole truth was even worse than the distorted glimpse which led to Distress. Maybe there was nothing ahead but madness.* 'Do you want me to prove that? Do you want me to read it first?'

Ve raised the notepad; I grabbed vis arm. 'Don't be stupid! There are too few people who even half understand what's going on, to risk losing one of you.'

We sat there, frozen. I stared at my hand where it held ver; I could see where I'd broken the skin, striking vis face.

I said, 'You think **Kaspar**'s view is too much for most people to swallow? You think someone has to step in and interpret it? To bridge the difference in perspectives?

'Then you don't want an expert – in TOEs, or in Anthrocosmology. You want a science journalist.'

Akili let me drag the notepad from vis hand.

I thought of the hopeless screaming woman thrashing on the floor in Miami, and the briefly lucid victims who'd clung to their sanity only minutes longer. I had no wish to follow them.

If there was one remaining purpose to my life, though, this was it: to prove that the truth could always be faced – explained, demystified, accepted. This was my job, this was my vocation. I had one last chance to try to live up to it.

I stood. 'I'll have to leave the camp. I can't concentrate with all this noise. But I'll do it.'

Akili was huddled on the ground with vis head bowed. Ve said quietly, without looking up, 'I know you will. I trust you.'

I left the tent quickly, and headed south. Stars still showed dimly in half the pale sky; the wind from the reefs was colder than ever.

A hundred metres into the desert, I stopped and raised the notepad. I said, 'Show me *A Tentative Theory of Everything*, by Violet Mosala.'

I took off the blindfold.

30

I kept walking as I read, half consciously retracing the steps I'd taken some eight hours before. The reef-rock hadn't fissured in the quake, but the ground's texture seemed to have been transformed in some subtle way. Maybe the pressure waves had realigned the polymer chains, forging a new kind of mineral; the island's first ever geological metamorphosis.

Out in the desert, away from all the factions of Anthrocosmology, the anarchists' heedless rejoicing, the mounting reports of Distress, I did not know what I believed. If I'd felt the weight of ten billion people slipping into madness around me, I know I would have been paralysed. I must have been saved in part by lingering scepticism – and in part by sheer curiosity. If I'd surrendered to the *appropriate human responses* – blind panic and awe-struck humility – in the face of the magnitude of everything which supposedly lay in the balance, I would have thrown the poisoned chalice of the notepad away.

So I emptied my mind of everything else, and let the words and equations take over. The **Kaspar** clonelet had done a good job; I had no trouble understanding the paper.

The first section contained no surprises at all. It summarised Mosala's ten canonical experiments, and the way in which she'd computed their symmetry-breaking properties. It ended with the TOE equation itself, which linked the ten parameters of broken symmetry to a sum over all topologies. The measure Mosala had chosen to give weight to each topology was the simplest, the most elegant, the most obvious of all the possible choices. Her equation couldn't grant the universe the 'inevitability' of freezing out of pre-space which Buzzo and Nishide had sought to contrive, but it showed how the ten experiments – and by extension, everything from mayflies to colliding stars – were bound together, were able to coexist. In an imaginary space of great abstraction, they all occupied exactly the same point.

Past and future were bound together, too. Down to the level of quantum randomness, Mosala's equation encoded the common order found in every process from the folding of a protein to the spreading of an eagle's wings. It delineated the fan of probabilities linking any system, at any moment, to anything it might become.

In the second section, **Kaspar** had trawled the databases for other references to the same mathematics, other resonances to the same abstractions – and in this scrupulously completist search, it had found enough parallels with information theory to push the TOE one step further. Everything Mosala would have spurned – and Helen Wu would have feared to combine – **Kaspar** had serenely brought together.

There could be no information without physics. Knowledge always had to be encoded as something. Marks on paper, knots on a string, pockets of charge in a semiconductor.

But there could be no physics without information. A universe of purely random events would be no universe at all. Deep patterns, powerful regularities, were the whole basis of existence.

So – having determined which physical systems could share a universe – **Kaspar** had asked the question: *which patterns of information could those systems encode?*

A second, analogous equation had emerged from the same mathematics, with almost no effort at all. The informational TOE was the flipside of the physical TOE, an inevitable corollary.

Then **Kaspar** had unified the two, fitting them together like interlocking mirror images (in spite of everything, I had a feeling that Symmetry's Champion would have been proud) . . . and all of the predictions of Anthrocosmology had come tumbling out. The terminology was different – **Kaspar** had innocently coined new jargon, unaware of the unpublished precedents – but the concepts were unmistakable.

The Aleph moment was as necessary as the Big Bang. The universe could never have existed without it. **Kaspar** had shied away from claiming the honour of being Keystone – and had even refused to grant the explanatory Big Bang primacy over the physical one – but the paper stated clearly that the TOE had to be *known*, had to be *understood*, to have ever had force.

Mixing, too, was inevitable. Latent knowledge of the TOE infected all of time and space – every system in this universe encoded it – but once it was understood explicitly, that hidden information would crystallise out wherever the possibility arose, percolating up through the foam of quantum randomness. It was more like cloud-seeding than telepathy; nobody would read the mind of the Keystone – but they'd follow the Keystone in reading the TOE which their own minds, their own flesh, already encoded.

And even before the Aleph moment, the mixing would happen, albeit imperfectly.

But not for long.

In the last section, **Kaspar** predicted the unravelling. The Aleph moment would be followed, on a timescale of seconds, by the degeneration of physics into pure mathematics. Just as the Big Bang implied pre-space before it – an infinitely symmetric roiling abstraction where nothing really existed or happened – the Aleph moment would bring on the informational mirror image, another infinite wasteland without time or space.

These words prophesying the end of the universe had been written half an hour before I was reading them.

Kaspar had not become the Keystone.

I lowered the notepad and looked around. The lagoon had come into view in the distance, silver-grey with the hint of dawn. A few bright stars remained in the west. I could still hear the music from the celebrations, faintly: a distant tuneless hum.

The mixing took place so smoothly that I barely knew when it began. Listening to Reynolds' Distress victims, I'd imagined them granted X-ray vision and more, assailed by images of molecules and galaxies, reeling at the universe in every grain of sand – and they were the lucky few. I'd steeled myself for the worst: the sky peeling open to reveal some Mystical Renaissance wet dream of stargate acid-trip stupefaction, the end of thought, the candied incineration of reason.

The reality could not have been more different. Like the coded markings of the reef-rock, the surface of the world began to speak of its depths, and its hidden connections. It was like learning to read a new language, in seconds, and seeing the beautiful but hitherto merely decorative calligraphy of a foreign alphabet transformed before my eyes – acquiring meaning, without changing its appearance in any way. The fading stars described their fusion fires, the crush of gravity held in check by the liberation of binding energy. The pale air, reddened in the east, deftly portrayed its own biased scatter of photons. The lightly rippled water hinted at the play of intermolecular forces, the strength of the hydrogen bond, the gentle elasticity of a surface trying to minimise its contact with air.

And all of these messages were written in a common language. It was clear at a glance that they belonged together.

No wheels within wheels, no dazzling cosmic technoporn, no infernal diagrams.

No visions. Just understanding.

I pocketed the notepad and spun around, laughing. There

414

was no overload, no crippling flood of information. The messages were always there – but I could take them or leave them. At first, it was like skipping over text with glazed eyes, requiring a conscious shift of focus – but with a few moments' practice, it became second nature.

This was the world as I'd always strived to see it: majestically beautiful, intricate and strange – but at its core harmonious, and hence ultimately comprehensible.

It was not a reason for terror. It was not a reason for awe.

The mixing began to cut deeper.

I grew aware of my own physicality, my own nature written in the TOE. The connections I'd seen in the world reached into me, and bound me to everything in sight. There was, still, no X-ray vision, no double-helix dream – but I felt the immutable grammar of the TOE in my limbs, in my blood, in the dark glide of consciousness.

It was the lesson of the cholera – only starker and clearer. *I was matter, like everything else.*

I could feel the slow decay of my body, the absolute certainty of death. Every heartbeat spelt out a new proof of mortality. Every moment was a premature burial.

I inhaled deeply, studying the events which followed the inrush of air. And I could trace the sweetness of the odour and the cooling of the nasal membranes, the satisfying fullness of the lungs, the surge of blood, the clarity delivered to the brain . . . all back to the TOE.

My claustrophobia evaporated. *To inhabit this universe – to coexist with anything – I had to be matter.* Physics was not a cage; its delineation between the possible and the impossible was the bare minimum that existence required. And the broken symmetry of the TOE – hacked out of the infinite paralysing choices of pre-space – was the bedrock on which I stood.

I was a dying machine of cells and molecules; I would never be able to doubt that again.

But it was not a path into madness.

The mixing had still more to show me; the messages of introspection grew richer. I'd read the explanatory threads fanning out from the TOE, binding me to the world – but now the threads which explained my thoughts began to turn back towards their source. So I followed them down, and I understood what my own mind was creating through understanding:

Interacting symbols coded as firing patterns in neural pathways. Rules of dendritic growth and connection, synaptic weight adjustment, neurotransmitter diffusion. A chemistry of membranes, ion pumps, proteins, amines. All the detailed behaviour of molecules and atoms, all the laws governing their necessary constituents. Layer after layer of converging regularity—

—right down to the TOE.

There was no arena of disinterested physics. There was no solid layer of objective laws. Just a deep circulating convection current of explanation, a causal magma upwelling from the underworld and then plunging down again into darkness, churning from TOE to body to mind to TOE – held up by nothing but the engine of understanding.

There was no bedrock, no fixed point, no place to rest.

I was endlessly treading water.

I sank to my knees, fighting away vertigo. I lay face down, clinging to the reef-rock. The cool solidity of the ground refuted nothing.

But did it need to? Held up by aloof, timeless laws, or held up by the bootstrap of explanation . . . it endured, regardless.

I thought of the inland divers who'd descended through every layer of the unnatural ecology which kept this island afloat, who'd witnessed the subterranean ocean ceaselessly corroding the rock from below.

They'd walked away – dazed, but exalted.

I could do the same.

I rose to my feet unsteadily. I thought it was over: I thought I'd come through the mixing, unscathed. **Kaspar** could not have become the Keystone – and yet somehow the Aleph moment must have passed safely, removing the distortion, banishing Distress. Maybe some mainstream AC had hacked into Mosala's account upon learning of her death and had grasped some crucial error in **Kaspar**'s analysis before I'd read a word of it.

Akili was approaching – an indistinct figure in the distance, but I knew it could be no one else. I raised a hand tentatively, then waved in triumph. The figure waved back, stretching vis giant shadow west across the desert.

And everything I'd learnt came together, like a thunderclap, like an ambush.

I was the Keystone. I'd explained the universe into being, wrapped it around the seed of this moment, layer after layer of beautiful convoluted necessity. The blazing wasteland of galaxies, twenty billion years of cosmic evolution, ten billion human cousins, forty billion species of life – the whole elaborate ancestry of consciousness flowed out of this singularity. I had no need to reach out and imagine every molecule, every planet, every face. This moment encoded them all.

My parents, friends, lovers . . . Gina, Angelo, Lydia, Sarah, Violet Mosala, Bill Munroe, Adelle Vunibobo, Karin De Groot. Akili. Even the helpless bellowing strangers, victims of the same revelation, had only been mouthing distorted echoes of my own horror at the understanding that I'd created them all.

This was the solipsistic madness I'd seen reflected in that first poor woman's face. *This was Distress*: not fear of the

417

glorious machinery of the TOE, but the realisation that I was alone in the darkness with a hundred billion dazzling cobwebs wrapped around my non-existent eyes—

—and now that I knew it, the breath of my own understanding would sweep them all away.

Nothing could have been created without the full knowledge of how it was done: without the unified TOE, physical and informational. No Keystone could have acted in innocence, forging the universe unaware.

But that knowledge was impossible to contain. **Kaspar** had been right. The moderates had been right. Everything which had breathed fire into the equations would now unravel into empty tautology.

I raised my face to the blank sky, ready to part the veil of the world and find nothing behind it.

Then Akili called my name, and I stopped dead. I looked down at ver – beautiful as ever, unreachable as ever.

Unknowable as ever.

And I saw the way through.

I saw the flaw in **Kaspar**'s reasoning which had kept it from becoming the Keystone: an unexamined assumption – an unasked question, not yet true or false.

Could one mind, alone, explain another into being?

The TOE equation said nothing. The canonical experiments said nothing. There was nowhere to look for the answer but my own memories, my own life.

And all I had to do to tear myself out of the centre of the universe – all I had to do to prevent the unravelling – was give up one last illusion.

EPILOGUE

As the plane touches down, I begin recording. **Witness** confirms: 'Cape Town, Wednesday 15 April, 2105. 7:12:10 GMT.'

Karin De Groot has come to the airport to meet me. She looks astonishingly healthy, much more so in the flesh – though, as with all of us ancients, the losses are etched deep. We exchange greetings, then I glance around trying to take in the profusion of styles in anatomy and dress – no more than anywhere else, but every place has a different mix, a different set of fashions. Imposing retractable cowls full of dark violet photosynthetic symbionts seem to be popular throughout Southern Africa. Back home, sleek amphibian adaptions for underwater breathing and feeding are common.

After the Aleph moment, people had feared that the mixing would impose uniformity. It had never happened – any more than, in the Age of Ignorance, the brutal, inescapable truths that water was wet and the sky was blue had forced everyone on the planet to think and act identically. There are infinitely many ways to respond to the single truth of the TOE. What's become impossible is maintaining the pretence that every culture could ever have created its own separate reality – while we all breathed the same air and walked the same ground.

De Groot checks some schedule in her mind's eye. 'So you didn't come straight from Stateless?'

'No. Malawi. There was someone I had to see. I wanted to say goodbye.'

We descend to the subway, where the train is expecting us and lights a path for our eyes to the carriage door. It's almost fifty years since I've been in this city, and most of the infrastructure has changed; in unfamiliar surroundings, the TOE blazes out of every surface, unbidden, like an exuberant child boasting of the bright new things ve's made. Even the simplest novelties – the non-slip dirt-eating coating on the floor tiles, the luminous pigments of the living sculptures – catch my attention as they spell out their unique ways of coexisting.

Nothing is incomprehensible. Nothing can be mistaken for magic.

I say, 'When I first heard that they were building the Violet Mosala Memorial *Kindergarten*, I imagined she would have been insulted. Which only goes to show how little I knew her. I don't know why I was invited.'

De Groot laughs. 'I'm just glad you didn't come all this way for the ceremony and nothing else. You could have done it on the net; no one would have minded.'

'There's nothing like being there.'

The train reminds us of our stop, holds the doors for us. We walk through the neat suburbs not far from the house where Mosala spent her childhood, though the streets now are lined with species of plants she would never have recognised. She never saw trees growing on Stateless, either. People stride past us, glancing up at the elegant logic of the cloudless blue sky.

The kindergarten is a small building, reconfigured into an auditorium for the occasion. Half a dozen speakers are here to address the fifty children. I lapse into reverie until one of Violet's grand-daughters, working on the *Halcyon*, explains the starship's drive; the core principle, close to the TOE, is easy to grasp. Karin De Groot speaks about Violet, anecdotes of generosity and intransigence. And one of the children sets the stage for me, telling the others about the Age of Ignorance.

'It hangs like a stalactite from the Information Cosmos.' The present tense is sophistication, not solecism; relativity demands it. 'It's not autonomous, it doesn't explain itself – it needs to be joined to the Information Cosmos, in order to exist. We need it, too, though. It's a necessary history, a logical outgrowth if you try to extend time before the Aleph moment.'

Ve summons vivid diagrams and equations into the air. The brilliant stellar cluster of the Information Cosmos, wrapped densely in explanatory threads, holds up the simple drab cone of the Age of Ignorance, which points back to the physical Big Bang. Vis audience of less precocious four year olds struggle with the concepts. *Time before the Aleph moment?* Grandparents notwithstanding, it almost defies belief.

I rise to my feet and recite my prepared version of the events of fifty years ago – getting laughs of incredulity in all the right places. Ownership of genes? Centralised authorities? *Ignorance Cults?*

Ancient history always sounds quaint, old victories preordained, but I try to convey some sense of how long and hard their ancestors struggled to learn everything they now take for granted: that law and morality, physics and metaphysics, space and time, pleasure, love, meaning . . . are all the burden of the participants. There are no immovable centres, dispensing absolutes like manna: no God, no Gaia, no beneficent rulers. No reality but the universe explained into being. No purpose to life unless we create it, together or alone.

Someone asks about the turmoil in the days after Aleph.

I say, 'Everyone found the truth hard to swallow. Orthodox scientists – because the TOE had turned out to be grounded in nothing but its own explanatory powers. The Ignorance Cults – because even the participatory universe, the most subjective reality possible, was no synthesis of their favourite myths – which could never have created anything – but the product of universal scientific understanding of what *coexistence* really meant. Even the Anthrocosmologists turned out to have been wrong; they'd been so obsessed with the idea of a single Keystone that they'd barely considered the possibility that everyone, equally, could play that role. They'd missed the most stable, and symmetrical, solution: where every mind obeys the TOE – but it takes all of them, together, to create it.'

One astute listener sees that I'm dodging the issue – a child I would have called 'human', in the days before the H-word exploded and it was finally understood: *the TOE is all we have in common.*

'Most people weren't scientists, cultists, or Anthrocosmologists, were they? They had no stake in these ideas. So why were they so sad?'

Sad. There were nine million suicides. Nine million people we could not hold up, when all illusions of solidity vanished. And I'm still not certain that there was no other way – that I found the only possible bridge into the Information Cosmos. *If I'd let myself descend into the madness of Distress, would someone else have asked a different last question, and found another way through?*

No one has accused me, no one has judged me. I've never been damned as a criminal, or hailed as a saviour. The idea that a single Keystone could ever have explained ten billion people into existence is absurd, now. In restrospect, Distress is seen as no different from the naive illusion that every galaxy is rushing away from us – when in truth, there is not, and cannot be, any centre at all.

I talk haltingly about Lamont's area. 'It made people think that they knew each other, and could speak for each other, understand each other – much more than they really could. Some of you might still have it in your brain – but in the face of the evidence, now, it's easy to ignore.'

I try to explain about the delusion of intimacy, and how much was invested in it once. They listen politely, but I can see that it makes no sense to them, because they know full well that they've lost nothing. Love in the face of the truth has turned out to be stronger than ever. Happiness never really depended on the old lies.

Not for these children, born without crutches.

In vis home in the dazzling bounteous engineered jungle of Malawi, I'd told Akili I was dying. *After you, there was no one*. And we'd touched for the last time.

I move on quickly.

'Other people,' I add, 'lamented the end of mystery. As if nothing would remain to be discovered, once we understood what lay beneath our feet. And it's true that there are no more "deep" surprises – there's nothing left to learn about the reasons for the TOE, or the reasons for our own existence. But there'll be no end to discovering what the universe can contain; there'll always be new stories written in the TOE – new systems, new structures, explained into being. There might even be other minds on other worlds, co-creators whose nature we can't even imagine yet.

'Violet Mosala once said: "Reaching the foundations doesn't mean hitting the ceiling." She helped us all touch the foundations; I only wish she could have lived to see you building on them, higher than anyone has built before.'

I take my seat. The children applaud politely – but I feel like a senile fool for telling them that *their future is unbounded*.

They already knew that, of course.

AUTHOR'S NOTE

Among many works which inspired me in the writing of this novel, I must single out *Dreams of a Final Theory* by Steven Weinberg, *Culture and Imperialism* by Edward W. Said, and 'Out of the Light, Back Into the Cave' by Andy Robertson (*Interzone 65*, November 1992). The excerpt from the poem *Technolibération* is modelled on a passage from Aimé Césaire's *Notebook of a Return to the Native Land*.

Thanks to Caroline Oakley, Deborah Beale, Anthony Cheetham, Peter Robinson, Lucy Blackburn, Annabelle Ager and Claudia Schaffer.